Praise for

MILE 21

"As a marathon runner, I've often thought that going out for a run is the perfect opportunity to examine my life. In *Mile 21*, Sarah Dunster expertly shows how Abish Miller flounders following a tragic loss, and ultimately, how she finds her way again by doing scary things, like running marathons and opening her heart to people who just might love her. Readers will be delighted to find themselves loving Abish, almost against their will, for her prickliness, her fragility, and her grit."

SHELAH MASTNY MINER, managing editor, segullah.org

"At turns almost painfully honest, deeply poignant, and very amusing, *Mile 21* is the story of what happens when the life we've planned for ourselves gets derailed. Abish Miller is a heroine on the edge, who speaks to everyone who's ever felt displaced or unsure about their future. I can't count how many times I teared up or laughed out loud while reading this book. Recommended."

AMBER GILCHRIST, author of *Glitch {A Comedy of Errors}*

Also by Sarah Dunster

Lightning Tree

Mile 21

SARAH DUNSTER

BONNEVILLE BOOKS
AN IMPRINT OF CEDAR FORT, INC.
SPRINGVILLE, UTAH

ISBN 13: 978-1-4621-1297-5

Published by Bonneville Books, an imprint of Cedar Fort, Inc.
2373 W. 700 S., Springville, UT, 84663
Distributed by Cedar Fort, Inc., www.cedarfort.com

LIBRARY OF CONGRESS CATALOGING-IN-PUBLICATION DATA

Dunster, Sarah.
  Mile 21 / by Sarah Dunster.
     pages cm
  ISBN 978-1-4621-1297-5 (Perfect : alk. paper)
  1. Grief--Fiction. 2. Mormon pioneers--Fiction. 3. Mormon girls--Fiction. 4. Frontier and pioneer life--Utah--Fiction. I. Title. II. Title: Mile twenty-one.
  PS3604.U577M56 2013
  813'.6--dc23
                              2013017854

Front cover design by Erica Dixon
Back cover design by Rebecca J. Greenwood
Cover design © 2013 by Lyle Mortimer
Edited and typeset by Melissa J. Caldwell

Printed in the United States of America

10 9 8 7 6 5 4 3 2 1

To Greg Roberts, George Handley,
and DelRay Davenport, who aren't turds.

To Eryn, Katrina and Tonio, Steve and Elizabeth, and
Deborah and Grandmasan, who know what it is to lose.

And to the Provo police department, who fasted for me.

Chapter

1

I'm Abish Miller. Abish *Cavendish* Miller.

The story goes, when I was born, Dad held me in his giant farmer hands for a few seconds before they whisked me off to the neonatal intensive care unit. I had a ton of dark hair lacquered to my scalp despite the fact that I was two months early, and he'd been reading Abish's story in the Book of Mormon, how she raised her king and queen from the dead with her pure faith. It's not surprising that the thought of naming me Abish seemed a good one at the time, especially considering how much of a miracle my birth really was. That you and Suzy came to this earth to stay, Dad likes to say, is a miracle.

I think Mama was still in the fog of anesthesia when she agreed to the name. Neither of them paused to consider how Abish fit with our surname, Cavendish. If they had, they might have changed it. Or they might not have; they might have thought I'd love the fact that I was a nursery rhyme.

My whimsical name resulted in some unpleasant days in grade school and in middle school. In high school too, but I sort of brought

1

that on myself. My nickname by then was Honest Abe. People didn't mean it nicely, like, "You can always count on Honest Abe." It was more because of how I talked to people; that is, not very tactfully, but honestly. Always honestly.

Name notwithstanding, I'm not ashamed of being a Cavendish. Annoyed sometimes, but never ashamed. My mom and dad met at school in the eighties. He served a Spanish-speaking mission, so he was partial to Latin-looking girls. My mother is Guatemalan. She caught Dad's eye as soon as she walked into that Physical Science 100 classroom. That's saying something, because Physical Science 100 is one of those freshman-weeder classes that stuffs the roster full of 300-plus students and meets in stadium-style seating. But Mama is extraordinarily beautiful; she's got dark, luscious curls and eyes like Esther from the Bible. Her nose is cute and small. Her smile surprises people, even me sometimes. It flashes suddenly and she gets this mischievous, almost wicked look.

Yeah. Dad didn't stand a chance.

Genetics are funny sometimes. I inherited Mama's dark hair, but it grows out bone-straight. I've got Dad's whale-belly complexion and his features: beaky nose, thick brows, and ice-blue irises. My face is pretty much Dad's except for one thing—instead of the soft, open smile that dimples his cheeks and occasionally renders him approachable-looking for a brief moment, Heavenly Father saw fit to bless me with Mama's smile. So I frighten people.

My only sister, Susannah—all of us except Mama call her Suzy—came out on top when it comes to looks. Her skin is a light tan, and it darkens in the summer to a stunning bronze. Her hair is brown like my dad's, with a hint of red in it. Her eyes are Mama's—large, dark, and melting. She has Dad's dimples. She's a soccer star, a straight-A student, and the homecoming princess this year. That's not supposed to happen. She's only a junior and the honor of fake-high-school-royalty is usually tucked into the sticky, glittering coiffure of a senior girl—fairness, you know.

But then, life really isn't fair. Suzy's life has always been easy and lucky, and lately, mine has been cosmically unfair in the other direction. I just turned twenty-one. Not many twenty-one-year-olds have gone through what I have in the last year.

Even now as I'm forced to sit in this office in front of this screen, fighting off the two p.m. drowsiness that comes from a belly full of lunch and being immobilized by a desk, the unfairness of it all grates on me, punctuated by the sharp gum-cracks sounding constantly in my ear.

I turn and glare at Adrian, who is sitting next to me. She's chewing away, her French-manicured nails self-righteously tapping at the keyboard. "You think you'll finish the payroll by the end of the day?" she asks. "Brother Barnes won't like it if the paperwork's late again."

"Yeah," I mutter, putting my unwilling fingers to the keys. The muscles in my legs are twitching. I shift my position so I'm leaning on another part of my back.

Adrian cracks her gum again. "Your thighs are getting big. You might want to go easy on those long runs of yours. You're going to have to go up a size in jeans pretty soon."

"Thanks for the advice."

She waits a moment, clearly disappointed.

Adrian, you see, is one of those girls who enjoys catty rejoinders. I used to dish her own meanness back to her with some to spare, just to see the grin hidden in her cheekbones as she turned back to her computer, feigning offended silence. A lot of things have changed in the last year. A lot of my relationships—not just my work relationships—have withered on the proverbial vine. It makes for monotonous afternoons.

I sigh and get going on the numbers again, tedium that requires too much concentration, and at the same time, too little. My feet are tapping restlessly on the floor. All I can think of is how in three minutes, I'll be running out the door.

My boss comes striding through the office. As usual, his bald head is shining, his duffel bag is slung over his shoulder, and a sour army-drill-sergeant expression is on his face. He stops and leans over the counter, glancing at both our screens. I see Adrian flinch and quickly exit out of a forbidden Facebook tab. After a few seconds of eagle-eye scrutiny, he straightens and gives me an icy glare. "Have a good weekend, ladies," he growls, and slams the door behind him.

When this girl called Jodi worked here before she left on her mission, she used to say sympathetic things about him. Like, he's antsy all the time because they won't let him on the field coaching anymore. Like, his back injury must give him a lot of trouble. Jodi is a very Christlike person.

I think my boss is a turd.

Burt the Turd. That's my secret name for him. We have an agreement, the Turd and I. Six months ago he brought me into his office and verbally ripped me up one side and down the other, telling me my job performance was falling, that he didn't tolerate sloppiness, and that I couldn't earn my living on sympathy.

Yeah, just like that.

And then he gave me a contract stating that from then on, I'd come in to work on a regular schedule every day. I'd work a certain number of hours a week. This would be my last semester deferring. He goaded me into signing the thing, and now I'm stuck, because while it's sort of hard to get fired at BYU-Idaho, that contract has my name on it. And it would likely stand because BYU-Idaho administration has a passion for contracts.

"Done," I say finally, raising a fist in jubilation. I jump up from my chair, sending it crashing sideways onto the floor.

It misses Adrian's knee by a mere three inches. She raises a drawn-on eyebrow but doesn't bother to glance my direction. "Have a good weekend."

"You too," I say with just as much sincerity. I open the glass double door, keeping my pace studiously grounded until I hit the sidewalk.

And then I'm running. My heart expands and warms. My lungs gasp open. My hips and legs ache with joy, gulping away at miles. I run out of campus on Viking Drive, then up along Second East. It's been an unseasonably warm December, so I don't have to deal with much snow on the little suburb streets that curl and wind around the Rexburg hill.

MILE 21

Sometimes running gets my thoughts going, helps me chew over things from the day. Sometimes my mind is completely blank and time feels suspended, and I don't even feel the street underneath me; it's like the scenery flashing past me is some movie I'm watching. Today is one of those days. I sink into my warm, blank place and just watch the horizon chug by.

Eventually I hit Temple View, coming down off the bench as the setting sun turns the sky to stripes of lemon-yellow and pink. When I reach the Yellowstone Highway, my tendons are warning me that it's time to be done. I slow down gradually, stopping just under the Big O sign. My blood races and my nerves tingle with warm energy.

My books are at home. I'll have to go by and get them.

When I hit campus again, I turn north and head past the giant line of complexes along Second West. Freshman Factories, I call them, or if it's family housing, Marriage Machines. Here at the campus of BYU-Idaho, marriage is quite a popular pastime.

Mama's fourplex is located almost in the center of town. She bought it at exactly the right time—nine years ago, before the college became a university, before land on or near the Rexburg Hill became worth a whole lot more. She runs her fourplex pretty much the way she runs everything else in her life: with Nazi-like organization, a hard set of rules, and a great deal of charm. It's a married-student complex. Mama dotes on young couples, so it's been a good venture for her. It's also helped our family financially, especially lately.

I live in the best unit, the south-facing apartment on the top floor. When Mark and I announced our engagement, Mama let the contract lapse on the couple who lived there and didn't sign any other contracts for three months. If you know my mother, you know that's a huge concession that she'd be willing to take a rent-cut just so her daughter could be slightly more under her thumb.

As I trot carefully up the icy steps, there's some guilt. *I need to remember to scrape them soon.* I fumble with the lock, open the door, and flick on the lights, then walk into the kitchen. I know exactly what's in my fridge. It's not a long list to memorize: 2-percent milk, a half-empty carton of eggs, and a jar of peanut butter. I take the frying pan out of the sink, rinse off the topmost layer of grease, and crack two eggs into it. While they sizzle, I glance at the answering machine.

Two messages.

And I bet I know who they're from.

I sigh and press the "play" button.

I'm the only person left that I know of who uses a landline and answering machine instead of a cell phone. Mark teases me about it too. I just don't feel like it's necessary that people should be able to get hold of me every loving minute of the day and night. Just because it's possible they *can* doesn't mean they *should*. The only cell phone I've ever owned is the one that was forced on me by my parents when I turned sixteen and started—supposedly—going on dates. I pretty much kept it off all the time.

The message comes on. *"Hi, this is Mark and Abish. Leave us a message and we'll call you when we can."* (My voice interrupts.) *"When we want to."* (Mark laughs.) *"When we want to. Thanks!"*

My lips curl up a little at the corners.

"Abish." It is, of course, Mama's voice. "You need to call the repair person to come fix the dryer in the laundry room. And the coins need to be emptied and stacked and put in the account. The cable will be installed Saturday morning. I asked the boy to be there as early as possible. And when are you going to be scraping off those stairs? It's a lawsuit waiting to happen. Abish, I—"

I press the button, cutting off the end of it, and sigh as her voice continues onto the next message. I press it again.

My eggs don't look appetizing. I add a piece of toast and a glass of milk and sit at the little round table in the dining nook. The picture sitting on the table is Mark's favorite of us. He's grinning, holding a giant blue cone of fluffy cotton candy, and I've got my head thrown back, laughing helplessly at something he just said. He wanted to make it our engagement photo, but Mama put a quick end to that idea.

I wrack my brain, trying to remember what it was he said to make me laugh so much, but it's gone. I throw on my silver snowboarding parka and sling my orange backpack over my shoulder, making sure to flick the light switch off and lock the door behind me.

It doesn't take me long to walk down Main Street to Second East. It's pitch-dark. I travel by the light of the Christmas reindeers and Santa's sleigh jauntily crossing Main and Second, toward the giant bank of lighted windows at the end of Main—Madison Memorial Hospital.

The receptionist on duty is Mara. Not my favorite. As I cross the threshold, I keep my face turned away from her and stroll past before she has a chance to say anything cranky.

They don't let me on ICU or Labor and Delivery anymore, not even in the lobbies. I make my way up the stairs to Med-Surg—that's hospital slang for the Medical-Surgical ward where any long-term patients tend to end up.

I'm a chaplain for the hospital. It happened kind of by accident. I was spending a lot of time here, and so they asked me to fill out the paperwork to make it official. I do the same stuff as a chaplain person as I did before—mainly sit with patients who don't have regular visitors. Usually it's Mr. Eems, who just lays there with his eyes permanently shut and a bunch of machines breathing for him and keeping his heart beating. They say coma patients can hear things, but I doubt he knows I'm here.

I find it restful, sitting in the chair by his bed. He doesn't try to make awkward conversation. Sometimes I read my anatomy and physiology notes aloud to him. I find that I can remember stuff better when I've read it aloud.

A nurse comes in carrying a giant binder and a clipboard. She smiles at me. "What's today? Have you got to the endocrine system yet?"

"Hypothalamus, pituitary, thyroid, parathyroid, adrenal, pineal, reproductive," I confirm.

Dalynne is a good sort of person. She was the one, actually, who found a way for me to be able to stick around here. "When's your lab final?" she asks.

"I passed cadavers when I took the class. The written test is two weeks from Saturday."

She watches the various monitors for a few minutes, making notes. "You're lucky you have Harrison. Baker would never have let you get away with deferring for a whole year on the final exam."

"I know." I stand, stretch, and lift my backpack to my shoulder. "Anybody else that could use a visit before I leave?"

She glances at the clock. We both know it is way past visiting hours. "Mrs. Downey's awake. Her daughter wasn't able to come today."

"Right." I head out the door.

"Hang on." Dalynne digs through her pockets, coming up with a bottle of bright-pink fingernail polish and a tube of lotion. "She's been wanting to do her nails."

"'Kay."

Mrs. Downey squints at me as I enter the room. She fumbles on her side table for her glasses and slides them on. "What are you doing in my room at this hour?"

I can't blame her for being cranky. She's been here three weeks, and from the stories she tells, she's not used to being in bed waited on hand and foot—in my case, literally. I grin at her, holding out the polish and lotion. "You want a midnight manicure?"

Her scowl softens. "I suppose this is the only time I'll be getting one. The staff has been too busy lately."

"It's Christmas," I murmur, spreading lotion onto my palms and taking one of her hands. "Hospitals are usually pretty busy this time of year."

By the time I get back to my apartment, it's past one in the morning. The living room is pitch dark. I don't feel like turning on any lights, so I toss my backpack in the general direction of the couch and trudge down the hall. As I pass the kitchen, I can see the answering machine light is blinking again, but I can't stomach the thought of pressing that button just now. When I get to my room, I tear off my jeans, sweater, and T-shirt. I grab my pajamas and slide the top over my head. Carefully, I climb into my side of the bed.

The room is silent. Empty, but not empty—the thick kind of quiet that makes you wonder if you're about to hear or see things.

M I L E 2 1

I reach over and pat the pillow next to me. It is cool and soft and smells faintly of Mark's favorite aftershave. The bottle sits in the medicine cabinet just above where we keep the toothbrushes.

I tuck the covers around my shoulders and shut my eyes. I shift positions several times—gingerly, careful not to mess up the smooth expanse of covers next to me. It might be one in the morning, but my body doesn't think it's time for sleep. But that's nothing new. That's pretty much the way things have gone this past year.

I can tell it's late when I wake up because light streams through my window. It's Rexburg, and at this time of year, the sun doesn't come up until around 8:30 or so. It means something is off kilter, because generally I get up early. And stay up late. I just don't sleep all that much.

As I sit up, there's this throbbing in my head and this horrible taste in my mouth. My eyes hurt. *Maybe those fingernail polish fumes got to me last night. Maybe I'm having a manicure hangover.*

I grimace and step onto the carpet. I stumble to the door, open it, and then freeze. A little boy is standing there. He looks to be about four. He's got a shiny bowl haircut and slanted blue eyes. He gazes up at me, a finger in his mouth, then turns and trots down the hall.

I stare at his retreating figure. *I must still be dreaming.* Feeling as if I'm in a trance, I follow him down the hall into my living room.

"Hello."

I turn and see a second apparition—a man sitting on my kitchen table. He's tall. His legs almost touch the floor. He's wearing dark-wash blue jeans, a tool belt, and a collared shirt with "Bob" embroidered on it. He's got dark eyes, a lot of tousled black hair, and five-o'clock shadow that's rather apparent. His thick eyebrows are furrowed. "Oh," he says. "I . . . guess you weren't expecting me."

It takes a moment for the realization to hit. *I am not dreaming; there really is a kid in my living room and a man in my kitchen.* I look down at myself. Other than underwear, I'm clad only in a thread-bare pajamas. My bare shins are covered with black bristles because I haven't shaved them for a while. It's like that terrible high-school nightmare where you dream you're suddenly naked in front of an audience, only it's not a nightmare. It's real.

"Sorry," I gasp, crossing my arms tight over my chest, turning to walk back to my room. About halfway down the hall reality sinks in further, and the walk turns into a run. I fling myself back into bed and pull the covers over my head. I have an inclination to break into a wild storm of weeping.

A guy just saw me in only pajamas in my living room.

My living room, I remind myself after a few moments. *On a Saturday morning. With no warning. I'm fairly certain I locked the door, so she must have provided a key and told him to go right in.*

My anger is rising at this point. *How could she do this to me? How can she be so invasive, so determined to interrupt my peaceful existence?*

Fury gives me a wave of courage. I jump out of bed, toss my hair up, and throw on jeans and a sweatshirt. When I step back into the living room, I nearly trip over a second kid I didn't notice before—a littler one with black curly hair. He's not old enough to walk yet. He looks up at me with a solemn expression in his wide, dark eyes, and he's sucking away at a fist containing a wooden block. I wonder where he got it, and then notice there's a pile of them in the corner of the room.

"You'll have to go," I say to the man. He's still sitting on the table, fiddling with a little white box.

He looks up. "Where's your computer?"

I shake my head. "What?"

"Show me where your computer is. Or tell me where you'd like your modem to be." He glances at the picture on the table. "Is your husband around?"

I shake my head. "I'm sorry. You must not have heard me. You need to leave. You see, my mom's the landlord, and she doesn't always respect boundaries like she should. She didn't warn me sufficiently that you'd be coming today. You can come back after I've had a little chat with her."

He narrows his eyes. "I was told . . . your mother is Lourdes Cavendish, the landlord?"

I nod.

"She told me you might forget. She gave me a key."

Suspicions confirmed. "Well I'm not okay with that," I say, striving to keep my voice level. "You can tell her that from me."

"Your mother wants the modem in this apartment, and the two other times we've tried to get in it's been locked and we have had to reschedule. Our schedules are pretty full, so this has been going on for three months now." He pauses. "I'm guessing you're managing the apartments for her?"

I fold my arms over my chest.

"If I had a manager who forgot two appointments for a cable install, I'd be tempted to fire them," he says blandly.

I stare at him for a few seconds. "You let yourself in without permission," I say slowly, "and now you're judging me and insulting me. I think I'll call the cops and charge you with trespassing. This is, after all, *my* apartment."

He sighs and passes his hand through his hair. "Let's just get this done. I need to install the modem and make sure your connection works. And I need to get a cable through a wall somewhere."

"You're not going to leave, then."

He gives me a direct look. "Your mother told me to stay and finish, no matter what the tenant said. I guess that's you. And I'm going to assume that if the cops showed up here, I could put them on the phone with your mom, and it wouldn't be *me* who was shown the door in the end."

"Right." I'm clenching my jaw so hard I think I hear a molar crack. "Well, have fun then." I whirl around and grab my coat, which is hanging from the doorknob, and my backpack, which is in the middle of the floor.

"You have to be here. I can't be on the premises without an owner or tenant present. Wouldn't want to be accused of walking off with anything." He glances around the kitchen. "Not that there's anything here to tempt me."

"You're a jerk."

He inclines his head. "Thank you for that. Where's your computer?"

"In the bedroom."

He glances down at the photo again. "Will your husband be back soon?"

"He died a year ago. So, no."

I gain immense satisfaction in seeing his cheekbones darken a bit. "Okay," he says after a long pause, scooping up the baby boy in one arm and tugging at the hand of the toddler. "Come on back with me for a minute, buddy."

I follow him down the hall. "You don't have to bring a chaperone. Believe me, I am in no way tempted to take advantage of you."

"Yeah. Well." Bob shrugs as he strolls through the doorway to my bedroom, stepping over my discarded clothes from last night, skirting the bed as if it might contain an explosive device. He shifts his overlarge frame into my little desk chair and settles the baby on his lap. He presses the power button on my Dell computer tower and flicks on the screen, glancing up at me as the password box appears.

"Cavendish," I say. "All lowercase." I'm standing in the doorway, arms folded, watching him. He logs onto my screen, sets the baby on the floor, and takes a drill from the case he's carrying. He plugs it in and begins drilling through the wall near the floor. He doesn't ask me if the spot's okay or anything; he just starts drilling.

The boy's watching me. His eyebrows are like his dad's. Yeah, I have to assume the kids are his, though why he'd bring them along on his job, I've no idea. Unless he is divorced or something. Which, frankly, wouldn't surprise me.

A wave of guilt hits me, dissipating my anger somewhat. *His wife might have died. You of all people shouldn't judge like that, Abish.*

The little boy's dark eyebrows contrast in a kind of compelling way with his light blue eyes. "Hey there," I find myself saying to him.

"Will you keep an eye on them a minute?" Bob asks, crawling out from under my desk. "I've got to feed the cable through." He doesn't wait for me to answer before he leaves the room. I step out of his way, but his shoulders are pretty broad. One brushes my cheek slightly as he passes.

Some father. For all he knows, I could be a serial killer or something.

I sit on the bed so that I can have a better view of the baby, who immediately starts bawling when his dad leaves. He cries harder when I go to pick him up, so I move back to the bed and try not to chew my nails. *Of course, most serial killers wouldn't run crying to their room because they got caught in their jammies.*

The boy gives me a shy little smile, walks over, and thrusts a toy into my lap. It's a black-and-red Transformer, bristling with complicated parts. I notice that one of the little feet-wheelies is missing.

"So cool. Does your toy have a name?" I make my voice loud enough so he can hear me over the baby's screaming.

"It's named Val'rie."

"A good name." I hide my surprise that a little boy would give his favorite action figure a girl's name. "Can she shoot people?"

"He."

I nod like I understand and hand him back the toy. "What's *your* name?"

"Todd. Is that your dad?" He points to the small bedside table where the lamp, as well as one of mine and Mark's wedding pictures, rests.

"My dad? My husband," I correct, stuttering a little.

"What's his name?"

"Mark."

"Is he at work?"

I shake my head.

Bob walks back into the room. He picks up the baby and sits

down at the desk, clicking the mouse and typing things occasionally. After a minute, the baby stops crying. My ears are ringing with the silence.

"My mom and dad got vorced," Todd informs me.

"Vorced?" *He means divorced. I guessed right the first time.*

"It works," Bob says abruptly, standing and nearly upsetting the chair. "Come on, Todd." He shifts the baby to his hip and puts a palm on the back of the kid's head to guide him out of the room.

I follow him down the hall. He gathers up his stuff. "If it doesn't work right, call the number," he snaps, slapping a magnet onto the refrigerator. "There it is."

"Excuse me." My blood is starting to warm again. "Have *I* done something to offend you? *I'm* the one that got walked in on."

"I'm pretty sure I'm the one who was walked in on," he retorts.

"I can't help that I didn't know you were supposed to be here today."

Bob gives me a skeptical look, reaches over, and punches the blinking button on my answering machine.

"Hi, this is Mark and Abish. Leave us a message and we'll call you when we can." (My voice interrupts,) *"When we want to."* (Mark laughs.) *"When we want to. Thanks!"*

He stares at me, his expression shifting from angry to somewhat-disturbed and possibly-a-little-concerned. He opens his mouth, then closes it. He shakes his head and turns away, packing his case.

"Yeah," I mumble. "Haven't really remembered to change it."

"I wanted to remind you, *hija,*" Mama's throaty voice blares into the room, "the boy is coming tomorrow morning. He will need to look at your computer. So make sure your room is clean." (Long pause). "I need you to make this work, Abish. All the tenants are complaining about Internet. I have to get this done or I'll lose two contracts. I love you. See you Sunday."

Bob gathers the pile of blocks into a zip-up plastic container sitting next to it. He lifts the baby, gestures to Todd, and walks out the door. He doesn't look at me. "Hope your connection works well. If you have trouble, again, the number's on your fridge."

"You already said."

"Bye."

I don't know if he means to, but the door closes hard enough that a sheet of snow falls off the eaves.

I'm sick with humiliation. The rage is starting to creep back too; at my mother, and at the cable guy—Bob, if his shirt is to be believed. I hate him for seeing me at my worst. For hearing my answering machine and thinking I'm messed up or something, just because I haven't changed the message.

At I don't know exactly what.

The phone shrills.

Slowly, reluctantly, I walk toward the kitchen, hoping it will run out of rings before I get there. I glance at the answering machine. My heart lightens instantly as I recognize the number, and I grab the receiver and press it to my cheek. "Hey, Pen." I'm laughing a little in my relief.

"Hey. You feel like shooting me today?"

"Yeah, I could do with some violence. Give me fifteen minutes or so."

"Cool."

I shower. Instead of my snowboarding jacket, I throw on a hoodie and some cotton gloves because running generally keeps me pretty warm. Pen's apartment is in west Rexburg, over by Kennedy Elementary. To be honest, it's not the nicest part of town. If Rexburg had a slum, this would be it: one of the town's two trailer parks, surrounded by a few ugly concrete industrial buildings.

Pen's not going to school this semester. Technically, if you're a single student at BYU-Idaho, you're supposed to go back home when you're not enrolled in school, but Pen doesn't. He sticks around. He's got a couple of part-time jobs in town. He just rents a non-approved apartment while he is out of school, until he can move back into student housing.

I take a few seconds to stretch my calves and get my breath back. The wet hair on the nape of my neck has frozen. I put my hand there to warm it. I knock and lean against the concrete wall of the stairwell.

He opens the door. His hair is studiously messy, and he's wearing jeans and an adorable wide-striped thermal shirt. His innocent blue eyes melt me for just a second. "Hey," I say, reaching for my ponytail and shoving the band higher up against my head. I stride past him and flop onto his broken-down couch. "*Halo* or *Warcraft*?"

Pen shrugs. He makes his way across the room slowly, likely so I can get a good look at him.

I know Pen's game, don't get me wrong. His natural instinct around women is slimy-ish flirtation, but I like to hang out with him because he doesn't judge me. He never calls me crazy. And . . . well . . . his lips are kind of like Mark's.

Yeah, it's totally sick. I know. We started kissing kind of by accident—I was over one time a few months ago and we'd just played five straight hours of *Halo*. I wasn't exactly thinking straight.

"I was playing Portal last night." Pen flicks on his 52-inch plasma screen. It dominates the tiny living room. It's such a *guy* living room: ugly couch, eighties-era shag, and giant gorgeous electronics. His speaker system spans all four walls.

"Portal's a one-person game," I reply. "Let's get some *Halo* on. I could use a heavy dose of frag grenades this morning."

Pen's lips curl into his trademark cynical smile. He slides in next to me and grabs a controller. I reach under the couch for the other one.

We destroy each other for hours. I take him several times with the grenades and once with a pistol-butt to the back of his head. He runs over me repeatedly with his tank and snipes me from his favorite hiding place. It's up high on the canyon wall; he won't show me exactly where. We take a break at around three p.m. for pizza. It's cold and likely at least a day old, but it's also refrigerated and still better than what I have at home. Pen reaches past me into the fridge and digs out two cans of my favorite beverage. He tosses one to me.

"Aw shucks—coconut water. You're keeping my drinks in your fridge. Pretty soon you'll be giving me a back door key."

"You only have to ask," Pen replies in a mock-sultry tone.

I gulp down that sweet, nutty goodness in one draw and crush the can in my fist before throwing it away.

"Hey," Pen says. "Let's go out for lunch. Sushi?"

"No thanks. I just had lunch." I indicate my two leftover crusts.

He reaches over and tosses them in the trash. "So? There's *always* room for sushi."

"Not now. I've got a hot date with the Millers tonight."

Pen furrows his brow. "Mark's parents?"

"Yeah. It's game night. We do it once a month."

I'm aware that my tone is slightly defensive. But after this morning, after Bob's face when he hit the button on my answering machine, it's kind of hard not to feel that way. *I'm not crazy. You'd understand that if you spent even one day in my shoes.*

"Right," Pen murmurs. "Fine, then." He grabs one of my shoulders and lays a kiss on me—warm, sweet, soft.

It startles me, but after a second or two I don't have a problem responding. How a boy like Pen can kiss like that, I'll never know. It's like in real life, he's that bratty still-a-teenager, spiky-haired kid you'd never give the time of day. But when he kisses you . . .

Well. I already said it. It's like Mark's lips were somehow put on someone else's body. I like to think of it as Heavenly Father's small consolation prize. I can't have Mark, but I can kiss Pen. And sort of have Mark. For like, three seconds.

Pen pulls away. "You know, I always thought girls who've been married would kiss differently."

I open my eyes. "Like how?"

"I don't know. Sexier, maybe?"

And that's done it—my warm, reflective moment is completely shattered. I roll my eyes. "Bye, Pendleton."

"Yeah, okay. Later." Pen walks with me into the living room and opens the front door—an oddly chivalrous gesture for him—and I'm already jogging when I hit the sidewalk.

Back at the apartment, I take my time cleaning up. I shower until the water runs cold and wrap up in my fuzzy blue bathrobe. It's one of Mark's presents to me from last year, which would have been our first Christmas as a married couple. We planned it to the last detail, gleefully bought presents, and prepared all kinds of pranks and jokes on each other.

Or at least, I did. I'm sure he did too. That was Mark.

I'll never know for sure though, because we didn't end up spending it together. On Christmas day last year, I opened the presents that Mark had wrapped for me one by one, imagining the smart remarks he might've been making if he was sitting next to me. And then I gathered up all of my presents to him—unopened, of course—and stuffed them in the suitcase we'd shared on our honeymoon seven months before.

They're there in my closet, still unopened. From where I'm sitting on the bed, wrapped in the warm robe, I can see the corner of the suitcase peeping through the fall of hanging clothing. Jeans, sweaters, shirts, and dresses. Mark's clothes are neatly lined up on one side of the closet. My side is a jumbled chaotic mess, as it usually is lately. There are five pairs of dirty running shorts tossed over the crossbar of one particularly loaded hanger. Shirts are sliding off all over the floor as I shove the clothes aside, looking for a particular black skirt.

The Millers like to dine formally on the weekends. It was completely intimidating for me at first, but then I got to like the fact I had an excuse to put on makeup and a hint of perfume every week to eat a fancy dinner. Saturday is less formal, but Anne always wears a skirt. So I do too.

I stand in front of the mirror and carefully dust my lids with a discreet red-brown tinted shadow—a present from Anne, actually—and line my eyes with black. I choose a wine-colored lipstick. I slide the boar-bristle brush through my hair until it falls, shiny and smooth, over my shoulders. Giving myself a brisk nod in the mirror, I throw on my coat and go sit on the couch to wait.

The horn honks at exactly 5:45, just as I knew it would.

"Hello," I say, opening the door and sliding into the passenger seat.

Andy—Mark's dad—smiles at me. "Hello. How have you been doing?"

I shrug. "Fine, thanks."

We chatter about this and that as we head out to Hibbard, which is where the Millers live. They built a house there about five years ago, before the explosion of McMansions began creeping their way into the subdivision (built by the BYU-I professors who were fleeing town in the wake of the Freshman Factories and Marriage Machines).

Mark's dad isn't a professor. He's an entrepreneur, and he's probably wealthier than most professors. On the outside, the Millers' home doesn't reflect that fact too much. It's a discreet brick two-story with a two-car garage. But as soon as you walk in the door, you're greeted with twenty-foot ceilings and a five-foot crystal chandelier hanging over the gleaming chestnut concert grand piano, which is angled off into the first living room. The parlor, I think Anne calls it.

Andy takes my coat. I stop and run my fingers over the keys. They're pristine and completely dust free.

I can't play, but Mark does, magnificently. Chopin and Debussy, Poulenc and Beethoven—let's just say I wasn't the only girl falling all over herself after the student ward talent show the year we met.

Anne meets me in the kitchen. "Well, hello," she says, giving me her best hostess's smile.

"Let me take that." I whisk the basket of rolls away from her and walk into the dining room. She follows me and lays out the napkins and silverware—just one extra fork this time. *Not too horribly fancy tonight, then.* She has the three of us up at the head of the table.

I settle into my chair. Andy says the prayer and then looks up at me. His eyes are moist. I feel my own throat thicken.

"A week ago," he says huskily.

"Tuesday," I correct him. "Four days."

We stare at each other for a moment. It's a comfort, seeing what I feel reflected in Andy's face. Half the time I don't even know what I feel. But I know it when I see it.

Mile 21

"I can't believe it's been a year already," Anne murmurs without looking at either of us. "Sweetheart, pass around the salmon, will you?"

It's a good meal. Good food, good talk. Andy makes me laugh a lot, just like Mark. Anne brings up genteel, interesting topics of conversation. She's good at that sort of thing—the perfect millionaire-entrepreneur's wife.

When we've had our fill of talk, we take our dishes to the sink (I never let Anne do it for me). We retreat to the den, where the board game *Clue* has already been set up.

I swallow and glance at Andy. "We haven't played this one for a while."

He nods. "I thought it would be appropriate, considering the anniversary."

Clue is Mark's favorite game. He always wins, for one thing. But he plays it unconventionally, asking all sorts of absurd questions that leave our little notepads a scramble of question marks and crossed-out symbols, and raising his eyebrows and frowning theatrically to put us off track. Honestly, playing Clue was mostly fun because of Mark.

As we play it now, I feel almost as if he's sitting with us, with the three of us who are sitting around a four-sided table. I glance occasionally at the empty side where his chair would be. I almost believe that I'll see him, with the warm light turning his sandy hair to gold, throwing his bony features into slight shadow.

Anne wins this time. It's a surprise. She never wins much; she's always too busy being the gracious hostess to pay attention. She's strangely silent tonight, though.

"Colonel Mustard in the Billiard Room with the dagger," she says abruptly. She grabs the envelope, pulls out the cards, and shows them to us. Andy and I gape for a moment before congratulating her.

"I'm a little tired," she says, rising from the table. She starts to tidy up the pieces and stack the cards, so I hurry to help her. We lower the lid onto the box together. "I've made cheesecake squares," she adds. "Abish, do you mind taking yours home with you?"

I frown. "Sure. Tiring week, it's been. I guess."

Anne nods, reaches for me, and embraces me for a long moment. "It's nice to see you, Abish." Her voice wobbles a little—it's completely uncharacteristic for her. I watch in disbelief as she leaves the den by way of the hall door.

She must be really tired, I think as I slide back in next to Andy. *But this week's a hard one for all of us. Maybe this year anniversary is the thing that's put her over the edge for the first time.*

I feel strangely tired myself. Andy and I don't say anything at all on the way back, but we both yawn a few times.

"Well, Abish," he says as he pulls up in front of the fourplex, "it's been nice seeing you."

I give him a nod and hop out of the car. "See you at the Christmas party."

"Yes. It will be a fun one. Anne's got a few special things planned."

"More than usual?" I grin at him. "Impossible. The famous Miller Christmas Extravaganza *cannot* get more special than it already is."

He smiles back. "Thanks for coming over."

"Bye." I slam the door, turn, and walk slowly up the stairs. The slick soles of my Sunday shoes have about the same traction as a pair of ice skates. I slip near the top and grab the rail, scrambling for dear life until I right myself.

As I walk into the apartment I feel strangely deflated. Usually these evenings with the Millers bolster me, fill me with warmth and courage to face the month ahead. *Every first Saturday. A recharge for me, a recharge for them.* Or so I thought. With Anne looking and acting the way she did, I feel more drained than bolstered tonight.

The answering machine is blinking on the counter. I stare at it for a few seconds, fighting my reluctance before I press the button.

"Abish, I want to make sure you are coming tomorrow. I have a few things to say to you. As your landlord and as your mother. Please be there."

I bite my lip and grimace, thinking of the incident this morning. *I hope he didn't tell her anything.* If Mom kicks me out, the next housing option is probably Aunt Cindy, and the thought makes every fiber of my being want to curl up and die.

I lean my elbow on the counter, thinking. Finally I pick up the receiver and punch a number in.

"Hey." Despite the late hour, Pen's voice holds no trace of fatigue, and I can hear some laughing in the background.

"Having a party?"

"Nothing big. Chad and Laura and Bloke."

I frown, because I'm not a big fan of Chad and Laura. They're all over each other every second you're around them. Laura's not a student at BYU-Idaho, but Chad is. And Bloke's an okay guy. His name's really Dave, and he drinks a lot of Coca-Cola. Once Pen introduced him to a bunch of annoying freshman coeds (using a fake English accent) as "the bloke who does coke" in order to scare them off. Bloke is the beefy-absent type. He's a decent person, but he's got no restraint when it comes to egging Pendleton on.

"'Kay," I say. "Pen, I need a favor."

"Oh?" The fake sultry tone is back. "And what do I get in return?"

"Oh, believe me," I say, chuckling, "I'll *have* to make it worth your while. It's Sunday dinner with my family."

"Huh?" he says in quite a different tone.

"C'mon, Pen," I plead. "It's not like I'm *taking you to see my parents*. I just need, I don't know, backup. I think Mama's on the warpath, and throwing you into the mix will toss a wrench into her plans to verbally disembowel me in public."

"Sounds pretty harsh."

"Mama's hard core."

"All right," he says after few seconds. "But you'd better make good on what you said before. About making it up to me."

"Oh, I will. I'll totally let you take me out. I won't even resist."

"Really? Deal." There's an unusually excited tone in his voice.

He must be getting addicted to Halo. "Seriously, you can beat me to a pulp. I won't even put up a fight."

A long silence. "You know, you're a weird chick, Abish."

"Wait till you meet my mom. Can we drive your car? I'll pay for gas. Then Dad won't have to come get us, and there won't be those awkward twenty minutes riding up and back from St. Anthony."

"'Kay."

"Bye."

I stumble into my room and lie down without bothering to remove my things. *I have early church tomorrow, but I can sleep in and run a comb through my hair. Brush a few wrinkles from my skirt . . .* I slide into bed, reach out, and touch Mark's pillow.

Sleep takes me away in a whorl of feverish warmth and confusing images—restless dreams I know I'll forget tomorrow. Dreams of his face, his eyes, his hands. Dreams of him here, talking to me.

Chapter 3

Mark and I chose the family ward over the student married one. I was (I think understandably) glad about this after he died. The problem is, a few months ago the Church changed policy. They dissolved the student-married wards and shifted them to the family wards. So now there are always a lot of young couples in the congregation, nuzzling and tickling and leaning on each other. I sit close to the front so that I don't have to watch. I wouldn't want to throw up all over some poor newlyweds.

The bishop reaches out to shake my hand as he passes me. "Hello, Sister Miller," he booms.

"Hey," I reply, and he lumbers on up to the stand to sit with his counselors. Bishop Snow. He's just like his name—an abominable snowman. Six-foot-four probably. A big, big guy with a mellow, bearlike voice. He has bright white hair and soft blue eyes.

He's great. He asks me in the hall once in a while how I am and I answer, "fine," and he understands what I mean, which is, *If I ever start going off the deep end I'll talk to you, but for now I'd like to be left alone, thanks.* Every once in a while his wife brings me over bread or cookies or something like that. Once she came in, and without even asking, swept and mopped my floor. Yeah, the Snows are one in a million. There when you need them, but hands off most of the time. I can't say there's anyone else in my life like that right now.

I sit through sacrament meeting. I take my place in the back of the room for Sunday School, and I'm in my usual quiet corner during Relief Society. Nobody really talks to me. They smile, say hi, then leave me alone. Which works for me. I have two empty seats on either side of me, and that's how I like it.

Okay, there might be a small, tiny piece of me that feels a bit . . . rebuffed, maybe, that I don't have any chatting-friends who I can just assume I'm sitting next to in Relief Society. But I know a lot of it's my own fault. I'm kind of a one-word-answer person at church. So I really can't blame them, and what would they say to me if I did encourage them? We have nothing in common . . . not anymore, at least. When things happen to you—things that aren't normal—people don't know what to say, so either they stutter and fall all over themselves and say all the wrong things, or they don't say anything at all. And let me tell you, I vastly prefer the second option.

After the last prayer is said, my visiting teachers stop me on the way out and we have a brief conversation. I semi-agree to an appointment next week but don't bother to write it on my hand or anything. My home teachers are basically nonexistent. I don't even know who they are.

Back at home, I step out of my skirt and nylons and rub my legs for a few minutes. They itch like nothing else after being in tights so long. I throw on my favorite worn-out pair of sweatpants, layer on two pairs of socks, and slip on my tennis shoes.

I head out toward Second East and hang a left at the intersection. The air smells nice today. It's warm for this time of year. The wind in my face feels and tastes so good, I wish I could drink it. The streets are empty. There's no sidewalk traffic.

I know some people would say running is too much like working, and that I shouldn't do it on Sunday, but Sunday is the most restful run of the week. My mind churns through things better when I don't have to stop at an intersection or avoid students loaded down with five bags of Walmart groceries on their bicycle handles. The road thins out, and suddenly I'm running through fields. I can see horizon on every side. Scenes from the week flash into my mind: the scene in my living room—that guy with his kids. My stomach twists with the memory. I close my eyes tightly for a few seconds and will it away.

I turn off at Cemetery Road and slow to a walk, glancing at the dusty weeds on the sides of the road. I'm not finding much, so finally I reach over and pluck a handful of dry grass with golden stalks and feathery, flowerlike tops. By the time I get to the cemetery, I've added a few withered Black-Eyed Susans and divided them into two semi-artistic bunches. They're actually kind of cute, like something someone might stick on their front door for fall decorations. The smaller one is just a black-eyed Susan, with a few little fronds tucked around it to frame its dark center and shriveled golden petals.

I pick my way through the headstones, stopping here and there to glance at some names I haven't looked at before. Finally I kneel in front of a shiny, flat granite stone, setting the bouquets in my lap.

"Hey, Mark. Just came by to see how you are. I'm sure you already know how I am." I run my hands over the smooth, cool surface. "Like I said the other day, I'm going to try to get back on track. I'm going to finish the degree like I promised you. But it's hard now that I'm so close to it, thinking of going back to classes, to all the *stuff*."

A thought comes into my head. It sounds, as it sometimes does, sort of like Mark's voice. *What stuff?*

I don't know if it's me making it up or if it's really Mark. But it's the only way I've talked to him since losing him, so I've never argued with it. "I don't know," I answer. "It's just been a strange year for me. I'm sure it's been a strange year for you too. I mean, you're somewhere completely new. And I'm still here. The only thing that tells me you're gone is that, well . . . you're gone."

But I'm not really gone.

"No, you're right." Abruptly, I lay the larger bundle on top of the stone. "You know how crafty I am. You're probably laughing at me right now. But, anyway, there you go."

It's cute. Definitely one of your craftier creations.

I smile and lay the tinier bouquet on the grass off to the side. I feel the beat of my heart in my throat as I stare down at it. "I'm glad you're with her. I'd rather you were with me, of course. But she probably needs you more."

I pause, stand, and trace the wet grass with the toe of my shoe for a few moments.

"She's probably pretty cute, isn't she? You'd only have cute kids. I bet she . . ." I glance around, suddenly feeling self-conscious. *Is someone watching me?*

I don't see anyone, but there's definitely something wrong. Usually my visits to the cemetery are so calming, so good—I have a nice chat with Mark and get stuff off my chest. But right now, my words seem hollow, and suddenly I can't get it out of my mind how crazy I'd probably sound to someone, talking to a slab of granite like it's a person.

Looking at that pathetic little bundle of flowers on the grass, I feel a blackness start to spread inside of me. A dull, terrible ache that seems to block everything out, to drain the sky of color. I stand up shakily and take off at once, fiercer, harder, faster than I generally run. By the time I'm back at the apartment, I'm pouring sweat and my breathing is ragged, but the sense of euphoria is worth it. The blackness is gone; I've outrun it.

My head aches, though. I go to the kitchen and make a slice of bread with peanut butter. I down it, along with the rest of the milk, which is starting to taste strange. After a long, hot shower, I call Pen.

"You ready?" I ask, glancing at myself in the mirror as I flick a brush through my wet hair. I've put on my purple high-neck sweater. Mama loves it; she says it brings out my eyes. It's itchy, but anything that will get me a little further into her grace today is worth it.

I hear a rustling of couch springs. "I guess," he replies.

"See you soon, then."

A few minutes later there's a knock on the door. I open it and follow Pen down to the driveway. His car smells funny—cigarette smoke, I think. He's got a couple friends who smoke.

We head out along Main Street. A few blocks from the entrance to Highway 20, he pulls into the Maverick.

I raise an eyebrow.

"You said you'd pay for gas."

I fish a five-dollar bill from my pocket. "You could buy it tomorrow."

He nods at the dashboard. "Tank's empty. We won't make it up there."

I hand over the five and watch as he goes inside to pay. I feel a little funny in my Sunday dress, sitting by the gas pump. I guess you could say I'm kind of a prude when it comes to Sabbath-breaking. I can't even bring myself to use a vending machine on Sunday; that's how deeply my father ground it into me.

The image of Dad's face presses into my thoughts—hawk-nose, hawk-brows. Unfathomable, ice-blue eyes. A smile that startles with its friendliness in such a strong face. It's been a while since we talked about anything serious.

"Saint Antoine," Pen drawls a while later as we curl off the highway onto the Bridge-Street exit.

"Slow down. The cops don't have much to do in this town—they *will* pull you over for going five miles over the limit."

Pen chuckles. "What a crap town."

"Yeah, well, with where you live, you're one to talk."

"I hit a sore spot."

"Nah," I mutter, smoothing the wrinkles of my skirt. Though to be honest, his comment did bother me. More than a little. You see, people can be snooty about St. Anthony. I get it all the time: the little frown, and the "St. Anthony, huh? Don't they have a lot of gang and drug problems up there?"

I mean, yeah, there's a handful of punks who like to write their names on walls now and then. Rexburg is a great town, don't get me wrong. There are a ton of things you can do in town because of the university. And the high school just built a million-dollar auditorium and has pretty much the best sports, arts, and music programs around.

But to put it quite simply, St. Anthony is heaven.

As we drive over the river, I glance at the icy green water roaring over the little rock outcrops of Keefer Park—an island in the middle of the Henry's Fork river. The rosy light from the street lamps illuminates the crumbling brick façades of the buildings all along Bridge Street. In the distance, the Tetons are turning golden in the light of the setting sun.

"Where do I turn?"

"Oh. Uh . . next intersection. Right after the stop light."

"*The* stop light." He grins.

I ignore him. Honestly, there's no energy to waste on being annoyed at Pen when much bigger things may be afoot. My fists are balled up in my lap, and I can feel my nails pricking my palms.

My house is a bit out of town, which I guess you'd say means it's in the middle of nowhere. We drive for a couple miles through vast expanses of fields with an occasional house here and there. I study the dull reflections on the frozen surface of the still-full irrigation ditches. The fields are great brown stretches of mud. If you went out there, you'd find frozen potatoes here and there left in the furrows.

I nod when we're supposed to turn. Pen doesn't say a word as we creep up the gravel driveway. The house, with its white siding, gleams in the twilight. It's not very big. *Big enough*, Dad has always said when Mom talks longingly of remodels.

I don't knock. I just open the door and walk in, Pen following. We're not greeted by any chandeliers, grand pianos, or twenty-foot ceilings. It's not bad, though. The little nook of a sitting room has a couple of bright orange couches that actually look sort of nice against the cheerful avocado color of the walls. Accent walls are stylish now. My mother was accent, though, before accent was cool.

Above one of the couches hangs Mama's favorite picture: a rendering of Christ with a crown of thorns, his eyes upturned so you almost see only white. I've always found it a tad creepy. It doesn't help that it's huge. Like, four feet tall.

Pen eyes the picture as we walk in, and his brow furrows. "Dude."

I walk through and into the dining room. "This way." We stop in the archway leading into the kitchen.

I love my mother's kitchen. It's corn-yellow with a red trim. She always cooks to music—Guatemalan or Mexican or sometimes Josh Groban—and the pulses of the music seem to carry the warmth and aroma to all corners of the home, like heartbeats.

Today, though, I enter with a crawling feeling in my spine. "Hello."

Mama's back is to me. She lifts the spoon to her mouth, tasting something from the pot she is stirring. As usual, the kitchen smells like heaven—tomatoes, fresh garlic, basil, cilantro. My heart leaps slightly when I see the corn-husk bundles piled onto two plates. *Tamales. She's going all out tonight.*

"Hi," I say, a little louder this time. "Should I take the food to the table, Mama?"

She turns around, brushing a curly dark tendril off her forehead with a small, graceful hand. Her neat little figure is wrapped in a cherry-red apron, and her eyes and cheeks glow in the heat of the stove. *How's a gawky teenage girl supposed to cope growing up with a mother like that? It's no wonder I'm a little messed up.*

The angelic impression immediately evaporates when her glance lights on Pen, who is gazing at her with a certain measure of appreciation. Her eyes narrow and harden. Her lips purse. "Come in," she growls, flicking the dish towel she holds in her hand as if she's cracking a whip. "You brought a boy?"

"Mom, meet Pendleton," I say, tugging Pen in by the sleeve cuff.

Mom studies him for a few seconds. The only sound in the kitchen is the bubbling of the pot. "Well, welcome," she says finally. "Take this in and put it on the table." She thrusts a plate of tamales into Pen's arms and one into mine. As I'm about to turn quickly and follow him, she grasps my upper arm.

"Who is he?" she asks in what she mistakenly thinks is a whisper.

"Just a boy. We've been hanging out." Immediately I cringe, knowing I've said the exact wrong thing.

"*Hanging out*? Do you not listen to the prophets, *niña*?"

"Dating," I amend, choking on the word. "Sorry, Mama. I meant we're . . . dating. Why else would I bring him here to meet you?"

The lines on her face smooth out. "All right. But you should have told me he was coming. I'm only glad I made *Tamales de Puerco* instead of a meatloaf, which was what I had planned."

Suzy walks into the dining room and sits down just as we're bringing the food in. She's wearing a jade-blue print skirt and a matching top, and a ribbon headband holding back her red-brown curls. She's wearing more makeup lately, I notice. It makes her look glamorous and older than her seventeen years.

"Hey," Pen says, sitting in the chair next to hers. He holds out a hand and gives her one of his cynical smiles—*gets 'em every time.*

Suzy glances at him, then down at his hand. "Hey," she replies.

"I'm Pendleton," Pen drawls, tucking his rejected hand back into his pocket.

"Mm-hm." Suzy turns to me. "Are you staying tonight? It's going to snow."

"Nope." I sit down in a chair directly across from them, feeling a tickle of amusement in my chest as I see the slightly incredulous look in Pen's eyes. *For this reason alone, it was worth it to bring him.* "Suzy, I've told you about Pendleton, haven't I?"

"No, you haven't." She smiles coolly. "Are you a BYU student?"

Pen gives her another slow, smirky grin. "Yup. Chemistry."

Pen's a mechanical engineering major. I can't wait to hear the lines I know are coming next: *You're majoring in chemistry? No, just saying I think there's some. Don't you?*

Of course, Suzy doesn't take the bait. "Oh?" She turns back to me. "I'd appreciate it if you could take some more of your boxes home tonight. I want to get a stationary bike and a desk in there. Mom said I could have it as a study and workout room."

"'Kay." My skin is heating up a little, because apparently, Mama's promised Suzy free reign of the space I grew up in without consulting me at all. *What am I supposed to do with boxes of my childhood stuff? Isn't that what spare rooms are for: keeping all those things that nobody knows what to do with but can't quite throw away? Are my parents completely exorcising me from their lives now?* "I don't really have a lot of room at the apartment, though," I reply, managing a civil tone.

"We could move some of it to the garage."

I nod. "Or we could just sell it all at the next yard sale."

Lucky for the both of us (and Pen), Dad walks into the room at just that moment. "Smells nice," he says, lowering himself slowly into his seat at the head of the table. He freezes for a moment, and his ice-blue eyes flash—instant dislike, I can tell. But that's nothing new. He's never liked any of the boys I've dated. Or married. He folds his arms and leans back in his chair. "Hello there."

"Hello, sir," Pen replies, rising to a standing position and leaning across the table with his hand extended. "Pendleton Walsch. Good to finally meet you." As he sits back down, he gives me a smirk. *You owe me, baby,* it says.

"Tone it down," I murmur, and grimace a little as Dad's eagle eye lands on me.

"You two are dating?"

Leave it to my dad to come right to the point without bothering about people's discomfort. That is the one thing Mama and Dad have in common. They both don't bother with niceties or euphemisms.

Mama seats herself, giving Pen a quick, sharp glance.

"Yup," I reply.

"Huh?" Pen murmurs.

I ignore it. "I'll say the prayer."

Dad nods, still watching us.

I mumble my way through a quick, generic prayer. Mama's mouth is tight and disapproving as she serves, using a soup dipper to pour the green sauce from the pot over the tamales with combative little flicks of her wrist.

We dig in.

"Oh man."

We all look at Pen, who is gazing at my mother with a look of utter adoration. "You cooked these?"

Mama's mouth softens. "My grandmother's recipe." She reaches across the table and pats Pen's hand. "You're too skinny. Make sure you take some home with you."

"I will. These are completely tripping."

Mama's smile twists into a slight frown of confusion. She nods and takes back her hand, focusing her gaze on me instead.

Immediately, I duck my head and pretend to be really busy cutting my food. "Yeah. Maybe the best you've made, Mama."

"Yeah," Suzy cuts in, annoyance sharpening her tone. "Completely *tripping*. Where did you say you went on your mission?"

"France," I answer for him.

"Toulouse," Pen adds. "It was a rough, rough mission." He shakes his head. "Hardest mission in the world, they say."

He's going for the sympathy angle. Maybe I should just put him out of his misery right now and tell him he's got about the chance of a snowball in . . . Toulouse.

Suzy gives him one of her stunning smiles, dimples and all. "I bet Paris is harder." She shoves another bite of tamale into her mouth.

We all chew for a few minutes. Finally my mom sets down her fork. "Abish, I have some things to say to you."

"But, Mom." I jerk my shoulder in Pen's direction.

She stands and blots her lips delicately with her napkin. "There are some things I need to ask you about. In your old room."

"Right now?" I gesture toward my half-full plate.

"It will take only a few minutes."

I glance at Pen, trying to will him to do something—follow us down the hall, maybe. *I'd love to see the room you grew up in,* he could say. Or anything. Pen's a pretty wily guy; that's why I brought him. I knew he'd be quick on his feet.

But at this moment, he's only aware of the food on his plate. He's in tamale heaven. He doesn't even notice we've gotten up from the table, he's so entirely focused on his food. Suzy gives me a slightly sympathetic glance.

Just me and my mom, then, head down the hall. I imagine I can hear drums beating a warpath, ending in a dramatic roll as she flings open the door and gestures impatiently for me to step inside.

"This is the last string," She hisses. "The neighbors are complaining; I promised them free wireless two months ago and you didn't schedule the repair boy and so I did it, and you send him away with a fly in his ear."

"A flea, Mom."

"What?"

"A flea in his ear."

"The apartment *better not* have fleas."

"Mama, I forgot about the cable install. I spend a lot time studying the night before. Nursing's a hard major. I got home and spaced it. I woke up and walked into the living room—"

"Naked." She throws her arms up. "You walked naked into the living room. Who does this?"

"I wasn't naked. The guy was completely rude. He was asking all sorts of personal questions."

"He was probably only being friendly. You don't know the meaning of that word anymore."

"He was *not* friendly."

We glare at each other.

"Abby," Mama finally says, "you need to get over whatever this slump is. If you want to live in the apartment at the special reduced family rate, you need to manage. I need a manager. If you can't be it, then I need to use the money to pay someone else."

I mumble something under my breath about the special reduced family rate and how it comes with a price.

"What was that?"

Her voice has that tone that I've known all my childhood; it means that the ice I'm walking on has evaporated and I'm basically treading water. "Nothing," I reply, looking her firmly in the eye. "It was a mistake. I had a long night. I was studying for my final. You know, the one I need to take to get rid of my incomplete? It's next Saturday."

"Yes. One test. What will happen in January? How are you going to handle a full load of credits if you can't even handle one class, Abby?"

I look at my shoes. "I'll do better. I know the ice needs to be scraped off the stairs. I know the laundry coins need to be emptied. And I know I screwed up with Bob. He was rude, but I admit I wasn't as nice as I could've been."

"Bob?"

"The Internet guy. I didn't mean to walk in on him like that. I was just wiped out. I stayed late at the hospital—"

At this, my mom truly loses it. She goes off in a tirade of Spanish. I don't understand any of it. Mama never speaks Spanish to us except when she is really, really mad, like right now.

When she finishes, she sighs and puts a hand on my shoulder. She's not looking angry anymore; it's more like worried. Very worried. And something I haven't seen in her ever before—a bone-weariness that sharpens the soft lines in her face and makes her look her age. It's awful—I suddenly want her to yell at me, take me by the shoulders and shake me. Anything. "*Querida*," she says, "you can't spend your days moping all around that place. You must get past this."

I take a step back and her hand falls away. "I'll get past it when I get past it."

"It's been a year, Abby. You should be functioning by now."

"I'm sorry if I'm cramping your style by having a hard time. When Dad dies, maybe we can talk about how easy it is for *you* to function." I stalk past her and slam the door, leaving her inside, and walk into the kitchen.

Just my luck, Suzy is in there, lowering a stack of plates into the sink. And of course she turns around and puts her hands on her hips.

"Don't," I say, holding up a hand as her lips part.

"What? I just wanted to know where you dug up that guy. You did bring him here to *meet* us, right?" The glitter of cynicism in her eyes would be hilarious to me in almost every other situation. Was, just a few minutes ago, in fact. *Pen, what a joke.*

"I've known him a while," I say finally. "I just brought him over . . . because."

"You mean you are really going out with that guy? That's messed up."

"Yeah, well." I shrug. "Sometimes life is messed up. You'll figure that out someday when you don't have Mom to tell you what to do every second of the day and night, and you have bigger problems to worry about than what color gown to buy for homecoming ball." I push past her, flip the water on, and begin loading dishes into the dishwasher.

"I don't like him. I don't think you should be hanging out with him."

I raise an eyebrow.

"He's not good enough for you, Abish."

I jam the plate into the loading rack and straighten. "Your definition of 'good' might be different from mine."

"Yeah," Suzy says emphatically, rolling her eyes a little.

"What does *that* mean?"

"Nothing. I guess we just have different taste in guys."

"You don't have to spell it out for me," I retort. "I knew that you and Dad were against me and Mark from the beginning. Too bad you never knew him well enough to judge."

Suzy's eyebrows draw down in the middle. "What, this is about *Mark* now? We were talking about that dude in there"—she jerks her thumb in the direction of the dining room— "not Mark. He's trouble. And a jerk. And not worth your time. Mom might gush over him, but she gushes over anyone who compliments her cooking or shows one of her precious little *bambinas* any attention at all. Dad's always been the better judge, and you know it."

"Yeah, and because Dad hated Mark, that means Mark was a jerk too."

"Dad didn't hate Mark; he just wanted you to wait to get married. He wanted you to go on a mission like you always talked about."

"Yeah, well, life happens." My voice is rising, enough that anyone in any room of the house can probably hear me. But at this point, I don't care.

I slide a casserole dish out of the fridge (strawberry Jell-O with banana slices, the dessert of Mormon champions) and restrain my first impulse, which is to dump it over her head. "I didn't choose for

Dad to name me Abish. I didn't choose for him to label me missionary material from the time I was born. And I didn't *choose*"—I grab a serving spoon from the drawer and plonk it into the Jell-O—"to fall in love with Mark. One thing you don't understand yet, Suzy, is that stuff just happens sometimes. You can lay out all the plans and write in all the journals you want, but—" I shrug, and there's a catch in my throat. "—sometimes you have to go with it. And sometimes you're happier when you do."

"You don't seem very happy to me."

"Yeah, well, my husband kicked it a year ago. Not many twenty-one-year-old widows are happy people, I'm guessing."

Suzy's face softens.

I can't stand it. I turn away abruptly and march back into the dining room.

"Jell-O?" I say, aggressively ladling about half the platter onto Pen's plate and setting the dish on the table with a resounding thump. I slide my chair back and sit down, folding my arms tightly over my chest. Dad regards me quietly from across the table. His icy gaze is softer than usual. There's something there, but like always, I can't really tell what. Maybe pain. *His or mine?*

I turn my face away, feeling my chest grow tight. "Let's go, Mark—Pen." I stutter. I stand up too fast, steady the chair with my hand, and turn on my heel. I remember to fling my coat across my shoulders and grab my gloves on the way out. The smell of cigarettes in Pen's car is like a disgusting version of smelling salts—it sharpens my senses and shakes me out of things a bit.

Crazy, I think. *It's not me; it's my family who are completely, utterly bonkers.* I look into the rearview mirror and attempt a hard, cynical smile, but the face that looks back at me is somber. Mouth trembling, eyes wide. Beaky nose red as Rudolph's. I reach into my pocket, bring out a crumpled Kleenex, and blow.

It takes Pen a while to get to the car. He's carrying a paper sack. I know what's in it. It does my heart just a little bit of good to see the sack's quite a bit smaller than the one Mark got sent home with when he first came to Sunday dinner with my family. Mark's stunned reaction to my mom's cooking that night overwhelmed her to the point that she got teary-eyed and cheek-pinchy, and it was a whole tin-foil covered pan she sent us home with. From the looks of things Pen got like, two, maybe. *Mom's not as dumb as you think, Suzy.*

"Ready to head out?" Pen gives me a sarcastic grin. "That was intense. Your dad is one scary dude. You completely owe me."

I poke at the bag at my feet with the toe of my Sunday shoe. "I think you got paid pretty well."

"Nope." Pen shakes his head emphatically. "Our deal made no mention of tamales. You said I could take you out and you wouldn't resist. I'm holding your feet to the fire on this one."

I give him a puzzled look. His tone is a kind of forceful for the subject matter, which is frag-grenades. But some guys do take their gaming very, very seriously.

As we approach the freeway on-ramp, a sigh escapes me. He gives me a curious look.

I touch his wrist. "Hey Pen, can we just drive around for a while before we head home?"

He shrugs, goes over the freeway bridge, and pulls a U-turn. "Whatever lights your fire, babe."

It starts to snow. The lamplight makes rosy haloes, outlining the drifting flakes. It piles up fast, furring the roads as I direct Pen to turn left at Main, heading in the direction of the Riverview Cemetery. We drive down the road for a while, heading through Parker, then Egin, then Plano.

"We're almost at Rexburg again," he says.

"Let's go back." *I'm not ready to go to the apartment.*

Pen shakes his head.

"I have someplace I want to show you. My five dollars in this car would cover five trips between Rexburg and Saint Anthony."

Pen pulls off the road and turns around. We drive for a while in silence. I'm starting to feel heavy around my eyes, so I know it must be at least nine-thirty. *Past my bedtime . . . if I could sleep.*

"Pull off here," I say when we get to the sign for the Riverview Cemetery. Pen drives into the parking lot, which is surrounded by wild, snow-covered nature and moving water. The peace settles over me.

"This thing with you and cemeteries is kind of creepy."

I shrug.

Pen unbuckles his seat belt, leans over, and kisses me.

For one blissful moment, Mark is kissing me again. My heart warms. I find myself returning the kiss with a tad more enthusiasm than usual. I lean in, taking his face in my hands.

"Yeah," Pen breathes when we break apart. "That's more like it." He leans in again.

This time it's kind of unpleasant. A bit too rough for my taste, a bit more passionate. Not that I'm not a passionate person; just . . . I know in my heart it's not Mark. It's Pen. Threadbare, slippery Pen.

I'm actually cringing a little as I lean away from him. "'Kay," I say. "I think I'm done. Let's go home."

There's a long moment of silence, then he grabs my arm. "Um, nope. You promised, kiddo. You can't do that to a guy." And he shifts over so that he's kind of leaning against me, so that his weight presses me into the seat's back. The smell of cigarettes leaches more strongly into my senses—his coat stinks of it too. His mouth lands on mine; greedy, forceful. A little slobbery, to be honest.

"Hey," I say, turning my head aside and pushing at him. "Hey!"

He doesn't let up. He shifts so that he's practically in my lap and begins making some overtures that no Mormon girl with any self-respect allows from someone she's not bound to for time and all eternity. After struggling a few minutes and getting continually more annoyed, I make the overture that (well, maybe not all) good Mormon girls with any self-respect will make if the guy just isn't getting it: I shove him away with as much force as I can muster, open the passenger-side door, and tumble out of the car. Pen tries following me, but I take my fist and lay a good one on his right eye.

This seems to give him the message. He stumbles back, holding his face, then stares at me for a few seconds. He lets off a single word—not one you would ever hear in Sunday School. He stalks around the car and flings himself into the driver's seat.

MILE 21

And he takes off, at noticeably more than thirty-five miles per hour.

I stand there watching him drive away, and I think how grateful Officer Jacobsen's going to be when Pen drives by his speed trap on Bridge Street. He has a hard time making his quota of speeding tickets. Yeah, that's me . . . making the world a better place.

Chapter 4

*I*t only takes me five minutes of walking aimlessly in the snow by the river, feeling my fingertips tingle and grow numb, to realize that I don't have anybody to call. Not a single person, even if I could find a phone. There's really only one thing I can do.

It's not a long run. Barely two miles. But I'm still wearing my Sunday shoes. They're Timberland Mary Janes and they've actually got a good arch in them, and they're pretty broken in. But with the snow melting against my bare shins and puddling inside of them, my feet are completely numb by the time I reach the front door. This is a blessing because it means I can't feel the blisters that likely line my ankles. Teeth chattering, I try the knob and murmur a heartfelt prayer of thanks as it turns in my hand.

I move carefully down the hall, hoping my dad isn't awake, because he hears everything. The one or two times as a teenager that I tried to creep in after curfew, he was in his bathrobe waiting for me at my door.

I make it to my old room without incident, though. I grab a

worn-out set of flannel pajamas from one of the boxes stacked in the corner. They smell like the rose potpourri sachet I made at girls' camp when I was fifteen. I creep back down the hall, step into the shower, and turn it on full-blast. At this point I'm a little past caring who might wake up. I didn't want anyone to see me in my bedraggled state coming in, but the fact is I'm going to be sleeping in my bed come morning. There'll be no avoiding the questions.

The warm water is all I can think about. I lie down on the shower floor and let it run over me until it starts to chill. I turn it off. I wait for fifteen minutes, shivering, and turn it back on again.

When it runs out again, I know it's no use stalling any longer. *I can't shower all night long.* I pull the pajamas on and flick a comb through my hair. I walk back into my old room and stare at the neatly made twin bed.

It's like I'm suddenly fifteen again. The smell of rose sachet, the feel of the flannel sticking to my skin. And the bed, with the blue-pattern comforter Mama gave me for my twelfth birthday—I slept under it until I left for college. As I walk toward it, my stomach twists and my throat tightens.

I force myself to get under the covers. *You need sleep, Abish. You have to be in to work at 8:00, and you'll need to have your wits about you tomorrow when Mama asks you a billion questions.*

I can't, though. I just can't do it. Lying here, it's like it never happened.

Mark.

It's like he never existed, like I dreamed him. Like I'm still fifteen and nothing has changed. *But it has,* I tell myself fiercely, tears welling in the corners of my eyes. *It has, no matter how much Mama and Dad wish it hadn't, wish Mark wasn't. He was. He is.*

I fling off the blankets and slide out of bed. Heart pounding, I pad down the hall barefoot, my wet hair clinging to my neck and cheeks. I hesitate outside their door, putting a hand to my mouth, closing my eyes tight. Finally I put up a hand and knock.

He's there an instant later, whisking the door open and staring down at me silently.

"Dad," I murmur. "Can you take me back, please? I lost my ride and I can't—" I shake my head. "I can't sleep here."

He doesn't say a word. He disappears back into the room, rustles around for a minute, and emerges with his old, ratty bathrobe and slippers on. He steps into the hallway and shuts the door quietly behind him.

Outside, with flakes lighting in his hair and on the dark tartan cloth of his robe, he holds open the passenger door to his fifteen-year-old four-by-four. The inside smells disturbingly familiar. *Sweat, earth, and sun-rotted vinyl—Dad.*

As we pass the exit to Sugar City, he breaks the silence. "I'm sorry, Abish. I heard you in the kitchen with Suzy. I didn't realize that was what . . ." He can't bring himself to say it: *what's made you shut me out these last couple of years.*

I put my knuckles to my mouth and turn to lean my head against the side window.

"I was wrong to get upset when you decided to marry Mark. I should have been happy for you. I could see you were happy. I was wrong to impose my wishes on you like that."

I'm glad that the darkness can hide my face. "Yeah," I manage. I don't trust myself to say another word. In fact, the muscles in my face kind of contract. I feel my mouth turn down. Tears choke my throat. I shake silently, the icy window turning my forehead numb.

He opens the door for me again when we reach the apartment. I keep my face turned away as I pass him.

He takes my shoulder in his large grip. "Abish."

The thing is, Dad and I aren't really the crying type. We get uncomfortable when people cry around us too. I don't think he's ever seen me cry. Heck, *I've* hardly ever seen me cry. So I can't bring myself to answer him just now because he'll hear the tears in my voice, and I can't look at him because then he'll see. So I put my hand on his for a moment, until he lets go of my shoulder, and then I hurry away, crossing the parking lot and running up the stairs, grabbing the rail to keep from slipping. I shut the door to the apartment behind me and lean against it, running my hands over my swollen, wet face. I breathe in deeply.

These smells soothe me. They're smells of the more recent past: musty couch cushions. Melon-scented candles—a wedding present. There's a hint of sourness from the kitchen. *The dishes need to be done.*

I stumble into the bedroom and climb into bed, but there's this annoying blue glare from the modem on the desk. I try putting the blanket over my head, but I can't get myself to sleep like that. I pull it off and glance at the bedside clock—2:12 a.m.

If I'm going to function at all tomorrow, I'm going to need at least a little sleep. I can't afford to tick off the Turd even one more time.

Finally, feeling like I'm about to cry from sheer frustration, I step out of bed, flip the lights on, and stalk over to the modem. There aren't any directions on the thing, no "off" or "on" switch, nothing. I try fiddling with a few buttons, but it doesn't do anything, so I flip the switch on the power strip sitting on the desktop. There are a half-dozen cords plugged into it but apparently the modem's not one of them, because the frenetic blue flickering continues.

Finally, I reach under the desk and yank the cord out of the wall. Then I collapse onto my bed and drift off.

A shrill sound pulls me out of my fretful sleep. I turn and squint at the alarm clock: seven fifteen. Strange, because I set it for seven-thirty, giving myself the bare minimum of time to make it to work by eight. I reach over to tap the button on top, climb out of bed, then head into the bathroom to brush my teeth. There's a pair of fairly-clean khaki pants hanging over the curtain rod; I put them on and glance down at my pajama shirt, which is plaid flannel. *Passable, at least. Nobody has to know it's a pajama shirt, or that I slept in it last night.*

The phone rings, and suddenly I realize that's what it was before—the shrill sound that woke me. It was the phone, not my alarm. I lope into the kitchen. The number isn't one I recognize, so I pick up the receiver. "Yeah?"

"Hi, Ms. Cavendish." The voice sounds world-worn and weary, so I don't bother to correct him about my last name. "This is Robert from CableOne. I'm calling on behalf of Lourdes Cavendish, the landlord. She's received some calls of complaint from the tenants this morning about the Internet going down."

"Oh!" I exclaim, setting the receiver on the counter. I dash into the bedroom and plug the cable to the modem back into its wall plug thing.

The light doesn't turn blue.

I stare at it, frowning. I kneel under my computer desk and jiggle the cable around, then peek over the edge of the desk—still nothing.

I look at the buttons and, again, try pressing a few of them. Nothing. *I killed it,* I'm thinking as I slink back down the hall. *I killed the Internet.*

"Hey," I say, picking up the receiver. "Sorry. I turned it off last night, and now I can't get it to go back on."

There's a long silence on the other end of the line. I hear a giggle somewhere in the background. It sounds like a little kid. Maybe a little boy.

Immediately the image of a toddler with brown hair cut straight across his forehead, dark eyebrows, and slightly slanted blue eyes swims into my vision.

Robert, he said. From the cable Internet company. Robert—that Bob guy. Of course it would be that Bob guy. How much more humiliating can my life get?

"You turned it off?" Bob finally asks. "How?"

"Well, I couldn't find an 'off' button, and it wasn't plugged into the power strip, and so I—"

"Pulled it out of the wall."

"Well, yeah. I didn't rip it out or anything, I just unplugged it—"

"And you've tried plugging it back in?"

"The blue lights won't go back on. I tried some of the buttons—"

There's a quiet groan. "Go into the room," he says. "Unplug it, and plug it back into the wall. Don't touch any buttons."

"But I did that al—"

"Unplug it," Bob interrupts me. "And plug it back in. Then come back and tell me what it did."

Dutifully, I walk into the room and kneel under the desk. I unplug the cable, leave it out for a few seconds, then plug it back in. "Still no dice," I say when I get back to the phone.

"Okay," Bob mutters. "I guess I'll have to come over there."

Immediately I feel defensive. *What, does he think I did it on purpose so I can spend more time with him or something? An ego and a half, this guy has.* "I can't wait for you," I retort. "I've got to get to work. I'll be late already." I glance at the clock and my heart speeds up because it's true. If I don't run the whole way and leave right now, I'll be really late instead of just a little bit late. *The Turd's not going to like this.*

"I can't come over if you—"

"Then call my mom," I say hurriedly, stretching the cord as long as it will go so I can grab my coat. I put the receiver between my cheek and shoulder as I tie on my tennis shoes. "She'll let you in. She can stay here. Sorry, I really do have to get going." I set the phone in the cradle and throw on my gloves. There's a jagged array of icicles hanging off the eaves, so I add a terry-cloth headband that covers my ears.

I go at a dead run and end up making it only fifteen minutes late.

Adrian glances up at me and cracks her gum. "You're lucky."

"What?" I gasp, looking wildly around the office.

"Burt's not here yet."

I blow out a relieved breath, hang my coat on the hook, and stuff the gloves and headband into the pockets. "*Burt's* late?"

The glass doors swing open just then. I shove my hands in my pants and walk away from the closet, trying to look like I was just going by it on my way to somewhere else.

My boss doesn't even glance at me; he brushes past me and heads straight for his office. I sit down at my desk, feeling oddly rebuffed. He might be a turd, but he's usually at least marginally polite.

"Don't take it personally," Adrian says, intercepting my expression. "He's had a tough weekend. He was made a singles' ward bishop on Sunday."

I stare at Adrian for a second and then double over, chuckling helplessly.

"What?"

"Just"—I shake my head—"whoever they are, I feel really sorry for them right now. The poor little freshmen don't know what's hit 'em."

Adrian shrugs and turns back to her screen, her long fingernails clacking on the keyboard.

I reach down and turn my computer on. *Man, I really wish I were with Pen right now. He'd get it, why it's so funny, the idea of Burt being a bishop.* Then I grimace, shoving the memory of last night out of my mind.

That incident—with the kissing, and then me clocking him in the eye—that was messy. *Pen'll get over it, but he's not going to be pleasant conversation for a while. Why he thought I'd be okay with him slobbering all over me, I cannot fathom.*

Actually, Pen's part of the reason why my boss has been mentally christened the Turd. Pen used to work here in the physical education department. In fact, that's how I met him; he was working here when I was hired. He kind of helped train me. It was before I met Mark. We went on a couple dates, but it didn't take me too long to realize he wasn't my type. And it wasn't too long after I was hired that the Turd sent him packing. I still don't know why. All I remember is it was sudden, with apparently no discussion. Pen and I stayed friends, even though we didn't have a reason to see each other every day anymore. We lost contact pretty much when I got married, but after Mark died, he was the only person who came around randomly to see how I was. He never talks about Mark. We just play video games. And occasionally kiss. *And sometimes punch each other in the face.*

Pen. For some reason, my chest is feeling a bit tight.

Seeing what happened to Pen is the thing that clued me in to how far I can push the Turd, which is the same distance I can push a John Deere tractor.

Which is why I signed that lame contract, even though I didn't feel like I could do all the things he asked me to do.

MILE 21

Imagine how he'll be, I think, clicking on the finances file folder icon on my desktop, *the first time someone comes to him because of roommate problems.*

The picture of my boss sitting behind a desk, glaring at a sobbing group of freshman girls, starts me up again. I snort and lean my head against the screen, my shoulders shaking with suppressed laughter. "He'll make them do push-ups," I murmur.

"Abish."

It's like my snarky thoughts have summoned him. His voice blares right in my ear, startling me so badly I sit up too fast and my cheap accordion-back office chair crashes to the ground. I manage not to fall along with it, gripping the desk with both hands and pulling myself upright.

The Turd plunks the chair back in place, gesturing for me to follow him into the hall.

I go after him reluctantly—warily, arms folded over my chest. Just before we get to his office, he turns. "Phone for you."

My eyebrows shoot up. Slowly, I reach for the cell phone he's holding out to me.

It's weird, putting the Turd's phone up to my face. It smells faintly of sweat and is still warm from being in his pocket. I don't like it at all. I hold it slightly away from my cheek. "Hello?"

My mom's voice immediately blasts over the line.

"Mama," I try to interrupt, "how did you get my boss's number?"

But she's going off in Spanish, and she's not listening to me. So I just stand there, waiting.

She's mad. I don't think I've gotten an incomprehensible tirade this long since I was . . . well, a teenager, when we lived in the same house. Finally her fury wanes, and she switches to English. "I'm sorry, Abish," she says. "This is it."

"This is what?"

"You're out. Pack up your things today. I'm going to advertise the apartment."

"What?" I screech. "You're being crazy! *Why,* Mama?"

"Because I had to drive down to Rexburg today to let Robert in.

Because you ruined the Internet. Susanna missed her PSAT session for your carelessness, *Hija*."

"Oh, *Susanna*," I snap. "Well, I understand now. Anything that interrupts *Suzy's* perfect life is clearly—"

"Abish, if you were any other person I would have fired you long ago. You have not been a good manager. You haven't done any of the things you said you would do. I have been picking up your smack—"

"I think you mean *slack*," I snap.

". . . for twelve months. And I have been giving you so much of a break on rent that I really can't afford the gas to come down there on a daily basis to resolve complaints. *I can't do it,* niña. Not anymore. I'm sorry, I just can't." Her voice breaks on the last word.

Shock completely displaces my frustration and anger as I listen to the uneven breathing—the gasps that sound suspiciously like sobs—on the other end of the line.

Like me and Dad, Mama doesn't cry much. I've only seen her cry three times in all my life: after my baptism when Dad placed his hands on my head to confirm me, when she lost Baby Andrew before Suzy was born and . . . well. When Mark died. Dad, Suzy and I didn't cry at the funeral. But Mama did. A little.

I realize, standing here listening, that she's not crying because she's sad or mad. She sounds more . . . exhausted. And it's completely out of character that she would fold like this, that there would be this defeated tone in her voice. *That's me,* I think. *I've done this to her.*

She's right. We can't do this anymore.

But it's like something is tearing at my innards. I can't bring myself to think about it. About finding someone to truck away the furniture, about packing up all my clothes, all my stuff. *All Mark's stuff.*

My knees are trembling a little. "Right," I manage. "I understand. I'm sorry." I take the phone away from my face. I hit the end button and hand it back to the Turd.

He studies me from under his bristly gray eyebrows. "Do you have a place to stay tonight?"

I glare at him. *Mama must have said something to him before he handed over the phone.*

MILE 21

She would. She may not cry easily, but Mama definitely has never had any issue with airing out the family laundry in front of whatever audience she can find. Especially if she's talking about me, her messed-up daughter. I clench my teeth and take a moment to shove down my red-hot rage, thinking how now would not be a good time to be out of a job. "That's really none of your business," I finally manage.

"I disagree," is the Turd's curt reply.

"You're allowed to disagree." I turn my back on him and walk down the hall. "I've got almost all the financial aid documents up to date. Should be completely finished by the end of the day."

He hovers there in the hall for a moment. Finally, he turns without a word and goes into his office.

Back at my desk, I set my forehead in my palm and say a little nonverbal prayer: *Thank you, Heavenly Father, for helping me to not go ballistic on my boss and get myself fired on top of all this.*

Adrian continues her clacking and cracking, pretending to be completely oblivious to the drama. I focus on my tasks, forcing myself not to dwell on what I'm going to have to face after work. Every time I think about it, I get this clenched, sick feeling in my stomach. I do such a good job focusing that when the clock hits five, I've not only finished financial aid, but every single niggling task on my list. I even spent time organizing my desk drawer.

I'm thinking of the Millers a lot—Andy, mostly. I feel lost, thinking of our last game night together. I feel like talking about Mark right now, but Adrian's not the best candidate.

I could call, I think, eyeing the phone.

But what if Anne picks up?

At precisely 5:00 p.m. I slide out of my chair and grab my coat. I get out the door before the Turd leaves his office. I start jogging a little even as I'm going down the hall.

I run as soon as I hit pavement. And run. And run. By the time twilight descends I'm stumbling, likely because I didn't eat lunch today. I don't mind. The empty, head-floating-off-my-shoulders sensation is better than the thing I can feel rearing up inside.

51

Chapter 5

When I finally get to the apartment, it is pitch black out, no light even from moon or stars. The security lamp on the balcony casts everything in a green-yellow glow. The door to the apartment is open slightly, key in the lock. Key and lock are shiny and new. *Mama's already re-keyed it.*

This should prepare me for what I'm going to find when I get inside, but it doesn't. I walk into the room, flick on the light, and freeze. *Blank, empty walls. Pristine counters.*

There's an overpowering chemical-fruity scent of carpet and upholstery shampoo.

I walk slowly into the kitchen and all the cupboards are standing open, empty. Mark's orange cup, which was always to the left of the sink, is gone. All the dishes are gone. The table is gone, and of course our picture, which stood on the table.

The shock is setting in. My stomach is so knotted, it feels like it must be folded in on itself. As I stumble down the hall, my only thought is, *They've killed him.*

My suitcase sits on the bare mattress. My backpack and my purse are on top of the suitcase. Next to them, there's a note in Mama's flowing handwriting. *Cynthia will pick you up at six. I've put the rest of the things in the storage unit.*

I don't move. I sit there feeling . . . what? Clenched. Blank. *Empty. There is nothing in this room, nothing except for me and my suitcase. There is nothing in this world left, except for me and my suitcase. I'm sitting here waiting. Waiting . . . waiting for what?* For Aunt Cindy. For eternity. For the clothes to magically appear in our closet, for the bed to suddenly have our wedding quilt on it, for the picture to be back on the kitchen table.

The loudest sound in the world is my heart beating in my ears. I don't know how long I sit there, feeling the room pound, before I hear someone treading up the stairs. I glance out the now-curtainless window and see Aunt Cindy's head appear over the top of the staircase. The yellow light shines eerily on her longish iron-gray hair, followed by her slim figure, which is wrapped in a cherry-red peacoat. As she walks past the window to the door she doesn't see me sitting there, but I can see she's put on makeup, lots of it. Her thread-thin eyebrows are drawn on in black.

What? I wonder as I rise from the bed and take my suitcase in my grip, slinging purse and backpack over one shoulder. *Does she think this is some kind of special occasion?*

She gets to the bedroom door before I do. "Well," she chirps, holding out a hand for my suitcase, "let's go."

I almost don't hand it over, but there's a no-nonsense tone in her voice that is completely incongruent with the false-cheery expression. *She's my bailiff. Mama can't deal with me and Dad can't deal with me, so they've passed the job off to Aunt Cindy.*

We drive in silence the whole way down to Rigby. She just sits there at the wheel with that cheery-hard expression firmly in place. The disapproval radiating from her is a palpable thing. Generally speaking, this situation would end in a display to put the annual Pioneer-Day fireworks program to shame. But right now, I just can't scrape together enough . . . initiative? Pride? Anger? . . . Enough of *anything*, to care.

"Well," she repeats as we pull into her garage, "I've made up the guest room for you. You know where that is, of course." She chuckles.

I feel the gorge rise in my throat. I open my door and step out, realizing vaguely that I've been clutching my suitcase handle the entire drive.

"Have you had dinner?"

"Please don't bother," I say, hating that I'm forming actual words, that I'm breaking my own silence. "Good night." I walk inside, through the kitchen, and down the hall.

"I made my agave cinnamon rolls," she calls after me. "When you're settled, come out and we'll have some warm milk with them."

"Agave," I mutter. *So I'm to be purified in body as well as soul. Likely she'll cook up some seaweed scrambled eggs for breakfast, and it'll be Tofurkey sandwiches for lunch.*

Tofurkey does taste like turkey—turkey that has been dead in the sun a few days. She brought some to Thanksgiving last year. It looked so much like real turkey I got a big mouthful by mistake and nearly vomited on Mark's lap, and he laughed so hard at my expression that a little Martinelli's came out his nose.

Thanksgiving.

One of the last real, clear memories I have of us. Just a couple weeks before.

The guest bedroom is at the very end. Cindy's right that I won't have any trouble finding it because I stayed in it for a week when I was twelve. Back then it was a huge treat to stay with Aunt Cindy. It was a sort of rite of passage; after we entered the Young Women's program, she invited each of us—me and Suzy—for "Aunt Cindy Week." She talked to us about what it meant to be Heavenly Father's daughters and showed us all her mission pictures. We put together scrapbooks and wrote in our journals. We made scrunchies patterned with anthropomorphized torches.

As a twelve-year-old I totally loved her, how girlish she seemed. Aunt Cindy doesn't really age; she just gets a bit grayer each year. She's so sweet, so innocent, so pure with her breathy Relief-Society-testimony voice whenever she starts talking about the gospel. Dad still falls for it. To him, Aunt Cindy walks on water. He sees in her everything he wants his daughters to become: a returned missionary, professionally successful. Aunt Cindy owns her own house. She has investments. She's completely independent financially, and as far as I can tell, emotionally too.

It wasn't until my wedding reception that I saw the other side of her. I was wearing my sparkly white dress and awkwardly adjusting my veil, loving the warmth of Mark's arm across my shoulders. Mama and Dad were standing next to me, and Anne and Andy were standing next to Mark, all of us with those frozen "I've been standing in a reception line for three hours" smiles on our faces.

Aunt Cindy greeted Mark's parents abruptly—it startled me. And then Mark leaned in to give her a hug, like he had every other person in the reception line, and she kind of took a step back and nodded stiffly at him. Then she leaned forward to give *me* a rib-creaking hug and murmured, "Well, we can't all follow the same path. He must be a wonderful young man to take you off *your* course like this."

What course? I'd wondered, feeling my blood rise as I watched her give Dad a sympathetic smile and a kiss on the cheek. *The Aunt Cindy course? A mission, and then a life full of scrapbooks, sugarless cookies, and sewing new window dressings for my empty house twice a year? Does Dad really want me to end up like her?*

If she says a single word, I think as I set my suitcase on the floor and sling my backpack and purse down next to it, *about me being free to serve a mission now . . .*

But instead of any scathing rejoinders, instead of a hot, rejuvenating surge of anger, I feel tired. Blank. *Empty.*

Without even thinking, I head into the guest bath. There's a tiny shower and a color-coordinated towel set stacked like a layer cake on a shelf above the toilet. There is also a picture of a young woman in a white dress holding a candle, her head turned rapturously skyward. Once upon a time I loved it; the fact the girl had dark hair and pale skin like me. The fact that, like her, I was special; I was a precious daughter of God. I was named by my father for a woman who could raise the dead with her testimony. I was Abish Cavendish, and I was set apart to preach the gospel to all the world one day.

I turn on the shower, strip, and step in. I stand for a few moments, then sink to the tile floor, resting my head on my knees as the hot water pelts my back and neck. After a few minutes, my skin starts to itch and I'm feeling like I can't breathe too well. I reach up and turn the heat down just a little.

I crouch there for what feels like an interminable amount of time. When I step out of the shower, I'm shaking, but not with cold, and not because of muscle weakness. Whatever it is, I'm shaking so hard, I can barely make it to the bed to sit down. I can barely pull on my flannel pajama pants and T-shirt.

The bed smells like dried roses and something stronger . . . gardenia, maybe. There's an irregular crack in the ceiling. Lying in this bed when I was twelve, I used to stare up at it and imagine it looked like the west coast of Africa. I used to fantasize about walking through jungles wearing a nametag and a loose blouse and skirt, crouching in huts with the Book of Mormon on my lap.

A pulse in my neck feels like it might strangle me, it's throbbing so hard.

I can't.

I just can't.

I look around the room wildly. My gaze comes to rest on a powder-blue rotary phone sitting on the nightstand. That's maybe the one thing Aunt Cindy and I have in common; a stubborn refusal to rise to the times when it comes to technology.

I pick up the receiver, pausing for a moment to get my head around the rotary and how it works. I dial a number in.

Anne answers. "Hello?"

There's a pang of dismay, because I was hoping Andy would be the one to pick up. "Hi, Anne. This is Abish."

"Oh." She pauses. "Hello, Abish. How are you?"

"Um, pretty good." I begin twisting the coils of the phone cord around my fingers. "Listen, would you guys mind if I stayed over at your place for a few days? Mom . . . well, she needs the apartment. She's sent me over to my aunt's place, but it's not going to work out. I don't want her to have to drive all the way up to Rexburg every day to drop me off."

"I . . ."

The pause is longer this time. Long enough for me to realize I've made a mistake. To know already what her answer is going to be and how much it's going to hurt. I feel like my heart, swollen and throbbing, has risen up to fill my throat.

"Abish," she says finally. "I love you dearly. And I understand you're hurting. But this has gotten to be too much for me. My therapist says I need to move on."

"Your therapist?"

"Yes." She pauses again. "Are *you* seeing someone, Abish? Someone to help you—"

"No." My tone is a little more snappish than I mean it to be. "I'm not the type to vent all my problems. You know me."

"Well, my therapist has told me that we can't have you over anymore, Abish. It's not good for me, for our grieving process. Andy's gotten stuck like you, and Rachel thinks that it's too easy for you to feed off each other."

You've talked to your therapist about me? I don't say it—I can't, but I can feel the anger stirring in my breast.

"I'm trying to get over this," Anne adds a few tense, silent moments later. "I *need* to get through this. And so do you. Rachel thinks that it'd be better for me, and especially for Andy and for you, if we just took . . ." She sighs. "Well, if we just took a breather for a while."

My jaw feels permanently hinged shut. I hold the receiver for another few seconds and then set it, carefully, down in its cradle. My teeth hurt because I'm grinding them together. The anger simmers inside me, scorching my lungs and prickling the corners of my eyes. The room feels suddenly poisonous. As if the air—damp and warm from the shower, with the cloying scent of flowers—is slowly suffocating me.

I gulp down the hardness in my throat and pick up the receiver again. I dial a different number this time.

"Hey," Pen says.

"Hey."

After what happened, I'm not sure how to begin. But he's all I've got left. Literally, the only person left to turn to. "Sorry for calling," I finally say. "You probably hate me right now, but, Pen, I really need a ride."

There's a long silence. "'Kay."

I'm so startled by his response, I nearly drop the phone. "Okay? Really?"

"Yeah. Where are you?"

"I'm in Rigby."

"Give me the address. I'll put it in my cell."

I give it to him, lowering my voice as I hear the creak of footsteps go past my door. "Thank you so much, Pen, I—"

He cuts me off. "Yeah. See you soon." The line goes dead.

Shivering, I sit up and wrap my coat around me. I grab my suitcase and backpack. I edge the door open.

All clear.

I walk quietly down the hall toward the kitchen, where I can see Aunt Cindy bent over the sink, washing dishes. She's got music blasting from a nineties-era boom box. It's tuned to KBYI, and Michael McClean—the Bryan Adams of LDS music—is playing. *We can be together forever someday,* the lyrics go.

It's a piece of Mormon doctrine that, contrary to what people might assume, hasn't brought me a whole lot of comfort lately. *Yeah. Someday in about eighty years when my abnormally healthy body finally runs down on me and I die, alone and shriveled, we can be together. Thanks for that.*

She doesn't turn or look up as I creep past the kitchen. I edge the door open and walk out into the yard. I walk carefully down the driveway, allowing my eyes to adjust to the dark, and stand next to the large cottonwood tree that borders her property.

It's a while before a pair of headlights heralds the arrival of Pen's little blue VW. My fingers and toes are numb. Wordlessly I fling the door open, shove my suitcase in the back seat, and sit down in the passenger seat. I keep my backpack in my lap, holding it to my stomach. He gives me a funny look, and I realize that I must seem a little strange, like a child clutching a stuffed animal or favorite pillow.

Pen doesn't speak until we get to exit 333, the turnoff to head up into Rexburg. "Where to?"

"Drop me by the school," I reply without even thinking, without even knowing why. But as I say it I realize that I need a plan or at least an idea of where I'm staying the night.

Glancing back, I notice Pen's ratty old sleeping bag behind the driver's seat. I point at it. "Can I borrow that?"

Pen frowns. "You need a place to stay?"

I shake my head.

"You can crash on my couch . . ."

"No thanks."

As we begin climbing the hill toward campus, he glances at me again. "Where on campus?"

I have the code to get into the office, and it's not quite ten o'clock, so the outer doors will still be open.

It's ludicrous, but really, it's the only acceptable option left to me. "Physical education building."

A few minutes later he pulls up alongside it, and I grab my suitcase and open the door. He reaches down and tosses me the sleeping bag. I can feel him watching me as I walk down the sidewalk toward the glass double-doors.

It feels odd, walking into the dark, deserted lobby. It looks cold and forbidding all of a sudden. I drop my backpack onto my desk and heft my suitcase up next to it.

What are you doing here? my cruddy accordion office chair seems to say to me. I stare at it for a second, then push it away from the desk and crawl into the shadowy space underneath. The tangle of cords and cables above me is kind of cozy. The floor—concrete, overlaid by a pathetic eighth-inch of cheap Berber carpet, is bruising. I pull the sleeping bag up over my body and lay on my side. I keep thinking I hear noises, maybe a janitor trying to get in. Once I see a beam of flashlight in the hall outside the glass doors. Finally I drift off.

❧

"Hey."

Something prods my hip. I open my eyes, blinking, and gasp as a face looms in my vision. It's male, blue eyed, and grim-mouthed. I rise to a sitting position and squint, taking in the uniform—light blue shirt, badge. He's holding a flashlight.

Oh, crap. Crapola.

Immediately I begin wrestling out of my sleeping bag. "I work here," I stammer. But being Honest Abe, I can't finish the lie that should easily flow from my lips. *I was working late and got tired and fell asleep, I decided to take a break for a few minutes, and I just happened to have my sleeping bag with me . . . and a suitcase . . .*

The officer glances at my running shoes, which are tucked up against the wall. He straightens and peers at my computer. It's turned off, of course.

He looks back at me. There's indecision in his expression. I start rolling up my sleeping bag and pray silently that he'll just issue me a warning and not look me up in his system.

"I'll need your student ID," he says. "Follow me, please."

And the sword falls. I close my eyes for a second before obediently walking after him down the hall. I leave my suitcase and the sleeping bag under the desk and my backpack on the chair and make sure to tuck my wallet into my back pocket.

He's going to find some stuff on me. Not bad stuff like real lawbreaking or anything. The problem is, the stuff he's going to find won't make my current situation look good.

Let's just say that this last spring and summer I spent some evenings in the park. Under a bush.

I'm fully aware that if people knew about this, they would probably associate me with those who wear Hefty bags over their shoulders and drive shopping carts around town. But it's not like that. It's just that, in the wake of Mark's sudden absence from my life, there were nights it was hard to lie down in that bed alone.

Sleeping out under the stars I could just sort of tell myself I was camping and that things hadn't changed as much as I thought they had. I could pretend that I had a warm apartment and a husband waiting for me back home. So sometimes I took my sleeping bag and hiked over to Smith Park, or Porter Park, or the Nature Park, or sometimes just an empty, unpaved lot, and slept under the bushes; you know, so that the cops who occasionally patrol places like that wouldn't find me.

Well, they found me. Twice. Both times in Smith Park. First time I was given a warning. The second time I had to pay some money and go to court. It was embarrassing. I just stood there and the guy—I guess I should call him the judge—looked at me with this incredulous expression. He asked me why I was sleeping in the park. He asked me if I didn't have an apartment. I shrugged and said that I did, and I just wanted some fresh air. Then he frowned, and I paid a hundred and fifty dollars. I guess he didn't like my answer . . . didn't think I was repentant enough for sucking in illegal gulps of park oxygen.

Anyway, the police at BYU-I are part of the Rexburg police department. So there isn't any separation of databases or anything. This guy's brought me to their base of operations on campus. It's a room in the Kimball building, but it's really just an annex of the normal city's police department, where I currently have a trespassing record. So basically, I'm fried.

I sit, trying not to fidget in an uncomfortable stiff-upholstered chair while he types some stuff into the computer at the desk, holding my ID up every once in a while.

"Drivers' license?" he asks tersely.

I've already dug it out of my wallet. I hand it over.

After several more minutes, he looks up again. His eyebrows are drawn down together. "This is your third offense."

"Second. I wasn't charged with anything before . . . the first time."

"We have record of a citation on February the twenty-fifth of two-thousand-twelve. It says here you were issued a warning."

"Yes, that's right." *February 25. Our anniversary.*

"And you had another on May thirteenth. You went before the judge and paid a fine."

"Yeah." I rub an imaginary spot off the knee of my jeans, avoiding his gaze.

"Do you have a place to live?"

"Yes. Well, I mean, I have places I *could* live."

"Hmm." The officer crosses his arms over his chest. "You know I can't let you off. Not when you've already been through court."

"I know."

"By all the rules, I should be arresting you right now and bringing you to the Women's Detention Facility."

My body goes cold. "Really?"

He studies me through narrowed eyes. "I don't want to, though."

I gaze back at him, waiting.

"I think I'll let you off this time." He draws the words out, as if he's not quite sure he's saying the right thing.

My heart gets going again. "Thank you," I reply fervently, pushing away the images that have poured into my mind—Mama's shocked expression, Dad's disappointed frown. Not to mention what would happen to me. Here at BYU-Idaho, you're booted out of school if you get arrested. It doesn't matter what it's for. Which I can understand, sort of. But, honestly, it's not like I'm breaking rules just to break rules. Or doing things that are going to interfere with my eternal salvation. I'm just . . .

I'm messed up. That's what I am.

He's saying something else. I turn my attention back in time to grasp the last few words, "honor code office."

The chill returns. I stand up. "Oh, no, please. I promise I won't be here after hours again. And it wasn't, I mean, it wasn't like I was"—I gesture helplessly—"boozing up, or . . . I didn't have a guy with me or anything."

"If you are a student at this school, you are supposed to be back in your BYU-approved housing by curfew."

"If you're a *single* student."

"Are you married, then?" He poises his pen over the piece of paper he's been scribbling on.

There is a long beat of silence.

"No." It comes out a whisper.

He nods. "Well, I think I'm about done here." He gives me a sudden disarming smile. "Don't worry about the honor code office. They are generally pretty understanding if you're willing to admit your error and agree not to do it again. I predict you'll come through with just a warning." He stands and holds the door for me.

Yeah. If you are a normal person with a normal boss. I slide into the corridor.

The brightening sky casts a pink glow on the tiles in the hall as I make my way back to the office. *It's probably about half an hour until I'm supposed to be at work anyway. No going back to sleep now. What am I going to do to kill thirty minutes?*

It's like my body responds before I even think about it—I'm running.

I dash out of the building and run to the track, passing one or two droopy-eyed students. It's cold enough to sting my nose, and my breath steams out in visible clouds. I circle the track a few times and then head out and make a circuit of campus. At this point I don't care if I'm late or not. I can't think about that. The sky just looks so beautiful, and my feet are an unstoppable train of motion driving me on and on and on. Driving the world away.

As I reach the top of the hill, the temple looms into my vision, the angel on the giant, towering steeple blazing with the sunrise. I stop, panting, and stare at it. Sweat is running down my cheeks. My heart throbs oddly in my chest.

It happens again, just like in the cemetery by Mark's grave. The whole world suddenly goes gray and two-dimensional. The sky is like a flat photograph. Moroni is a shapeless blob. The temple—the place that has always been a refuge for me, the place Mark and I were married—it's just a building. Boring, rectangular like a Lego block.

Suddenly I wonder what I'm doing, why I'm standing here. Why I'm panting.

Why I'm breathing at all.

I walk back slowly, to the only place I know to walk right now, which is right into the lion's den. By the time I get to the office, there's a dark ring forming around my field of vision.

"You're pretty late. Burt's not happy."

Adrian's voice sounds odd, tinny. I make my way to my chair and sit in it, then remember my backpack. I peel it off, drop it to the floor, and lean my forehead on my palm.

Adrian bends over me; I can tell because of the cloying fragrance of Bath and Body Works Apple Blossom lotion. "Are you okay?" she asks. "You look a little pale."

I rub my fingers on my face. "I'm fine," I reply, straightening so quickly that I almost bash her in the chin with the top of my head. "Just forgot to have breakfast."

She slides into her chair and reaches into her own backpack. Wordlessly, she hands me a bottle. It's a store-bought smoothie.

"No thanks."

"Don't be stupid," she hisses, and practically throws it at me. "You're about to pass out."

I stare down at it. After a moment I unscrew the cap and gulp some down. It does make me feel a little better. I flick on my screen and log into my employee account, glancing down the list of emails.

It takes the Turd all of three minutes. His door slams, and I wince at the thunder of intent in the footsteps—heading down the hall, moving toward the circle of desks, coming up behind me. I flinch as his palm lands on my shoulder.

"We need to talk." His gruff voice resonates in my bones, sending shock waves down my spine. I rise and follow him back to his office.

Once we're both sitting, he doesn't say anything for a few long, agonizing moments. He just stares at me, his mouth in its usual tight, disapproving frown. I feel entranced, like some small creature caught in a predator's gaze. I swallow—it's loud in my ears.

He whisks his glasses onto his face, picks up a yellow paper, and begins reading from it.

It's the summons to the honor code office.

MILE 21

"How did you get that?" I snap, welcoming the feeling of indignation that replaces my nervousness. "That's private."

"They didn't know where else to find you. You don't have a phone, and your email account hasn't had any activity for a year. If you were living in approved student housing with a manager, they would have notified your manager." He passes the paper across the desk.

"That doesn't—that didn't . . ." My voice trails off. I'm supposed to go this morning at ten. That's in less than two hours. *These people sure work fast in their campaign to keep their school free of illegal park-air breathers.*

"Abish."

"Yeah?" I mumble, crumpling the paper and sticking it in my jeans pocket.

"It is unacceptable that you don't have a place to live."

"I'll *get* a place to live."

"Where?"

I glare at him. He holds my glare until I look away. "It's none of your business."

"Yes, it is." He bends and rustles through a drawer and brings out a familiar-looking sheaf of papers, stapled at the corner. The paper is folded down over the staple. I did that, fiddling with it as I read it before I signed it a few months ago. *The Contract. That's what it is, the hated Contract.*

He glances down at the top page. "It says here that you agree to abide by the honor code, to come in regularly during assigned shift hours, and to be handling a full load of credits starting January 2012."

"That has nothing to do with where I live."

He digs through his desk again and hands across another piece of paper; special BYU-Idaho stationary. It's the honor code. I recognize it immediately because I've signed it half a dozen times since starting school.

"Yeah, so? It says here"—I punch my forefinger down on the page—"that if a spouse has passed away, I'm exception to the rule."

"It says that you need to get approval to live in student housing.

The problem is, you are a single student. Read the paragraph above that."

"All single students must live in BYU-approved housing unless they choose to reside with a relative . . ." I feel like something icy has passed through my blood. "That doesn't apply to me. I'm sure they'd say—"

"I've talked to them already," he interrupts. "You don't have to go to that honor code meeting. I've taken care of it. But the administration agrees with me. The best option for you, Abish, is to move into student housing."

"You mean *single* student housing?" It comes out in a screech of pure outrage. "You're kidding, right?"

"I've also talked to your parents," the Turd continues. He's never looked turdier than he does now with his hands on the desk as he leans down to gaze at me with those cold, evil eyes, made all the more evil by the magnification of his reading glasses. "They tell me you have a relative that you could live with."

"No," I choke out.

"Your mother said that situation is not ideal because you'd need a ride to campus every day."

"That's right." Warm relief washes over me. I slump back in my chair, feeling tired. So, so tired. The room is starting to grow fuzzy around the edges again.

"Your best option is to find a contract in an apartment close to campus. You could rent a married apartment—I think the housing office would allow that—but the problem is money. You and I both know that you can't afford to pay a contract on family housing by yourself."

Not without the special reduced family rate.

"Of course, if you had something else that worked . . ." He shrugs. "What was your plan?"

I give him a blank look.

His brow furrows. "Surely you weren't planning on spending the entire winter semester sleeping on the floor of this office."

I shake my head. That's all I can do—just shake my head. *I have no plans. My plan was for Mark and me to live and grow old together.*

He sighs and removes his glasses, setting them back on the desk next to his shiny brass name card: *Burt Barnes, Chair of Health, Recreation & Human Performance.* "I'll find you a place," he says finally. "You go back to work. No—take a lunch break," he amends, glancing down at my hands, which I suddenly notice are shaking a little. He digs into his pocket.

"No thanks." I shove away his hand, which contains a five-dollar bill.

He glares at me and slaps it down on the desk. "Take it. Take two hours. Then come back here and finish sorting the files on the hard drive. I can't find anything in the system. You've done a sloppy job archiving the payroll documents."

I take the bill, look at it for a few seconds, and tuck it into my pocket. At the door, I turn. "Why are you doing this? Why don't you just fire me like you fired Pen?"

He looks taken aback. "Pendleton Walsch?"

"Yeah. You just fired him. No questions, no comments. Why are you giving *me* a break?" *If you say you feel sorry for me*, I'm thinking as I glare at him, *then we're done. Job or no job.*

"It's my business who I fire and who I retain."

I shake my head.

"Somebody's got to intervene, Abish. You aren't coping. You've alienated yourself from friends. Your family apparently isn't capable of helping you right now."

"So you feel sorry for me."

He studies me for a few seconds. "No. I just don't enjoy watching train wrecks."

Well, when you put it like that.

Chapter 6

The turkey wrap I buy in the cafeteria tastes like glue. Sitting and forcing myself to swallow down mouthfuls, I think back on my first year of college, living in an apartment with five other girls. Goosebumps rise up on my arms. *I can't do it.*

But what other choice do I have?

I could get another job so I can afford family housing.

The job I have now is likely the highest paying I'll ever be able to snag, supposing I managed to snag a different one at all with the way the market in Rexburg is so completely saturated. Plus, I doubt the Turd would give me a good reference.

Live with Aunt Cindy.

No. No, no, no. I'll take a hundred yapping freshmen over Aunt Cindy.

Go home to St. Anthony.

And do what? Apply to be a waitress at Big J's or Chiz's? Serve gravy and fries the rest of my life?

The Turd is right. It's the only real choice.

I swallow hard, feeling like I'm swallowing my own bile. It's like

68

taking a step backward in my life with the idea of roommates, of singles' wards. When I married Mark, I willingly left that stage behind.

I dust off my jeans and throw away the crumpled ball of saran wrap. I do feel somewhat better. *Odd how bodies actually need food, whether you feel hungry or not.*

My feet drag on the way back to the office. I don't know what I'm going to find there. I don't know what's going to happen next. A stab of feeling injects itself through the muffled layers of my usual numbness—fear.

Where do I go from here?

Did you consider that, Heavenly Father, when you decided to stick your giant thumb into my perfectly normal, perfectly happy life? Do you have some kind of plan for me? Well, I'd sure appreciate hearing about it.

I whisk through the glass office doors and allow them to crash together behind me. I trudge over to my desk, jab at the keyboard, and watch the colorful moving pipes of the screen saver dissolve into long columns of boring texts and numbers.

It takes him three minutes this time too. Hearing his footsteps advance down the hall, I shut my eyes for a long moment, then turn and put on my best glare.

He leans over and places some papers next to my keyboard. "I found four apartments with open contracts for winter semester that aren't currently occupied. You can pro-rate these last couple of weeks of December. Two aren't listed on the housing website yet. Call and go look at them. Choose one by the end of the day."

"You said you wanted me to work this afternoon."

"This is work. I'm giving you a job to do; go find yourself an apartment so that I can keep you on my payroll. If you haven't signed a contract by the end of the day, you're fired."

"I don't have money saved up to pay an advance contract," I contend, folding my arms over my chest. "Single housing isn't month-to-month. You have to pay a semester ahead."

"I'll pay it. It'll come out of your salary on a month-to-month basis until the end of winter semester. But you'll have to set aside money to save for spring semester's contract."

"How?" I growl at him. "Am I going to live on peanut butter and spoiled milk for the next four months?"

The Turd breathes out through his nose and squints at me. "I know how much I pay you. You'll get by if you work hard to make it work."

"I still have to save for tuition—"

"You need to apply for a Pell Grant."

"I'm not married anymore."

"The government will consider you independent because of your marital status. You're not single; you're widowed."

Hearing that word, *widowed*, drains my angst completely, leaving me limp as a cooked noodle. I turn away from him and nod. "'Kay."

He steps away, then turns back. "I forgot that you don't have a phone. I give you permission to call from here and set up appointments—"

"I can handle it. Thanks."

"And you should call your mother and let her know where you are."

"No." My tone is weary but absolute. *I will not call my parents. You can't make me. I'll move to Mexico and start an agave farm first.*

The Turd hesitates, then gives an abrupt nod and heads down the hall. I wait for the door to slam before I reach for the knobby black receiver of the office phone. I glance down at the papers.

Fifteen minutes later I have appointments lined up for the rest of the afternoon. Adrian glances up as I leave.

"Bye," I say. I don't know why I say it. She and I don't exactly stand on ceremony. She nods in return, and I feel her eyes on me even after I've gone through the door, until I turn the corner to the stairwell.

The first apartment is on the north side of campus—one of those mid-size complexes. The manager meets me at the door. We walk in, and I know within five seconds that I won't be able to swing it. There are posters of Johnny Depp and Dieter F. Uchtdorf on the wall. There's a pink smear on Dieter's forehead. I lean closer and realize it's lipstick.

I glance around for ten more seconds, taking in the framed yarn-embroidered sampler on the wall and the spilled trail of cereal on the kitchen floor.

I kind of blank out during the rest of the tour, nodding and smiling mechanically. "I'll let you know," I say. "Thanks."

I walk down to the parking lot. I shudder and take a moment to breathe in the clean, fresh air.

The next apartment is a pretty run-down place off Second East, two blocks up from Main. It's a house that's been divided into a couple of apartments with three rooms each. The room that's vacant doesn't have anybody else in it. Of course, it's about the size of a broom cupboard. The one bathroom in the apartment is kind of dank, with water-stained linoleum on the floor and sixties-era wallpaper, and paint peeling off the toilet seat. It's got a bank of mirrors outside the toilet area, though, with lots of drawer space, and it's the best price.

The third and fourth apartments are nice. New two-tone paint, new carpet, new everything. They're in the Freshman Factories west of campus, and they're both rooms that already have an occupant—a ready-made room-roommate. As I walk into the last bedroom of the last apartment and take in the rumpled bedclothes, pile of dirty laundry, and the cut-out digital pictures of some missionary taped to the wall, I think how much more bearable things might be if I could have my own space. Nobody fighting me for room in the closet. No one trying to get me to engage in late-night girl talk.

I call the manager of the second apartment. We meet in front of it. I sign and tell her the check will come by the end of the day, squirming inside as I think about the Turd's . . . *generosity? High-handedness? Psychopathic need to control the lives of his employees?*

When I make it back to the office, it's five minutes past five. The Turd's waiting there for me. I hand him the paper for the apartment I've agreed on. He glances at it, and I see something flick across his features—concern, resignation? I can't quite make it out. "Fine," he says. "I'll call her and drop the check off on the way home." "One problem. I can't move in until tomorrow."

"You're coming home with me," he replies, punching the number into his cell phone.

"Um, no."

He glances up. "You'd rather your parents came to pick you up?"

He has a point. I let out a sigh, air hissing through my gritted teeth, and nod. I can't quite make myself say "Okay," or "Thank you," or anything else productive.

I follow him outside. He holds the passenger door. I slide in and buckle up. He shuts the door and then walks around and sits against the hood.

After a few moments, I frown at him through the glass. *Is he getting in?*

Suddenly he raises a hand and smiles at some kid who is trotting toward us across the parking lot. He's got sandy blond hair and a smattering of acne across his forehead. He's pretty young—not RM-age yet. *A preemie, then. A freshman.*

"This is my son, Andrew," the Turd says when they've both settled into their seats. "Andrew, this is Abish. She's going to stay at our place tonight until she can move into her apartment."

Andrew nods and reaches over. "Nice to meet you, Abish."

I take his hand and shake it. "Hey."

I keep my forehead against the cool glass of the window and my eyes fixed on the scenery during the entire drive. The Turd is chatting with his son about school and classes and such. He sounds so different from what I'm used to. I feel completely out of place.

The car comes to a stop in a driveway in front of a yellow one-story house just off of Taurus Drive in west Rexburg—the older, but still respectable, part of town. There's a weathered basketball hoop over the garage, and one of those weighted freestanding ones off to the side at the end of the driveway.

The door opens before anyone knocks. I'm a little taken aback by Mrs. Turd. Well, I guess I shouldn't call her that. I've got nothing against her. *Mrs. Barnes. Sister Barnes.*

Sister Barnes is a clean-faced, decently good-looking woman in her early fifties. She's fit but not skinny, and there's this sort of bustling energy about her. She's got clear blue eyes with smile-wrinkles at the corners. She doesn't ask any questions; she just herds us all inside in a friendly bossy sort of way. She tells us to put our things in the closet and take a seat at the table in the dining room.

It's me, Andrew, the Turd, Sister Barnes, and a brown-haired girl about Suzy's age at the table. The girl looks curiously at me as I sit down.

The Turd hasn't introduced me. He is busy dishing up food and murmuring to his wife. "Abish," I say, my voice cracking a little.

"I'm Molly," the girl replies, giving me a half-smile. "Are you in my dad's new ward?"

"No." *Thank you, Heavenly Father.*

The casserole dish has come around to me. It's some mix of stuffing and chicken and cheese and Campbell's soup—delicious and delightfully down-home. I suddenly realize that I'm pretty hungry. I take the biggest breast left in the pan and ladle the gooey mix generously over the top.

The Turd gives the blessing. He says it in a sort of confident, public-speaking way, almost like a Baptist minister leading a prayer meeting. It's a little surreal, hearing him say the kinds of words you say in blessings. Asking, instead of pushing everyone around.

"The spare room's in the basement," Sister Barnes says when I rise with my empty plate. "Thank you," she adds as I turn on the faucet and rinse my dishes.

She leads me through the living room, where I grab my suitcase and backpack, and down the stairs. The basement is mostly a hallway with rooms off to each side. There's a large open space at the end with leather couches, a fireplace, and a sixty-inch plasma screen. There are big square banners on the walls in red and white: U of U. It surprises me a little. *I would have pegged him as a BYU fan.*

She opens a door at the end of the hall. The guest room feels cool and stagnant, like it doesn't get aired much. There's a peach-colored comforter on the bed and a white lamp on an oak stand next to it. On one wall is a painting, one of those muted landscapes that you don't really remember even if you've slept in the room every day for a decade. It feels homey, but not too homey. If I try, I could imagine this as a hotel room. *I'm on a trip somewhere, and Mark is at home, asleep in our bed.*

"Thanks," I say, shifting my balance from foot to foot as I watch her fuss with the pillows, taking off the shams and putting them on the nightstand.

"The bathroom is two doors down the hall on your right. You'll be the only one sleeping down here, so don't worry about sharing. We used to fill these rooms up, but now most of the kids have moved on." She gives me a confiding, slightly sad smile and moves toward the door. I step out of her way.

"There are fresh towels under the sink," she adds.

"Thanks," I reply.

As soon as the door closes, I unzip my suitcase and rustle around until I find a set of sweats. I pull them on and fall into the bed. For a moment I'm tempted to just fall asleep there on top of the covers, but I muster the energy to climb underneath them, pulling them up over my head.

It's not the most comfortable mattress I've ever slept on, but when I wake up, light is streaming through the little basement window. I blink incredulously at the clock. *7:17 am.*

Somehow I have achieved the deepest, most un-interrupted, most blissfully dreamless stretch of sleep I've had in a long time.

The Turd drives me and Andrew to campus the next morning. It's kind of nice not worrying about ticking him off by being late. I focus hard all day, and when work's done I don't wait for the offer of a ride. I sling my backpack over one shoulder, purse over the other, and drag the suitcase out the door just as the clock ticks to five.

It's a laborious walk down Second East, and I feel a little foolish when I find the Turd's silver-colored sedan waiting in the driveway of my new apartment. To his credit, he doesn't make any smart remarks as I walk past him; he just gets out and walks around to the trunk, where he lifts out two large cardboard boxes stacked on top of each other.

My stuff.

"Where . . ." I start to ask, then stop. I really don't want to know. I don't want to think about my family right now.

I follow him into the apartment. There are four girls crowded into the living room. One of them jumps up immediately and takes my suitcase. "Hi," she says. "I'm Shelley."

I nod, taking in her appearance: large blue eyes with just a hint of eye-shadow, hair pulled into a tidy ponytail with an artistic twist of bangs in front to frame her face. She's got a fitted long-sleeved shirt on. She's wearing jeans, and her small leather shoes are immaculately polished, gleaming in the soft lamplight.

A total Molly Mormon, in other words.

"Hey," I reply, glancing down at my own scuffed Adidas.

"Let's take your stuff up and then come back down and introduce you to everyone else."

I don't argue. I follow her up the stairs. The Turd makes a third, carrying my boxes with apparently little strain, though they must be heavy if they contain all my essential possessions. *Guess that makes Jodi-the-missionary wrong about the back injury. He's a turd because he likes being a turd.*

Somehow the thought feels a little off, though, as I watch him haul my stuff. I feel a twinge of uneasiness and wonder again why he's doing all this for me.

Because he doesn't enjoy watching train wrecks. Right.

I set my stuff on the bare mattress and gesture for Shelley and the Turd to do the same. Reluctantly, I follow them back into the living room.

"This is Stephanie." Shelley gestures to a girl with a riot of soft, dirt-colored curls standing up all over the crown of her head. She's tall and lanky, with a slightly upturned nose.

"Call me Steve," she says.

Shelley points to the girl sitting next to Steve. "Julie."

Julie is heavyset and short, with straight dark hair. Her upper lip has a little scar and quirk to it. She gives me a look that is almost a roll of the eyes. "Hey," she says, and then glances back down at her cell phone. "Jeff and Noah want to play." It takes me a moment to realize she's directing this at Steve, not at me. "They'll feed us pizza."

"Tell them it has to be Hawaiian and from Papa John's," Steve replies, jumping up from the couch. "I'll get my soccer cleats. Do you play?" she shoots at me.

Startled, I stumble a little in my reply. "I used to play a mean center forward in high school. Nothing like college standards, though."

"You'll be fine. We're just playing 'smear' rules anyway. It'll be mostly mud wrestling." She gives me a smile similar to the Cheshire cat's—wide, enthusiastic, and just slightly evil.

Maybe this won't be so bad, I think to myself. Then I catch Julie's expression. It's the meanest look I think I've ever seen on a face: eyes narrowed and dark with malevolence, lips curled. I shiver and take a step back, I'm so startled by it. *Well, all right then.*

"No thanks," I say, smiling coolly at her.

"And this is Maddie," Shelley finishes, glancing from me to Julie and then sitting down next to the remaining girl. "She's my room-roomie." She puts an arm around Maddie's shoulders.

Maddie is tiny and blonde, and when she turns to me I'm startled by the color of her eyes—a deep, sea-blue tint that I have serious doubts about. They're heavily lined, and she's wearing a violent pink shade of lipstick that turns her mouth into a voluptuous little pout. "Hi," she says, looking me up and down. "I'm so glad you're moving in. You look kind of normal, and Andrea was such a complete weirdo."

"All right," the Turd interjects, clearly impatient with the girl-talk. "Do you have everything you need?"

I shrug. "Yeah. I think. I can walk to Broullim's to get stuff for dinner."

"I'll take you," Shelley says. "That way you can stock up for the week. We all have early finals—we'll be leaving for Christmas by the seventeenth."

Of course. Christmas, and finals. This is dead-week, then—I have a test to take in four days.

I'd completely forgotten. "Thanks," I reply. "You really don't have to, though."

She tilts her head, considering me. "No, but I want to."

The Turd nods and turns on his heel.

"Bye, Bishop," Maddie calls as he heads out the door.

I freeze.

The Turd freezes for a moment too and then slowly turns to face me.

"No," I say when I've got my voice under control.

"I didn't tell you to move into this apartment," he replies calmly. "I found everything I could, everything I happened to know about. You chose this, not me."

"But when you handed me the listings, you didn't tell me that if I chose it, I'd be in your *ward*."

"I didn't think it should influence your decision. Heavenly Father chooses bishops and boundaries. You needed to find the place that was right for you."

"No." I follow him out onto the sidewalk and shut the door tightly behind me, practically in Shelley's face. "No. You should have told me. You can't do this to me!"

The Turd raises his eyebrows. "Do what?"

"That you would be . . . that I would have to . . . it's a conflict of interest!"

"How is my being your bishop and your boss a conflict of interest?"

Because you want to have complete control over my life. "Well, for one thing," I reply unsteadily, "you're not supposed to hire people you know."

"I didn't hire you when I was your bishop; I became your bishop after I hired you."

I put my hands on my hips. "I'm not living here, then. I've changed my mind."

He frowns. "If the idea of my being your bishop is that awful to you, feel free to look around. But I don't think I'll be able to get a refund on that deposit unless you can sell this contract as well. I'm not funding another deposit."

It's a kill-shot—the reminder of what he's done for me, and

therefore, how badly I'm acting considering my circumstances. I can't think of anything to say in response. I even have a strange, infuriating impulse to apologize as I watch him climb back into his car.

It stinks, I think helplessly as he drives away. *It stinks like the cigarette smoke in Pen's upholstery. Like Aunt Cindy's potpourri. What did I do to deserve this?*

I go inside and relieve my feelings by stalking through the living room without acknowledging anyone. I rip open my boxes and strew things around the room. My anger builds as I see what my mom has packed—clothing, bedding, toiletries. All the essentials. Nothing to remind me of Mark. I ache, looking at the empty room—just a mattress and a tiny window. Blank walls.

My new life.

I can't quite believe it. I feel like I'm on an alien planet.

I walk back into the living room. "Sorry about that," I say. "Are you ready to go, Shelley?"

The trip to Broullims is mostly silence. Shelley glances at me from time to time but doesn't say anything. I thank her as we get out of the car. We both grab shopping carts. I turn down the first clear aisle I find, and she follows me. I make another abrupt turn and head toward dairy, leaving her to contemplate the price of eggs.

Milk. What kind of milk? There's whole milk and two percent and one percent, there's chocolate and strawberry and dairy-free . . . I stare into the refrigerator, closing my eyes for a moment to savor the cool air on my cheeks. The milk cartons are blinding white, blurring in my vision into a long stream of tiresome choice. *Who cares about brands, about prices per ounce? Who cares about milk?*

"This is a steal." It's Shelley's voice that breaks my reverie. She plunks a carton into my shopping cart. "Fifty cents off the usual price."

I glance down at the milk sitting in my cart and feel strangely grateful.

It takes us an hour to find everything. Shelley walks along beside me, occasionally engaging me in small talk. I answer with only half my brain. I'm thinking about the time Mama took me shopping when I was first moving out. I fought her on every decision, from what brand of bread to how many forks and spoons I'd need. I didn't want her to be able to take credit for anything. Now, I don't care enough to muster the energy to make any decisions at all.

Grocery shopping with Mark was always an experience. He would smile at anyone we met in the aisles, and they always smiled back. He would sometimes engage complete strangers in conversation. It was embarrassing, but people seemed to like it. And he'd always put one or two completely improbable things in the cart. I would try to catch him and put them back before we got to check out, but inevitably I'd be loading things onto the conveyor and find a jar of jalapeño jam or a package of glittery press-on nails. One time it was an orthopedic neck brace, and I bought it without batting an eyelash. *Good idea*, I told him. *You can never have too many first-aid supplies.*

Shelley goes first. I load my groceries up as she finishes and watch the checker scan everything, seeing the price add up to a lot more than I've spent on groceries in a while. I swipe my own card through and pray I have enough. I have no idea what's in my account, and I'm at that dangerous time just before the next pay period.

It goes through. In my relief, I feel a little warmer toward Shelley. "Thanks for taking me," I say after I've loaded the groceries into her trunk. The sky is an off-black color, and the streetlamps and headlights light up the lazy flakes that have started drifting down over the crowded parking lot.

She shrugs and smiles, holding the door for me.

"He's really not bad," Shelley ventures just as we pull up to the driveway. "Bishop Barnes. He just comes across at first as pretty . . . well . . . I don't know." She shrugs again.

"Turd-like?" I supply.

Her brow furrows. "Bishop Barnes is kind. Even though he seems kind of stern." She leans over to open the trunk.

"You don't have to tell me about *Bishop Barnes*. We've known each other a while."

"Hmm," she replies as she gathers up her own groceries. There's a hint of disapproval in her tone.

It pains me to admit it, but she's right. I don't think Heavenly Father would consider it proper sustaining if I call him Bishop Turd, even in my head.

Which means, I think as I load up my arms with plastic bags, *that I've got to sell this contract as fast as I can, because it's not going to happen. And I don't want to end up in whatever lower heavenly kingdom is allocated to bishop non-sustainers.*

Chapter

7

Cooking in a kitchen with four other girls is exactly what I remember from being a freshman: chaos, bumping elbows, and people getting annoyed at each other. While preparing breakfast this morning, Julie gave Maddie a royal chewing-out for leaving a plastic spatula burning in a pan of eggs, a spatula that would be easily replaced with a trip to the dollar store. But who am I to intervene. I don't even want to be a part of this. So while Julie was yelling, I quietly heated up my bean burrito, poured on some salsa verde and cheese, and made a beeline for my room.

I sit here on the bare mattress and contemplate an ugly brownish stain while I eat. I try to draw it out, but a frozen burrito is a frozen burrito. I don't have work today, either, to take my mind off things. Nothing at all to do, in fact, except unpack.

Burrito consumed, I kneel next to my boxes and start putting stuff away. I hesitate when I pull out our wedding quilt, the one Grandma Cavendish made and sent over because she wasn't in good enough health to drive from Moscow (Idaho) to attend.

I was wrong. Mama did pack one reminder.

Spreading it on the bed, doubling it up so it will fit, I start shaking my head even before I'm finished. I pull it off and shove it under the bed.

After I finish putting away my clothes, I bring an armful of toiletries and hygiene products to the bank of mirrors in the bathroom area and shove them in an empty drawer. It's shallow, so not everything fits. I take my shampoo and conditioner and line it up on the ledge in the shower next to half-a-dozen other pastel-colored bottles. Looking at them, I wonder what happened to Mark's aftershave. *Did Mama just chuck it? Did she give it to Dad?*

As I walk back down the narrow hallway toward my room, one of the two other bedroom doors swings open and Steve comes barreling right into me.

"Oh, geez." She grabs my shoulder to keep me from falling. "Sorry, I didn't see you."

"Seeing through doors isn't one of the usual gifts of the Spirit," I agree.

She gives me a startled look, then laughs. My lips curl up a little at the corners. *That smile of hers is just too much.*

For a moment I'm tempted to follow her into the living room, but when she opens the door, the sound of Maddie's yappy little voice changes my mind. I head back to my room and grab my backpack.

"Where are you going?" Shelley asks pleasantly as I stroll through the living room toward the front door a few minutes later.

"Study." I shut the door behind me and take a moment to breathe in the fresh air.

The snow is still coming down. There's a fluffy carpet three inches thick on the sidewalk. I make my way along it, savoring the soft compression of snow under my feet and blinking at the white falling world around me. It's so soft. So quiet and peaceful.

I wonder if it snows a lot in heaven.

The hospital is only five blocks away, a much closer walk than before. I slip a little as the sidewalk gets steep, headed up the last stretch. I'm so calm and almost zoned out that I forget to avoid the reception desk and earn myself a nasty suspicious glance from Mara.

MILE 21

The head nurse on Med-Surg is Andrea this time. She's okay, I guess.

"Hello," I say politely. "Does Mr. Eems have visitors right now?"

"No." Andrea taps her pencil on the chart spread out in front of her on the desk. "But we could use you in room 243. Donald Rigby."

I nod and stride past the nurses' station.

"He'll be glad to see you," Andrea adds. "He's really craving some conversation. His family's in Ashton and haven't been able to get down to see him. He came in two days ago with a pulmonary embolism."

I freeze. I turn and look at her.

She glances up from the chart. Catching my expression, her eyebrows shoot up. There's a moment, and then recognition dawns on her face. "I'm sorry, Abish. I forgot. Don't worry about it—go see Mr. Eems."

"I'm not worried," I reply stiffly. "It's fine. I'll visit Donald."

"You should call him Mr. Rigby," she reminds me.

As I walk slowly toward room 243, her words are echoing in my mind. *I'm sorry, Abish. I forgot.*

It's only been a little more than a year, but she's forgot. Likely Mama and Dad have too . . . they've forgotten little details, events in the day that changed my life completely.

I don't have the luxury of forgetting.

A little of the tightness in my chest dissolves when Mr. Rigby's face lights up as I walk into the room. "Hi," he says, holding out a gnarled hand. From the hitchhiker thumb and the sheer size of it, I'm guessing he does something manual for a living, like farm or fix cars.

"Hey, I'm Abish." I return the firmness of his grip with plenty of my own. He grins at me, revealing teeth that are slightly yellowed.

He doesn't have all that many tubes coming from him. Just an IV and cardiac monitoring stuff. In fact, he looks pretty good. "Like from the Book of Mormon," he says, breaking through my thoughts.

I nod and brace myself for what's coming. *The one who raised the Lamanite king and queen from the dead.*

He doesn't say it; he just observes me through slightly narrowed eyes for a moment. Then he smiles, the lines in his face smoothing out. "Sit." He pats the upholstered chair next to his hospital bed.

We chat for a while about his grandkids. He shows me pictures from his wallet, and I make the obligatory admiring noises. I'm used to the routine by this point, and I'm usually pretty comfortable with it, but I can't stop glancing at his body, at the few monitors in the room. The steady beat of his heart, fifty-four beats per minute. He's pretty healthy.

Mark was pretty healthy too. And much younger.

Finally I rise from my chair. "It was nice visiting."

"Thank you." His smile fades and he gazes at me for another long moment.

He can feel it, I think as I leave the room. *The weirdness inside of me. Jealousy. That's what I'm feeling—jealousy.*

Because I have to wonder why an old man can come out the other side—*pulmonary embolism; the two words that changed my life*—looking as good as he does.

I walk to a little alcove I know, far down near the end of the hall. Nobody ever uses it.

I sit down, leaning my head against the top of the leather chair. The memory I've been suppressing all during the hour I talked to Mr. Rigby floods in.

It starts with him on the court; indoor soccer. He's got on a yellow polo shirt with thin blue stripes. The fluorescent light pours down on him—his golden hair, his tan arms and legs. He's like something from a vision or maybe a Greek legend.

I decided to sit out that game. No, he convinced me to sit it out. I'm on a white plastic chair on the sideline. There are a few other chairs—other young wives. I'm listening to a conversation about Pinterest recipes with one half of my brain and watching Mark with my other half.

He's playing. The ball goes out of bounds. He runs over, grabs the ball, and flings it over his head toward James Bennion, another of the young married men in our ward. And then suddenly something changes; I can see it even from all the way over here on the side where I'm sitting.

84

MILE 21

I'm standing by the time he gets to me. He's running with a strangely jerky pace, clutching his chest. He stops in front of me, reaches out for my shoulders, and fixes me with a gaze more intense, more serious than any I've seen on his face. And then, suddenly, he collapses at my feet.

We found out after the EMTs came that he died almost instantly. They called it a saddleback clot—a lump of hard blood that had started in his calf. He had been complaining that week about it, cramps in his leg. The clot sat there in his superior vena cava, waiting, and then with all the activity of the soccer game it came loose, shooting up to lodge in both bronchial tubes.

My knees are trembling. My hands and fingers feel twitchy. I open my eyes and notice the picture across the wall from me—that portrait you always see in obstetricians' offices of a woman wearing a loose white nightgown, looking out the window as she holds the round head of her child against her shoulder.

Staring at it, I feel like there's something bad there for me—the blackness, maybe. I wait, clutching my knees. I close my eyes.

Strangely, it doesn't come. It's almost frustrating, like that feeling crouched next to the toilet, waiting to vomit. There's all the terrible anticipation and none of the relief I'd feel if the blackness actually swept down on me and claimed me and I could see if it was as bad as I thought. I stand, gripping the strap of my backpack with both hands.

Mr. Eems welcomes me with the usual science-fiction beeps and lines. I sit in my chair and try to focus on the processes of ovulation, conception, and gestation—to focus without focusing too hard. This is the point in the semester when I found I had to drop out last year. *It's all coming at once. The move. Mr. Rigby. The chapter on pregnancy. Heavenly Father, what are you trying to do to me?*

Fallopian tubes. Just a name, Abish. Everybody has them.

Well, half the population at least.

I muddle through, focusing on keywords and review questions. Finally I sigh, shut my book, and glance up at the clock. I've put in three hours; that should be enough to satisfy anybody.

As I walk home, I savor the silence. The snow has stopped, and the absolute stillness of snow-covered Rexburg fills my heart with icy comfort. I find I'm limping. I don't know why.

The week goes by fast. I flit from one distraction to another—work, study, sleep, study, work, sleep. I spend my nights on the floor in the corner of my room because I can't bring myself to climb up onto the neatly made bed. Luckily, I still have Pen's sleeping bag. Pen hasn't called and asked for it or anything.

Not that I'm wanting him to. Honestly, I'm kind of relieved.

Except it would be nice to be able to get a little angst out my system by blowing stuff up. Or just hanging out with him a little. He never asks me questions or even expects me to talk much. Everybody *else* seems excessively curious about my day-to-day activities.

Each morning I go to work, the Turd gives me the hairy eyeball and asks me how my evening went. And Shelley tries to talk to me when I come home from work, asking me how my day went. It's like they're taking shifts. I wonder if they're reporting to each other.

Steve seems the most normal of all my new roommates. She doesn't try to force me into conversation as I pass through the living room on the way to the hall or to go out the door. One time she invites me to come with her to a Christmas party at some guy's apartment in the ward. If I hadn't already been inclined to say no, the look Julie gave me from over her shoulder would have convinced me. Julie and Steve are like conjoined twins. Or maybe Julie's more like the tail to Steve's comet of reckless energy. They are very social, always either gone somewhere or sitting in the living room with a few of their countless noisy friends, laughing so loud that not even my shut door will keep the noise out. Those are the days I spend the evening hours at the hospital.

Maddie is something else. It's like her tongue operates independent of her brain. Sometimes it's inconsiderate questions she'd figure out the answers to if she thought long enough. Or knowing when something's not very tactful. Like when she asks me what the ring on my left hand is for, and then informs me that I'm weird to still be wearing it.

Yeah, it is a little weird, I guess. But, I mean, is it really? Would she say that to an elderly woman who was widowed? What am I supposed to do, stuff it in the back of a drawer somewhere? Is it so bad that I still think of myself as a wife . . . as married, in fact?

Sometimes Maddie is just downright clueless too. Either that or purposely rude; I still haven't decided. Like when, after I explained that I'm married but he passed away, she props her pointy little chin on her fist, stares at me for a long moment, and then says, "So, you've totally done it."

"It?" I ask, hoping against hope she doesn't mean what I think she means.

"Slept with a guy."

"Um, yeah. My husband."

"Oh yeah. It's totally okay, of course."

"Thank you for the dispensation."

"It's just"—she gives me an unnerving sea-green stare—"I mean, what is it like?"

I let out a half snort, half chuckle of complete disbelief. "Just about what everybody says it's like," I reply, and turn to walk back to my room so that I don't give in to my impulse, which is to grab her by the hair and shake her until her teeth rattle and her color-change contacts are rolling on the floor.

Overall it's livable.

I just can't think too hard about it.

On Saturday morning I find myself sitting in a small empty classroom with Professor Harrison for my anatomy and physiology test, and it feels like kindergarten. I've spent so much time and energy over the last few days focusing my thoughts and attention away from the stinky turns my life has taken and toward anatomical processes and terms, that it's like answers flow directly from my pen onto the paper without much help from my working memory. When I finish the last question, I'm almost 100 percent sure that I've aced it.

I've got this, I think as I hand over my bluebook. *If I can beat Anatomy and Physiology, I can do anything. Bring it on, winter semester.*

It's a triumph that I badly need. As I walk home, the jubilation of success comes over me, and I feel almost like skipping. The air is icy and sweet. I'm walking down the hill and I can see the horizon all the way to the mountains. My knit hat makes my ears itch pleasantly, reminding me that I am alive.

I start running, a route that takes in all of campus and most of the streets on the hill and winds back down around University Boulevard, down Yellowstone, and back. My mind churns away, digesting the week, the day. The feeling is so good, it's scary. I'm so high . . . so much higher than I've been lately.

You are happy, Abish.

Life can be good, Abish, see?

I'm pretty sure, as I collapse onto the front porch, that I've done at least fourteen.

Fourteen miles. That's the most I've ever run.

Mark was the runner. He got me into it when we were dating. After we got married, we even started training for a marathon together.

And then I had to stop training. But he kept going, still determined to do it alone. He'd already done three half-marathons, and he wanted to beat those twenty-six miles. He signed up for the Ogden marathon. He never ended up running it, of course.

As I sit here on the step and stretch my calf muscles, thinking of Mark training for his marathon, I feel a stir of something I've been missing lately. The sort of smiling-warmth feeling I have sometimes, like maybe he's thinking of me. Like maybe he's proud of me right now.

Good run, Abish. Next Saturday we'll try for a sixteen. Your shoes need to be replaced, though.

I look down ruefully at my beat-up Adidas. *You're right. It really is time to get new running shoes.*

I shake my head suddenly, violently. I stand, putting a hand to my forehead. I open the door to the apartment and let out a deep, relieved sigh—it's dark. Empty. I have the kitchen to myself.

I take a little extra time over my tuna sandwich, slicing a handful of green onions, adding pickles. I take it to my room and wolf it down, looking around at my empty walls. What should I do with the rest of my afternoon? I feel a little like celebrating—*fourteen miles, and my incomplete finally gone.* I have my coat back on, and I'm weighing the merits of Kiwi Loco against the various frozen custard places in town. As I reach for the doorknob, someone knocks.

Somehow I know who it is. The image is in my mind: Dad and Mama standing there on the doorstep. I open the door slowly, carefully, like peeling off a Band-Aid.

There they are. My dad's arms are folded across his chest. We exchange a long look. His ice-blue eyes are enigmatic and his mouth is a tight, unsmiling line—*Pain? Anger? Frustration? Nerves?* Mama's wearing her fake-polite smile. She's shivering a little, but not with cold, because she's got her rabbit-fur coat on. She's clutching a pan of something to her chest.

I swallow hard. "Come in."

Mama puts her offering on the kitchen counter. It's empanadas—caramel apple, my favorite kind. It's what she brings people when they're sick or their house has burned down.

"Did the T—Bishop Barnes tell you where I was?" I ask.

"We've been in contact with Burt," Dad confirms, setting his palms on either side of the doorway to the kitchen as if he's testing its strength.

I nod and clear my throat. My heart is throbbing in my chest. As I said before, we Cavendishes don't do drama very well.

"Pretty sure I aced the A&P final," I find myself saying. "And I ran fourteen miles today."

Mama's forehead wrinkles. "Fourteen miles? Why would you run that much?"

Dad's face lightens a bit. "I didn't know you ran. I ran track in high school."

I trace the lines of grout on the counter. "I thought you were a wrestler."

"That too."

There's another long silence.

"Are you training for a marathon?" he asks.

I look up at him quickly and see only a general sort of inquiry in his face. "Maybe," I reply. "I'm still deciding."

He nods. "I wouldn't mind training for one someday. I've thought about it."

I frown and pull the tinfoil off the top of the plate, which is piled high with succulent empanadas. I take a corner of pastry off and pop it in my mouth. "So why are you guys here?"

Another interminable silence.

It's my mom who finally speaks up this time. "We want . . ." She glances at my father and bites her lip. "Abby, I think it might be a good idea if you went to see a scientologist."

I raise an eyebrow as images of Tom Cruise hopping up and down on Oprah's couch come to mind.

The corners of Dad's eyes wrinkle and the dimples make a slight appearance. "Psychologist," he amends.

I don't smile back. "If I need therapy, it'll be my decision."

"Of course. But therapy is expensive. We want you to know we would be willing to help with that. And if you needed medicines."

"What makes you think something is wrong with me? You realize that my *husband* died a year ago."

"Yes, Abish," Dad replies. "A *year* ago."

"So there's like, a year cutoff date on how long people are allowed to be sad their spouses die?"

Dad shakes his head impatiently, and his mouth is back in its grim line.

"Of course we understand that you are sad," Mama adds. "We all loved Mark—"

Now I'm shaking my head, so violently my dark hair swings around my face. "You never liked Mark."

"We did not dislike Mark," Dad says shortly. "Mark was fine."

"It was my decision to get married you didn't like."

Dad's face grows weary—that too-tired expression I've become so familiar with in these last few days. For some reason it makes me extremely angry this time. *Who are they to be so tired out by* my *pain?*

To act like I'm some kind of burden. My glance lights on the empanadas. *Or invalid.*

"Well, bye," I say shortly. "Thanks for the visit. I'm sure you have other stuff to do while you're in town."

Dad grabs my upper arm as I walk past him. It startles me; he's so silent and still, standing there, and then suddenly I'm brought up short. It shocks me too, because Dad has never laid a hand on any of us—Mom, me, or Suzy. Ever.

"What can we do for you, Abish?" His voice is odd—there's a strange, pleading sort of note in it.

I'm shivering now, like Mama. *We're all making each other nervous. This is what happens when the Cavendishes try to talk to each other about hard stuff.* "Nothing," I reply. "Just let me figure things out."

"Can I give you a blessing?"

I can remember one time—just one, in my life—when I got a father's blessing. It was when I was ten years old. I was sick with measles. Actually I can't remember much of it; my temperature was up around 105 and I wasn't very aware of my surroundings. All I recall are the cool drops of oil, and then the feeling of warmth and heaviness when he put his hands on my head. So it's indescribably weird that he's asking me now.

I look up at him, and his eyes hold mine. Again, I cannot tell what he's feeling, much less what he might be thinking.

"No, thank you," I reply. It comes out sounding prim, timid almost. I jiggle my arm a little, and he releases me. "I've got to head out. Thanks for coming over. Thanks for the sweets, Mama." I don't look back to see if they follow me; I just walk out the door.

My feet automatically take me to the hospital. This time I don't bother to check in with the nurses on Med-Surg. I walk past the station and head down the hall to room 243 and fling the door open without knocking. This isn't something I'd usually do, but I'm really not thinking clearly.

Donald looks up from a crossword he's doing and gives me a

little smile, or really, more a slight narrowing of his eyes. "I need help," he says.

"Oh?" I plop myself down in the chair next to his bed and run my fingers along my scalp. I'm tempted to rip a hunk of it out. Find some sackcloth and ashes. *Something.*

"Do you know an eight-letter word for hygiene?"

I think for a few seconds. The distraction helps; I feel my heart slowing a bit. "Grooming," I finally say.

"Well now," he murmurs, scratching in the letters with his pencil, "I think that might be it. That's done." He flings down the folded newspaper, slides the pencil behind his ear, and looks at me.

"So," I say, "how are you feeling?"

"Just fine. Nurses say that I can go home tomorrow."

"Mm-hmm." I glance at his wires. They've taken out the IV. His monitor is beeping regularly. "How do you sleep at night with that thing?"

"Don't sleep much," he says. "To be honest, I'm glad to be getting out of here. Shop's suffering. I've got two transmissions waiting for me. They won't let any of my boys touch it. Real loyal customers." He laughs, glances at me, and then looks away. "I'm sorry about your husband."

That throws me for a loop.

"Yeah?" I finally stutter. "Who told?" *Because they're about to get an earful on confidentiality policies and the seventeen million rules they've broken.*

"Nobody."

"Somebody must have."

"I heard the nurses talking after you visited last time. Stopped right outside my door . . . I don't think they noticed you left it open a crack." He studies me for a moment, his gaze penetrating. "Are you angry?"

I frown at him. "What do you mean?"

"Angry that I lived and he didn't."

It's such a question. It takes me completely by storm for a moment; so many emotions pass through me. First it's the anger he mentioned, then bleakness. Then a deep and bone-grinding ache that I can't identify.

"Don't I have a right to be?" I finally respond. "No offense. But you're what, like sixty?"

"Seventy-four," he corrects with a slight grin.

"Man. You've taken care of yourself, then."

He shrugs. "Good genetics. Don't smoke or drink, but I eat my fill of steak and potatoes."

"Hmm."

"You can't always prevent crap from happening."

I stare, startled at his use of the crude word.

He grins. "It's a fact of life. Crap happens."

"That's not the way the saying goes."

He shrugs.

"Yeah," I say, rising from my chair. "I think the nurse might have put a little something extra in your applesauce."

He flashes a grin, cynical and amused at the same time. I notice that his center bottom teeth are crooked and worn down, extra yellow. "You can't live this life without getting hurt—Abish, isn't it?"

I nod, then shake my head. "If that's true, what's the point, then? What about the plan of happiness?"

"It doesn't cut out hurt. Even being born hurts."

"Well, that's a real comfort. Thanks." I stalk to the door and shut it behind me, forcing myself to do it gently and not slam it like I want to. As I go back through the hall and down the stairs to the main entrance, everything seems to have a kind of reddish tint. Intense, unnamable feelings are roiling inside me. One moment I want to shred something or kick a hole in the wall, and the next I feel like I might collapse.

I walk around behind the hospital and sit on the curb at the back of the parking lot. I close my eyes and let the sun hit my neck for a few minutes, and then I'm up, off. Running.

I don't get far before I keel over to the side of the road, kneel, and empty my stomach in the irrigation ditch. My temples are throbbing and there's this deep, sick kind of pain in my gut. *What is wrong with me?*

It's called grieving, Abish.

Yeah? So what am I supposed to do with this?

Just keep moving through it.

I sit up and clasp my knees to my chest, shivering. A running girl in white spandex pants and a pink sweatshirt slows to a walk. She glances at me and removes one of her earphones. I give her a curt nod. "I'm fine. Just got the wind knocked out of me."

She smiles uncertainly. "Okay," she says, and starts running again. I watch her slim legs, the lightness of her gait. She's practically leaping, like a gazelle or something. Like she doesn't have a burden in the world.

I stand and begin to walk. I circle the southeast corner of campus, then cut across the Kimball parking lot and head to the computer lab on the first floor of the humanities building. The CSR gives me a doubtful look, taking in my wet and slightly muddy jeans.

I sit down at the computer and log onto the site for the Ogden marathon. It only takes me a few minutes and a visa debit of fifty dollars and I'm signed up. I breathe in slowly, seeing my name, number, and the date there on the screen. A thrill of fear races through me as I click onto a tab where I have downloaded a training schedule. Twenty miles, one of the weekend runs. *Twenty miles. How am I going to run twenty miles?*

For that matter, how am I going to run twenty-one miles? And twenty-six? In the moment, it seems impossible. Like climbing Everest.

People have climbed Mt. Everest. In for a penny, Abish. Five thousand of them.

When the paper comes out of the printer, I fold it and stick it in my pocket, then hand my I-card to the CSR for him to swipe.

Just keep moving through it, I think as I trudge back to the apartment.

Chapter

8

Sunday dawns gray and muggy. A bank of clouds hovers, fogging up the windows of Shelley's car and refusing to provide any relief in the form of real precipitation. As we step out—me, Steve, Julie, and Maddie—a gale-force wind rips at our carefully coiffed hair (well, mine isn't all that coiffed) and attempts to lift our skirts above our armpits. I'm feeling kind of scattered as I follow my new roommates to the bank of glass doors, holding my hem to my kneecaps.

I was on the verge of not coming this morning. I woke up entirely intending to spend another hour bed instead of making the mad dash to be ready for 9:00 sacrament meeting. Then Shelley knocked on my door, stuck her head in, and told me the Turd called.

The Turd. Yeah, I mean Bishop Barnes. I guess I have to call him that if I'm actually attending the ward. Shelley said he told her to make sure I knew that ecclesiastical endorsements are coming up so he wanted me in for an interview after meetings were over. Which is a veiled way of saying come to meetings or I won't ecclesiastically endorse you. *I knew it wouldn't take long for the power trip to set in.*

So here I am, breezing along the Manwaring corridors with a crumpled skirt and witch's hair. Maddie makes a stop in the girls' bathroom to smooth herself down again, but the rest of us apparently can't be bothered. Which in a way makes me feel a smidge better—we're low-maintenance girls, us Manor tenants.

Apparently that's the nickname for the house we live in: the Manor. It's so singles ward-y, living in a house with a nickname. It makes me squirm every time someone says it.

I glance down at my empty left hand and shiver. It was a hard decision: keep the ring on defiantly, or remove it so I don't have to answer a hundred awkward questions that really are nobody's business but my own. In the end the ring ended up on a chain around my throat, resting against my chest under the snug cotton of my under-tee.

Sacrament meeting is in one of the classrooms with stadium-style seating. My roommates file in and sit in an empty space in the third row. I'm tempted to head off to the very back of the room. But I realize that will make me even more conspicuous because there's no way this entire room is going to be full. So I sit down next to Maddie, who smiles and raises a hand at someone. I glance over and see that a group of boys has wandered in. Most of them have tall, athletic builds and tolerably regular features.

The hot-guy apartment, I think to myself.

There's one in every ward. When I was dating Mark, he was in that apartment. His roommates were all bores. I kind of judged him for it. I assumed he was brainless jock who was too full of himself to pay attention to anyone else, until we had our first real conversation.

Maddie is pretty starstruck with this group of guys. A few of them wave at her casually and go to sit down, but she doesn't take her eyes off them. She's straining, she's concentrating so hard. I think I can see a vein popping out on her temple. When she finally turns away, she notices me watching her and blushes bright red.

"Cute," I say.

She shrugs. "The guy in the blue shirt? That's Dave Cannon.

I've been on a couple dates with him. He's the elder's quorum president."

I nod. *Ah. The EQ prez.* If he's attractive at all, the elder's quorum president is usually the most sought-after guy in any LDS singles' ward. "Cute," I repeat, and turn my attention to the front of the room.

The Turd—*Bishop Barnes, Abish, Bishop Barnes*—is there sitting next to the podium. He's got a notebook on his lap, and he's concentrating hard on it. I don't know how, what with the rays of fury that are emanating from my eyes in a direct line to his soul.

The room fills rapidly, the soft prelude music stops, and the bishop rises and moves to the microphone. "Welcome," he says in his gruff voice. He goes on to outline the program, and I start to zone out. I look at my knees. I look at Shelley's adorably wind-tumbled hair. I glance over at the hot guys and quickly look away when I see one of them looking at me. *Who's the new girl?* is written plainly on his face.

Yeah, I'd like to know the same thing. *Who am I going to be? Jock girl? Antisocial witch? That crazy person who sits at the back of Sunday School muttering under her breath?* I don't fit in here. They can tell, and I can't help but know it. *What sort of favor does the . . . does the bishop think he's doing, forcing me into this situation?*

It's the last Sunday before the semester ends, and so people all around me are being gooey and chummy, talking about good times they've had these last few months. When sacrament meeting is over, I negotiate my way through the crowded hall. Nobody speaks to me. I'm not sure if I'm glad about this or not. I know I'm walking all hunched-over tense, making it obvious I feel uncomfortable and would like to be considered invisible. I try to force myself to relax, take deep breaths, and straighten my spine. There's this terrible tight feeling inside of me, like my innards have been vacuum-packed.

In Sunday School, Shelley sits on one side of me. Nobody sits on the other. The small room fills up and grows hot and humid with everybody's breathing. After the opening prayer, the teacher begins by theatrically rolling up his sleeves. "Today's topic," he says, "is eternal marriage."

Someone in the room groans. I'm glad to hear I'm not the only one who doesn't really want to stick around for this. I sit through the discussion of the sealing covenant and why it's important to eternal salvation, and I try hard not to listen. Mark's face—that serious, intense thing in his eyes just before he collapsed on the ground at my feet—keeps drifting into my mind. *Did marrying me get you the goods, Mark? Are you in the best of the best degrees? Enjoying life up there under the sun in your celestial hammock?*

A dart of awful guilt chases my anger away.

Shelley takes my arm on the way to Relief Society. "That lesson was hard for you. You must miss your husband."

"Yeah," I reply. *I don't want to talk about it, thanks.*

"At least you know for sure you have him forever." She gives me a quick timid, anxious glance. I resist the urge to swat her arm away.

Shelley allows me to lead the way this time, and we end up in the back row. I concentrate during the opening song and prayer. I take a few quiet, deep breaths and attempt to compose myself.

A perky-looking blonde girl gets up. "Hey, ladies," she says. "Today's lesson is about something very important." She pauses for a long moment. "Chastity."

Heavenly Father, you're playing a joke on me. I half rise from my seat, then sit down again quickly as a couple of girls give me curious glances. The silence in the room is thick. She starts with the usual analogy. I've heard it before in half-a-dozen forms—*women are like crock-pots, men are like microwaves. Men are blow-torches, women are candles. Women are the tortoises, men are the hares; slow and steady wins the . . .*

No, that one wasn't from a singles' ward sex discussion. It was the marriage enhancement class Mark and I took. *It really wouldn't do to get the two mixed up.*

I hear whispering. I glance up and see Maddie, a few rows in front of me, busily talking to her neighbor. She looks over her shoulder and smiles at me, then continues whispering, nodding in my direction.

MILE 21

Lovely. So that's who I'm going to be. The girl who's done it.

And that's about done it for me too. I stand and edge past all the knees in my row of seats. I practically jog out of the room, I'm in such a hurry to get away from there.

Bishop Barnes is in the hall as I come rocketing out. He's busily discussing something with *EQ prez* Dave Cannon, but he stops when he sees me. "Something wrong, Abish?"

I shake my head. "I'm not feeling well. I'm going to go home."

"All right. My schedule's filled up for this afternoon, anyway. We'll see you this evening at six. You can stay after for ward prayer."

I don't waste time arguing. I nod and walk past him, stumbling a little as I round the corner to take the stairs down to the parking lot.

I run, even though I'm wearing my battered Timberland Mary Janes, and I haven't quite recovered from the blisters I raised the night I jogged home after punching Pen in the face. The pain helps a little—focuses my rage.

Because that's what I'm feeling: boiling, red rage. I could *kick* someone in the face right now. And the people on my shortlist for face-kicking really aren't hard to come up with. *Mom, how could you? Dad, you're useless. Bishop, are you sure Heavenly Father approves of the torture regimen you've forced me into? Maddie, you deserve to be shaken. Aunt Cindy, you deserve to be shoved under a bus. Shelley, I want to see the look on your face if I were to say some of the words in my head out loud. Mark . . .*

My knees give, and I find myself sitting on the sidewalk outside the apartment, trembling.

Mark, why did you leave me?

Eventually I rise and go in. The refrigerator is stocked with useless food, most of it not mine. I don't feel like eating anyway. I walk unsteadily down the hall to the bathroom. There's moisture on my ankles; blood, maybe.

I sit on the toilet and pull off my shoes to see that my blisters have broken open and are bleeding on both of my insteps. I swab them with alcohol and put Band-Aids on. I examine my feet. My toenails are pretty bad—bruised, especially the last three. My left pinky nail looks like it's about to fall off.

Time to buy new shoes.

Are you sure? What if I like my new shoes better than the old ones?

Well, that's kind of the point. Off with the old, on with the new.

But the old shoes fit so well. They brought me through hundreds of miles.

They're not working anymore, Abish.

My chest feels tight as I walk into my room and look down at my old Adidas—their busted soles and cracked uppers.

Mark and I bought them together. He bought a pair at the same time. They were on the floor of our closet. Who knows where they are now: in a box, at a thrift shop, maybe in a dumpster somewhere.

I lie stomach-down on the mattress. It smells dusty, with an undertone of sweat. I don't care. I close my eyes and press my nose against it. I don't sleep, I just lay there trying to wipe my mind blank, but all the images keep coming. *Mark's face . . . Mark falling . . . cotton candy at Lagoon . . . Mark laughing as we run together and telling me to slow down, it's not soccer practice. Mark's incredulous, happy grin when I told him the news . . . the new tenderness in his eyes when he looked at me after . . .*

Even though my eyes are pressed tight shut so that I can't see anything, I can tell the room goes scary-flat around me. Not just the room.

The *world.*

The world suddenly becomes insipid and two dimensional and worthless. I'm hungry, but I don't feel like eating. I'm exhausted, but I don't care about sleeping. School is pointless. Running is a fruitless activity. Even thoughts of Mark . . .

Even Mark . . .

The blackness descends on me like a shroud, and I go completely limp. My thoughts are listless and bleak and half-formed. I don't care if I breathe in or out, or even if the ceiling collapses on top of me. The pain and the end would both be welcome.

MILE 21

I hear the apartment door open and the chatter of the girls as they rush in.

A few minutes later, footsteps come down the hall. There's a tentative knock on my door. I don't bother to answer or even to turn over. I feel a small dart of annoyance as the door eases open, scraping over the brown shag carpet on the floor. I know it's Shelley. *Nobody else would.*

I stay completely still, not because I want her to think I'm asleep, but because I don't have the impetus to move a single muscle. After a few moments she shuts the door and pads back to the kitchen.

I lie there for what is probably hours. Eventually I feel the change in the light coming through my tiny window, and a small crab of worry creeps over me. I stir, sit up slowly, and glance at my clock. 5:15.

I don't want to go. I don't have to go.

But he could refuse to endorse you, and then you'd be out of school.

Do I really care about school?

What else is there? What other plans do you have?

I walk down the hall to the bathroom, squinting against the artificial light, and glance at myself in the mirror.

I look terrible: eyes swollen, hair a mess. I run a brush through it and put it up with a few random twists of rubber band. I glance down at my crumpled skirt and head back to my room, reaching into my suitcase to grab the first thing that touches my fingers: a pair of dark corduroy pants. They're dressy enough, I decide. I slip them on, then pull on my Adidas, savoring the way the old rubber hugs my feet perfectly as I walk into the kitchen.

"Hey," Steve says. She looks me up and down. Her face is so completely guileless that I can see her thoughts perfectly. *Ratty tennis shoes and nice pants. And Sunday evening. These things do not compute.* "You going somewhere?"

I shrug and grab a box of Captain Crunch.

"That's Julie's."

I shrug again and pour a generous portion into a bowl. *I've gotta eat something. The last thing I want to do is collapse in front of the Tu—Bishop Barnes.*

"Julie's, like, really territorial about her food."

I nod. "I'll buy her some more. If she throws a fit, tell her I took it."

"Oh, I will," Steve says emphatically. "Or else she'll blame me." She considers me, head tilted slightly. "You really don't care what anybody thinks of you, do you, Abish?"

I finish pouring milk and tuck the carton back into the fridge before I answer. "I can't."

"Can't what? Can't care?"

I shrug, sit, and start wolfing down the cereal. "I've got too many other things to worry about," I reply, my words muffled with chewing.

Steve sits across from me and leans on her elbow. "Like what?"

I look up. Her face is genuinely curious. "I don't know. School. Work. Stuff."

Steve nods slowly, narrowing her eyes a little. I can see she wants to ask. But she doesn't. I'm grateful.

I finish my cereal and turn on the tap to rinse the bowl. I stick it in the dishwasher. "See you," I say awkwardly, grabbing for my coat, which I'd left slung over the arm of a couch.

The air is dead cold. Icy. Lung-scalding. My nose hairs freeze and my chest aches as I breathe in. In a way it's nice. It distracts from the other aches in that general vicinity. I walk slowly, drinking in the dark sky above me, savoring the way the street lights and the illumination from windows casts such contrast.

My cheeks sting as I enter the physical education building. I walk up the stairs to the same office where I work because that is where the Good Bishop runs his church business too. It's a little surreal, coming through those glass doors and seeing lots of Sunday-clad young men and women sitting in the chairs in the lobby. Everyone looks over as I walk in. A few people do a double take, eyeing my pants and unkempt tennis shoes, and then return to their small-talk.

I glance around to see who's in charge. There's an unfamiliar water bottle on the desk where Adrian and I work, but nobody is sitting there. I settle myself in a chair in the corner and try not to make eye contact with anybody.

Bishop Barnes strides into the lobby a few minutes later. "Abish," he says. I glance up, and he jerks his thumb in the direction of his office. "Let's go."

His authoritarian tone sparks a reaction. "No," I say. "All these people have been waiting longer."

The lobby has gone quiet. The people all look at me with expression ranging from bored-curious to mildly scandalized. Bishop Barnes frowns, his eyes doing that cold-disapproval thing.

I shrug and rise to my feet. I'm more tempted than I ever have been to push the tractor, but I know just where it'll get me.

He sits down behind his desk, and like so many times before, I sit opposite him. We stare at each other for a few minutes.

"Well, let's get a move on," I say finally. "Ask the questions. I'll give you the answers. Sign my paper and I'll turn it in."

"I believe you're worthy to go to school, Abish." He grabs a pen, takes an ecclesiastical endorsement paper from the stack on his desk, and signs it. He hands it to me. "I'll spare you the interview this time."

"Gee, thanks," I murmur. I scrawl my signature at the bottom, feeling slightly self-conscious. I fold the paper and tuck it into my pants pocket.

"Do you have somewhere to go for Christmas?"

I glance up at him. "What?"

"If you don't, my wife has offered for you to come. It wouldn't be any trouble for us."

"Um, no thanks." I rise to my feet. "But thanks." *I'm thanking him too much.*

"Just know the offer's on the table. And I want to see you back in here." He eyes me as if he's unsure about his next words. Something I've never seen before. "Next Sunday," he finishes finally.

"What for?"

"To discuss your situation."

"We've already resolved my situation. I'm living in single housing. Going to a student ward. Starting school in January." I raise my hands in a gesture of surrender. "You win."

"No . . . I mean, your . . ." Again he hesitates.

I frown at him. *What is his problem?*

"I meant more your mental health. Have you considered seeing a therapist?"

"No," I reply before he's finished. "But thanks."

"The ward could provide some of the funds."

"I still wouldn't be able to afford it."

"Your parents have offered to help."

At this, I feel a sudden throb of the same disabling anger that overcame me when I was running. It scares me so bad my knees start shaking again. "Um," I manage, "please keep out of my business. Don't talk to my parents."

"I'm not the one calling them. They're really concerned for you, Abish. And so am I. I want to make sure that you—"

"Well, I'm fine," I cut him off. "So stop worrying. Let me try to pick up the pieces, all right? Give me a chance before you decide to commit me."

"Nobody's talking about committing you."

I snort and raise my eyes to the ceiling. "That was a *joke*, but apparently not to you. What is wrong with people? My husband died. Dead, *muerto*. Why can't anyone see I can't just go back to life before? That I can't just erase him from me . . . from my—" And at this, I turn and stalk out of the office. My lips are trembling and my throat is thick and there is no way, absolutely no way in this universe, that I will cry in front of Bishop Barnes. I'd cry in front of Dad first.

Well, okay. Maybe they're tied for first place on my unacceptable-to-cry-in-front-of list.

I am feeling angry enough to explode. Angry that I let Bishop get to me, and also that all the people sitting and waiting for appointments will see me undone and wonder about it. I keep my eyes on the ground, my arms tightly folded, as I stride down the hall.

"About five more minutes," a voice is saying as I walk into the lobby. It's an oddly familiar voice. "Don't worry, we'll take a break for ward prayer," he adds.

I stop suddenly, ending my mad dash for the door, and turn slowly to look at him. *Bob, the Internet guy.*

I blink, closing my eyes so tightly that I see stars, and then open them again.

No, it's really him. It's Bob.

But it can't be.

Because of my emotionally overwrought state, I actually blurt it out. "You can't be in this ward!"

Bob turns. He actually looks pretty good in a suit. It turns his bulk into something kind of gracefully massive. He's shaved today; there's only slight evidence of the five o'clock shadow. His shoulders look impossibly broad, and his hair is slicked back in a classy way completely unlike the mess of dark curls I remember from the time in my kitchen, when he sat on my table with his legs dangling clear to the ground. When he was installing my cable Internet. When he saw me in my pajamas.

No, I say furiously with myself. *Not my fault. Heavenly Father, you* are *playing a trick on me. You must be.*

Everyone in the room is staring at me because of the words that have flown out of my mouth. "Hello again," Bob says, and his voice sounds just about as enthusiastic as I feel. "Abish, right?"

"Right."

"Internet working okay?"

"I wouldn't know. My mom kicked me out. Because of you."

His frown turns to an expression of mild amusement. "Because of *me?*"

I step closer to him, glance around at the people staring at us, and lower my voice. "Yes. Because you told my mom that I walked in on you in my . . ." I gesture helplessly. "Like I did it on purpose. And then you called her when I broke the Internet."

"You *told* me to call her."

"Yes, but I didn't . . . it's not because I . . ." The red-hot rage now seasoned by the embarrassment and disbelief I feel at this ridiculous turn of events has rendered me incapable of speech. "I can't believe you're here!" I hiss when I've gotten hold of myself. "You're such a complete jerk!"

He looks a little taken aback for a moment. Then his eyes harden. He gives me a cool smile. "Singles wards are full of jerks."

I badly want, in that moment, to give him a taste of the Pen treatment. "Yeah," I say, shoving my fists safely into my pockets. "But this is impossible! This can't be a coincidence. Mama somehow must have . . ." I shake my head. "You have kids! You *can't* be in a singles' ward."

"Well, here I am. Did Bishop Barnes want you to schedule another appointment?" He opens his notebook and lowers his eyes to the page, pen poised and waiting.

"*You're* the executive secretary?"

He nods.

"Of a BYU-Idaho singles' ward."

"I'll just write you down for after church next week, all right?" He glances at the people sitting in the chairs in the lobby, and I think I see some uneasiness in his eyes.

I narrow my own. "Wait. Does the Turd know you're divorced? That you have kids?"

His brows shoot up. "*Who?*"

"The T—I mean, Bishop Barnes." My face grows a little warm in the wake of the horribly disapproving look he gives me. "Yeah, write me down. He said to come in next week."

"Fine," he says after he's scrawled my name on the page under *weekly appointments.*

"My last name's Miller, not Cavendish," I correct him.

He scratches out Cavendish—how he remembered that, I don't know, because he must have hundreds of Internet customers each month—and scrawls Miller instead. He looks up at me. "And, *yes,* the bishop knows I have kids."

"Does anyone else?" I glance around at the people sitting in the lobby.

"That's not your business."

"Where are they? Your kids, I mean."

Bob sighs, passing a hand over his face. "At my mother's house."

"You pawn your kids off on your mom so you can go to the singles' ward and troll for clueless freshmen?"

MILE 21

"Abish!" Bishop Barnes' tone cracks like a whip across the room. He's standing at the end of the hall, glaring at me ferociously. I worry that in a moment the lightning of his righteous indignation might burn me to the ground. And, of course, all the eyes in the room are fixed on us.

"Apologize," Bishop Barnes says. "That remark was completely uncalled for."

He's right, and I know it. Anger and bewilderment completely made me lose my head. I mean, I'd never say something like that to someone. I never thought I could be that mean. *Usually I'm completely easygoing—nice. Accepting. A little on the blunt side, but nonjudgmental to a fault to make up for it. What's wrong with me?*

"I'm sorry," I mutter to my shoes.

I walk through the room, feeling like my face is on fire from the glare of a couple dozen pairs of eyes. *I'm not only going to be the girl who's done it. I'll be the girl who had to be reprimanded publicly by the bishop.*

A guy gets up to hold the door for me. His expression is cold, and a little disapproving.

I give him the meanest smile I can muster. "Your fly's undone."

I relish the slightly panicked expression on his face as he looks down—it's only slightly unzipped. Not enough for real concern, certainly not enough to warrant my embarrassing him in front of everybody. I stalk past him and head down the corridor, my heart pumping like I've already run my marathon.

I will put notices up in every stall in every girls' bathroom on campus, I promise myself. *I'll get out of this apartment, even if it means . . .*

Well, no; Aunt Cindy's still worse. It'd just be another person trying to control my life, to tell me what to do. To make me forget.

I can't forget. I feel helplessness rise up and overtake my anger, leaving me bone-weary and on the verge of either weeping or laughing hysterically. *Heavenly Father, it's not funny. Things have to be subtle to be funny. Bob the Internet guy? Really? Because that pushes things beyond subtle and into the territory of cruelty. Why are you torturing me like this?*

I don't even think about going to ward prayer. I just head back to my dank, dark, empty apartment and climb into my dank, dark (hopefully empty; I've noticed scuffling noises in the walls at night) sleeping bag.

Chapter

9

Over the next few days, all the roommates pack up and leave. I can't say I'm sorry. After the last of them has gone (Maddie flirting outrageously with Dave Cannon, who has come over to help her load up her tiny silver Mazda) I feel like I can breathe a little better. I spend time over my morning cereal and then head to the library to check my class schedule.

Am I ready for this?

It's a valid question. I glance at the list of credits. Fourteen in all; some nursing classes, a couple other prerequisites for my degree. *It'll be okay,* I tell myself as I click out of the screen and type in the address to my email account. *You can handle it.*

I haven't checked my email for a while—there are twelve new messages. I glance down the list and am surprised to see that four are from Pen. Pen's not the type to email you four times or leave stalker-messages on an answering machine. Girls generally follow him around or he isn't interested.

I click on the most recent message.

Hey, Abish. You're not answering your emails, and your mom says you've moved out of the apartment. I'm getting sort of worried. Please give me a jingle or something, soon.
Pendleton

My curiosity piqued, I click on the others. They're all variations of *hey, where are you, I have no way to get hold of you, call me.* I am puzzled and also a little weirded out. I mean, I punched him in the face, then stole his sleeping bag. And especially with Pen, it should take me crawling back on hands and knees, begging and offering to watch him play Portal for three weeks straight in exchange for forgiveness. If forgiveness is even possible.

I press the reply button and start rattling off an answer, then change my mind, log out of my email account, and go to the courtesy phone in the library foyer. He answers on the third ring.

"Hey." I twist the cord between my fingers.

"Abe."

"Yeah. Listen, Pen. I'm sorry." I don't say for what, because honestly I'm not sure.

"Okay," Pen says. "Do you have my sleeping bag?"

"Yeah. Do you mind if I still borrow it, though?"

"Sure, no prob. Hey, do you want to hang out? I've got a new joystick. You can use it."

I shake my head. *Curiouser and curiouser.* "Um, okay, I guess. When are you going home for Christmas?"

"I can't afford the gas this year."

"Oh." I look down at my shoes, scuffing them against the tile floor, and suddenly I have an idea. "Hey, Pen, do you want to go shopping with me for shoes?"

"*What?*"

"Running shoes," I explain hastily. "My Adidas are coming apart."

"Oh. Yeah, okay. Where are you at? I'll pick you up now, if you want."

"Okay. If you're not doing anything."

"No, man. I'm bored. And I know a good place down in Idaho Falls."

110

"All right." I hesitate, wondering if I can push my luck. "I'm all out of groceries too . . . do you need to go by Winco?"

"We can go by Winco," is his astonishing reply. "See you in five minutes. Meet me in the Manwaring parking lot."

He meets me right on time. I climb into the passenger seat. We're pretty quiet for a while. There is literally nothing to say, nothing at all. He glances at me from time to time. "Hey," he finally breaks the silence. "How are you doing, Abe?"

"Fine. And you?" *This is so strange and so completely awkward.*

"Good, I guess. I signed up for classes."

"What are you taking?"

"Not what I wanted to be taking." He gives me a little grin. "Don't start on me about procrastinating."

"I wasn't going to."

"'Kay." There's a hint of disappointment in his voice. When the silence stretches out again, he reaches over and presses the radio button. He tunes to a rock and roll station and we listen to wailing electric guitars for the rest of the way. I get lost in my thoughts—a mixed up jumble of what happened in the bishop's office, my parents' visit, and planning for the new semester. *I'll have to make sure to look in the syllabi for texts so I can order them online instead of breaking the bank with books from the BYU-I Bookstore.* The sky is starting to grow dim as we pull off the freeway onto the old Main Street. The river is translucent in the twilight. The lights of the temple run in long lines in the water. We pull up next to a small storefront. It's in the posh section of shops off of the mall complex—Teton Running Company.

We climb out of the car and walk in. It's a nice place with all kinds of running paraphernalia—from shoes to wristwatch-heart-monitors to nutritional supplements. There is a treadmill tucked in an alcove, where someone is chugging away with a shop attendant looking on.

A girl approaches me. She's tall, with the slim build of a runner. She gives me a friendly smile. "Are you here for shoes?"

"Yeah."

"Those have seen some good times." She tilts her head in the direction of my feet, encased in my battered Adidas. "Do you have any idea of what you want?"

I glance at Pendleton. "You don't have to stay and watch if you don't want to."

He shrugs and walks over to where a screen is mounted on the wall, playing a video about running technique.

I'm incredibly self-conscious at first, trying on pair after pair of brightly patterned shoes. I feel out of place—disembodied. I keep glancing at my old shoes sitting there on the bench. I'm tempted to just leave, say I don't really need new shoes yet, but I know that's ridiculous. And there's the marathon I signed up for. *There's no way my current shoes will last through training. They'll fall apart, and probably cripple me in the process.*

Finally I choose a pair of Asics. They're light and comfortable, and they feel good running. It actually makes an astounding difference. Pen steps up to the counter when I pay for them. As we leave the store, I feel like hiding the bag, which is emblazoned with the store's logo.

Winco isn't as crowded as usual. *It's because all the students are gone for Christmas.* I realize suddenly that I should be buying my own Christmas dinner on this trip if I'm going to do something special. I glance at Pen and wonder what his plans are. We get through checkout and load up the trunk.

"Are you going to your parents' for Christmas?" Pen asks as he settles behind the steering wheel.

"Yeah," I say. It's a lie. The first lie I've told in . . . I can't remember how long. Maybe ever.

I just can't hold it. "I mean, maybe not. Bishop Barnes—Burt, you know, our old boss? He invited me to his place. You could go with me to Burt's if you don't have any place else."

Pen rolls his eyes. "I'll opt out."

Just then, a slim, erect figure moves through the sliding-glass doors, pushing a cart heaped with bagged groceries. It's Anne Miller.

When I see her, longing hits me so acute and so painful that I can't say anything. My throat feels thick—closed off—as I watch her

walk past me. She doesn't see me. Or at least, she doesn't say anything; I think I see her eyes flick in my direction for a second before
she turns down another line of cars.

She couldn't have seen me, I think as we pull out of the parking
lot. *Anne wouldn't ignore me. She's an adult, for crying out loud. And
she's polite. She'd never cut someone dead on purpose.*

Still, I feel like the world has caved in over me. I see the Teton
Running carrier bag at my feet, and it's like a glaring neon sign. *I'm
moving on.*

From what, though? From Mark?

Anne sure seems to be moving on from me.

But I love Mark. And he's my eternal companion. There is *no
moving on.*

I only speak to give Pen directions to my new apartment. We
pull into the driveway. He turns off the car, hops out, and opens the
trunk, and then helps bring in my groceries. This is completely out
of character, but I don't have the energy to feel surprised.

"You want to make dinner together?" he asks, glancing around
the empty kitchen. "All your roommates split already?"

"Yeah. No thanks, Mark. Pen," I correct myself quickly, but not
soon enough.

He about-faces and stalks over to the door. I can see from his
expression that he's pretty bothered. *About what? That I called him
Mark? That I didn't want him to stay?*

"Sorry," I say dully. "See you sometime." I hold the door open
and after a moments' hesitation, Pen walks out to his car. He starts
up the engine and takes off, tires screeching as he backs up and then
tears off down Second East.

Bishop Barnes meets me at the office the next morning. It's just
the two of us with Adrian gone.

"This'll be the last day of work. We're closing up shop for Christmas," he says.

"Okay," I reply. I feel like something fuzzy grew in my mouth overnight. I brushed like three times this morning, but the feeling won't go away. My shoulder also hurts, like I slept on it wrong.

"Are you coming for Christmas? My wife would like to know."

"No."

"No? You're going with your parents, then."

"That's not your concern."

"Your welfare is my concern."

"Not as my boss," I snap, raising my face to glare at him.

"I'm your bishop *and* your boss."

"Well, what are you right now? My boss or my bishop? Because as my bishop, you shouldn't be in a room alone with me. You either need to go to your office, or call Bob to come sit in the foyer or something while we finish this fun conversation."

He frowns. "Consider coming for Christmas, Abish."

"I've considered it."

"I'll tell my wife to expect you, just in case you change your mind."

I watch his paunchy figure retreat down the hall. *The last thing I want to do is spend what is shaping up to be a completely depressing holiday with you, Bishop Barnes. With you and a bunch of people I don't know at all.*

It's a long work day. I enter grades for most of it. That's usually Adrian's job, but of course she's home in sunny Arizona by now, likely taking the mall by storm with all her catty, long-fingernailed friends. By the time I'm done with grades I've got a splitting headache. I look down at the carrier bag, wondering for a moment if I really ought to attempt a run in my new shoes in this state.

I slip them on and take off down the hall. I've mapped the route already—sixteen miles. I focus on the sky, on the pavement, on the trees. My headache disappears along with the rest of the world. By mile fourteen I'm sweating and start to feel nauseated. The new shoes are hurting me. The hot spots on my ankles and instep are burning like fire and my throat feels like sandpaper.

I'm thinking about Anne. I can't get her face out of my mind. *Did she see me? Didn't she?* Her face is so much like Mark's. He has her coloring. He has her smile.

M ILE 21

My throat is becoming unbearably scratchy, and I feel like my lungs are rasping with every breath, so I take a moment to slip into the restroom at Frontier Pies Restaurant to chug some water.

Scenes from the week flash through my mind. Feelings start to overwhelm me—anger, guilt, and something else that I keep pushing away because it makes me feel weak. By the time I reach fifteen miles, my knees are starting to shake and I feel like my skin might be chafing off. I keep going until I reach the big-0 sign, then slow to a weary jog and finally, a walk.

Sixteen miles, I think as I wait at the stoplight. *Just one more. You have to do it, Abish. You have to get past twenty. Are you going to run a marathon or aren't you?*

You're bleeding.

I look down and see a wash of red up the inside of both ankles. Suddenly the pain is completely unbearable. Trying not to wince, I hobble my way back to the apartment. I head straight for the bathroom, sit on the closed toilet, and unlace the shoes. I groan as I pull them off and see the blisters. *Not just blisters; gaping wounds.*

Silly. You're supposed to break them in before you run in them.

I made the same mistake with my first pair. Mark advised for me to walk around the house and around campus in them, but I kept forgetting to slip them on. When we went on our first run—a measly three miles that had me with my out-of-shape body gasping for breath and nearly throwing up by the end—I had blisters on my heels and pinky toes.

How could I forget that?

Mark, I'm forgetting. It scares me.

I spend Christmas Eve at the hospital. Mr. Eems seems glad to see me, or at least, I imagine he does; that his still, austere features hold a hint of a smile; that the electronic beeping is a touch faster than usual. Donald is gone. Discharged. *Moved on.* I don't feel the relief I expected to feel.

I get home around eight and find that the lights are on in the apartment and a car is parked in the driveway. My heart skips a beat when I see the bulky outline of the old truck—*Dad.*

I'm surprised and also a little disappointed, when I walk through the door and see Suzy sitting there on the couch. She's got her reading glasses on, and one of those giant SAT prep books on her lap.

"Hi," I say.

She glances up. "Oh. Hi. Door was unlocked."

"What brings you to my neck of the woods? Did you have a fight with Mom?"

"No. I just came over to say Merry Christmas. And bring your presents." She slides the book back into her backpack, then pulls out two packages wrapped in red and green paper. "Oh, and this is from me," she adds, digging in her pocket. She comes up with a beautiful bracelet—silver and different shades of blue polished stone. "I made it."

"Thanks." I'm thrown. I have absolutely no idea what to say.

"Merry Christmas, Abe." She reaches over to hug me and our shoulders clash awkwardly. She slings her backpack over her shoulder and hurries out the door.

I watch through the window as the headlights turn on, as they slowly back down the driveway. Then I turn my attention to the presents in my lap. My mother's is predictable—an angora sweater. It's nice, actually, a pale yellow color like sunlight. The color does surprise me a little. Generally, she goes for bold tones. It's Dad's present that brings me up short, though.

Nestled in the little cardboard box is a necklace. A smooth green stone on a leather thong, with a painted wood bead on either side. *Jewelry.* Dad *bought me jewelry.*

I know he picked it himself too. It's too earthy to be something Mama or Suzy selected.

Dad went into a jewelry store, held this necklace in his work-rough palm, and thought of me.

My throat is tight as I take it from its nest of cotton. There's something underneath it; a picture. I pull it out, and my heart stops beating for a moment.

Me and dad. On my wedding day. I'm half-smiling, half-wincing

as the wind blows my bangs into my eyes. My dad is staring straight
at the camera, jaw lifted, smile broad enough to bring the dimples to
his cheeks. He looks happy. He looks . . .

Proud.

I bring my hand to my mouth as I gaze at it, curling my fingers
against my lips. Was it just an odd moment captured? The proud
expression not for me, but for the person behind the camera? Was
there a joke told in the background that brought such a smile to
his face?

He wanted me to go on a mission. I lower the photo back into the
box and curl the necklace carefully on top of it.

I glance at the clock on the wall—it's 12:21 a.m. *Merry Christmas to me.* An impulse flares up. *Just ask Mom and Dad if you can
come over.*

I look down at the presents. *They had Suzy deliver them for a
reason. They can't handle me right now. They don't want me. I'll ruin
Christmas for them.* I think suddenly of my mother's tamales. She
makes them on Christmas along with a giant slow-cooked ham.
Guatemalan and American Christmas, meeting in the middle so
that all traditions are satisfied. The thought of peanut butter banana
sandwiches and skim milk for Christmas dinner seems unbearable
by comparison.

*You could take Bishop Barnes up on his offer. He'd likely be nice to
you with his family there, or whatever guests they're inviting. And with
Sister Barnes cooking, the food is going to be good.*

Hm, I think as I slide into Pen's sleeping bag. *We'll see how things
look in the morning.*

I wake up to falling snow. I stand at my window and watch for
a few minutes. Large, flat flakes are drifting down gently, adding to
the smooth white piles on the ground already. I shower and change
the Band-Aids on my ankles, comb out my hair, and get dressed.
The new sweater looks nice on me. I walk into the kitchen and have
my peanut butter banana sandwich. It doesn't take long to finish. I

sit, drum my fingers on the table, pick up all the crumbs, and put my dishes in the dishwasher.

Finally I throw on my coat, step outside, and begin walking.

Taurus Drive is on the opposite corner of town, but I'm used to long distances. I take the walk slowly and carefully for the sake of my blisters, enjoying the feeling of clean, breathless energy that infuses my system. At the bishop's door, I hesitate. My arm shakes a little as I raise my hand to knock.

Bishop Barnes answers it. He's wearing old jeans and a Utah Jazz T-shirt, and he's got a big grin on his face. He stops short when he sees me. The grin hardens into something more businesslike. "I'm glad you've come, Abish."

He holds the door, turning sideways so I can get past him. I walk in feeling like I'm bringing a rain cloud in with me. There are several small children running around screaming, chasing each other, and all the available sitting space in the living room is taken up with people. Several look about the right age to be Bishop Barnes' kids. *And their spouses.*

"This is Abish," the bishop calls across the room. "She's in my ward. Didn't have a place to go for Christmas, so I invited her here."

"Hi." A girl with strawberry blonde hair smiles at me. "That's a nice name. I haven't heard it before. Well, except in the Book of Mormon, of course."

She's young like me, and she's got that sort of newlywed glow about her. Her husband sits next to her on the couch. He's got a hand on her knee.

"My dad chose it," I reply, feeling my stomach start to knot. *This was a bad idea.* "He's got a funny way of seeing the world, I guess you could say." Attempting a smile that I'm pretty sure comes off more as a pained grimace, I head straight for the kitchen.

Mrs. Barnes and one other woman are in there, stirring pots. Immediately she makes shooing motions at me. "I'm glad you came, Abish. Go, sit. We've got it covered."

"No. Let me help you. Please."

Some of my desperation must come across in my tone, because

she hesitates, then nods. "You could throw together a couple of dishes of green bean casserole. Do you know how?"

"I know Mama's recipe."

She hands me a can opener. I cut notches in the lids of eight cans and begin draining green-bean juice into the sink. "Do you have any chili powder and cumin?"

Sister Barnes gives me a puzzled look. "For bean casserole?"

I take the opener and start cutting the rest of the way around the can lids. "Trust me. Mama's a scary good cook. If you want, we can do one pan regular and one pan with the extra spices."

"Sounds adventurous." She reaches into her cupboard and pulls out cumin and chili powder. "Is your mother Mexican?"

"Guatemalan."

"What does she make for Christmas dinner?"

Visions of tamales dance in my head, and my mouth waters a little. I suddenly realize how hungry I am. It's strange; I can't remember the last time I actually felt hungry. As in, not just weak and wasted inside, but craving actual food.

The last time you were over here. Remember? The chicken casserole.

I snitch a green bean and chew on it. "Mostly the usual stuff," I reply.

When I've finished, she gives me cherries to pit, then salad to chop. She keeps me going all morning. The other woman in the kitchen is her oldest daughter, Pam. She's nice, but mostly talks about her kids. In fact, Sister Barnes and Pam chatter pretty much the whole time about the family, the grandkids, what other relatives are doing. It leaves me out of the conversation, but I don't mind at all.

I hear a lot of laughter and, occasionally, some loud thumps and bangs. Some guy in a Utes' cap sticks his head into the kitchen and asks Sister Barnes if they can borrow some spoons. It takes me a second to recognize Andrew, Bishop Barnes's son, who I met the day before moving into the new apartment.

Sister Barnes grabs a handful from the drawer. "Don't lose any.

And you get to wash them before the meal is served, or I won't have enough to go around."

"Thanks, Mom." The guy glances at me. "You ever played spoons before?"

"Not for a while."

"Come play with us."

I shrug and gesture at the cutting board in front of me, full of chopped iceberg lettuce.

Sister Barnes takes the knife from my hands. "Go on. Everything's just about done anyway."

I open my mouth to argue and meet Sister Barnes's gaze, which has a distinctly no-nonsense look to it. "Go have fun."

I turn and slink out of the kitchen, following Andrew down the stairs to Bishop Barnes's Man-Cave, where a large circle of people is sitting on the blood-red area rug.

"This is Abish," Andrew says, as if he is presenting the president of the United States. "She's going to play spoons with us. I bet you're good at it," he adds, turning to me.

"Then you're going to be disappointed," I reply. "I haven't played since junior high school." I don't mean for it to come out sounding nasty, but somehow it does. "Thanks for asking me," I add hurriedly. I sit, cross-legged, in the open space they've made.

We play a few rounds. I lose every single one. It's pretty humiliating. It would be okay if I knew everybody; they could tease and poke fun at me. Instead it's awkward, and I'm wondering how much of an idiot these people think I am. Finally during one round I manage to keep from being last, but it's at the expense of an eight-year-old girl who looks visibly crushed when she realizes all the spoons are gone. I catch myself before I apologize, and I'm relieved to hear Sister Barnes call everyone up for dinner before we can start a new game.

They've laid tables end-to-end across the living room. The kids have a reserved area in the kitchen. I take a chair just about as far away from Bishop Barnes as possible. He sits at the head, of course, looking fierce and patriarchal.

And proud.

For some reason, his expression reminds me of the picture that came with Dad's necklace. I stare at my plate, feeling suddenly like I don't want to eat.

There's a loud knock on the door. Sister Barnes gets up to answer it.

"Sorry I'm late," a familiar voice says.

"No, not at all," Sister Barnes replies. "Come on in. There's a spot for you at the table."

A little boy with blue slanted eyes and a bowl cut trots into the room, and my stomach sinks to somewhere in the vicinity of my ankles.

"Go on into the kitchen, Todd. The kid food is in there." Sister Barnes takes his hand and leads him through the doorway.

Bob's wearing kind of the same thing he wore the first time I met him—dark jeans, black tennis shoes. He doesn't have on his work shirt, though. He's got on this deep blue v-neck sweater that makes his hair seem extra black, and he's carrying the dark-haired baby against his hip.

Sister Barnes comes out of the kitchen and walks across the room, arms outstretched. "Let me take him."

Bob hands her the baby. She sits down, tucks him into her lap, and starts feeding him bits of roll from her plate.

My gaze goes from him to Bishop Barnes. *You didn't tell me you were inviting Bob too.*

"Welcome, Robert," Bishop Barnes is saying. "Glad you could make it. You didn't pull the all-day shift after all."

Bob grins. "I got time off for good behavior."

"Right." Bishop Barnes half rises in his seat, shakes Bob's hand, and slaps his shoulder. He looks down the table. "There's a seat empty next to Abish."

I feel my cheeks go suddenly hot. I narrow my eyes at Bishop, but he's still not looking at me.

Bob's movement falters as he sees me, and his brow furrows. "Hey," he says. He approaches the empty chair. A guy across from us leans over the table toward him, holding out a hand. He and Bob do some kind of complicated handshake. "You going to join us in our game tonight?"

"Wouldn't miss it." Bob sits, grabs his napkin, and spreads it out on his lap. "You playing tackle this time or touch?"

"Tackle, of course. Hey, man, it's nice to see you." The guy gives Bob a smile that makes the words utterly believable.

Bishop Barnes says the blessing. The chatter rises as platters and bowls are passed around the table.

I take a little of this and that, but my appetite is completely gone. I feel like I'm at sea, a stranger in a strange land. I stir my potatoes around with my fork and watch Bob out of the corner of my eye as he laughs with his friend, as he answers questions flung at him from people all down the table. He teases Sister Barnes about her rolls—"You bought them at Broullim's this year, right?"—and seems to thoroughly enjoy the fake scolding she gives him. He's a completely different person here. Laughing, smiling. He's got nice teeth, actually. Something I didn't have the opportunity to notice before.

How does Bob know them? Clearly, I'm the only outsider here.

Bishop's voice cuts into my thoughts. "Abish, you know Bob from the ward, of course. Bob was star quarterback on the high school team for two years when I was still assistant coaching. He's also my son Daniel's best friend." He gestures to the guy across from us. "Abish and Bob are both in my singles' ward," he adds for the benefit of those who might not have fully picked up on the awkwardness of the situation.

"Ah," I say quietly, and glance at the clock. *How much longer can I stay without seeming rude?*

"Not by choice," Bob mumbles, forking up a piece of turkey.

I glance over at him, surprised.

Daniel laughs. "My dad's a hard one to refuse."

"You don't have to tell me." Bob and I say it at the same time. He glances over at me, and his dark eyes wrinkle at the corners. My face warms. I begin eating for a distraction, but the turkey tastes like sawdust in my mouth.

"This is good," Daniel exclaims a few minutes later, jerking his fork at the pile of green bean casserole on his plate. "Did you try a new recipe, Mom?"

Sister Barnes smiles across at me. "You can thank Abish for that. She added a few spices."

"She tends to do that," Bishop Barnes says drily, sending up a chuckle around the table and a wave of curious glances in my direction.

I raise my head and glare at him. I'm not pretending, but for some reason it sends Bob into a spasm of uncontrolled, silent laughter. "Sorry," he has the grace to say when he's gotten himself under control.

But I just can't take it. I rise from my chair, plate clutched in my hands, and step into the kitchen. All the kids stop chattering and look up at me. There's about a half dozen of them seated around a low, round table on primary-sized chairs.

I notice Todd sitting close to the door. His blue eyes find my face. "You're the lady who came into the kitchen with pajamas on," he declares.

"Yeah." I squeeze around the table and place my dishes in the sink. "That's me. And you're the kid with the robot named Valerie."

Todd smiles. "I've changed him to Sauron." He growls the name in a monster voice. It's actually quite good—he even pronounces it "sow-rawn," like in the movie.

I walk back over and crouch down next to him. "You like *Lord of the Rings?*"

"Yup." He turns back to his plate and begins attacking a pile of pink Jell-O-marshmallow salad. "I'm going to be Aragorn for Halloween."

"Aragorn? Not Gandalf?"

"Nah. I'm going to get a sword, like when he gets all those ghosts in the cave . . ." he goes off, repeating the scene action for action, gesturing with his whole body, nearly dumping his plate on the ground. I move it away from his elbow.

Actually, the Jell-O looks kind of good. And there's a big bowl of it on the counter.

"Hey," I interrupt him. "Do you mind if I sit next to you?"

Promptly he scoots his chair to the side, making room for me. I grab a paper plate and sit cross-legged on the floor. The table comes up to about my neck, but it works. I serve myself a good helping of the pink stuff, adding several olives and some mashed potatoes.

"I don't like olives," Todd declares, watching me spear one with my fork. "They make good hats, but they taste gross."

"Hats?"

Todd demonstrates, sticking olives on two of his fingers. "Or they might be shoes." He walks the fingers olive-side down like a pair of legs with shiny black shoes on.

"Those are some fancy shoes."

"That's nothing. I can do it too." A little redheaded boy—clearly of Barnes stock—sticks olives on all his fingers and begins wiggling them across the table top.

Todd gives it a critical glance. "That guy has too many legs."

"He's an octopus."

"Octopuses don't wear shoes."

"Sure they do," I cut in, seeing the way the redheaded boy's eyes narrow and how Todd's face is flushing. "And they can tap dance. Look." I take several olives from the bowl, stick them on all my fingers, and begin drumming them on the table. "Tea for two, two for tea," I sing. The eight-year-old girl looks at me like I'm completely crazy, but the rest of them are grinning like it's the best show they've ever seen.

I change tunes and do a slightly more intricate routine, acting like my two hands are octopus dance partners. "I'm gonna wash that man right out of my hair," I sing, just as the kitchen door opens, nearly walloping me in the rear, and Bob sticks his head in. His glance travels from my startled face to my olive-clad fingers.

"What are you teaching my son?" he asks finally, leaning over to ruffle Todd's hair.

"She's showing us how octopuses can tap dance," Todd replies calmly, stuffing his face with pink Jell-O fluff.

"Are the octopuses feminists?"

"The song's from *South Pacific*—you know, the musical." I remove the olives one by one, piling them on my plate.

"Sure it is." Bob's expression doesn't change, so I can't tell if he's serious or not.

I study him for a moment, then rise carefully to my feet, avoiding stepping on anyone's feet or jostling the table. "Tell Bishop thanks."

"You're going?"

"Well . . ." I shrug.

"You have to stay for football."

"Yeah." I give him an up-and-down glance. "So you can break every bone in my body?"

"I've got a feeling you could hold your own."

"Hm."

"The whole family plays. It's not just the men."

"Why do you care whether I stay or not?" My tone is sharper than I mean it to be.

Bob's expression goes from guarded, maybe slightly friendly, to that bleak, blank sort of look I'm used to seeing on him. "I'll tell Sister Barnes for you," he says. He ruffles Todd's hair again. "You okay in here, bud?"

Todd nods, studying two olive clad fingers. He wiggles one and murmurs something under his breath.

Bob leaves the room.

"Please stay," I think I hear Todd say as he wiggles the other olive-man. "Don't yell. You're waking up the babies." After a moment he sighs, pulls the olives off his fingers, and stuffs them in his mouth. "Bye," he adds, meeting my gaze. His eyes have that same bleak, defeated expression.

As I walk back, there's a lump in my throat. My boots chafe against my Band-Aids, but I force myself to go the whole eight miles I'd planned. It's still pretty awkward, but it's better than the unbroken Asics of death. *I wish I'd thought to keep the old tennis shoes around for another couple of weeks.*

My blisters are pretty bad, and Pen's place is only about half a block away. It's not a hard decision.

"Want some company this fine Christmas Day?"

There's a moment of awkwardness. Finally he shrugs, then nods. "Sure."

We while away the rest of the afternoon cheerfully maiming one another. I even let him play Portal for a while. Watching isn't usually fun, but he actually follows some of my suggestions, and we spend a lot of time laughing at our combined disastrous efforts to work our way through the game's obstacles. It's around eleven by the time Pen drives me home. As we pull up along the sidewalk, I notice a car parked in the driveway. The drivers' door immediately opens.

It's the bishop. He's carrying something that looks suspiciously like a Christmas gift. I get out of the car. Pen stays in the drivers' seat, eyeing Bishop Barnes with a mixture of anxiety and intense dislike.

"It's a journal," the bishop says, putting the package into my hands.

"You're not supposed to tell people what their presents are."

"I want you to start writing in it after you read scriptures in the morning."

"I don't read scriptures in the morning. I read them at night." I feel a slight wash of guilt, not just because I don't seem to be able to control unending flow of back talk that comes out of my mouth. *When was the last time I read my scriptures? I honestly can't remember.*

"It's better to read in the morning." Bishop Barnes holds the present out to me. "You pay attention more, and it's a good way to wake up. A good start to the day. You should try it."

"Okay. Thanks." I hesitate and then take it. "Nice of you. Tell Sister Barnes thanks too."

He glances at the car. "I hope you're not planning on bringing Pendleton inside the apartment at this time of night."

My guilt evaporates in a hot wave of annoyance. "It's not curfew yet, and it's not against the rules to have boys in the apartments as long as they stay in the living room."

"I'd advise against you letting Pendleton even into your living room with all your roommates gone."

"What are you saying? You think I'm the kind of girl who

would . . ." I can't bring myself to finish. I'm all out of guts for the day.

"No." Bishop Barnes shrugs. "It's just an observation. A friendly suggestion. Merry Christmas, Abish."

As I watch him back his car down the drive, I'm feeling a little churlish. I turn and give Pen a wave. "Thanks for the ride. See you later."

He expected me to ask him to stay. He's already halfway out of the car by the time I finish talking, so there's this awkward moment where he freezes, one foot on the pavement. Slowly, he pulls his leg back in and sits down. He gives me an enigmatic nod and shuts the door.

$\mathcal{T}$he next morning, I open the fridge to get my milk and find that Steve's sesame seed oil (put in the side door without cap) has toppled and spilled over half the contents of the fridge. I spend a meditative hour taking everything out, washing it, and giving the shelves a good going over with Palmolive and a Scotch Brite pad.

I'm pretty disgusted, but not surprised, at what I find. A moldy cucumber in one of the crispers, just sitting in a puddle of its own dank juice; several Ziploc containers with unrecognizable contents. Expired yogurt, and at the back of the top shelf, a withered apple with several bites taken out of it. I throw out the trash, including the containers (in the end I decide that at a dollar apiece, they just aren't worth cleaning out) and give it all a good scrubbing. When I'm finished, I move on to the freezer just because I'm on a roll. It's a little better, but there's some frozen juice residue and a strange collection of several plastic cups with half-melted ice cubes in them.

I'm not really a neat freak, but I do like a tidy fridge. It's an area where Mark and I are different—he likes a tidy room, organized possessions, socks folded just so. But he wouldn't notice if a bomb went off in the fridge; he'd just rinse off his tomatoes and be fine. Not me. I need to know my food is resting on clean surfaces.

I'm almost done when a knock sounds on the door. I sigh, shut the freezer door, and set the ice-cups next to the sink. I give my hands a quick rinse before I trot over and answer it.

Pen's standing there, and he's obviously taken some trouble with his appearance. He's wearing what I think is a new striped polo and his most flattering dark-wash jeans, and his studiously messy do is even more studious than usual.

"Hey," I say, running my hand over my bangs, which have escaped from the rolled bandana I've tied around my head. "What's up?"

He shrugs and saunters in. "Just seeing what you're up to. Brought the Xbox just in case. You don't have to work?"

"Office is closed. Burt decreed it. " I give him a grin and gesture to the couch. "Sit. Do you want a drink?"

"Sure. What do you have?"

I open the fridge door again and examine the contents critically. "Milk. Or water," I finally say. "Or ABC ice." I gesture toward the cups lined up next to the sink.

"ABC?"

"ABC . . . already been chewed."

Pen squints at me.

"Didn't you ever say that in grade school? Like with gum?"

"Yeah, but I didn't think ice could be chewed more than once."

"Well, I guess not chewed, then, but used. Saved, in the freezer, after use."

Pen smiles. "That's weird. Who saves ice? It's just frozen water."

I shrug, dump the cups down the sink, then nestle them into the top rack of the already-full dishwasher. "Yeah . . ." I sigh, sitting down next to him. "Living with four girls again is just weird in itself, though."

"You holding out okay?"

I feel a little uncomfortable with the way he's looking at me, so I give him one of my frightening smiles. "Fine, thanks. And now I'm going to hand your camo-clad behind to you on a platter. Let's go play some *Halo*."

"Okay, if you want. I was kind of thinking I could make you dinner tonight, though. Today's Wednesday. You're probably at the end of your groceries."

I am totally flummoxed. *How does Pen know I do my grocery shopping on Thursdays?*

Well, I guess I've asked him to take me once or twice. Okay, maybe several times. "Thanks," I say. "But you'll have to let me make dessert, then. I do have a few things."

"Deal." He stands and holds a hand to help me up.

An hour and a half into our game, I begin to worry about him. "You feeling okay, Pen?" I ask as I blast his head from his shoulders with one well-placed shot from my semiautomatic rifle.

"Yeah. Why?"

"I've just killed you five times in the last ten minutes."

"I'm fine. I'm trying a new strategy."

"Well, your new strategy stinks." I shoot him down again, watching his limbs flail pathetically as his body hits the ground.

"Do you want to play *Portal*? I'll watch, and you can ask me if you want, like, a hint to get through the puzzles."

I turn and stare at him for a few seconds. "What's going on, Pen?"

"You don't have to. It was just a suggestion."

I take him up on his suggestion and get so involved in the game that I don't even notice the hours passing. I end up finishing the whole thing. By the time I'm done, my ribs hurt from laughing, and Pen's arm is around my shoulder. I don't remove it, because it just feels friendly. Comfortable. *I've been friends with Pen for two years, right? We're buds. And we got that whole crossed-signals thing behind us.*

We make a grocery store run. Pen buys noodles and cream and other ingredients. "You've never had my fettuccine Alfredo," he says as he loads up the cart. "You're going to be blown away."

"And you've never tried my chocolate chip cookies."

Pen gives me a confused look. "You make chocolate chip cookies all the time."

"Yeah, but it's the only dessert I can make with what I've got in the cupboards back at the apartment, so we're stuck with it."

Pen shrugs. "We could get some, like, fresh strawberries and shortcake shells, and I could—"

"No," I say, frowning. "No, Pen, don't. Let me split the tab with you on this one. You don't need to apologize for what happened; let's just put it behind us. Don't forget I gave you a black eye."

"I wasn't . . ." Pen shakes his head. "Okay. Let's check out then."

It's pretty late when we get back to the apartment. By the time we tuck into the food, the clock says eleven thirty. I glance up at it and feel a little nag of guilt. I'm not used to following curfew. For almost two years, I've been living in married housing, where curfew doesn't exist. But Shelley's always pretty strict about making sure any boys leave before the clock ticks to eleven on a weeknight. *Technically it's sort of like a weekend*, I tell myself. *It's a holiday. Not a school night.*

I kick him out promptly at midnight, though. He's kind of taken aback by it—I can tell by his expression—but he doesn't argue. He gathers up his stuff and walks out. "Thanks for hanging out, Abe."

"Thanks for dinner." I stand at the door and give a little wave before I shut it.

I spend the next day at the hospital with Mr. Eems. Mara the grouchy receptionist is in attendance as I walk in. She looks even grouchier than ever. I can't blame her too much. I'm really glad to have work off to have some time to process the holiday. But I still feel sorry for the lady who comes in after me when I hear Mara cutting her off mid-explanation and testily telling her to wait on the couches by admittance.

I nod to Dalynne, who gives me a smile and an absent hand gesture and goes back to her charting.

I settle into my usual spot and close my eyes for a minute. I rest my head on the back of the chair and absorb the familiar music of the electronics controlling and monitoring Mr. Eem's biology: heart, lungs, bladder, and bowels. But not brain.

I don't know Mr. Eem's situation of course. Privacy laws. But I can't help wondering why he's still on all these wires and monitors. He was here when I was admitted here, so it's been at least a year. Does he have some son or daughter in a distant city who can't handle making the decision to shut things down? Did he sign some kind of ironclad "resuscitate in every circumstance" mandate?

Is he happy? Is he even really alive? I wonder what the spirit does when the brain is dead. Is it maybe trapped in some kind of limbo, or hibernation, or something?

He's alive, though. The machine beeps away, reminding me every second. It echoes my own heartbeats and is oddly comforting. I take the journal out of my backpack, the one Bishop Barnes gave me. It's dark-blue suede cover with silver-edged pages. Practical but classy. It was clearly chosen by Sister Barnes. The blue color actually reminds me of the sweater Bob wore at Christmas dinner . . . that dark, almost-black blue.

I'm still thinking about Bob as I walk home and as I prepare a mediocre lunch with the dregs of my end-of-grocery-week supplies. What is his situation, exactly? Obviously he's a decent guy. Or at least, the Barneses think he is, and Bishop Barnes isn't exactly your most open-minded sort.

Bishop Barnes called him as executive secretary. And his divorce must be pretty recent, considering the age of the baby. So whatever lead to Bob's single-parent state obviously wasn't something that got him in trouble Church-wise.

So did that mean it was *her* fault, what happened?

I can't stop picturing Todd playing with his fingers like they were people talking to each other. I can't stop remembering the words he said: *Please stay. Don't yell.*

It's not your business, I tell myself sternly as I lace up my Asics, wincing as the lip comes in contact with my raw ankle. *How do you feel when people get all nosy about your life?*

I run a new route today. I charted it a few days before Christmas, using MapMyRun at one of the computer labs on campus. It stretches all around town and down toward Archer and back. Eighteen miles. I've actually been kind of nervous about it. These runs have not been fun, even without moleskin-covered blisters. I've had to force myself to finish. I've planted water bottles in a couple of places too. This time I hope that eating a little something before makes a difference.

But just like before, thoughts and memories from the week are seeping through my usual mental blankness. Usually, running is blissful rest from my thoughts. Usually, my heart pumping and the power in my legs distracts me from all the unpleasantness of things that have happened, or are happening. Why am I thinking about Pen's fettuccine, and what's this creeping discomfort that's coming over me?

A friendly suggestion.

Why am I seeing Todd's face?

Are the octopuses feminists?

Suddenly, I'm laughing. And coughing.

I'm approaching sixteen miles, and every muscle in my body is screaming at me to quit. My stomach is queasy. My lungs are irritated. The coughing has turned somewhat violent. It's like, once started, I can't stop.

Your body might not be able to take this, Abish.

I've got to try. You've done it. We were going to do it together.

I push myself. I count steps. I hum "Chariots of Fire" under my breath and picture myself running in slow-motion. I think of crossing the finish line of my marathon, a look of triumph on my face.

Finally I make it—eighteen, just as I run back into town. I slow my pace, continuing to jog for another quarter mile or so, so that my muscles don't seize up with the sudden halt in exercise.

I feel like my lungs might just turn themselves inside out. Like my quadriceps muscles are about to explode. *How on this earth am I going to run twenty-six? That's almost ten more miles.*

The next morning, I can barely walk. I stumble out of bed early and stretch for a good half hour after I shower, but still the trek to work is somewhat agonizing. I catch myself thinking about all those elderly people at the hospital, bent over their walkers . . . *If someone offered me a walker right now, I'd take it.*

I'm in the door five minutes before eight. I settle into my desk and start attacking my list of tasks, which is not very long because it's break. It's more complex than usual, though, because Adrian's gone and I'm shouldering stuff I'm not that familiar with.

I hold my hand up when Bishop Barnes walks in.

"Good morning," he grunts, and stalks past me toward his office. If he weren't Mormon, I'd say he was suffering from a hangover. *Well, if he weren't Mormon and he wasn't Burt Barnes, who doesn't need an excuse to be in a bad mood.*

About an hour into my day, the door opens again. I glance up and am startled to see Bob. In fact, I don't quite believe my eyes for a moment, seeing him walk across the lobby. I've been thinking of him—well, of Todd, really—so much lately, and then he's here.

"Um," I say, blinking at him. "Hi."

He places his hands on the desk and leans over me. "Hi. You look pretty busy, sorry. Is Bishop here?"

"Yep." I jerk my thumb in the direction of the hallway. I watch him out of the corner of my eye as he walks down the hall. His shoulders are maybe the broadest I've seen on a person. They make his torso triangular—that kind of wedge shape, you know. That fit guys have.

What am I doing?

I give my head a little shake and turn back to my boring screen of numbers.

He's in there quite a while. It's probably only my imagination because anything coming from that far down the hallway is pretty muffled by the time it reaches me, but I think I hear raised voices. My eyes lift automatically when the door opens and Bob heads back down the hallway in my direction. It's strange; in those seconds he's walking toward me I suddenly want to say something. Anything that will make him stop for a second and talk to me.

I feel oddly gratified as he walks over and sits down beside me in Adrian's spot. He swishes the mouse around on the pad to wake up the machine. "Burt tells me the network is having issues," he says. "Have you noticed anything?"

"It's been a little slow connecting to the backup systems," I agree. I watch him for a few minutes as he clicks through the sign in. *Bishop Barnes must have given him the password.* I force myself to turn back to my own screen. It's no use, though. It's like my curiosity is an untamed beast. The questions are tickling my mind. *Is Todd okay? Why are you divorced? Are you ticked that you're executive secretary in the singles' ward? Does your wife ever take the kids or are they completely your responsibility right now?*

"How's Todd?" I blurt out finally, swinging my chair around to face him and crossing my arms over my chest.

He starts, then glances over at me. "Fine. He's at my mom's."

"Does she watch him a lot?"

He shrugs. "I'm in school too. And cable Internet guys don't make much money—I can't afford a day care."

"Well, he probably likes being with his grandma anyway." *This is awkward. So awkward. Why am I doing this?* "You know," I continue, "if you ever needed someone to watch them . . ."

His eyebrows shoot up. "Thanks." His expression clearly says, *Not if you were the last choice on earth.*

I glare at him. "I'm a good person. I'm good with kids. I was the most popular babysitter in town when I was a teenager."

"Uh-huh." Bob turns back to his screen. "Babysitting's not the same as parenting."

A giant solar flare of anger and hurt rears up inside of me. "Yeah," I say, and to my horror, my voice is wobbly. I stand, and my knees are also wobbly. "You know what, Bob? You're a jerk. A total jerk. I was just being nice. I guess you don't know the meaning of friendliness." Even as I say it, I hear my mother's voice: *Friendly. You don't know what the word means anymore.*

I stumble past him and out the door, breaking into a run. My muscles are so tired that I stop after just a few steps. I walk until I find a sheltered spot of landscaping and sit, knees drawn up against my chest.

The tears turn into real sobs. My whole body is shaking.

I don't know where this is coming from.

Don't you?

Yeah, well. That's silly, then. Lots of people lose babies. He's right. I've never been a parent. I never got a chance to be one.

You are *a parent, Abish.*

Yeah, but I don't have a real, flesh-and-blood baby as proof of that, do I?

How old would she be now?

I picture the dark-haired baby in Sister Barnes arms and suddenly a longing comes over me, so strong and powerful I feel like my heart might stop beating. I sit and tremble with it and wait for it to subside. Eventually it does, but new bursts of pain keep breaking over me, flooding my heart and mind like the backwash of a giant tidal wave.

Eventually I stand and walk back to the health building. I go into the locker room and wash my face. It doesn't help; the puffiness around my eyes betrays me completely, so I head over to the showers. *Bishop Barnes is already going to be hopping mad I left. Fifteen minutes won't make a difference, and I'd rather face him without the humiliation that he'll know what I've been doing for the last thirty.*

I take my time in the hot water. When I'm done, I towel off with my locker towel and get dressed. I can't do much about my clumpy wet hair with no conditioner and no brush, but at least my face looks normal again. I trudge back up to the office to face the wrath of Bishop Barnes.

It's like that old expression—waiting for the axe to descend—as I sit at the desk and type. But I see no sign of Bishop Barnes. Bob's gone too, thank goodness. After about an hour I'm calm enough to actually work on what I'm supposed to do. I get all the scholarship applications processed and the TA applications sent off to student employment.

Bishop Barnes stalks past my desk at 5:03. He turns to me, and I hold my breath. "Have a good evening, Abish," he says.

I nod. "Yeah. Thanks," I manage.

The week crawls by. It's back to the familiar endless cycle of sleep, work, hospital, and an empty apartment until Pen gets off his shift at Taco Bell. The strange thing is, this is what my life has been like for a year. I can't help but wonder what's changed to make it suddenly seem monotonous—almost unbearably so. I find myself almost looking forward to the girls coming back to the apartment.

At this point, Pen's been bringing his gaming system over to my place. The TV's tiny and totally cruddy and there's no surround sound, but generally I've been saying no to going over to his apartment, so I guess he figures he's willing to put up with less quality in order to have someone to play with. We're in the middle of a knock-down-drag-out battle in an abandoned army base when Julie and Steve walk through the door, loaded down with their baggage.

I look up at Steve. "Hey," I say. I hesitate a moment, then add, "Want to join us?"

She gives me a puzzled smile and glances at the clock on the wall. "No thanks. Who's this?"

I look up at the clock as well. *12:45 a.m.* "Crud," I say, just as Julie steps into the living room. "We kind of lost track of time."

Julie looks down at us. Her expression becomes grim. "It's a weeknight. Curfew was almost two hours ago."

I suppose the tableau of Pen and I could seem a little compromising to a person of a certain mind-set. I'm kind of draped over Pen's lap because I tend to "drive" when I use a joystick—contorting and bending my body as if it will make my characters move faster. And it's a small couch.

I feel my cheeks warm a bit under her forbidding gaze. "We're playing *Halo*. You ever played?"

"No." Julie stalks down the hall, lugging her suitcase and a full duffel bag. "Tell him to go home before I call the RA."

"Sorry," I call after her. "I haven't lived in a singles apartment for a while. I'm not used to the rules yet."

"The rules don't change," she snaps, just before she slams her bedroom door.

I'm feeling unsettled and annoyed at this point. "What's her problem?" I ask Steve. "I meant the curfew. Pen and I weren't doing anything inappropriate. I know *those* rules don't change."

Pen jumps up from the couch and begins packing up his gaming stuff. His face is pink.

Steve winces. "I'll make sure she doesn't call the RA. You didn't mean anything by it, I'm sure."

But even those words, *you didn't mean anything by it*, make my skin crawl a little. I'd forgotten how serious curfew violation is when you're a single student at BYU-Idaho. I really could be in big trouble, especially considering my previous recent encounter with the honor code office.

In fact, I can't help but wonder why Pen didn't keep an eye on the clock either. He is, after all, a single "I" student himself.

I grab the other side of the box Pen's carrying and help him lug it out to his car.

"You want to play tomorrow?" he asks as he shuts the trunk.

"No, classes are Wednesday. I have to go buy books, make sure my schedule works . . . all that stuff."

"'Kay. Run by my place sometime."

I grin at him. "Thanks for hanging with me, Pen. You're a lifesaver."

"No prob." He smiles back at me.

You know, he's really not a bad guy, I think as he drives away. *And whatever else I might object to, he's got a pretty good personality. He's laid back, easygoing. He might be scrawny, but his features are kind of nice. He just has to clean up a bit . . . kind of rub some of those rough corners off.*

I step back inside. Julie's got her head in the fridge and Steve is busily unloading groceries into the cupboards. I'm on my way down the hall to my room when the explosion occurs.

"*Who* moved my food?"

The way Julie shrieks the words makes my hair stand up on my neck.

I jog down the hall and step into the kitchen. "I cleaned the fridge over break. The stuff should be in the same place; I put it all back where it was before."

"All my containers are gone."

"I threw away some stuff that'd gone bad. I figured the containers weren't worth saving . . . not at a dollar for a pack of three, with the effort of cleaning them."

Julie stands there a moment, her body still half inside the refrigerator. She slowly backs out and turns to face me, and I admit, there's a thrill of trepidation. It gets worse as I see her expression. Her lips are twisted, her eyes narrowed. Her face is crimson.

Steve's words come back to me—*she can be kinda territorial about her food.*

I thought Steve meant the usual stuff. Squabbles over who-ate-what, who moved my cheese, etcetera. But now I realize that Steve meant something much more than ordinary roommate issues.

Julie's not normal.

The words float through my mind with the images of stacked, carefully preserved Ziploc plastic containers of molding foods, and cups lined up against the back of the freezer full of half-melted ice.

"I'm sorry," I say, preempting her as she opens her mouth. "I'm sorry; I didn't realize."

"Realize *what*?"

"That you are—that you keep stuff," I finish lamely. "I understand, though—we studied it when I took abnormal psych. I promise, I won't touch your stuff. Ever again. If I clean the fridge"—I shrug—"I'll just leave your corners alone." I pause, because her face has twisted into an expression that is, if possible, even more ugly than before. "I'm not saying this right. I'm not that great at words sometimes. But I'm sorry."

"You did just fine," she hisses. "I'm *abnormal*."

I shrug. "No more abnormal than anybody else. I'm not the sanest person on the planet either. I'm sure you've noticed."

Julie doesn't dignify my words with a response. And, frankly, I can't blame her. Watching her stomp down the hallway toward the room she shares with Steve, I think, *You really botched that one, Abish.*

The front door swings open again. It's Maddie—breathless, loaded down with bags, with Dave Cannon in tow. "You can't come in," she gasps. "Past curfew. Just put them on the floor. Abe, can you help take this stuff back to my room?"

"Sure," I reply. I stride over and grab the handles of the two suitcases that Dave has deposited on our living room floor.

"Thank you." Maddie wrinkles her nose and gives him a studiously rueful smile. "I don't know what I would've done if you hadn't come to meet my bus. I'm so spacey sometimes. I completely forgot it only stops at campus."

Yeah, right. I don't say the words out loud, but they're definitely there, reflected on Dave Cannon's face.

The chuckle escapes my lips in spite of all effort to suppress it. Dave meets my gaze and gives me a conspiratorial grin. "Hey," he says, stepping out onto the porch. "Saw you running the other day. You're pretty hard core, aren't you?"

I shrug, suddenly regretting meeting his eyes. "Uh, yeah. I'm training."

"For what? Are you running the Teton Dam? I did that last year."

"Nope. Ogden."

He shoves his hands in his pockets and grins at me. "Cool."

Maddie is stifling a pout. I can tell by the way her jaw is twitching. "See ya, Dave," she says, stepping between us and placing a light kiss on his cheek. "That's for helping me out."

He smiles down at her and gives her a little wink before he heads out into the night.

"Thank you," Maddie says after I've got her suitcases stacked next to her bed. Her expression is far less friendly than the one she gave Dave as she thanked him.

Back in my room, I turn off the lights and slide into my sleeping bag, feeling oddly uneasy.

It's not as if the roommates and I were buds or anything.

I mean, it seemed like things might work, to be friends with

Steve. There might have been that possibility of friendship, maybe. But thanks to my ever-present bluntness, Julie's got some ammo to use against me now. And Steve will side with her; their friendship is obviously a long-standing, loyal one.

Indignation rises as I remember her reaction when we first met—that dismissive, almost loathing expression. I hadn't even opened my mouth yet. She had no real basis to judge me other than how I looked. *What about me walking into that living room made her decide to dislike me?*

I shake my head and chuckle at myself. *Why do I care so much, anyway?*

Chapter 11

$\mathcal{T}$he morning dawns bright and white. Again, it's snowing outside, this time in little flurries of individual flakes that would look like perfect lace under a magnifying glass.

I slide on my new running shoes. They're feeling a little better now. Before I get going, I lift my face to the sky and stick out my tongue, feeling dots of soft ice melt into it while the cinched edge of my hoodie cuts into my throat.

It makes me think of times during my childhood when I'd wander out into the white, piled velvet of our potato field. I'd stand in the middle with my face lifted up, watching the snow descend. I used to picture God sitting up there with something like a giant saltshaker, sending it down toward me in blessings. Right now I feel strange. Frightened almost, looking up and thinking how tall the sky really is.

I hike up along the sidewalk toward the university bookstore. There's a long line of students waiting inside to pay for their giant stacks of books.

I hate the bookstore during move-in. In the past I bought my textbooks online, but I kind of missed the boat this year, what with moving suddenly and then dealing with the nuclear fallout of my life. I don't have time to wait for a shipment from Amazon because classes start tomorrow.

So I slink along the crowded aisles with my class schedule clutched in one hand, grabbing the last of everything listed with the other. One or two books have run out. I'll have to go ahead and buy those ones online, and hope those teachers are abnormally slackish ones who won't be assigning something from them during the first week.

The line takes me an hour. They try to make it pleasant, handing out mini-candy bars and such, but by the end I'm tempted to say something snarky to the checker like, "What, no free gift-wrapping?" But I decide not to as I see the weary lines of her face. *This can't be a fun time for the bookstore employees, either.*

Back outside, I suddenly get this overwhelming urge to do something outdoorsy. The air is warmer, but the snow is still coming down. The earth smells fresh and icy sweet. I want to snowshoe on the Ashton hill. I want to go skiing at Targhee. Dad always used to bring me ice fishing at the Ashton Reservoir on days like these. There were a couple of times he even picked me up from school so I could sluff with him.

His face comes to mind—angular nose red and eyes glowing with the cold—and I feel as if something is clutching at my throat. I start to jog, cutting through the parking lot. My now heavily loaded backpack weighs me down, making me skid a little. It's hard to see with the snow coming down like it is. I slide, flailing to keep my balance, and stumble into a big, bulky figure.

"Whoa." He grabs my shoulder to keep me from falling. In the process, he drops his books all over the slushy asphalt.

It's Bob.

Of course.

"Man, I'm sorry," I mumble, leaning over to help pick up the books. He kneels next to me. I avoid looking at him and try not to think of the juvenile outburst that ended our previous interaction. *You know what, Bob? You're a jerk. A total jerk.*

Well, he was. Though he didn't know it would hurt like it did. But everybody has bad days . . . heaven knows I've had plenty of them. In any case, he doesn't deserve to have two hundred dollars worth of text-books ruined.

I wipe the slush off the books I'm holding on the inside of my coat, then reach for the two he's got. "Here, let me dry those."

He looks down at me. "You don't have to do that. You're getting your jacket lining muddy."

"No, I don't want your books to be ruined. This coat'll wash out." I grab them, wipe them off, and hand them back. I rise to my feet and give him this awkward kind of army-ish salute and immediately feel stupid. I turn and trot away with my face hot enough to fry an egg. *Yes, sir, Private Abish Cavendish Miller, reporting for book-wiping duty.*

"Hey, Abish."

I pretend not to hear him.

"Hey," he repeats, trotting after me. "Do you need a ride?"

I turn, blinking away the snowflakes that have caked my eye-lashes. I want this interaction, and my self-consciousness, to be over as soon as possible. "Not really. I mean, it's just a few blocks away."

"But it's snowing pretty hard, and you've got a load on." He lays a hand on the top of my backpack. "Come on. My car's just over here."

It turns out to be an old semi-restored Camero. The paint hasn't been redone. It has worn away on the hood and rusted through. The inside reminds me of the smell of my dad's old truck. *Baking vinyl.* The dashboard has a crack running down it.

He slides into the driver's seat. I can't help but grin a little as the motor gets going. *Such a nice purr.*

He looks at me out of the corner of his eye and gives me a smile. "You like cars?"

I shrug. "Everybody likes cars."

"I've been planning to fix this one up for a while. I just haven't had the time yet. It's not very pretty, but it's a classic."

"Engine's what matters. Paint won't change that."

"Brakes also matter." His tone is wry. "And water pumps. This one's been leaking for a year. I can't drive it much in the summer because the engine overheats. My . . . the people who've ridden in it complain about me turning the heater on full tilt in July."

I don't miss the byplay. He was going to say, "my wife." "Wish I knew how to fix a water pump," I reply, trying to cover the awkward moment. I'm feeling sort of puzzled. I'm not sure why Bob's being like this.

It's like he hears my thoughts or something. "Abish, I wanted to apologize," he says.

I nod, keeping my eyes trained on the crack in the dashboard.

"The other day when you offered to watch the kids, you were just trying to be nice." He shrugs. "I'm not usually like that. I don't know what got into me. You're right, I was being a jerk."

I chew my lip and glance out the side window. We're coming up on my street. "Yeah," I reply. "I have that problem too. Just so you know, though, I'd like watching Todd and the baby, sometime."

"Gabriel."

"Gabriel." I picture the baby with his large dark eyes and black curlicues standing up all over his head. *A good name for him.*

"Nice of you to offer. I'm betting you're pretty busy, though."

"If I didn't have class or work, I mean. There'll be some empty evenings, I'm sure."

It's my turn to feel awkward. I don't mean to say it like that, *empty evenings*, like I'm feeling sorry for myself. "I really wouldn't mind," I add, trying to brush past it. "I mean, I was almost a mother myself, so it's not like I don't understand . . ." And then I stop, feeling my heart pounding in my throat.

What made me say that? I haven't told anyone that before. Only Mark. Only Mark knew, and the knowledge died with him. Except for the hospital staff. Well, and her. Really, it died with her.

I look up and see Bob's expression in the mirror: a mix of surprise and something else I can't quite translate.

We pull to a stop in my driveway and sit for a few moments in silence. The snow is falling on the windshield. If I don't get a move on, Bob'll have to come out and scrape it off.

I grab the door handle. "Yeah. Anyway, thanks for the ride. I remember when you came to do the Internet, you had to bring the kids. That's probably hard, to try to do your job with them there."

"I'll keep your offer in mind," he replies, reaching across me and pushing my door open. The gesture—chivalrous in a kind of sly, spontaneous way—leaves me without words. I step out of the car, clutching my backpack to my chest. "I'm usually okay, though," he continues. "That time I came to your place was unusual. My mom's always available, and like you said, Todd loves being with her."

"Okay. But you know, if you wanted to go out some night or something, and she had something to do . . ."

"Yeah." There's a hint of irony in his tone. "In spite of what you think, I don't date much right now. Not really into trolling for freshman at this point."

My face warms. "As long as we're apologizing . . ."

"How about we just call it even?"

"Sure." And then suddenly I think of what happened the other day, of coming out of Bishop Barnes's office into the lobby bustling with college kids and seeing Bob leaning over the desk. It put me in a state of complete shock then. Right now I'm seeing a semi-miserable expression on his face as he sits there in his suit, hands clasped on the desk, waiting for the evening to be over so he can get back to his kids.

Suddenly a wave of sympathy comes over me. *He's trapped in this situation just like me. And all because Bishop Barnes is sure he knows what's best for everybody.*

I stop before shutting the door behind me. "No, I really am sorry for what I said." It comes out in a rush. "And for not being dressed appropriately when you came that day."

"It wasn't your fault."

"It kind of was. But I didn't mean to, like, assault you, or be disrespectful or anything. It really was kind of an accident."

His eyes brighten. Slowly, he smiles. It's like watching a spotlight turn on or a star get born in a cloudless sky or some other sappy analogy that would only cheapen the startling change Bob's smile effects in his face. "I didn't feel assaulted," he says, and glances over his shoulder. "Snowplow's coming."

I nod and slam the door shut and Bob barely makes it out of the drive before the plow hums by, leaving a three-foot drift that blocks the entrance entirely.

The roommates aren't going to be able to get in.

I trudge around to the utility room and grab the snow shovel. With each heave, I try to get rid of the embarrassed, tense feeling in my stomach, to get rid of the image of Bob smiling at me, and those words he said. *I didn't feel assaulted.*

Really, Bob? With my hairy legs and blotchy, sleep-deprived face? Besides, you acted like you were afraid I was trying to vamp you or something.

He's just trying to make me feel better, I decide as I shift clumps of snow out of the driveway entrance.

The next morning, I am up with the dawn.

A good day, I think as I tie on my running shoes. They're feeling much better now, but my blisters haven't completely healed, so I've still got some moleskin on them.

I go into the kitchen to pour myself a half-bowl of Raisin Bran with skim milk. It's a delicate balance. I don't want to make myself ill, but I also don't want to be passing out somewhere on the bustling streets of Rexburg.

Just as I'm finishing up, I hear footsteps in the hall, and the light turns on in the kitchen. Julie blinks at me. "You taking my milk?" she asks, her eyes flitting over the carton sitting on the counter. I lift the cap to show her my sharpie initials, and some of the tension leaves her face. She goes to the fridge and grabs her own milk. "Why are you up so early?"

"I want to get a run in before class."

"Hey, you're going running?" another voice chimes in. Maddie comes into the kitchen, her hair adorably disheveled. She's not wearing her contacts. For the first time I see her true eye color, which is that kind of golden, root-beer-brown. They seem to glow in the dim light. "Me too." She yawns. "Want to run together?"

I start to rinse my bowl and spoon under the faucet. "I'm doing an eight-mile loop."

"Whoa. I've never run that far before."

I nod and head into the living room.

She follows me. "Can I come with?"

"I don't know if that's a good idea, Mad."

"I'll turn back when I'm spent. I just don't like the idea of going running alone in the dark."

I turn to face her. "I'm leaving right now. I won't have time to do the whole thing if I have to wait for you to get ready."

Apparently she takes this as an invitation because her face lights up and she turns and runs to her room. And to my chagrin, she's back in the living room by the time I've got my coat and fingerless gloves on. She's wearing pink everything; from her track pants to her fleece headband, and her running shoes have silver sparkles.

We set off together. It's a little confusing, hearing and feeling her pace beside me. But after a while I slide into my usual block-out-the-world mind-set. My legs are pumping pistons. My heart and lungs are combusting engines. The world explodes all around me with the illumination of the rising sun as I crest the top of the Rexburg hill. The steam clouds of my breath can't even keep up; they trail behind me like exhaust from a jet engine.

The world kind of fades out, and my thoughts take over.

School again. A sick feeling comes to my gut.

No, it won't be the same, Abish. Don't worry. You're not erasing it. You're going back with a new perspective.

Memories start to come—Mark, walking me to classes. His arm on the back of my chair in Marriage Enhancement.

"Hey, how much further do we have?" a voice gasps, breaking me loose from the image of the little table in the Crossroads cafeteria where Mark and I met for lunch sometimes.

I glance over and see that Maddie's still with me. It's kind of a surprise, but there she is, right beside me, running. Her legs are longer than mine—I have an abnormally long torso—and her body is lighter, but she's obviously struggling. Her cheeks are bright red, her face is pale, and she's gasping with every breath.

"All right," I say, slowing my pace. "It's time for you to stop."

She gives me a strange look—lidded eyes, set mouth—and doesn't slow down at all. I quicken my pace again to keep up with her.

She wants to outdo you.

She needs *to outdo me. Why?*

She's looking pretty pale. Paler than me; paler than I've seen anyone. *Alive, that is.* "C'mon, Maddie. I've been training for months for these distances. You can't just get out and run eight miles because you suddenly decide you want to." I grab her upper arm and slow to a walk, then stop.

She's too weak to fight me, so she comes to a stumbling standstill. It's a good thing I've got her in my grip, because her knees buckle. I grab her other arm and hold her steady until she gets her feet under her. "You should walk around for a bit. It's not a good idea to stop cold."

She waves me away and digs into her pocket, bringing out a little foil package. Lips trembling, she rips the corner off with her teeth and squeezes the contents into her mouth.

"Here." I put a palm in the middle of her back and force her to take some steps with me. After a few minutes, she seems okay. I glance at my watch. *Shoot—it's later than I thought.* "Here, give me your phone. We'll need a ride back if we're going to make class on time."

"Don't call Shelley," Maddie rasps. "She'll kick my behind."

"Who else do we know with a car?"

She shrugs. "I can walk just fine. And half the time the first class of the semester is just passing out a syllabus. We'll be okay."

I glance at her still-trembling hands. *No, you won't.* "I won't call Shelley. But I really don't want to be late. This is my first semester after deferring for a year. I'm already kind of stressing over it."

Maddie relinquishes her phone, her brown eyes suddenly bright with curiosity.

"Thanks." I punch a number in and press it to my cheek.

"Did you defer because of your husband dying?"

Inappropriate personal questions. She must be feeling better. Luckily Pen answers right then. I roll my eyes slightly and turn away from her. "Hey."

"Hey," Pen says. "You're calling pretty early."

"Yeah, I know. I'm kind of stranded. Do you think you could give us a ride? We're out toward Archer, along Yellowstone."

Pen is quiet for a few seconds. I hear some muffled noises in the background.

"Do you have people over? Sorry."

"Bloke crashed on my couch. His landlord wouldn't let him in the apartment because it was past curfew."

"Tell Bloke I'm sorry I woke him. Will you come get us?"

"Who is *us?*"

"Me and my roommate Maddie."

"Oh." He hesitates for a few more seconds. "Yeah, okay. It'll take me a little bit to get dressed."

"We'll start walking back, then, and you can meet us on the way. Thanks so much, Pen."

"See you in a few."

When Pen's little blue car pulls up to the curb and he steps out, Maddie goes rather quickly from hunched-over-exhausted to upright and perky. She wrinkles her nose, smiles, and holds out a hand for him to shake when he approaches us.

I'll admit it, he looks pretty good. He's got on his usual dark jeans and an orange rugby shirt, and his hair is messed into an adorable little ducktail over his forehead.

"I'm Maddie," she says. "Thank you." She slides into the passenger seat.

"Hey," Pen replies. He glances at me, still standing on the sidewalk, then back down at her. "Pendleton."

"How come I haven't seen you around before?"

"I don't know." Pen reaches down for the handle to the back door, but I beat him to it.

MILE 21

"The apartment," I say once I've settled in the back seat.

In the same exact moment Maddie says, "Kiwi Loco."

I glance at Maddie's still-trembling hands, resting on her knees. "Kiwi Loco," I agree. "But make it quick, please. I really don't want to be late for my first class."

"Yeah, I'm pretty sure we're going to be late at this point, Abe." Brow furrowed, Pen yanks the steering wheel around in order to turn in time.

I squint at him in the rearview mirror. "Are you mad, or something? I didn't plan on being stranded. You didn't have to come pick me up."

His face relaxes. "No, it's no problem. I could handle a yogurt too," he adds as we pull into a parking space in front of Kiwi Loco.

"I'll hang out here until you guys get back," I reply.

Pen hesitates, then shrugs and steps out onto the pavement. He forgets to open Maddie's door for her. *I guess chivalry's not an easy habit to acquire.*

They take a long time. I can see them through the bank of glass windows, talking. Maddie laughs, throwing her head back. As the minutes tick my, my insides start to crawl. I glance down at my watch—7:45.

There is no way I'm going to be on time unless I get out of the car right now and head up to class, sweaty and bookless.

I take another glance through the windows. Maddie and Pen don't appear to be moving along in their choosing process, so I fling open the door and begin to run, this time in the direction of campus. *I'll bum a pen and a piece of paper off someone,* I reassure myself. *Get the assignment down. There's never homework due on the first day of class.*

I just hope they don't kick me out because of the way I smell.

It is kind of surreal, running along those thin stretches of concrete in between the campus buildings, passing through crowds of students. It's like two halves of my life have come to meet the middle: me, running sweaty in my track pants and new tennis shoes; and young men in collared shirts, girls in bright-print skirts. The smell of new concrete. The squeak of my soles on light-colored tile.

The feel of my muscle-sore rump in a hard plastic chair. The trickle of sweat down my temples against the cool breath of the central air in the classroom, which still smells of new plaster. The people filing in, filling in seats all around me—well, not all around *me*. There's sort of a buffer one empty seat-wide on every side of me. *Either I smell bad, or I exert some kind of "don't touch me, don't talk to me" aura. Likely both.*

It's five minutes past the hour by the time the professor strides in, and what's left of my confidence dissolves instantly. *Professor Harrison.*

"Professor Baker has decided on a last-minute sabbatical," Harrison announces to the class, "and I have agreed to take this section." He glances over the classroom and nods when he sees me. I return his nod, suppressing a groan.

It's not that I don't like the guy. Harrison's great—friendly, upbeat, smart, a good teacher. It's just that he's the one who I had to retake the final from. Who I royally fell apart in front of last year and had to ask for slack. *I wanted to start fresh. With a clean slate and teachers who aren't going to watch me with concern, or worse, pity. I'm so done with that. I'll transfer as soon as I get a free hour.*

Yeah, just like you sold your contract and changed wards.

Harrison's saying something about midterms. I turn and ask the guy behind me if I can borrow a pen and paper. He gives me a slight eye-roll and goes digging through his bag.

My inner voice proves to be right. I don't find time for a visit to the registration office because I'm too busy dashing back to the apartment for my books before my next class. I get there late, and for the rest of the day, I feel like I never gain back those ten minutes. I feel disjointed—off, somehow.

I feel like I'm isolated in an impenetrable, invisible bubble. Like the world moves past me without realizing I'm there. I feel like suddenly I speak another language. All around me is chatter I've heard before and used to participate in, about people, about dating. About activities, worries over petty things like too many pages in an assignment, or a roommate who's hogging cupboard space.

I feel like everyone around me knows everybody else. They talk across me if they have to, but never to me. More often than not, the seats around me remain empty. *Yeah, well, it doesn't help that you're a hot mess wearing sweaty track pants.*

No, it's more than that. They know it. Somehow, they can sense I'm not one of them, not anymore.

One girl makes a tentative attempt at conversation, asking me who I had for a previous prerequisite course. I try to dig words out of my throat, words that will reassure her and show her I'm a human being capable of human speech, but I can only come up with a one-word answer: the professor's name. She doesn't try again. In that moment, I suddenly miss Mark. The feeling is like a fist in my stomach. *I don't belong anywhere. I don't belong to anybody.*

An image comes to mind—us sitting in the Marriage Enhancement class that we took the semester after we got married. He'd scoot his chair close enough so that he could put an arm around me, and we'd whisper wisecracks or insights to each other during the lectures.

I can see his face now, more clearly than I've been able to remember it for a while without looking at a photograph. *The warmth of blue eyes, the handsome crook of his nose, the way the light plays on his golden hair.* Sometimes he'd have stubble on his face. Being blond, he didn't have to worry much about that dreaded phenomenon, the five-o'clock shadow. *Not like Bob, who probably needs to shave twice a day in order to—*

"Hey." The kid sitting next to me prods me with the corner of his notebook. I glance up and see that everyone in the classroom is looking expectantly at me.

"Sorry?" I look at the professor. "I drifted off there for a minute."

She smiles. "I could see that. I'm just having everyone introduce themselves. Give us your name, your major, where you're from, and something interesting about yourself. You're supposed to be writing down a seating chart and memorizing the information for a quiz next class."

"Yeah." I glance around at the faces. "I'm Abish Miller—"

"Stand up."

"Abish Miller," I repeat, standing. "Nursing major. From St. Anthony just up the road. And I . . . I'm . . ." *A widow.*

"I like to run," I manage finally. My classmates are politely smiling. One or two of them nod, then glance at the guy behind me. I sit, he stands, and my moment in the spotlight is over, thank goodness.

Somehow the afternoon goes by. I head over to the hospital and do my studying with Mr. Eems. Dalynne is working; she asks me how my first day of classes. I say fine. *Back in the saddle, or something like that.* When I get back to the apartment, it's about dinner time, but nobody's home except Maddie, who is sitting at the table with a bowl of cereal. She's poring over the fresh new ward directory, probably delivered by our home teachers, whoever they are. "Hey," she says when she sees me. "Pendleton said he'd be coming by later."

"Great." I grab my bread and begin slathering on some peanut butter. "Did he want me to come over to his place and play? I don't think our living room will be an option tonight."

Maddie takes a bite of Raisin Bran. "Actually, I told him I'd make him a pie."

I stop, mid-slather, and turn to her. "A pie? What for?"

"For rescuing us today, of course. He's such a nice guy, Abe. You've been holding out on us."

Abe. So we're on one-syllable terms now? "Yeah," I murmur, going for the grape jelly. It's not mine. I glance at the top to make sure of initials. *Shelley's. Okay.* "He's pretty cute, I guess."

"Yeah. You're not, like, seeing him or anything, are you?"

"We hang out."

"But you aren't dating?"

A snort escapes me. "Sorry," I say when she frowns. "Pen's just not my type. And I'm married."

MILE 21

"Were married," Maddie corrects, tilting her bowl to get the last of the milk.

"*Am* married." I turn to glare at her. "Just because he's dead doesn't mean we aren't still married."

Maddie sets the bowl down and looks at me thoughtfully. "Yeah," she says. "You know, you're really pretty lucky, Abish."

"Lucky how?"

"Well, you found your eternal companion. You're totally taken care of. Like, you get to be in the top tier. You're not even, like, divorced or something where you have to go looking again to gain celestial glory."

"Yeah," I say dryly. "I should go join a convent or something."

Maddie's eyes are round and serious. "Well, it wouldn't be a sin if you did. And now I think of it, I mean, it *would* be kind of selfish for you to . . ." She shrugs. "I mean, you've had your chance, and there are only so many good guys in the world. And it's not like you can get married in the temple again. Women can't get sealed to more than one man."

Well, when you put it that way.

"So you really don't care if, like, I were to—"

"Have at it. Just leave me a night or two a week to toast his behind in *Halo*." As I head out of the kitchen down the hall, I'm chuckling to myself. I mean, I just can't take offense; Maddie is only saying out loud the things everyone else thinks. The things that *I* have thought, over and over.

Chapter 12

So today's my second time attending the singles' ward. I skipped church during Christmas break. It was sort of an accident. They called to tell me the wards were combining during break and meeting at nine, but I forgot and slept in until 9:20. And then it seemed kind of pointless to go to Sunday School or Relief Society, especially considering the fact that with all my roommates gone, I wouldn't know anybody except for Bob and Bishop Barnes.

And for some reason, I have nerves this time. I don't know why it is, but I feel jittery, like I've had a liter of Mountain Dew. And I feel completely, utterly self-conscious.

I cannot, for the life of me, straighten my spine or un-hunch my shoulders as we head out the door to go to church. It's windy enough to take the shingles off the roof, so we squeeze into Shelley's car. Steve and Julie get in the front seat together. They're leaning on each other, shoving, elbowing, and laughing their heads off each time we turn a corner.

"Stop," Julie gasps. "You're going to ruin my hair."

"Who're you trying to impress, Jules?" Steve grabs her head and presses her face against the side window. "Huh?"

"Cut it out, guys," Shelley snaps. "Act your age."

Maddie, Steve, and I all look at her, shocked.

Julie fires up immediately. "Don't be so anal. We're just having fun."

"Just cut it out. I can't think with so much noise. And you're going to make me get in an accident." She sounds annoyed, which I never would have thought possible. *Shelley does not get annoyed. Shelley is a bottomless bucket of patience, goodwill, and good grooming.*

I notice that there are circles under her eyes, like maybe she got about the same amount of sleep I did last night.

Julie opens her mouth, but Steve gives her one more well-placed elbow, and she grunts and closes it again.

We file in during the second verse of the opening hymn. I glance up at the stand. Bishop Barnes and his two counselors are there. Not Bob, though.

I kind of zone out during opening prayer and announcements. There is a huge number of sustainings, which is normal at the beginning of a semester in a singles' ward. I raise my hand over and over, not really listening to names and callings at all until Shelley rises from her chair with a rustle of starched cotton.

I glance up at her and raise my hand again, a little more tentatively this time. *I really should have been paying attention. For all I know, they called her to be the ward sacrificial virgin, and I've just agreed to help cast her off the Menan Buttes.*

Maddie pats her on the elbow when she sits. "Way to go," she whispers.

Shelley grimaces. "Thanks."

I lean across Maddie to ask. "What's your calling?"

Shelley blows out a gust of air, stirring a tendril on her forehead. "Relief Society president."

"Oh. You'll be great."

"I hope so."

Something about the way she says it makes me wonder a

little. I watch her during the sacrament hymn. She's got one arm wrapped tight around her waist in the universal defensive-girl gesture, and she's barely mouthing the words. *She is totally freaked out by this.*

Bob walks by our row just then. There's this strange little twist in my stomach as he glances down our row, counting silently and making notes on his little notebook. Seeing my gaze, he gives me a slight, unsmiling nod and continues on down the aisle.

"Hey, Julie," Steve mutters, nudging her with an elbow. "It's Robert Hartley."

I glance quickly at Julie and see her cheeks redden. I look at Bob again—he's completely oblivious. He's got this resigned, almost weary, expression on his face, and his broad shoulders are slightly hunched. Kind of like mine.

But he's still kind of . . . well. Imposing. It's hard not to look at him. I don't blame Julie for having a bit of a crush. *But does she know? Does anyone know about him? That he's been divorced? That he has kids?*

I tear my eyes away and look down at my hands. They're knit so tightly together, the knuckles are white. *Oh, Abish. What on earth are you doing here?*

After we get back home, I head straight to my room and remove my dress and tights. I spend a few minutes scratching my legs, which are unbearably itchy from being in tights for three hours straight, and then slide into sweats and my Asics.

Shelley gives me a slightly disapproving glance as I head for the door.

"It's not work," I throw over my shoulder. "It's a hobby." *Why am I explaining myself again?*

These girls are getting under your skin, Abish. Shake it off.

Run *it off.*

It's too much for my body. By the time get to the spot where Maddie and I broke down, my heart is thumping weirdly, my thighs are on fire, and I'm hallucinating. For some reason I cannot get the image of Bob smiling at me out of my head. I try to meditate, to focus, because I'm losing my gait and stumbling. *Chariots of fire, Abish. Think chariots of fire. Muscular legs, running in the sand. I wonder if Bob works out. He's in pretty good shape, but some people are just that way genetically.*

Okay, this is not working.

Think of Mark. His lithe, lean-but-still-solid form, torso rippling as he leaps to snatch a Frisbee out of the air. His smile . . .

I stumble, feeling a dart of panic. *What does his smile look like? I can't remember. I can't remember how it felt—his arms around me. When was the last time anyone put an arm around me?*

My pulse is throbbing in my throat. My insides are starting to twist with nausea.

Focus, Abish. Think of his eyes. His eyes, that day. You know *you'll remember that. That serious expression—almost asking something, pleading with me to do something; to take his hand, to pray warmth and life into those veins. To staunch the flow of his spirit. To tie him to earth and keep him here.*

My father named me Abish.

The bile rises in my throat. In a moment, I'm going to collapse on the side of the road. I slow to a walk and bend over, gasping for breath.

I give myself a minute and try to start again, but for some reason my legs refuse to get going, to leave the ground so that I'm running instead of just walking.

"Hey," Maddie calls as I limp through the door. "They called and said you're supposed to go in tonight after ward prayer. You and Julie."

I pause on my way to the bathroom. "They?"

"The ward. Bishop Barnes."

"Oh, crud." I glance in the mirror. My skin is all blotchy, my hair's a mess, my shirt is soaked in sweat, and my knees are trembling. I look and smell, basically, like a newborn calf. "What time is it?"

"Quarter-to. You'll have to get going if you want to make ward prayer."

"I don't think it's in the cards tonight," I reply, stepping into the shower.

After a long, hot soak, I'm sorely tempted to put on pajamas and pretend I didn't get the message. I don't, though; I put on one of my few decent pairs of jeans and a coral-colored top that I know makes my skin look nice. I even take time to quickly blow out my hair and put on a little lip gloss. I have no idea why.

These girls must be rubbing off on me.

Even a barn looks better painted. Who was it that said that—Kimball? Benson?

The office is teeming with people this time, all waiting to be called to some position in the ward or confess the sins they committed over Christmas break, or something. I lower myself into one of the few open chairs and drum my fingers on a side table, waiting.

Bob's sitting at my computer. He's reading a book—not really socializing or paying much attention to anyone. On impulse I rise from my chair, walk over, and lean on the desk.

He looks up. "Hi."

"Hi."

His eyes narrow slightly—amusement, I think. "Do you need something?"

I shrug. "Nope. Just kind of bored."

He looks out at the crowded lobby. "You don't feel like socializing?"

"Do you?"

He smiles. "You should have brought a book, like me."

"What is it?"

He holds it up.

"Terry Warner. Good one. We . . . I mean, I . . . well. Mark and I read it for our marriage enhancement class."

"Bishop assigned it to me."

I don't say anything for a few seconds because of all the thoughts and questions that are crowding my mind. Bob leans back in the chair, opens the book on his lap, and starts reading again.

A clear sign. But for some reason I feel like I'm caught here, watching him. Like there's some half-born sentence that needs to come unstuck before I can leave. "Be careful, that chair tips really easily," I finally say.

"Yeah, I noticed the first Sunday I sat here."

"Did you fall on the floor?"

He glances up. "You'd like it if I did, wouldn't you?"

"Misery loves company. That chair's tried to kill me several times."

He sits up straight again and swivels a little. "This is your spot, then."

"Yep."

There's a long silence. I can see the indecision in his face: *what do I want to do more, read a boring book or talk to a crazy person?* Finally he gives a little sigh, closes the book, and sets it aside. "So, how long have you worked for Burt?"

I open my mouth to reply, but just then the man in question stalks down the hall. His eyes find me. "Abish," he says, jerking his thumb in the direction of the office. I follow him, wondering what he can possibly have to say to me tonight. Hasn't he pretty much said it all already?

"So," he grunts when I've taken a seat. "How's the apartment hunt coming?"

"Uh, yeah. Haven't had a whole lot of time."

"So you're planning on staying."

"No, I . . ." Suddenly I feel completely overwhelmed. I pass my hand over my forehead. "No. Maybe. I don't know."

"We'll just assume you're here for now, then. We've assigned your apartment some good home teachers, and the Relief Society will want to know if you want to be a visiting teacher—"

"Probably not a good idea," I cut in. "On both counts."

He raises a bristly eyebrow.

"I don't need home teachers. Anyone I visit teach at this point will probably end up going inactive. I'm not really . . ." I shrug.

"Yes?"

With Bishop Barnes regarding me through those glasses of his, what started as an inappropriate joke seems suddenly more serious. "Yeah, well, I'm not really fully charged, I think you'd say."

"I would?"

"*You* were the one who called me a train wreck. Are you sure you want me spreading that around?"

Bishop Barnes narrows his eyes. The magnified effect through the lenses of his glasses is terrifying. "Just because you're struggling in life," he growls, "doesn't mean your faith has to suffer."

I'm starting to feel annoyed. "I'm fine. I'm not breaking commandments. I'm doing what I'm supposed to be doing."

He removes the glasses. His eyes look tired without them. "How's your faith doing?"

"Yeah," I say, lowering my gaze. "I'm doing my best. I just wasn't up to this particular trial Heavenly Father decided to bless me with. Maybe he should have measured my faith before he . . ." I shake my head. "Before."

And I'm feeling, again, like I might lose it and end up a blubbering mess in front of Bishop Barnes. I bite my lip and glare down at my shoes. "Anyone would struggle," I finally say.

"Yes." Bishop Barnes edges a box of Kleenex toward me.

"No thanks," I snap, edging it back.

"When was the last time you went to the temple?"

I shake my head. "A while."

"You need to involve Heavenly Father in this process, Abish. It's not optional. Not even you are strong enough to get through it completely on your own." He hesitates a moment, then leans forward on his elbows. "I want you to promise me that you will do all the Sunday School things. *Make* yourself do them."

"Sunday School things?"

"The Sunday School answers: read scriptures, pray each day, attend the temple often. It's trite, but it's true. It works."

I want to argue. Tell him he's wrong, that those things aren't going to change the fact that my entire life has been screwed up. *Praying isn't going to make Mark answer, and scripture reading isn't going to raise the dead. Theoretically, I know that God wants me happy, that there must be a way.*

I just don't see it.

"Yeah. I'll try to do better." I rise from the chair. "Scriptures, prayers, temple. Check."

"Journal," he adds. "Write in that journal."

"Yeah, the journal. Tell Sister Barnes thanks. She's got good taste."

He frowns.

"The Christmas present? Tell her thanks."

"Oh." Bishop stands and holds the door for me. "I chose it. You're welcome. I want to visit with you next Sunday too, Abish. Same time, if it works."

I'm not sure exactly what to say. I give him a stiff nod, turn, and head down the hall. The lobby is even more packed than it was before. I spot Julie sitting next to the window. "Hey," I say. "It's pretty dark out. I'll wait and we can walk back together."

Julie glances at the girl next to her. I recognize her; she's one of the people Steve and Julie hang around with a lot. She's been in our apartment a few times. I think her name is Amy, or Emily, or something like that.

Actually, it's more like an exchange of glances. Not one that I like too much, if you know what I mean.

"No thanks," Julie says shortly. "I'm sure your boyfriend wouldn't mind coming to get you. He seems to keep pretty late hours anyway."

"Yeah, well, I have to pay him by the hour, and I'm fresh out of cash."

Amy-or-Emily's eyes widen. I give her an evil smile.

"Or maybe you can ask him." Julie jerks her shoulder in Bob's direction.

The smile falls off of my face. "Why would I ask Bob for a ride? He's got to be here until everyone leaves."

"You seemed to be getting along just fine with him before."

"Before when?"

Julie shrugs and her face reddens a bit, but she's got that deadly look in her eyes. "You were just talking to him before you went in to your interview. You're not exactly a one-man woman, are you? I mean, you were married before, weren't you?"

Since she's hardly said more than half-a-dozen words to me in one sitting, I have to assume she's talking mostly for the benefit of those around her—considering the volume at which she's talking, for the benefit of the entire lobby. Everyone certainly heard the last part about me being married before. Even Bob, clear across the room behind the desk, is looking at us.

I don't trust myself to speak. I know I could come up with something truly eviscerating, and that's the problem. I don't want to rile Julie any more, because I don't know exactly what she is capable of. I don't want to find out what she is capable of, and I don't want to complicate my life any further by starting a brawl in the bishop's office.

"See you at home, then," I reply in a deceptively mild tone. I walk out into the hall, closing the glass doors quietly behind me.

I've already run myself to exhaustion today. But I have nothing else to do with this boiling mass inside my chest, so I walk down Second East.

It's a long distance, and the cemetery's a kind of spooky place to go at night. Particularly this cemetery—unlit, in the middle of fields. But kneeling by Mark's grave, I feel a kinship that I did not feel back there. *If he were here now, Mark would tell me that I shouldn't care what others think.* It's an unusually warm night; all the snow has melted off the stone. I kneel on it and pull my snowboarding jacket off.

I mean, I don't care. At all. But all those curious gazes at once, and the way Julie just spilled my business in front of them. How she made it sound so *bad*, too . . .

I hate them. I hate them. I hate them.

Shelley's face comes to mind, and Steve's, and Maddie's.

And Bob's. *No, you don't, Abish.*

They don't know what I'm feeling, I argue. *What I've been through. Why I am the way I am.* I run my hand over the stone, letting my index finger rest in the dip of the M—*Marcus Andrew Miller.*

Yeah, well, if you can't even face it yourself, then why would anyone else understand?

It's almost curfew by the time I get back. As I slide in the door,

Amy-or-Emily is just coming out. She gives me a hard look and walks by without saying a word. Julie's sitting on the couch. When I look at her, she averts her gaze and starts fiddling with her phone.

I pause for a moment, trying to dig up something that might be productive. Finally I shake my head. "Good night, Julie."

I walk to my room and sit down on the bed. I pull out the journal. *Bishop Barnes picked it out.* I still can't quite get my head around that. It's completely incongruent. My dad, buying a necklace. Bishop Barnes, picking out something classy like this. *Why did he?*

Sunday School answers.

My scriptures are on the little nightstand, under a toppling pile of textbooks. I pull them out and let them open randomly. The pages part, revealing a section of scripture that I know well. It's in the New Testament—one of Paul's epistles. *Neither life, nor death . . . nor any other thing, shall separate us . . .*

Mark's favorite scripture. *Nothing can separate us.* But we're *separated, aren't we?*

From the love of Christ. It's talking about the love of Christ.

I shut my scriptures, set them on the floor, and sit, running my fingers over the soft edges of the journal. I open it, ingesting the smell of new pages. New, blank pages. It frightens me, the thought of filling them.

I know there's life after death. But what about my life, right now, after your death? I don't remember any lessons in the Young Women's manual about what you're supposed to do if something unexpected happens, leaving you without the life you prepared so carefully for.

I honestly don't know what comes next, Mark. I'm stumped. And frightened. I feel guilty that I might want to move on.

This brings the tears that were waiting before. They come quick and hard, leaving my throat and chest aching like I've undergone some kind of surgical procedure. *I feel like my heart is breaking. Like I'm losing you all over again. Like I'm doing it, this time. But I can't keep this up, Mark. I just can't. I need something other than the prospect of us together after a long, lonely life pining away down here. I don't think God made me strong enough to be alone.*

I lie down on the sleeping bag and wrap my arms around my chest, shivering. *I don't know what you want me to do, Heavenly Father. It would be nice if you gave me a little direction.*

My heart swells and a random thought works its way into my mind: *be happy.*

"Be happy with my current situation? Or do you mean, do the things that make me happy? I'm not happy right now."

The silence presses me. My temples are aching. I close my eyes and try to will myself to sleep, but I lie there for a long time, shivering and listening to the drip of melting snow off the eaves outside my window.

⁓

There's something about a term of school that makes time fly. Weeks get eaten up. It's midterms before I realize what happens. My life goes by in flashes; I live from quiz to quiz, from project to project. Other than school and church, I spend a lot of quality time at the hospital with Mr. Eems.

I get my racing bib and information in the mail. The marathon is another worry now. I run seven miles or so on weekdays, and I try once every other weekend in February and March for a longer run, but my body won't go any further than sixteen. If I've got the time I can rally around and do a twenty in two pieces—a sixteen and then a four—but not all at once. It frightens me.

At Bishop Barnes's urging, I try going to a Relief Society activity in the middle of February. Shelley would usually keep me company, I think, but she is busier than a queen bee presiding over her hive. She's literally making herself crazy trying to have everything perfect, I can tell. I want to pull her aside and tell her to chill, but I haven't had a great track record lately when it comes to counseling roommates, so I figure it's better to mind my own business. Maddie doesn't think to say hi to me either, not that this surprises me. It's not really productive to sit on a metal chair in a corner by yourself, even if there are raspberry cupcakes to eat.

I glance at the clock. *You've only been here fifteen minutes, Abish.*

Give it a try. I stand, throw my cupcake wrapper in the trash, and walk over to Steve. "Hey," I say.

Julie, sitting next to her, gives me a nasty look.

"Hey, Julie," I add. "That color looks nice on you."

She turns to Steve. "As I was saying . . ." and she goes off on some random spiel about a group date they went on the week before. We're right next to the refreshments table. I reach over and grab a piece of cake—one for the road.

"I made that," a girl sitting next to Julie remarks. "It's called 'better than sex cake.' No, that's really the name," she adds as Steve laughs.

Julie looks up at me. "Well, is it?"

There's a long silence. I remove the fork from my mouth. "Nope," I reply, looking her right in the eye. I turn on my heel and head for the door, and bump right into . . . who else?

"Stephanie, the bishop would like to meet with you for a moment, if that's okay," Bob says. Only he's not looking at Steve; he's looking at me. And there's this kind of quiver in his voice, and a smile hidden in the corners of his mouth.

Yeah, well. I guess the universe has decided that Bob must see every single one of my low moments.

For some reason, I feel a little bit like crying as I walk home. After that, I avoid ward activities, and Julie and I fall into a rhythm that works: I ignore her and she ignores me. I say no when Steve asks me to do stuff even if I occasionally kind of want to say yes.

And as for my other roommates, Shelley occasionally surfaces from her fog of stress and hyper-involvement in the ward to say hello to me as we pass in the hall. Maddie sometimes asks me questions about Pen. After she baked him that pie they went out on a date, but against my prediction, he hasn't seemed all that interested. He'll come over occasionally and play games with me, but when Maddie comes around to sit next to him he won't say much, in spite of her attempts to engage him in conversation. Of course, guys don't really like to talk while they're gaming. But I've never known Pen to keep a controller in his hand and his eyes on the screen when he could be chatting up some girl. And he'll do things like suggest we go somewhere to get a burger when I've got a perfectly good sandwich on my plate. Like he's trying to avoid her, almost.

It's really getting to her, I can tell. She's pretty quiet most of the time, and when I say something like, "Hey, how are midterms going," she'll just shrug.

One wind-tossed Friday in March, I'm relaxing on one of the couches with a peanut butter sandwich and a glass of milk. I've just gotten back from my usual study date with Mr. Eems.

The front door opens and Shelley walks in. She's loaded down with groceries, so I set my plate down and jump up to help her.

"Thanks," she says when the last plastic grocery bag has been knotted and thrown in the trash.

I shrug and head back to the couch.

"Hey, come with me to talent night. You're going, right?"

I give her a puzzled look. "Why would I want to go?"

"It'll be fun." She plops down on the cushion next to me. "If you stay inside all day and all night, your eyelids will start growing together like those cave fish."

I smile in spite of myself. "No thanks. I've found that the Seventeenth Ward and I don't mix well. Besides, my only talent at this point is running long distances, and since I can't cart around the entire ward in a jogging stroller . . ." I shrug.

Shelley laughs. "You should get up there and tell jokes."

"I don't think they'd like the sorts of jokes I'd want to tell."

The smile melts away, and I regret my facetiousness. "You should give it a chance, Abish," she scolds. "I know you probably feel uncomfortable sometimes, but it's your ward. We all have stewardship over each other. You need us, and we need you."

I snort. "Believe me, I'm doing the ward a big favor by keeping my presence to a minimum. I don't fit in, Shelley. You have to see that."

"Don't say that. You're a good person, Abish, and you can't let people treat you like you aren't." There's a fierceness to her tone that surprises me.

MILE 21

"Yeah?" I rise from my seat and carry my plate to the kitchen. "Well, you can't force people to see you a certain way. People are judgmental. And, honestly, they can judge me any way they want, because it's not really my problem, is it?"

"No," Shelley says slowly, twisting her hands in her lap. "But you should try, Abish. Give people a chance to know and accept you. I know it's hard, laying yourself open to criticism, but nobody says life is easy . . ."

"Only that it's worth it," I cut in. "You say that, Shelley, but you don't know what it really means." I stalk down the hall to my room before she can answer.

Immediately I feel guilty, though. I think of her sitting there, obviously nervous about asking me to come with her.

She's just a poor little Molly Mormon; ignorant and annoying, but she didn't mean anything by it. I sigh and walk over to my closet. I've not done enough laundry lately, but I think there might be one decent pair of jeans I've only worn three times. And I can wear Mama's sweater that she gave me for Christmas. I haven't put it on since dinner at the Barneses.

"I'm sorry," I say when I emerge from my room five minutes later. "Thanks. I'll come if we can sit in the back."

Shelley looks up from her giant binder full of ward-council notes and pastel-colored tabs. "You look nice," she says, setting it aside. She stands and stretches her arms. "We'd better get going, then. I'll buy ice cream after."

"You don't have to do that." I pull on my snowboarding jacket, zip it up, and begin snapping it down my chest.

"But I want to, so shut up." She's glaring at me. It's nothing as fierce as either Julie or I could produce, but there's no mistaking how serious she is. When it comes down to it, I'm pretty sure I could win in an arm-wrestling match, but in a contest of stubborn, self-righteous determination . . .

"Fine," I say after a few seconds. "We'll go to the show, and then you can funnel Kiwi Loco down my throat. It's a date."

Her frown melts into a grim smile, and she holds the door for me.

It's being held in the old stadium of the Hart building. There's tons of space for the small amount of people in our ward. I'm tempted to make a beeline for the balcony, but Shelley reaches out and grabs my elbow, leading me to last row in the section of seats where everybody seems to be gathering. It's a compromise I can handle, maybe. I sit, fold my arms, and people-watch.

Maddie's with the Cute Boys, chattering away. They're not really listening to her, though Dave Cannon glances down at her every once in a while and gives her a nod. Steve and Julie are with their friends on the first two rows. They are making a lot of boisterous noise. People come in groups by apartment, mostly. There are a few couples—the near-engagees of the ward. Soon, Bishop Barnes will be able to start his running total of couples married off.

Bob walks in just before the lights dim.

Julie notices. She throws a glance over her shoulder, reddens, then looks straight ahead like she's not paying attention.

I watch him waver, trying to decide between sitting with the bishop at the end of one of the crowded front rows or doing what he really wants to do, which is find an unobtrusive watching spot like me.

He glances at the sparsely populated back row and sees me looking at him. I give him a nod, fold my hands in my lap, and look down at the stage, where Steve has started the evening's program by standing at the podium and making wisecracks while her group of friends laugh (in my opinion, more than they need to).

"Hey." Bob's voice startles me.

I take a deep breath and let it out slowly. "Hey."

Bob settles into the seat next to me. "Mind if I sit here?"

"It's a free country."

He frowns. "I can sit somewhere else."

"Nope." I swat his knee. "You're fine."

He looks down at his knee. It's incredibly awkward. I fold my arms tight across my chest and glance over at Shelley. She's laughing helplessly. *Okay, so maybe Steve is legitimately funny.*

Man, I think as I watch her up there, grinning her Cheshire-cat grin and rattling off jokes. *I wish Julie didn't exist. This whole ward thing might actually work, then. Steve and I would get along just fine. I'd have friends, maybe.*

Steve steps down and a series of acts follow with varying degrees of talent and awkwardness. Steve and Julie's friend—Amy-or-Emily, I still can't remember her name—plays Für Elise on the piano. Shelley rises from her seat and goes to the stage to participate in a little lip-sync skit with Julie and a couple of other girls: a rendition of Beyoncé's "All the Single Ladies," with dance and funny expressions.

"This song is so tired." I don't mean to say it, but it just slips out. "Cute," I add hastily. "But, I mean . . ."

Bob looks at me out of the corner of his eye. "How many times do you think it's been performed at singles' ward talent shows up to this point?"

"A lot."

"Before this song, it was that one . . . I don't know the name. The bride dance from that chick flick . . ."

"*My Best Friend's Wedding.*" I look at him with a measure of astonishment. "*You* watch chick flicks?"

He shrugs. "It was Valerie's favorite movie."

The urge to tease struggles with the awkwardness I feel, and wins. "Right," I say. "*Her* favorite movie. That's why you've seen the credits at the beginning enough times to remember the dance."

"I might have teared up a little the first time I saw it. When Julia Roberts and what's his name go under the bridge and she just can't get out the words, 'I love you.' Good thing I was in a dark theater or it might have been embarrassing."

His tone and expression are completely bland. I honestly can't tell if he's joking or not. But I figure it won't hurt to test the waters further. "You saw it in the *theater*? Dude, how old are you?"

He grins. "I was eleven. I went with my mom."

"*Right.*" I try to give him an evil smile but I laugh instead and turn quickly back to the stage.

We get through all the ready volunteers and move on to the reluctant who need their arms twisted. Finally, Bishop Barnes gets up on stage and starts talking into the microphone. *Great, it's over. Time to blow this popsicle stand and go get some ice cream.*

Except for some reason, I'm not in that much of a hurry to leave. Shelley's back in her seat smiling and having a good time; I don't want to pull her away before she's ready. And with Bob sitting next to me, I feel like I badly need to say something. Like there are *still* words. It's completely baffling. I mean, I've already apologized to him for everything. And offered to babysit, for crying out loud. What more could I need to say to the guy?

He feels my gaze and looks over at me.

". . . just one more act tonight," Bishop Barnes says. "Robert Hartley, come up here."

We both start and turn back toward the stage. Everyone's craning their necks, looking at Bob over their shoulders.

Bob stands and waves his arm in a depreciating gesture. "No. Thanks, Bishop. I haven't prepared anything."

Suddenly I notice a guitar in the Bishop's hands. "Come on up, Robert," he repeats. "I know you've got a few songs you could do."

"No thanks, I . . ." He glances down at me.

I shrug and give him a sympathetic smile. *It's a lost cause when you're dealing with Bishop Barnes.*

"Fine," he grumbles. He edges his way out of our row and stalks down the aisle toward the stage. Someone finds a chair. Bob sits down, strums experimentally, and begins playing.

It's kind of amazing, actually. His hands are so big, I wonder how he can have such dexterity in his fingers, but there he is, playing. And each note is perfect, ringing out over the stage. And then he starts to sing, and a visible swoon passes over the audience.

Bob is . . . well, he's *good*. His voice deep and clear, mellow with a velvety sort of rasp. He could totally front for a band. He could play at weddings and stuff.

Maybe he does. You know barely anything about him.

It's such a huge contrast from my first impression of him; blue collared shirt, disheveled hair, surly expression. I can't quite believe I ever saw him that way at all. It makes me wonder how people see me.

Because lately—if I'm going to be completely honest with myself—I haven't made much effort. I've been Abish, raw and unedited. No apologies, but no display of redeeming qualities, either.

After he finishes to wild applause and hands the guitar back to the Bishop, all eyes are following him as he heads back to the seat next to me. It's like Mark and the singles' ward talent show all over again.

No, I chastise myself immediately, feeling the guilt hit me in the gut. *No, Abish, it's not.* "Okay, I'm ready to go now," I hiss at Shelley, just as someone stands to say the closing prayer.

She doesn't hear me. When the prayer is over, she gets up and starts to mingle. The crowd is breaking up. People are standing, milling around, chattering, laughing. Bob and I are the only ones still sitting.

"Good song," I say gruffly. "I never would have guessed."

He shrugs. "I don't do a whole lot with it lately. A long time ago I was in a garage band. We played at all the high school dances."

"I bet you were pretty popular. Football . . . in a band . . ."

"Yeah. Maybe."

"I bet you dated all the cheerleaders too."

Something seems to close off in his face. "Yeah," he repeats, and rises from his seat. "Well, I've got studying to do. See ya." He's about to turn and leave, but a group of girls streams up the aisle, blocking his path. It's Steve and Julie and their noisy bunch.

"Good job," I call out.

"Yeah, thanks," Steve replies, then turns to talk to someone in the row ahead of us.

Julie leans in. "Yeah, Abish," she says quietly. "All the *single* ladies, though. I mean, you don't really qualify."

"Nope," I reply. "I don't."

She puts a hand on her hip. "Why're you *here*, then?" Her eyes go to Bob for a fraction of a second, then land on me again. I look over and realize that Bob's not missed a word of this little interaction.

Ah. This is for Bob's benefit, then. Well, I won't spoil her fun. "Yeah, I'm trolling for gullible freshman," I say. "Preemies. I've always found them attractive."

I feel a hand on my elbow. "Let's go get that ice cream, Abish," Shelley says.

I glance back at her. A flare of annoyance sears through me. *What, is she afraid I'm going to punch someone?*

"Ice cream sounds good," Bob interjects. "Where are you two headed?"

I shrug. "We were just thinking Kiwi Loco."

"That fruity stuff isn't ice cream. I'll take you guys to IBC's. My treat." And to my astonishment, he puts an arm around each of our shoulders—mine and Shelley's—and leads us toward the exit.

"I don't need you to defend me," I say when we enter the lobby.

"It's not *you* I was worried about." Bob releases us and heads for the door. He holds it open.

"What's that supposed to mean?" I ask as we walk past him out into the parking lot.

Bob gives me a look.

"Okay. Sorry. I'm kind of out of the habit of being teased."

"He was trying to help, Abish," Shelley murmurs as we slide into the backseat of his car. "You say things you don't mean. A lot. And it puts people off. And with your situation . . ." She shrugs.

"What situation is that?" I whisper. "The fact that I have a dead husband? Excuse me if I don't feel a need to excuse *myself* and kiss up to people because I've had tragedy foisted on me."

"The point is sound." Bob's voice, from the front seat, makes me jump a little.

I'm turning red too. I didn't mean for him to hear. "What the crud does that mean?" I finally say.

"It might not be fair. People don't handle things as well as they should, but you make people uncomfortable, sometimes on purpose."

I glare at him in the rearview mirror. "I don't see *you* making much of an effort either."

Bob shrugs. "I know I need to try harder eventually. I'm not quite ready yet."

"And you think *I* should be? It's only been a year since Mark died. How long has it been since your divorce?"

"Three months."

That silences things pretty well. I keep looking at Bob's face in the mirror during the drive . . . it's like I can't look away. Good thing he's keeping his attention on the road. Shelley is sitting next to me, probably feeling like a giant third wheel, but I'm glad she's there.

The mood lightens a bit when we walk inside the ice cream place. We order and sit. It's pretty good ice cream. Maybe even better than the stuff at Fall's Drug in St. Anthony.

"Thanks," I say after a few bites.

Bob meets my eyes. "You're welcome," he replies, in a tone that I know means more than just ice cream.

We get back an hour before curfew. Bob walks us to the door of our apartment. When he opens it, a blast of noise hits us full-frontal. "What?" I yell over the noise. "Did someone forget to tell me about the free rock concert?"

It really is out of control. I don't know what's in the air tonight, but whatever it is, it doesn't look legal. People are jumping up and down on the couch, a couple of guys are contorting their bodies in realistic impression of air-guitar à la Jimi Hendrix, and there's a lot of long hair swinging around.

"It's the post-talent-night talent night," Steve yells over the music. "Hey, Bob. You should hang out." She looks over her shoulder at Julie, who is pretending not to see us in the doorway, but who immediately toned her dancing down as soon as we came in.

"No thanks," Bob replies. "See you guys." He gives a wave, steps out, and shuts the door.

"Are you okay leaving your car by campus?" I shout at Shelley. "It's dark. You should walk with someone if you're going to go get it."

"The weather is supposed to be nice tomorrow. I'll walk in the morning and bring it back after classes."

"'Kay! Night-night." I nearly trip over Maddie, who is sitting in the hallway with her back against the wall, texting. She gets up and follows me.

"Yeah?" I ask, turning when we reach my door.

"Do you know if Pen's got plans this weekend?"

"Not that I know of. Why don't you ask him?"

"He's been busy lately. He hasn't always been remembering to return my calls."

I sigh and run my fingers through my bangs. "Maddie, you should forget about him. He's kind of flaky. I mean, I've never known him to stay with one girl for more than a couple dates. If he's not returning your calls, believe me, it's not you. It's him."

"He answers *your* calls."

"Yeah, but I'm his bud, not his NCMO partner. Sorry," I add quickly when her eyes flash. "I didn't mean anything by that. Look, Maddie, you can find much a much better guy than Pen, trust me."

"I thought he was your friend."

"He *is* my friend. So I know him better than any girl he's ever dated, and I'm telling you now, he's not worth it. Maybe in, I don't know . . . five years or so, he'll have pulled it together enough to be a project worth taking on. But he's kind of rough material at this point. With guys like Dave Cannon hanging around, I wouldn't waste my time on Pen."

Her expression turns utterly bleak. "Dave doesn't want to date me."

It kills me to see her looking like that. I mean, she can be annoying and insensitive, but she's still a human being. She's inappropriately curious, but she's open. In spite of her occasional lack of tact, she's got a good heart. And she's *cute. Any guy should be so lucky.* "I'm sorry," I finally say.

"He just treats me like a little kid. Like when I was little, and I used to love my brothers' guy friends. I crawled all over them and followed them around. Did you ever do that?"

"I only have a little sister."

"Oh. Well, Dave Cannon looks at me the same way they did. Like he's about to pat me on the head."

"So what? Don't let one jerky guy get you down, Mad."

"It's the same with *all* guys. Dave, Pen. They think I'm cute but then they get bored. Or annoyed. I don't know what to do differently."

"Well, you're so . . ." I'm at a loss for words. "You are kind of adorable, Maddie. You can't help that. Maybe you should just be yourself a little more. Like, get rid of those weird contacts. Every-body can tell they're not real, and guys *love* big brown eyes. It's not a bad thing to be cute."

"It is when you're trying to get people to take you seriously." Her voice cracks. She takes her hands and presses them onto her face for a moment. "Oh, man. If I could just get rid of some of this puppy fat." She gestures her body. "Get lean and mean and fit. But I can't."

"You're not fat. Don't change yourself for someone else." I reach over and put an arm around her back, giving her a brief, awkward squeeze.

"You can say that because it's easy for *you* to be yourself."

"Yeah." I roll my eyes. "Real easy."

She pulls away and gives me a long, hard look. "You know, Abish, you'd be more attractive if you weren't so sarcastic all the time."

"You're the third person to tell me that tonight."

Her expression immediately switches from woebegone to avidly curious. "Did you and Bob and Shelley go somewhere together?"

I shrug. "He just bought us some ice cream."

"You know Julie likes him, right? You should probably back off him a little. You don't mean to, but it kind of looks like you're flirt-ing with him sometimes."

I sigh and shut my eyes tightly for a second. *I really, really don't want to be having this conversation.* "If Julie ever asks you, tell her not to worry. Bob is all hers."

Maddie nods, her face completely serious. "I will."

But honestly, I just don't picture Bob and Julie together. It's not just that he's totally good-looking and several echelons more mature that Julie; I'm also trying to imagine Julie getting along with Todd, and it's not computing. Julie's not the type to be good with children. "Make sure, though, that she's also aware that he's a single parent of two kids." I feel guilty saying it, but there it is.

Maddie eyes widen. "You're joking, right?"

"Nope." I reach back and turn my doorknob. "Night, Maddie."

I feel another surge of guilt as I sit down on Pen's sleeping bag. *Yeah, maybe I should have kept my mouth shut. But honestly, Maddie can't handle Pen. And Bob is a single parent. It's not like I'm telling some big secret or something.*

Maybe Bob doesn't want the whole world knowing his business. Maybe he's looking for a fresh start. Everyone deserves a fresh start.

I can't have a fresh start. I made an eternal covenant. I get one chance at that. Like Maddie's said, I've got my spot reserved if I can manage not to mess things up too badly for the rest of my life.

Be sensible, Abish.

"I *am* being sensible." I shout the words, startling even myself. "What else am I supposed to be doing, Mark?"

Shelley sticks her head in just then. Her brow furrows as she takes in the sight of me with my fists clutching two handfuls of my hair and the angry, frustrated expression on my face. "Sorry," she murmurs. "I tried knocking."

I sigh and let my hands fall into my lap. "What's up?"

"Bob's on the phone. He wants to talk to you."

The silence is measured with the rhythm of my pulse pounding in my ears. "Um," I finally say, "now's not a good time. Can you take a message?"

She puts the phone to her ear. "Abish is kind of preoccupied. What's up?" She nods a couple times, then presses the cell to her shoulder. "He wants to know if you can babysit tomorrow at seven. I guess you offered at some point?"

My heart quickens. "Yeah. Yeah—tell him it's okay."

Shelley relays my acceptance, closes her phone, and frowns. "Are *you* okay?"

"I'm fine. Thanks. Good night."

The door shuts. I sit there, struggling against the burning humiliation that threatens to overwhelm me as I imagine how things must have seemed just now from Shelley's perspective. *I am crazy. Truly crazy. She's probably going to advise Bob not to trust me with his kids.*

And maybe she would be right to do so. Maybe it's time you stopped talking to yourself.

But there's nothing else. I don't have anything else. Dead ends all around—that's my life.

MILE 21

There's no answer, because I don't *have* an answer to this one. The journal is on the floor near where my head is resting. I pick it up, flip to the first page, and stare at it for a while. Finally I take a pen and write it: *There's nothing else. I can stay in this state forever, becoming lonelier and lonelier as I push people away further. Or I can move on with my life. Those are the only options.*

It doesn't help in any way, having the words actually on paper. In fact, it seems to lend a terrible finality to the whole thing. I lie down on the sleeping bag and gaze up at my window. The stars shine, clear pinpricks of light. The moon is a silver pendant against the black sky. My breaths become deeper, and it all blurs together.

Chapter

13

*H*ey."

I'm gathering up my books and papers, stuffing my binder with the notes I've taken. The buzz of conversation is actually kind of nice after the aching quiet of lecture and jerking awake every few minutes.

"Hey." The voice is accompanied by a shoulder nudge this time.

I turn and smile politely at Nathan. He's in my study group. He's got these pale, washed-out eyes and an unnerving tendency to stare. He also doesn't have any eyebrows and his overbite is kind of noticeable. But he's a nice enough guy. "What's up?"

He shrugs and takes a couple of my textbooks under his arm. "Where's your next class at?"

I'm a little surprised by the gesture, but I definitely don't mind. I've got a lot of books to carry today. "The Hart building. Not class, I'm going to work."

"Cool."

We walk along in silence. It's a touch awkward, but nothing I can't handle gracefully. "Well, thanks," I say as the front doors of the Hart come into view. I reach for my books. He pulls them to his chest.

Okay, seeing him this close, I realize that he does have eyebrows. They're blond, and they kind of grow together in the middle. "I was wondering," he says, "if you'd like to get pizza sometime. Tonight, maybe. Pizza Pie Café has a five-dollar special if you go after eight tonight."

It takes me a moment to remove my focus from his eyebrows and absorb the fact that Nathan from biology has just asked me out on a date. "I can't," I finally reply. "I'm babysitting for a friend. But thanks for asking."

"Okay." He shrugs again. "Maybe this weekend?"

"I . . ." I shake my head. "You see, I'm kind of not dating now."

He frowns. "Not dating?"

I understand his confusion, because here in Rexburg, if you aren't married, saying you're not dating is kind like saying you're taking a short break from breathing oxygen. Even though I have every legitimate excuse in the book to turn Nathan down, in the back of my head a voice is nagging. It sounds kind of like Sister Simmons, the Sunday School teacher I had when I was sixteen. *Always say yes to the first date. It's the polite thing to do.*

Yeah, but this is different.

Just because you're not attracted to him at first doesn't mean you won't like him if you try. Always say yes to the first date because you might miss out on your eternal companion.

I'm. Already. Married.

"No," I repeat. "Sorry. You seem like a nice guy, though." I give him a smile that is more like a grimace. "Thanks for carrying my books."

"Yeah."

I turn away, but he's speaking again. "You know, you can just be honest with me. Say you're not attracted to me or whatever. I wish girls would just be *honest*."

I turn back, reluctantly, to face him. "Oh, believe me," I reply, "honesty's not a problem for me. And honestly I'm not dating. Anyone. Sorry."

His expression is growing mulish. It's making me uneasy. "Okay," he says. "Well, how long do you think you won't be dating anyone? Can I get your number so I can call you in six months or something?"

Dude. This guy doesn't know when to quit. "I probably won't be dating then, either."

"Probably?"

"I'm fairly certain."

He shrugs and looks down at his shoes. "If you don't want to go out on a formal date, we could just go for a walk or something. If you wanted."

"No, thank you. But thanks."

"Are you, like, preparing for a mission or something? Because the prophets say you should prioritize marriage over a mission."

My veneer of sympathy for this guy is cracking up like the Arctic Circle during spring melt. "So we'd go for a walk, and then it's on to the sealing room after that?"

He squints at me.

"Yeah, see you later. Thanks again." I march up the stairs to the office, feeling both sick to the stomach and irritated because Nathan kind of reminds me of a guy friend I had in high school. He was a senior when I was a freshman. We were outcasts together because neither of us was in the popular group, and at our small high school, either you were popular or you were unpopular. For me, unpopularity was because of bluntness and the fact that I didn't care what people thought of me. For him it was appearance and the way he tended to rattle on about science-fiction series. He ended up going to MIT and marrying a girl just as nerdy and nice as he was. They have two redheaded, nearsighted children. Couldn't be happier.

But even if I were dating, isn't it wrong to say yes to a date out of pity for the guy; to make him spend the money, time, and emotional investment on you when you know he's not your type?

Yeah. It still really stinks to say no.

By the time I reach the second floor, I'm tempted to gnash my teeth and growl right there in the hallway. I hate to admit this even to myself, but I'm pretty sure that some of my rotten feeling comes from the fact that he thought he had a chance with me. A really guilty, unrighteous prideful corner of my soul is amazed that he wouldn't just walk away the first time I said no.

Have I really fallen so much in attractiveness, in self-confidence, that someone like Nathan-from-bio-class thinks he should be able to bully me into a date?

Yeah, Abish. Why are you worried about that if you're not planning on dating again?

At some point in the afternoon, Adrian makes a veiled remark about my hairstyle. Generally I can take it, but this time, I can't resist muttering something under my breath.

"What was that?" Adrian asks.

I tremble on the brink for a moment, then let it spill. "Just that at least I'm not such a slave to fashion that I walk around looking like a zebra." I lift my chin in the direction of her hair, which is high-lighted in chunky blond-and-dark-brown streaks.

She's smiling. She's suppressing it, but I can tell by the way her eyes narrow. "Better a zebra than a half-drowned alley cat. Get an appointment at Reflections, why don't you."

I wag my index finger at her. "Don't have a lot of time for fancy haircuts. I actually take school seriously. I study."

She turns back to her screen. After a few moments she glances over at me with a smile. "Glad to see you're back among the living, Abe."

I feel for a few seconds like I've been punched, but I manage a nod and a tight smile and continue with my work until the clock says five. My mind is running in circles as I change in the locker room and walk out to the parking lot. As I start to run, the touchy subject I've been suppressing rears its ugly head.

I'm moving on.

How can I, though? What am I moving on to? I can't forget about Mark because he still exists, and I'm still married to him. And I don't want that to go away. I love Mark. And there's also the baby. Amelia.

The name is thick in my throat. It's pouring over me—the bleak grayness of that first month without Mark. And as the month ended—the agony that was more than muscle spasms. More than an issue of blood. When I knew I was losing our baby.

I failed both of you, I think as I sweep by the Maverick on Main Street and grab the water bottle I've left under the tree there. *Utterly. And I'm failing you again now because I can't keep this up. I can't keep thinking about you all the time. It's making me crazy, Mark. I'm lonely, and it just doesn't feel real enough anymore. If only I could see you once in a while. If only I could have seen her look up into my face and know that she knew me even for a second.*

There's no answer.

I'm plodding along on mile fourteen. Mile fifteen. I channel all my angst and grief as I approach sixteen and try to push through, but it's no use. I start getting the tearing feeling in my chest, the trembling in my knees. My stomach spasms and I know in another second I'll be heaving into the Rexburg canal, so I slow, stop, and lean over, gasping and coughing. My shins are throbbing and my knees ache.

Too many long runs, too close together. Give it time, Abish.

When I've gotten hold of myself, I walk back to the apartment. The clock on the microwave says 6:10. Todd and Gabriel are coming over in forty minutes.

I shower and throw on a hoodie and sweatpants. I put my wet hair into two braids; I don't know why. Mark always thought I looked cute that way, but I think it makes me look like a little girl. I'm sitting on one of the sofas with my biochemistry text, trying to ingest little-known facts about nucleic acids, when the doorbell rings.

"Come in," I call. There's a slight flutter in my stomach. It almost masks the sharp edge of pain left over from my run.

Todd trots in with Valerie (or Sauron, or whatever his name is this week) and a brown paper bag clutched in his hand. Bob follows with Gabriel propped on one shoulder and a diaper bag slung over the other. The baby is in a fuzzy sleeper the color of astro-turf. His dark eyes find my face, and his lips tremble and turn down into the most adorable pout I think I've ever seen.

"Oh," I say, stretching my arms out. Bob hands him over. "Hey." I try to guide his head onto my shoulder. "I'm Abish. I promise I'm not going to eat you for lunch."

"Thanks for doing this."

I gesture toward Todd's paper bag. "You didn't have to bring dinner."

"Yeah." Bob smiles. "I know what kind of food you college girls eat." He sets the diaper bag on the table—pink and brown polka dots.

"Nice bag."

"People tell me it doesn't go with any of my outfits."

"Nah. I'd say it's a good match."

Bob glances around. I wince—the kitchen's not all that tidy. "You have a candle burning somewhere?" he asks.

"We're not allowed."

"Huh. Well, something smells nice."

"Probably just shampoo. I took a shower."

His eyes move over my wet braids, faded sweats, and the purple furry slippers I'm wearing. "You look cute." He says it in this casual, serious way, like he's commenting on the weather.

My cheeks warm. "Yeah. I know I look like a twelve-year-old. Aren't you going to be late?"

"Yes. Okay, diapers are in there. Formula and bottle too. Todd might fall asleep on the couch if he doesn't get too wired up. There's a couple of DVDs in there he'll sit and watch if you need a break. I don't have your cell number." He pulls a phone out of his back pocket.

I shake my head. "You can call Shelley's like you did before. She'll probably be here some of the night."

"You don't have a cell phone?"

"I don't like cell phones. As soon as you get one, people are offended if they can't talk to you every second of the day or night."

"Sounds like a good idea." Bob looks at his cell phone for a few seconds, sighs, and puts it back in the pocket. "I'll be back by eleven; the job shouldn't take longer than that. You're a lifesaver."

"Do you usually have to work this late?" I ask as he heads for the door.

"Nope. Regular hours end at nine, but there's an outage in a neighborhood in south Rigby. They tried to fix it at the street level but the short's not there. So I have to climb some poles. I might find it right away. In that case, I'll be done early."

"Climb poles . . . like *telephone* poles?"

He gives me a smile. *Gotcha,* it seems to say. "Don't worry. Linemen have special equipment to keep them from falling."

"I'm *not* worried," I retort, feeling my face warm again. "It's just not a very usual thing. I don't know a whole lot of people who climb telephone poles for a living."

He steps through the doorway. "I've got to go."

"Yeah. See you at ten or eleven." I shut the door as he turns to head down the stairs.

The baby starts to wail. I bounce him on my hip and look down at Todd. He has a solemn expression on his face, and his eyes are following his father's retreating figure through the window.

"Hey you," I say. "Let's play Uno. Do you know how?"

"No."

"I'll teach you, then. It's pretty easy. You just have to know your colors and your numbers."

His face brightens, and he looks up at me. "I know all my numbers up to twenty."

"I was hoping you didn't so I could beat you."

He grins. "You're sorry out of luck."

"Sorry out of luck, huh? We'll see about that."

We sit on the floor cross-legged and play for a good hour. Then I pull out his dinner, which turns out to be a tuna fish sandwich, sliced apples, and a juice box. Not bad for dad food. *I can do better.*

I look in the fridge. My section has exactly three things: peanut butter, two-week-old milk, and a jar of pickles. I look in my cupboard: olives, a can of tuna, a box of Malt-O-Meal.

Yeah. Maybe not.

Nothing I do makes the baby happy. He alternates between crying and pouting quietly, a terrible, pathetic baby-pout that makes me want to pick him up and hold him in the hollow of my neck and rock him, but that doesn't seem to make things any better when I try it. Finally he cries himself into a light sleep. After Todd finishes his food, I suggest a DVD, and he agrees. I pop in *The Incredibles*, and within the first fifteen minutes, Todd is blinking and yawning. I shift his position so he can lean against my side. I'm starting to zone too, and I'm kind of wondering where all the roomies are. Usually at least one of them is home by now.

I get my answer when Steve and Julie and a couple of guys burst through the door, chattering and laughing. Todd's obviously a good sleeper because he doesn't even twitch a muscle, but it wakes up Gabriel, who immediately starts wailing up a storm.

Steve gives Gabe a startled look. "Oh, geez. Sorry."

I reach down and gather Gabe's rigid, protesting body against mine.

The guys, still chattering away, head to the kitchen, where Julie is digging through her cupboard, coming up with ingredients. Chocolate chip cookies, it looks like. "I'll try to keep things quiet," Steve murmurs. "Whose are they?"

"Bob's."

Steve's eyes widen. "Bob. Like, Robert Hartley from the ward? He's got *kids*?"

"C'mon, Steve." Julie's tone is sharp with annoyance. "I need you to get the pasta going."

Gabe isn't crying as loudly anymore, but he is shuddering and his pout is a permanent fixture. He won't look me in the eye when I try to hold his gaze; he turns his head away. I stand, shifting my weight from foot to foot, rocking him. After a while, he relaxes and starts breathing like he's sleeping, so I stretch out on my side of the couch, being careful not to disturb Todd, and lie with him on my chest.

Steve and Julie and their following settle onto the floor and on the other couch and start eating. I watch them idly, counting Gabe's heartbeats. His soft, dark hair is like silk on my cheek. He smells sweet. Not flower-sweet; more musky. Human.

"Whose kids?" one of the guys ventures, breaking the silence.

I glance at Steve. "A friend's."

They finish eating, gather up their plates, and stack them in the sink. As they file past me, they're debating between playing a game of tag in an empty building on campus or catching a movie. Julie's the last one to head out. When she reaches the door, she turns suddenly. "It's totally inappropriate to bring kids to the apartment," she says. "I babysit for my sister in town. She'd never let me watch them at a college apartment."

"It wasn't exactly planned," I reply. "I'm sure that if he could have, Bob would have found somebody more appropriate."

Julie frowns. "What?"

"Usually his mom watches them, but she was probably busy tonight."

"Did you say Bob? As in, Robert Hartley from the ward?" She looks at Todd, then at the baby, and finally me again. "You're such a liar."

"Okay," I say agreeably. "Have a good time. Don't sprain an ankle."

She shakes her head, turns on her heel, and shuts the door behind her.

I doze off for a while. When I wake up, I'm sticky with sweat. *A sleeping baby in fleece pajamas is even better than a hot water bottle.* I shift his head a little, settling his cheek on my shoulder. There are white washes of salt down his face where his tears have dried. In the warm lamplight, I can almost imagine . . . almost see her. Amelia. She might have had dark hair like this. She'd be about this age, maybe.

I count the months. *Yeah, maybe. Maybe she'd be a little younger. Not much younger, though.*

I watch him sleep. *His face is so perfectly formed.*

My vision blurs, and my chest convulses. I fight it, but I lose.

MILE 21

I try not to make any noise, but I'm crying hard enough that I'm almost choking on it. It just keeps coming and coming. It's like I've struck a well of feeling I didn't know I had inside me.

When I'm done, I'm so completely exhausted that I'm not thinking clearly. I lie down on my side and pull Gabriel up against my stomach. We're like two commas, like a set of parentheses curled together.

Something shakes my shoulder, jostling me from my half-asleep state. I open my eyes and spring to a sitting position when I see Bob staring down at me. The movement wakes the baby. He immediately begins wailing again.

"I'm sorry," I say, handing the baby up to Bob. "I lost track of things."

"Sorry for what?"

"I just . . . I fell asleep . . ."

"You guys must have played hard." Bob looks over at Todd, who is sprawled facedown on the couch, his left arm dangling toward the floor.

I brush my fingers through my bangs to straighten them. "How'd it go?"

"What?"

"Telephone pole."

He leans over Todd. "Wake up, bud. It's time to go."

Todd turns over, rubbing at his face. "Okay," he murmurs.

Gabriel is still crying. Bob lifts him up so they're looking at each other. "Hey there. Did you get a good nap? Hopefully not too good so you'll sleep the night. Yeah, it took a little bit of time to find, but we got it up and running again. How did things go here?"

"Fine." I stand and stretch my arms. "Todd was a little worried at first, but he got over it."

"Did Gabe ever let up?"

"He slept for an hour or so. But yeah, he cried pretty much the whole time he was awake."

"Well, thanks." Bob looks over at me and hesitates for a moment. "You okay?"

"Of course." I turn away from him and walk around the kitchen, gathering the remains of Todd's lunch and stuffing them in the diaper bag. *He can tell I was crying. I should have taken the time to wash my face before he came home.*

When I walk back into the living room, Bob leans toward me, balancing the baby on his hip. I hesitate for a moment, then sling the diaper bag onto his shoulder.

"It can be tough to deal with Gabe's crying. Believe me, I get it."

I glance at Gabriel. He's fallen back to sleep, his face pressed against Bob's shoulder.

I look away because suddenly, it hurts. It really hurts thinking how in a few minutes, the baby isn't going to be here anymore for me to hold, and that this is the way things are supposed to be. That Amelia could have looked just like that, felt just like that on my chest, but I don't get to hold her like I held Gabe.

"Hey," he says, taking a step toward me.

"No." I pass a hand over my eyes again. "No, I'm fine. Thank you for letting me watch them."

There's a long pause. "You're welcome . . ." He says it like a question.

I force myself to smile at him. "Really, thank you. I'd love to do it again sometime. And I don't mind the crying. It was okay. I'm glad I got to . . . yeah."

"If you carry Gabe, then I can get Todd and the diaper bag, and we can do this in one trip."

Unable to speak, I gather Gabriel into my arms. When we get to the car, I give him a last, gentle squeeze under cover of darkness before I slide him carefully into his car seat and snap the belts around him. It really is dark outside. So dark I can't see much at all when I shut the door and the car's interior light turns off. *There must be clouds covering the stars.*

"Abish." Bob's voice seems spectral, coming out of nowhere.

"Yeah?"

There's a long pause. I feel almost breathless, waiting for him to speak again.

"Thanks again," he says finally. "Good night."

"Good night."

As I walk back to the apartment, a stunning wave of some dark, bleak feeling overtakes me. I sit on the couch with my head bowed, struggling to keep a grip on my emotions.

Maddie stumbles in the door. She looks strange. Pale, not quite right. Her legs are shaking as she walks down the hall.

I don't even think. I jump off the couch, rush over, and put an arm across her back. "What's wrong?"

"Nothing," she mumbles. "Nothing. My medicine."

I hold the door to her room. She enters and collapses onto her bed.

"What medicine?"

"It's in my top drawer."

Inside the drawer are several baggies full of syringes and two small glass bottles. I pick one up and read the label. *Insulin.*

"How much?" I ask, hiding my surprise.

She holds out her hand. "Half. I can do it. Just fill it up, please."

I glance at her shaking arm. "You sure?"

"Give it to me," she snaps.

"Okay." I poke the syringe into the rubber top of the medicine bottle and draw it out until it fills the tube halfway. I flick out the air bubbles and hand it to her. She lowers her waistband and plunges it into her hip. I wince a little but watch until she's done, then take the needle from her, cap it, and slide it into the empty milk carton that is also stowed in the top drawer. I sit on the bed next to her and wait.

After a few minutes, she turns to me. "You can go. I'll be all right."

"I want to make sure. I don't want you on my conscience."

"I'll be fine. Good night, Abish."

"All right." I stand, trying not to shake the bed too much. "Good night." I step out of the room and watch as she slides under the covers, clothes and all. I turn the light out for her and walk to the bank of sinks outside the bathroom. I reach for my toothbrush and toothpaste and stare at my own tired, blotchy face in the mirror, my mind a confusing whirl of emotions. There's surprise and worry because of Maddie. Also loneliness and utter longing as I remember Gabe's face as he slept and the warmth of his little body curled up next to me.

Chapter
14

*I*f it was Bishop Barnes's intent in compelling Bob up onto the stage to get girls in the ward to notice him, then he has succeeded in spades. They glance at him as he walks into sacrament meeting. They keep an eye on him as he makes the rounds of the chapel doing his head count.

I have to admit it's not just his performance. All they needed was a reason to look at him. The real problem is that Bob is the perfect romance-novel character: tall, dark, and brooding.

He has two kids. You all know that, right?

They have to by now. Maddie's not the type to keep secrets.

Well, Seventeenth-Ward girls, kudos for your nonjudgmentalness. Apparently a divorced guy is acceptable dating material, while a widowed woman is too much damaged goods to consider.

Calm down, Abish. Remember? Singles wards are full of jerks. Don't let them upset you. I tap the sole of my shoe on the thin carpet, trying to focus on the sacrament meeting talks, but it's no use. I don't know why I'm so bothered, either. I mean, I've been ignored for three months straight and never felt all that bad about it before.

I watch him walk up onto the stand to sit with Bishop Barnes and his two counselors. *Don't be so selfish. Maybe he really does want to date and get married again. He's likely to, at some point. He has two kids to raise, and apparently Mom's not in the picture. And don't forget the fact that he can be sealed for time and all eternity in the temple again, while you cannot. That's going to deter potential suitors. Not that you care, Abish, right?*

Bob looks out at the congregation. His eyes land on me and I think he winks.

I mean, it's so subtle I can't be sure, but I feel the heat creeping up my neck just the same, and there's a kind of tightness to my chest, like I can't quite catch a good breath. I give him a stern little nod and shift my gaze back to the speaker.

In Sunday School, I find my usual spot in the back row (two open chairs on either side.) Shelley comes in late, talking in low tones to a couple of girls. She glances around the room, sees me, and smiles.

"You don't have to sit here," I say when she settles into the chair next to me. "If you have people you need to talk to."

"Nobody that I want to," she replies.

I suppress a chuckle. "How's the calling going?"

She turns to me. "It's fine. I'm sorry; that was flippant. For some reason, I say things I wouldn't when I'm around you."

"I tend to do that to people."

After the prayer, a vaguely familiar-looking guy walks to the front of the room. "I've been asked to substitute this week. Since the topic is such a sacred one, I'd like to open with a hymn: 'The Spirit of God.' Who can play for us?"

Shelley hesitates, glancing at me. She bites her lip as the silence continues.

"I'm not going to sneak out the back," I whisper. "Go play. It's what you want to do."

She stands, smiling and nodding at people as she walks to the piano. I sigh and rustle around under the chairs until I find a hymn-book. We're in the middle of the first verse when someone slides into the spot Shelley has vacated.

MILE 21

Bob.

I give him a sideways glance and continue singing, only a lot more quietly now . . . more like musical mumbling.

He leans over and hunts around for a hymnbook. There aren't any. I turn on the chair so that I'm angled slightly away from him, hoping it'll discourage the request I know is coming.

"Can I share?" he finally asks.

I edge the hymnbook slightly in his direction. He grabs one side of it and starts singing—a clear, smooth baritone. *Pavarotti. I'm sitting next to Pavarotti.* I keep my face angled away from him and start to mouth words instead of singing.

He glances at me. "You okay?"

"Yes," I whisper. *I'm making myself look even more of an idiot than if I just braced myself and got it over with.* I sigh and begin singing.

After a few seconds he's laughing. I can hear the tremble in his voice.

"Yeah, so I'm a lousy singer," I hiss, flinging my half of the hymnbook toward him. It nearly clocks him in the eye.

He fumbles and manages not to drop it. "Understatement of the year."

"You really know how to make someone feel good about herself."

"How did you get through Primary?"

"Tone-deafness is a rare gift. About as rare as perfect pitch, I'm told. And they mostly stuck me in the back during sacrament meeting programs and Father's Day performances."

"Remind me never to share a hymnbook with you again. Not only are you a bad singer, you almost gave me a black eye."

"Oh, believe me . . ."

I have no intention of sharing with you again. It's the response that belongs in the conversation, but for some reason the words won't form in my throat. And suddenly I'm having a hard time suppressing a smile because it actually is pretty funny. I never realized before how funny it is that I'm tone deaf, but I sing at church because it's what you do. I raise my voice, giving Bob a belligerent look as I continue. He smiles and sings louder too, holding the book between us again so that I can read the words of the second verse.

Actually, it was kind of a tense thing between me and Mark. With his piano playing, he was pretty serious about music. Anytime we sang together—pretty much just hymns in church like this—things got really uncomfortable. He probably didn't even know he was doing it, but he'd turn slightly away from me and raise his book higher to cover his face. And I'd sing more and more quietly because I hated that I was making him feel embarrassed.

While I'm churning away mentally, the song has ended and the lesson gets going. It's a familiar topic: temple covenants. I've heard all the quotes and scriptures before and so I'm kind of zoning a little. The heat doesn't help.

And then Bob raises his hand. It jolts me out of my reverie. In fact, the entire room turns to him. I don't think Bob's ever commented in Sunday School. Or at any activity, really. "There are more eternal covenants than just marriage," he says when the teacher calls on him.

"There are other covenants," the teacher agrees. The expression on his face is vaguely familiar. *Zipper guy,* I realize. *The one I lashed out at that first time I talked to the bishop. He gave me that same kind of smug-disapproving glance as I walked by, and so I announced to the room that his fly was undone.*

Now that I think of it, I vaguely recall seeing him at our apartment a couple times. *Yeah—he was doing the air guitar on our couch the other night.*

"But," zipper guy continues, still addressing Bob's comment, "according to the scriptures, marriage is the highest of the covenants. It kind of"—he shrugs—"umbrellas all the others. Marriage is what it's all about. If you fail in marriage, you've failed at all the other covenants too."

Bob's face, the way it kind of flushes and his jaw tightens, makes me act without thinking.

"The sealing covenant isn't just about marriage, either," I blurt out.

Zipper guy glances at me and then turns away—literally turns his back on me—and stares down at his manual. "To continue," he says, "the marriage covenant requires sacrifice. It's a perfecting process. I'd like to read something President Kimball said—"

My cheeks are hot, and my pulse is throbbing in my throat. "Did he just, like, completely ignore me?" I murmur.

"He's just a kid. Don't let it get to you."

"It got to you too." I raise my hand again. The guy looks directly at me twice, then looks away and continues on with the lesson. He calls on several others, even asks a question. I've caught the attention of the majority of the people in room. They keep looking at me with puzzled or nervous expressions.

Shelley finally speaks up. "Abish has something to say, Noah."

Noah-the-zipper-guy gives me a cold smile. "Oh. Okay, Abish, go ahead."

"Yeah, I can't remember what I *originally* wanted to say anymore. But I think I should ask how many times you've been married. You seem to know a lot about it."

Noah tilts his head and considers me for a moment. "No, I haven't," he replies. "But since it's something you should only do once, I figure it's good to wait until you're ready to make the right choice. Divorce is never a good option."

I raise an eyebrow. "Never? I'd say there are some situations where it's necessary. And as to the 'just once'; what about death? What about when a spouse dies?"

The silence is electric.

Noah shakes his head. "We have *one* shot at our eternal companion. I believe people don't respect that anymore. They don't think of marriage as real, as binding beyond the grave. I'd hate to get married when I'm not ready to make that full eternal commitment and end up being unfaithful to my eternal companion if it so happened we were divided for the short span of mortality."

"I think we'd all agree," I reply, my voice a little unsteady. Something warm touches my shoulder. I realize it is Bob's hand when I feel the fingers tighten. It completely melts my anger for a moment and leaves me with the real thing I'm feeling, which is sorrow. Deep, blinding sadness like I've never felt before.

Noah is talking like he isn't aware how pointed this is for me. *But he has to, doesn't he? Just like Bob and his kids, there's no way that with Shelley and Maddie and Steve and Julie knowing, the whole ward doesn't know about Mark.*

So why is he being so rude and condescending? Is it just the zipper thing? Has Julie been venting to him about me?

"This life," he continues, "is just a blip on the timeline of eternity. What we go through here isn't really much at all. Not compared to eternity. Not compared to the Atonement. Let's keep this from getting personal, guys," he adds, looking down at his manual again. "I wanted to touch on some things that the Apostle Paul said about the marriage covenant . . ."

It's too much.

I stand. Bob's hand falls away and I edge past him, heading out the door to the foyer. I sit there on a chair and put my fingers on my temples, trying to get my anger under control.

By the time Sunday School's out, I've gotten my breath back and I'm not seeing the world in a reddish tint anymore, so I wander into Relief Society with all the other girls. Avoiding eye contact, I make my way over to a deserted corner.

Someone who is not Shelley sits down next to me, surprising me. It's a girl I don't know: short brown hair, yellow flowered skirt. She gives me a small smile as the lesson begins.

That girl Steve and Julie hang out with—Amy-or-Emily—is teaching the lesson. I try to calm myself further by reading all the scriptures she's using. Something pops into my head while we're reading out of Jacob, so I raise my hand.

She doesn't notice me at first. When she does, it's a repeat of Sunday School: me with my hand raised stubbornly for three, four, then five minutes, and Amy-or-Emily ignoring me. Oh, she's noticed me—she glances at me a couple times. Most of the girls in the room are looking from one of us to the other with slightly nervous expressions. I see Shelley near the front of the room. She moves as if she's about to speak, but Amy-or-Emily manages to blurt out a quick testimony and end the lesson before Shelley can stand up for me again.

MILE 21

Someone gets up to say the closing prayer. I bow my head and close my eyes, but my thoughts are racing. *Am I suddenly in bad standing or something? Did Bishop Barnes tell people I'm not allowed to speak in class?*

I walk home slowly by myself. When I get there, the kitchen is crammed, as it is on most Sundays, with Shelley and Maddie and Steve and Julie all making Sunday dinner. Amy-or-Emily is also there. She gives me this weirdly triumphant look as I walk past them on the way to my room. As I'm changing, I'm wondering if the whole world is crazy or if it's just me.

My Asics feel comfortable now, hugging my feet but not binding them. *You can do it,* I say to myself as I stop in the bathroom, turn on the faucet, and take a long drink. I glare into the mirror, swipe my hair away from my face, and twist a rubber band around it.

Heading on up Second toward campus, I go slow and steady, paying attention to the power and spring in my legs. *Twenty miles. You've got enough energy. You've got the muscle. Do it.*

But I don't even come close. It falls on me early this time; I start feeling sick and dizzy at about ten miles. *Please, please . . . I just need to get to twenty miles.* The soles of my shoes on the pavement seem to whisper it: *Please, please . . .*

The world starts spinning. Before I know it, I've tripped up against a concrete planter, and I almost tumble into it.

A firm hand grabs my elbow and helps me up. In my daze, for a moment I'm sure it's Bob. After a few good breaths of oxygen, there's a strange sort of disappointment when the guy's face becomes sharper and I see it's a stranger.

"Hey, thanks," I say.

"Are you okay?"

"Just got out of breath. I'm fine. Have a good Sunday." I give him a wave, and he walks away.

Pen's waiting outside the apartment when I get back. He stands immediately when he sees me jogging slowly into the driveway. "Are you okay?"

"Um, yeah." I come to a stop and begin stretching. "What's up?"

"I thought it might be fun to play a little *Halo*."

I shake my head before he's done speaking. "Can't. Early day tomorrow."

"We can play for just an hour."

I give him a look. "You know it wouldn't turn out that way."

He grins. "'Kay. Sometime this week, then?"

"It's pretty busy with dead week just around the corner. Then finals. Haven't you been busy too?"

"Yeah. I just thought it's been a while."

I shrug. "Well, when your life is as messy as mine has gotten lately, video games kind of have a way of falling off the table. I don't need a fake apocalypse when I'm living in one."

"I'm cool with that."

"Thanks, Pen." I walk past him and start up the stairs.

"Do you want to hang out, then?"

I turn slowly and face him again. "Hang out, like what?"

"I don't know. Go out to eat? I could cook for you again."

I bite my lip. *I don't have the energy for this. Not today.* "Pen, please stop, okay? I'm busy right now. Why don't you hang out with Maddie?"

"Because I don't *want* to hang out with Maddie."

I sigh and brush my hand over my sweaty forehead. "Okay. Well, I've got to go to bed early, and I still haven't eaten."

Pen's face is pale, his jaw oddly set. "You really don't miss hanging out with me?"

"I like playing with you, Pen. It's just kind of a big deal for me to get things right this semester. Bishop Barnes has this contract. I can't mess up, or I'll end up at Aunt Cindy's or back with my parents. You saw how things are with them."

"I could help. We could maybe study together."

I manage a smile. "I don't think so. See you sometime, though, okay?"

He shrugs and walks down the driveway to his car. His door slams a little harder than necessary. He revs the engine and drives off with a squeal of tires.

MILE 21

I make my way into the kitchen. *Thank goodness it's empty of people.* I open the fridge: peanut butter, pickles, milk. I look in the cupboard even though I already know the rest of the list. *Cereal and several spoonfuls of peanut butter it is then. Not a very good meal after an exhausting run, but what can you do?*

I chow down a bowl and a half and down a third of my jar of Skippy. The veins in my forehead are throbbing and I'm starting to get an ache just above the nape of my neck when the doorbell rings.

I trot over and open it, and there stands zipper guy—*Noah*—and some other kid I don't know.

"Julie's not here," I say when I've gotten over my shock.

Noah narrows his eyes and smiles. "Abish, right?"

"Um, yeah." *Like you didn't say my name without any trouble just a few hours ago in Sunday School, when you were in the process of publicly humiliating and belittling me.* "So what's up?"

"We're your home teachers."

"You haven't come by before."

"We just got reassigned. Dave's mixing things up. Can we come in?"

It's the smile that does it—supercilious, condescending. The eyes cold, without a hint of apology.

I mean, I can't claim any credit for my actions. My body just seems to act on its own. My hand reaches for the doorknob and the next second the door slams shut, hard enough to cause a gust of wind that flutters a sticky note off the bulletin board on the wall.

I stand there for a few moments, completely surprised at what I've done. Through the window, I see Noah turn on his heel and march away. The kid who came with him looks at me through the window with wide, startled eyes. He turns around slowly and follows his companion down the driveway.

I walk into my room and sit on my bed. I'm half-frightened at my own actions, that I could do such an inexcusably rude thing. The other half of me is angry. So, so angry. It's that kind of anger that chokes you, that melts you, that leaks saltwater all over you without your permission. I kneel, put my face in my mattress, and suppress a scream.

I don't deserve this.

I didn't ask for Mark to die suddenly and leave me with eighty more years to figure out. I didn't ask to be put back in the singles ward. I didn't ask to have a gossipy, likely borderline-psychotic roommate who thinks I'm after her man . . . who happens to be an okay guy with problems of his own that I can't seem to stop thinking about.

I hate the fact that I care. Hate, hate it. *When did I start caring?*

There's a knock on the door. I stay quiet, hoping that whoever it is—*probably Shelley*—will go away. After a few minutes, though, the door opens and she walks in. "Oh," she says. "Sorry. I just wanted to . . ." She shrugs and takes a step toward me. "Noah was wrong to act the way he did. And Emory too in Relief Society. I've talked to the bishop about it. I just thought you should know he's going to call them in and resolve the issue, and I wanted to see if you'd like to be involved."

I stare at her, kind of at a loss for words. "No," I finally say.

"Okay. That's fine." She shrugs. "Don't let them get to you, Abish." She gives me a smile that is half-real, half-worried about how I'm going to react.

"Yeah, thanks."

She pauses before she shuts the door. "Your Savior loves you. You can always count on that."

"Thanks," I say abruptly. "I need to get to bed."

"Good night."

"Good night, Shelley."

A week passes. Classes are getting more intense; I can tell we're on a race to the finish. I'm handling it okay. Honestly, the only thing I'm not handling too well is seeing Nathan in biochem. He hasn't said much to me since I turned him down, and I've kind of removed myself from the study group. It makes things harder, but I've decided that maybe I don't belong in study groups. Apparently study groups at BYU-Idaho are half study-group and half group-date.

I stay long hours at the hospital. The nurses occasionally ask if

MILE 21

I'll visit one or two people when I finish up, but mostly I'm sitting, as always, with Mr. Eems. As the saying goes, I've grown accustomed to his face, and the music of his beeps and clicks helps me think.

One afternoon, Dalynne stops me as I pass the nurses' station on the way to his room. "He's passed," she says.

I turn so I'm facing her but still walking backwards down the hall. "Who's past what?"

"Mr. Eems. He passed away last night."

I stop. "He died? Mr. Eems?"

"Yes."

"But"—I shake my head—"he's been on the respirator for months. Why would he just die suddenly?"

There's conflict on her face. She looks at me, then frowns down at the open chart on her desk. "I'm not supposed to tell you for confidentiality reasons," she finally says, "but his next of kin decided it was time. We pulled the plug last night."

I feel cold. Achy. "Why didn't anyone tell me?"

"You're not in his family, Abish. You didn't know him when he was alive. You honestly feel you should have been notified? What would you have done?"

"I don't know. Watch it happen, maybe. Be there. His *next of kin* was never here."

"He was last night."

And you would have been intruding. The message is as clear as if she's said the words aloud.

I glance around, looking at the various chairs and alcoves that satellite the nurses' station. I want to say, "Where am I going to study, then?" But it would sound callous, like Mr. Eems was just an excuse for me to be here.

Well, he kind of was, wasn't he?

Sort of. I don't know. Then why do I feel like I've been punched in the stomach? "Can I see his room?"

"It's been cleared of all his things."

"But nobody else is in it yet?"

Dalynne sighs. "Not yet. Go ahead."

The fact that it looks just like any other hospital room isn't comforting at all. I glance around at the empty walls and the bare bedside table, trying to see if there's any sign Mr. Eems lived here for so long. I remember he had a few pictures, but I couldn't tell you what they were. The bed is neatly made with hospital corners. All the machines are gone.

I sit in my chair. It shapes itself around me, I've broken it in so well. There on the arm is that highlighter mark from when I was going over my notes to re-take my A&P final. *This was my room.*

Not anymore. Someone new will come. Probably not a coma patient, either. They'll probably be crotchety or private and won't want a regular visitor.

There's no place for me here anymore.

It hits me in the gut as I walk back through the nurses' station. "Bye, Dalynne," I manage.

"You aren't staying?"

I shake my head.

She smiles like she understands. Maybe she does. "See you, Abish."

I pause on my way down the stairs. After a few seconds of indecision, I exit the stairwell on the second floor and walk up to the double doors that lead to Labor and Delivery. Nobody's at the desk, so I walk over to the phone on the wall and pick up the receiver. "Hey," I say, closing my eyes and crossing my fingers. "This is Abish Miller. I just want to stop in one last time."

There are a few seconds of silence, then: "Hello, Abish."

I feel a warm rush of relief. "Hello, Amelia."

"How are you doing?"

"I'm . . . this is my last day here. At least, that's my plan. Unless, like, I have to come to the hospital again for some other reason, but hopefully that doesn't happen, right?"

Amelia's chuckle sounds tinny through the telephone receiver. "All right. I'll buzz you in. But you know the protocol."

"Yup."

The doors open and I walk into the world I've tried not to dream about or think about but still I've chewed over, like a dog worrying a bone, for the last fifteen months.

Amelia walks up to me. Her eyes are light blue and her black, cheek-length hair is as shiny as ever.

It was so surreal, having her be the one who helped me, because she is exactly the way I've always imagined my daughter would look. It's why I named the baby after her. It kind of gave her a tie to the living.

"Did you want to see the nursery?" Amelia asks, correctly interpreting my glance down the hall.

"Please." It comes out a whisper.

We walk slowly, almost like a wedding march or a funeral procession, or something even more sacred. I feel like there's a spotlight shining on me from somewhere, an invisible illumination that is more a warmth in my chest than anything else.

We pause at the glass windows and look in at the newborns resting in their little rolling cribs. There are three in there right now.

"All boys," Amelia says.

I watch the nurse, rocking in the corner with one of them. He has a fine feathering of dark hair. He's got his eyes closed but he's not asleep; he's concentrating hard on suckling the bottle she holds.

"Do you remember?" I ask. "How tiny she was."

"I do."

"She didn't take a breath."

"They can't when they're that young." She pauses and glances over at me. "She didn't feel a thing, Abish. She wasn't in pain."

"How do you know?"

She smiles. "I don't, but she seemed very peaceful. She just slowly left us. Do *you* remember?"

I nod, allowing the picture to come into my head: the tiny, human-like creature barely bigger than my hand. The redness of her skin against the soft white blanket they wrapped her in. The pursed lips, the eyelids with wisps of purple veins almost too small to see.

She didn't ever seem to wake up; she just changed colors and left. They weren't going to let me, but I insisted. And I held her, wondering.

One of the newborns is close enough to the window that I can see the flickering under *his* eyelids. *He's dreaming about something. Mama always said they dream about where they've just come from.*

"Thanks," I say, finally. "I think I can go now."

Bye, Amelia. I whisper it as I walk back through the doors. I watch them shut behind me, hiding the hall and nursing station from view. The tears are there, in my throat and at the corners of my eyes. I choke them back as I walk through the front lobby because there sits Mara, my least favorite receptionist.

Mara's the one who threatened to call security on me. It was after the Labor and Delivery unit put a notice out that I was no longer allowed in the hospital. I did it to myself; I kept asking to come back on the unit, and once I followed someone through the doors after they were buzzed in. Then Dalynne came up with the solution of me being a chaplain for Med-Surg so I could be here. *And now that's over too.*

Mara watches me through her square, rimless glasses with her usual sour expression. "I heard that your friend died," she calls as I'm about to walk through the doors.

I turn slowly. "Mr. Eems. Yeah."

"I'm sorry." She says it completely unconvincingly. "Is there anything I can do for you?"

"No. Thanks for asking."

As I walk down the street, I see that the trees are budding with bright green nubs all along their outstretched branches. I can smell cut grass. I feel a little bit like I'm waking up, or like I've been under a turned-down dimmer switch and someone just flicked the light all the way on. My black hair soaks in the sunshine, making my scalp tingle with warmth.

I open the door to the apartment and am startled to see Noah sitting on one of the couches. "Hello, Abish Miller." There's something odd about the way he says it. Mocking me, maybe.

"Hey," I reply. I walk into the kitchen and am met by the *other* lesson-giver who snubbed me last Sunday. There she is, leaning against the refrigerator with her arms folded and a belligerent look on her face. *Amy-or-Emily. Except I remember now that Shelley called her . . .*

"Hi, Emory," I say dryly, reaching around her to open the fridge.

She steps away. "You and I both know that I didn't do anything that you didn't deserve."

"Yeah? How's that?" I grab my cereal out of the cupboard. "Where's Julie?"

"She's not here. She said you usually come home around this time. Noah and I wanted to talk to you alone."

"Okay."

"Bishop Barnes told us to apologize."

I pause, about to take a bite of cereal, and lower the spoon back to the bowl. "The bishop asked you to apologize? To *me*?"

"And we are sorry," Noah puts in, rising from the couch and walking into the kitchen. "We didn't handle things the way we should have. What we *should* have done is what we *did* do on Sunday, which was tell Bishop Barnes directly about what you've been doing."

"What I've been doing? What have I been doing?"

Emory's face turns puce. "You know *exactly* what we're talking about. Julie told us all about that guy you hang out with. How he was here all during Christmas break and staying past curfew, how you guys were practically *living* together!"

It takes a moment for me to process this. When I do, I laugh. "Pendleton?"

Emory shrugs.

"I've never done anything with Pen except try to kill him with frag grenades. Sorry to disappoint you."

"Doesn't matter," Noah says. "Breaking curfew alone is bad. You signed the honor code."

"Yeah," I say, standing and folding my arms. "But it was an accident. I'm not used to single student rules. I was married for a year."

He smiles. "Well then, maybe you don't really belong in single-student housing."

"Oh, I don't disagree with you," I reply. "But that definitely is something you'd have to talk to the T—Bishop Barnes about, since *he's* the one who forced me to move into this apartment."

They exchange a glance. It is so frustrating and annoying, I'm tempted to say some things that definitely wouldn't meet the standards of single-student housing. Somehow I manage to keep my mouth shut and stalk down the hall to my bedroom instead. I sit on the bed for a few minutes, simmering.

My stomach rumbles. I remember my abandoned bowl of cereal there on the kitchen table. It's the last of the stuff from this week's shopping trip. *I don't really have any other food, and my next paycheck won't come in until tomorrow morning.*

". . . touch football," Emory is saying as I walk back into the kitchen.

Julie and Steve have both come in too. *They must have been waiting outside somewhere for Emory and Noah to finish with me.*

"You going to play, Abe?"

I look up at Steve, my mouth agape and full of Raisin Bran.

Julie, Emory, and Noah are looking at Steve too, with expressions similar to mine.

I swallow. "What?"

"They're putting together a football game in Porter Park. It'll be nice and muddy. You need to get out more. Meet some of the other people in the ward."

"But . . ." Emory starts, then stops when Steve glances at her.

"Mud football, huh?" I reply after a few beats of silence.

Steve gives me her Cheshire-cat grin. "We're starting at seven. Be there or be trapezoidal." Emory and Noah are pretending not to listen at this point; they're talking to each other. Julie's looking daggers at me.

Something inside me snaps. I narrow my eyes at Julie and give her the full benefit of my most evil, intimidating smile. "Oh, I'll be there," I say. I turn to Steve. "I might be a little late. I still have some studying to do."

Mile 21

People are already playing when I get there. Not everyone's participating in the game. There are clusters watching from the sidelines, Shelley among them. "Hey, Abish!" she calls, trotting over to me.

"Hey." I fold my arms, watching Steve wrest the ball from some girl who is laughing her head off. "Are you going to play at all?"

"Not this time."

"Yeah, you're not really dressed for it. Isn't it a little warm for long sleeves?"

She grins at me. "Modest is hottest. Sometimes literally."

"You wouldn't want someone to catch a stray glance of elbow."

"Hey, I've got to see about the refreshments, but"—she pats my shoulder—"nice to see you."

I survey the crowd and almost immediately notice Bishop Barnes and Bob. They're watching and chatting near the sideline. "Go!" Bishop Barnes yells suddenly. "Take him down, Stephanie."

"You said no tackling," I think I hear Bob say.

Yeah. I turn around, fully planning to slink away back to the apartment. *Maybe not.*

"Abe!" Steve calls my name across the field and makes emphatic gestures for me to join. She's got a rolled-up bandana tied across her forehead and mud streaks down her shins; she basically looks insane. "Be on my team. We're one short!"

I pause a moment, considering.

I really want to play. Not just to spite Julie; I'm aching for this kind of mindless, lighthearted silliness. But Bishop Barnes and Bob are here. They'll be watching.

Yeah. Why do you care so much? As I jog out onto the field, I'm feeling decidedly less cheery than I did on the way over.

We get through a few downs before I find myself sprawled in the mud. I do okay, but I'm feeling a bit timid, like Bob's eyes are burning holes in the back of my shirt, even though every time I glance their direction, he and Bishop are chatting and laughing with each other and not really paying all that much attention. Steve throws a long pass to me. I end up catching it and scoring the touchdown just before we take a halftime break.

The ward has provided sodas and taco salad. I feel pretty hungry, so I serve myself a large helping.

"Whoa." Maddie's voice surprises me. "That is a *lot* of calories."

I turn and face her. "Yep." I take a chip and shove it in my mouth. "Have some."

"No thanks. Have you heard from Pen lately?"

"Um." I glance over at Noah, who's standing not too far away, chatting quietly with Julie and Emory. "He came by the other day."

"Really?" Maddie looks completely crestfallen. She sets her diet soda down on the ground.

I study her for a moment. "You look a little shaky." I grab a plate off the table and put some chips on it, adding chili and cheese and some lettuce for good measure. I hand it to her.

She backs away. "No thanks."

"Maddie, you can't play with your blood sugar like that. Eat. Please."

Maddie has turned bright red. She glances around like she's looking to see if anybody heard. "Shut up," she hisses.

"Dude," I reply, lowering my voice, "don't mess with diabetes. You won't win."

"Thanks but no thanks," she snaps, whirling around and stalking in the direction of the bathrooms.

"There's Abish, making friends wherever she goes," Emory calls across to me. Julie puts a hand to her face, not successfully concealing her laughter, and Noah throws his head back, making a dramatic show of it. A few heads turn and look at me curiously.

"She'll be fine," I reply, but I feel my cheeks warm. As I go back out on the field, anger is taking hold of me again.

What did I do to deserve their enmity? Very little except rearrange some leftovers and make a cutting remark when I wasn't in my right mind. I'd think that being pulled into the bishop's office and chewed out would be enough to help them see how ridiculous they are being. *Apparently not.*

"You okay?" Steve asks when I join her at the centerline.

"Fine." I bend over, stretching my hamstrings.

"We need two more players," the captain of the other team calls. "Blake and Devon went home to study."

"I'll join you." Noah trots onto the field.

"Me too," Emory adds quickly, glancing at Noah.

As I watch them take their positions, I feel almost as if the heavens have opened. *Hello, angst. Meet your appropriate outlet: contact sports, a muddy field, and the very people you feel like grinding into the dirt.*

Trying not to make it obvious, I wait until someone passes her the ball before I tackle Emory. I half-land on her, sending her skidding across the deepest patch of mud on the field. I roll off her after a couple of seconds of feeling her squirm around. She comes up sputtering. Her shirt is covered, her pants are covered, and her hair hangs in slimy, brown tentacles around her mud-spattered face. "This isn't tackle," she manages. "You're not supposed to tackle me."

"Well, shoot," I reply. I don't say sorry, because that would be a lie. "Hope they don't give me a penalty." I pluck the ball from the ground where she dropped it and trip out onto the field, nimbly evading the other team's forwards.

"That was hard core," Steve murmurs as I pass her. "I'm all for a little smear tactics now and then, but you're going to have to be more careful. The bish specifically said no tackling. He'll make you sit out. I want you on the field."

In spite of Steve's admonishment, my jubilation carries me clear through the end zone for another touchdown. Or maybe it's not jubilation; maybe everyone's a little bit afraid of me now. I don't know and I don't care. I continue to play in the thick of things as the ball changes possession several times. We're not making much headway. I keep an eye on Noah, feeling anticipation fill my gut. *How good that will feel to press that patronizing smile into the mud.*

"Abish," Steve calls. She backtracks, running downfield, doubles up, and throws me a perfect long spiral, right over the heads of the scrapping mob in the center. I sprint hard and catch it, then turn on my heel and run for it. Someone makes a grab for me just before

I cross the goal line, but I squeak by with inches to spare. There's general outcry and applause, and someone whistles.

It's Bob. He's standing there, watching me with an amused expression. I give him a mock salute before I run back to the center of the field for the next hike.

My chance comes a little while later. Someone tosses Noah the ball and he looks surprised for a minute. He starts running. It's a little awkward, but he's doing an okay job dodging people. He's fast too. But I'm faster.

He changes directions.

I do too.

And then . . . and then, he passes the ball.

I'm so disappointed I could cry. I run after the ball, but what I want to do is run after Noah and send him face-first into the mud like I did Emory.

I glance over at the sidelines and see that Emory's been offered a towel and a water bottle, and she's busy talking to Bishop Barnes. *Yeah, she can't prove anything.*

I turn my attention back to the game, but my heart's not in it for the win anymore. I'm running slower, taking turns with less precision, not watching for fumbles.

And then—miracle of miracles—someone throws the ball to Noah again.

I speed after him. *I'm not letting you get away this time.*

"Hey, Robert, you playing?" someone calls from behind me.

"Yup."

I falter for a moment, watching Bob trot onto the field, and then turn I back toward Noah. I quicken my pace until I'm all-out running. The logo on the back of his T-shirt is my bull's-eye. I'm coming for him.

And then, suddenly I'm down in the dirt with the wind completely knocked out of me. "What?" I wheeze, looking up into Bob's grim countenance. "This isn't tackle."

"No," he says pointedly. "It's not." He stands and holds out a hand, but I scramble to my feet on my own.

MILE 21

"What'd you do that for? You're on my team, aren't you?"

"Yes." He turns and runs toward the melee, which is now at the end of the field near the other team's goal line. I stand there stupidly, watching him and wondering what just happened.

"Goooooo, Noah!" someone screams. It's Emory. She's jumping up and down on the sideline.

He's still got possession. Thank you, Heavenly Father. Rage makes a good engine. It gets me across the field faster than I've ever run before. I'm like a heat-seeking missile. I can taste sweet, sweet victory on my tongue.

But then I notice that Bob is headed toward me again full tilt. I try not to pay attention, to keep after my target, but as I see that determined look on his face, as I sense his large form gaining rapidly on me, I feel a strange thrill along with a healthy measure of sheer, cold terror. *"Nooo!"* I manage to shriek before he takes me down again.

This time it hurts. It really does.

As I rise from the mud, gasping, I mask my pain with my most supercilious smile. "Thank you for that," I gasp. "Maybe we should run after the ball, though?"

Noah's still in possession somehow. And he's coming my way. *It's like Heavenly Father's blessing me*, I think as I rise back to my feet. In a second, he'll be within a few feet of me. *It's like he wants me to—*

Yeah. It's like a bear cuffing a kitten. I'm on the ground again. "Stop it!" I shout. I try to sit up, but Bob won't even let me do that. He puts a hand on the crown of my head and casually pushes me down again. Then he leans over me and puts his hands on my shoulders, holding me there.

He doesn't say anything. I try to squirm out from under his hold, but yeah. There's no way on this planet. I'm so angry, I'm in danger of saying a few words that are not usually heard at BYU-I singles' activities. "Let go of me!"

"Nope."

I stare at him for a moment. His dark eyes are completely calm.

213

Suddenly—don't ask me why—I'm laughing, hard. So hard, I'm almost crying.

His eyes narrow, and he breaks into a smile. It's completely devastating. I couldn't move even if he didn't have me thoroughly pinned. "Learned your lesson?" he asks.

"Um." I bend my neck, trying to brush an itchy spot of mud off my cheek onto my shoulder. "Maybe."

"No maybe."

"Uncle. Open Sesame. Okay, *yes*, I've learned my lesson."

He backs off me and kneels, offering me a hand. I take it this time.

"What the crud do you think you're doing? I don't even have the ball, and I'm on your *team*!"

"Saving you," he says, leading me off the field, "from yourself."

"They're jerks. They deserve to be massacred."

"Massacring people is not the way to make friends. Do you want to be labeled as the ward you-know-what?"

I stop in my tracks and look up at him. "No. I don't know, Bob. What?"

He grins at me again—it kind of makes my knees wobble a bit—and then he turns and walks away.

"You still playing, Bob?" someone shouts.

"No."

"Abish?" Steve calls.

"I think I'm going home." I glance at Bob. He's busy chatting with Bishop, who is chuckling. *How come Bob never talks to me like that? He barely has more than three words for me, ever.*

I walk home wincing and rubbing my lower back. Yeah, I'm going to have some interesting bruises tomorrow.

Chapter

15

When I get back to the apartment, there's a surprise waiting for me in the living room. On my living room couch, to be exact. At first I can't quite believe what I'm seeing; I mean, Maddie is essentially a good girl. But there she is with Pen, and it doesn't look all that G-rated from where I'm standing.

"Uh," I say.

Maddie immediately stops kissing him. She pulls away, stands, and walks quickly to her room, keeping her face averted as she passes me.

My surprise has worn away, leaving a rising tide of annoyance and—yes—anger. "Hey, Pen," I say as I head to the kitchen. I grab an enormous bag of peas out of the freezer. "A word?"

"Hang on a sec."

I glance over. He's running his fingers through his hair. He looks up at me and raises his eyebrows. *A challenge.*

"Don't be a jerk," I growl.

He pulls on his shoes, tying them carefully. Slowly he rises from the couch, stretching his arms. "Yeah?" he asks as he saunters, finally, into the kitchen.

I wrinkle my nose at an overpowering whiff of Armani cologne. "What are you doing?" I ask, keeping my voice quiet. It's not easy.

"You said she and I should hang out. I'm just taking your suggestion. Why?" He gives me a sly look. "Are you jealous?"

I narrow my eyes at him. He looks back at me, his face the picture of innocence. It takes me a few moments to get myself under control, to try to come up with a way to say what I want to say without baiting him. "Please don't mess with Maddie, Pen."

He shrugs. "She's having fun."

"She's fragile. You don't want to deal with the fallout, believe me. She's not one of those hardened . . ." I swallow the word I want to use, ". . . girls you usually go out with one or two times."

"I'm just playing." There's a sulky note in Pen's voice.

And that's done it. "Not with Maddie, you're not," I hiss, glancing down the hall. "Unless you want another black eye."

One word escapes his lips—one that I'm kind of tired of hearing from him, to be honest. He turns and walks out of the kitchen to the door.

"You know better, Pen," I call after him. "Are you really this much of a jerk?"

He whirls around in the doorway. "No, I'd say that'd be you," he replies, and shuts the door, hard.

I stare at it for a few moments. *Does he mean I'm a jerk, like, I'm jerking him around?*

I didn't ask him to make me dinner. I didn't ask him for anything except fun. Games.

There was the kissing.

Yeah, there was that.

I head down the hall. I pause, then knock quietly on Maddie's door.

When she doesn't answer, I open it anyway and find Maddie huddled in her covers.

"What did you say to him?" Her voice is muffled by her pillow.

"You don't want to know."

"He's into you, isn't he?"

"Maybe. Oh, no," I add, as I see her shoulders start to shake. "Don't, Maddie. He's not worth it."

"You keep saying that," she chokes. "Not just you. I keep hearing that: *He's not worth it.* Why does it keep happening to me, then? Maybe *I'm* the one who's not worth it."

I walk over to the bed and sit down next to her. "No, it just means you need to choose a different kind of guy. You need to find people who treat people around them with respect, who aren't just looking for people to use."

She shudders away from the hand I put on her arm. "Go away, please," she says. "Please, just leave me alone."

Somehow I make it through the rest of the week sitting on hard plastic chairs, in spite of my sore tailbone and other various bruised anatomy. When Saturday finally rolls around, though, I'm glad for the break. I study for hours lying on my bare mattress. It's more comfortable but also smelly.

Well, there's something you can do about that.

I lean down and reach under the bed. The wedding quilt is crumpled, but still clean. Not smelly. After I'm done making the bed, I stare at it for a few minutes before I lay down on top of it.

It's okay. Warm, soft. Reminds me of Mark. Reminds me of our marriage, of the life I lived for a year, and then refused to let go of for another year.

I almost decide to stay home from church the next morning. I'm so tired of it. Not just the Noah and Emory and Julie drama—it's everything. How ridiculous people can be. I feel ashamed that I got sucked into it. My cheeks burn as I remember the football game.

And of course, there's the whole thing with people spreading rumors about me and Pen. I'm sure it didn't stop with Julie and her friends. How many people in the ward believe the things Julie's spread about me? Does Bishop Barnes believe it? Emory and Noah said he told them "he would address the issue." Does that mean I'm in for it? Is Bishop Barnes going to ask me for another interview?

I should just play sick and stay home.

I pull the covers over my head and doze off for a while. There's a rap on the door. I don't answer, but it opens anyway.

"Are you getting up?" Shelley asks. "We leave in fifteen minutes."

"Don't you have, like, morning meetings and stuff?"

"No. Ward council is after church. Come on, hurry up. I hate walking in late."

I pull the covers off my face and give her a good, hard glare.

She smiles sweetly. "Don't let immaturity and spite win."

"Honestly, I don't care."

"Really. Then how come you're not getting ready to go? If you really didn't care, you wouldn't mind walking into sacrament meeting, and Sunday School, and Relief Society . . ."

I shudder and prop myself up on my elbows so I can see her face. "It's not that I care. It's just that I don't have the energy to deal with it. Not today."

"Well, deal with it." Her voice hardens. "Or else they'll think they've won. Come on!" She tears the comforter off my bed, grabs a skirt and blouse out of my closet, and tosses them to me. "Fifteen minutes," she repeats, striding out the door and shutting it behind her.

The internal debate is rather contentious. In the end I get dressed, slide on my Sunday shoes, and head to the bathroom area to run a comb through my hair. I pause in front of the mirror and fiddle with my bangs for a few seconds, trying to get them to do the cute twist thing Shelley's so good at. I give up and smooth it back into the usual neat ponytail. As I put the comb back, I find my fingers closing around my old clutch purse, which contains makeup that I haven't worn for many moons.

The mascara's a little clumpy, so I put a couple of drops of water in and shake it up. I'm just finishing with my lipstick when Shelley puts her head around the doorway to say it's time to go. We walk out to the parking lot—Shelley, me, and Maddie. Shelley starts the engine with just the three of us in the car.

"What about Steve and Julie?" I ask.

"Walking's good exercise. Twenty minutes until church starts; they have plenty of time."

"Why are we leaving right now, then?" Maddie pouts. "You didn't let me finish ratting my hair."

Shelley doesn't answer. I eye her in the rearview mirror. She catches my gaze, colors, and pretends to check her blind spot. "You look nice," she murmurs.

At this, Maddie looks over her shoulder. "Oh yeah, wow. Your face looks so much better with makeup."

"Thanks."

Her eyes narrow. "Who're you trying to impress?"

"Nobody. It's war paint."

We get to sacrament meeting early enough that the room is pretty much empty, and we sit in the second row. Bishop Barnes stands when he sees us. "Abish, come see me after sacrament meeting, please," he calls over the slightly-out-of-tune tinkling of prelude music.

My face gets hot. *Is he trying to make me look bad, calling me out in sacrament meeting? He didn't believe what Emory and Nathan told him, did he?* I glance around the room. Thankfully the few people here don't seem to be paying much attention. "Sure," I reply, trying to sound careless. "Your place or mine?"

He gives me a grim smile and mutters something to one of his counselors.

After everyone files in and the prayer and opening hymn are over, Bob starts making his way up and down aisles. He's still drawing the eyes of every female in the room. I force my own away and focus studiously on the second counselor, who is making announcements.

Maddie, sitting next to me, lets out a little squeal.

"What?" I whisper.

"Didn't you hear? He just said we're having a Cinderella Ball the last day of finals. I've always wanted to do one of those!"

"What is a Cinderella Ball?"

Shelley leans in. "You bring a shoe, toss it in the pile with all the other shoes. The men pick one and dance with you if it's yours."

I groan.

Shelley pinches my shoulder. "You're coming, Abish, so you can just quit right now."

"I am *not* coming."

Bob walks up to his assigned seating next to the bishop and his counselors. The sacrament hymn starts. As I drone tonelessly through "There Is a Green Hill Far Away," he looks down at me sitting here in the second row and gives me a quick smile. I can't tell if it's approval or amusement at my terrible singing.

I slip away right after the closing prayer, edging through the bunches of people chatting, flirting, and otherwise getting their money's worth out of the five-minute buffer between sacrament and Sunday School meetings. I slink down the hall toward the office. I get there before anyone else, even Bob and the bishop.

It's kind of restful sitting in the empty room, but it also gives me a bit of time to stew. *If he accuses me of doing stuff with Pen, I'm going to go postal.*

I mean, why should I have to defend myself? I'm honestly starting to wonder if maybe I did something to deserve this. And that's pathetic. What I should do is tell Bishop Barnes this ward is getting to me and he needs to let me leave it and figure out something else that actually works.

I'm going over the words in my head—how I'm going to convince him—when Bob bumps into the glass door. He's carrying two large boxes. I leap from my seat and open the door for him, then close it behind him as he edges past me. He sets the boxes under the desk, then takes his place in my chair. "Hey," he says.

"Hey."

We look at each other for a few seconds. And I don't know if it's the football or what, but seeing him sitting there in his suit, looking kind of like Marlon Brando, I totally feel like tackling him to the floor.

Maybe that's not the right way to put it.

Well, no. It's *exactly* the right way to put it.

"Abish." Bishop Barnes enters the glass doors and gestures curtly with two raised fingers.

I jump up and follow him down the hall, feeling distinctly queasy. Because all the planned conversations in the world kind of go out the window when you're talking to Bishop Barnes.

"I didn't do anything with Pen," I say as soon as we're sitting. "Julie's upset at me because I rearranged the refrigerator. She's got some kind of OCD thing. She's a complete nutcase if you ask me. Not because of the OCD, I mean, but because ever since I moved in, she's looked at me like I'm . . ." I trail off, seeing the confusion on his face. "All righty then. What did you want to see me about?"

He shakes his head. "I just wanted to give you a break from Sunday School after last week. What Noah did was inexcusable. I thought it would be too much to expect you to walk back in again."

I'm completely dumbfounded. I stare at him for a few moments. "Um, thanks. I'm okay, though."

He meets and holds my gaze. "You are?"

"Noah is kind of a jerk. I wasn't really courting his good opinion."

He doesn't smile but some lines make an appearance around his eyes and in his cheeks that tell me he's feeling like smiling. "If only I could dilute you, Abish," he says. "Spread you out through this ward."

"*What?*"

"You come on a little strong sometimes, but you don't let immaturity rattle you. I can't tell you how many people I've had come to my office with petty offenses and roommate problems."

"Did you make them do push-ups?"

He frowns.

I shrug. "Never mind. So did you actually have something to tell me, or am I just here so I don't have to be in Sunday School?"

There's a silence. He looks down and fiddles with a pad of paper he has sitting there in front of him.

Bishop Barnes, nervous to say something to me? Whatever it is, it's got to be pretty good.

"How is the journal writing going?" he finally asks, looking up again.

I shrug. "It's hard to reinstate habits. I've written a couple times. I tried reading my scriptures once and . . ." I shake my head.

"And what?"

"I just . . . the scripture I turned to reminded me of Mark. They all remind me of Mark."

"They all remind you of Mark."

"The one I read was about how life and death can't separate us from the love of God, but I couldn't help thinking about Mark. How we're separated."

I don't know why I'm spilling like this, but once started, it's like a faucet I can't turn off. "I just don't know how to deal with it, to be honest," I continue. "I don't know what to think. What am I supposed to do with the rest of my life now that I've already attained the 'highest level of glory,' or whatever, but I don't have a life here to live with him? I don't know why you have me in this singles ward. I can't get sealed again, so I can't date. I've—"

"Hold on," he says, raising a hand. "Back up. You can't date?"

I blink. "Well, I mean, no. A woman can only be sealed once. Right?"

Bishop Barnes nods.

"And even if they would cancel my sealing with Mark, I'd never want that. I'd never . . ." and suddenly I'm choking up again. "Man," I say, rubbing a hand over my face.

"I'd offer you a Kleenex, but I'm afraid you'd take my hand off."

I glare at him and pull the box across the desk, whipping out two and crumpling them in my fist. "What am I supposed to do? I can't date. I can't saddle some poor guy with me for time but no eternal glory. And if I ever had more kids, they wouldn't be . . ."

"*More* kids?"

And I'm gone. I don't want to be crying, but my body has decided for me. It goes on a couple minutes. I cover my face with my hands, but my shoulders are shaking and I have to make full use of the Kleenexes in my hand. I grab several more too. "Um," I say when I get my voice back again. I hate the way I sound—all pathetic and trembly. "Mark and I were pregnant before he died. We didn't tell anyone because we were waiting four months. My mom had a lot of miscarriages, and I didn't want . . ." and I lose it again.

MILE 21

A hand reaches across the desk and covers mine.

"I lost her at twenty weeks."

"How long after Mark died?" His voice brings me back to earth. I take the crumpled Kleenex and scrub savagely at my nose, then meet his gaze. "I don't know. A few weeks."

He just looks at me with those keen, gray eyes. There's sympathy, but not pity.

Which I'm grateful for. Sympathy I can handle, but I can't stand pity . . . it's like people taking your tragedy and hanging it like a millstone around your neck. *You must be so traumatized. You must miss them so much all the time. You must.*

I clear my throat and take my hand away, tucking it into my lap. "So, I mean, I can't really entertain any ideas of dating. I've got an eternal family already. And I can't break that. I can't lose them— Mark or Amelia."

"They wouldn't let you," Bishop replies. "Nobody would want you to. But you've got things a little mixed up, Abish. Shelley told me what Noah said to you during Sunday School, about being unfaithful to a spouse who dies. You don't really believe that, do you?"

I pause a moment and consider. *Do I? If I dated again, but I'm already married, isn't that the definition of being unfaithful?*

"Man wasn't meant to be alone, Abish. Woman, either."

It so closely mirrors a few thoughts I've been having lately that I can't discount it. "How does that work, though?" I argue. "If I ever got married again, the person I married would be completely cheated. We'd go through this life and then in the next, it'd be all over. And like I said, any kids we had wouldn't be born in the covenant. How does that work? I couldn't do that to someone I . . . I loved." I pause and take another swipe at my nose, then crumple all the Kleenexes into a large ball and toss toward the can by the door. I'm actually kind of surprised I make it; it's pretty far away.

"Good shot," he says. "And technically, any children you have would be born in the covenant—the one you made with Mark."

"Great. Then I'd be taking all his kids away too."

"Well, let's consider this for a minute. Do you believe in the plan of happiness?"

"Of course."

"Do you believe that it is a plan of happiness? That we're meant to be *happy*?"

"I believe we will all be ecstatically happy if we can manage to get through this life without screwing up so bad that we forfeit what comes next."

Bishop shakes his head. "It's about this life too, Abish. Heavenly Father wants you to be happy here too. Living life the way you've lived it since your husband passed, can you say that you've been happy?"

I sigh. "Sometimes. Not as much lately. But maybe that's because I'm human, you know? I'm not perfect. I could be happy if I just had enough faith in the next life, and in what will happen once I've made it through all this"—I shrug—"what I've been given to go through."

"So your plan is to live out the rest of your life alone."

I nod.

"I believe you're meant for more than that. You are meant to be a mother. You are meant to be a wife. You are meant to be whatever it is you want to be apart from those things too."

"But how?" I explode, throwing up my arms. "How can I? The gospel doesn't have a little footnote for my situation. I can't be sealed again, period. And I'm not sure I'd want to be, either! I mean, what happens in the next life, then? Do I have two husbands? What happens when I live the next sixty years of my life falling more and more deeply in love with some guy and raising kids with him, and then when we die, we don't get to be together?"

"The gospel *does* have a footnote, Abish. It's called, 'we don't know everything right now.' It's called faith."

I stare at him. I so badly want to believe it. I don't think I realized up to this point how much I want to be able to move on. It's not that I don't love Mark. It's not that I don't mourn for Amelia and want to be with her. It's just that what he says makes such terrible sense. He's voicing all the thoughts I haven't let myself think these last few months. "I need more than that," I croak. "I can't build my life on just that. I can't expect some poor guy to build his life on such a shaky foundation."

"It's not shaky, Abish. It's truth. The wise man builds his life on Christ. On mercy, the Atonement . . . trusting that God knows what we need and can give it to us."

I'm feeling so scattered, I don't know what I'm thinking. "I'm . . . I . . ."

"I'm not asking you to go out and date someone tomorrow. Just consider. Ponder, pray, and read your scriptures. While you are doing those things, be open to all options so that God can tell you what he wants for you. Let Him bless you the way *He* wants to. I have a feeling you're not done with marriage, with children, in this life." He gives me a nod. "You can go now if you want. Go home, and get out that journal. Open those scriptures and look beyond your tragedy. Let yourself *look*. That's all I'm asking."

Oh, that's all, is it? I rise from my seat, keeping my face carefully turned away.

"And cut that out," he snaps. He walks around so we're facing each other. "You've got a right to mourn. Don't be ashamed. You should let others mourn with you." He puts a hand on my shoulder, squeezes it, and opens the door for me.

When I step out into the hall, my mind is reeling. I'm thankful that the office is still empty of people. *Guess Bishop Barnes planned that one pretty well.*

Except for one thing.

"Hey," Bob says as I walk past. "Are—"

"I'm fine," I snap, and then for some reason, I'm running. You'd think I'd have learned by now that Sunday shoes—even if they're Timberland—aren't the best running equipment, but apparently I'm not always in charge of my body.

It's warm outside. The sun glares down on my exposed neck. The wind whips my skirt around, but I can't care. The feelings—mortification, guilt, and yes, maybe a bit of longing—don't leave me; they run with me. *The world is full of pain. Pain in my feet. Pain, sending my hair in a dark cyclone around my face.*

I lean into the turn as I peel off along Cemetery Drive. I'm running fast, so fast that I'm panting and coughing when I come to a stop.

It's the same manicured grass. The same smooth marble. Looking at it, seeing how nothing about it has changed since the day the grass grew over the grave, I realize with a bleak sort of finality that he's gone. *Not forever.*

But for a good long time.

There aren't any tears, but my chest and throat are aching. I turn and scout for proper ornamentation. Across the road is a tree loaded with white blossoms. I trot over and break off a couple branches, a big one and a little one, barely more than a sprig. I kneel there and look at the grave for a couple of minutes, then lay the larger branch across the stone right under his name, obscuring the dates. The little sprig I lay off to the side, as usual.

"Hey." The voice from behind me is startling, not just because it's a voice in the silence, but because it's Bob's.

I shut my eyes tightly for a moment and grimace. I take a deep breath, stand, and turn to face him.

He's still got his suit on. "You're hard to catch," he gasps. "Of course, I'd probably do better in track pants."

I open my mouth, then shut it and just look at him: solemn dark eyes; broad, handsome face. Big shoulders. *Does he know how imposing he looks in that suit?*

Probably.

"I just wanted to make sure you were all right," he ventures finally, breaking our long silence.

"I'm fine." I glance at the stone behind me. "Just paying a visit. You know."

Bob kneels down next to it. He glances up at me. "Do you mind?"

I shake my head. It's surreal, seeing him kneel there on the dirt over where Mark's body rests. It's like I'm dreaming and awake at the same time, and the two images have superimposed.

He moves the branch so he can read the dates. "He died pretty young."

I kneel down next to him. "Twenty-three."

"That's sad."

"Yeah." He's so close. *Have I ever been this close to Bob before? Well, yeah. There was the tackling thing.* My face colors. I shake my head. "Yeah, it was sad. Very, very sad."

He gives me a look that says, *Go on.*

"It happened during an indoor soccer game. He was playing, and I was watching because I was . . . because I didn't feel well. The ball went out of bounds and he ran over and grabbed it, and lifted it over his head to throw it back, but something funny happened. Something was wrong, I could tell. He dropped the ball and then he ran across the gym toward me. The way he was running was weird too. He stopped in front of me and gave me this look . . ." I glance at Bob. "Do you mind me telling you all this?"

"No."

"He had this really intense expression, like he wanted something from me. And then he . . . fell." I sigh and stretch my legs out in the grass. "My whole life, my dad has told me the story of Abish in the Book of Mormon."

Bob's face is troubled. "She converted a bunch of people. She touched the Lamanite queen and king and they woke up."

I nod. "Yeah, you got it. I thought I was supposed to save him. In that moment I was sure I was going to bring him back. I knelt down right there and prayed. I touched him, and when nothing happened—I'm a nursing major, so I knew some things—I turned him over and began CPR. I kept trying and trying to resuscitate him even though I could tell his chest wasn't rising or falling and I wasn't going to be able to do anything with mouth-to-mouth. The EMT had to pull me off him. It was kind of stupid."

"No," Bob says quietly. "Not stupid."

"He died almost instantly. Those few seconds as he ran across to me were his last. He was dead that moment he fell. By the time the EMT got there, he would have been brain-dead even if they could have bypassed the clot . . . blood clot, which blocked off the two main passages of his lungs."

The breeze whips up, blowing over us. It makes the trees sway and rustle. It ruffles Bob's hair and sends mine lashing around my head again.

Bob reaches over and touches the smaller branch.

"We were expecting. I didn't carry her to term. It happened three weeks later."

"How far along were you?"

"Twenty weeks. They let me hold her, but she never opened her eyes. I guess in a way, she wasn't really ever alive, maybe. She didn't take a breath."

"What was her name?"

I pause for a moment. "Amelia."

"A good name." His voice cracks as he says it, and then suddenly he reaches over, circles an arm around my shoulders, and gathers me against his chest. It's painful, the way he holds me so tightly there for a minute. I feel like my heart is in my throat. When he lets go, I'm startled to see tears on his face. He brushes them off with the back of his hand. "Life," he says. "It's pain, isn't it?"

The words are out of my mouth before I give them permission. "Life is pain, highness. Anyone who tells you otherwise is selling something."

He laughs. We look at each other. It's suddenly a little awkward. "Well." He rises to his feet and offers me a hand. "I'm not really up to running back. I can't afford to dry-clean this suit right now."

I take his hand and he pulls me up. As we walk back toward town, he keeps an arm around my shoulders. It's kind of nice, because now that I'm not running, the wind is cold. It's nice in other ways too, but I can't quite face such things.

"Thanks," I say abruptly as we approach the apartment.

He lets his arm fall away. "I could use someone to watch the kids Saturday morning. If you think . . . if you want to."

"I love your kids." My face heats up. Again, it's my mouth speaking without my brain's permission. "I mean, sure."

He gives me a half smile. "See you Saturday, then." He turns and walks up the street.

I wonder for a moment where he's going, and then realize his car is probably still parked up on campus.

The kitchen and living room are bustling with people. A good portion of them are people who don't want to acknowledge my presence.

"Hello, Noah," I say as I pass him. "Hi, Emory." They both nod without making eye contact. "That color looks nice on you, Julie." I add, reaching past her for my Raisin Bran.

Maddie comes up beside me and pulls an apple from her cupboard. I notice her hands are shaking. I frown at her, and she gives me a look like, *You don't want to go there.* She takes a bite of apple and walks slowly out of the kitchen, leaning on the doorway for support as she passes it.

"Shelley," I ask, "may I borrow your phone?"

"Sure." She hands it to me. I punch in a number and wait through the rings, tapping my fingertips on the counter. *If he doesn't pick up, it might actually be nicer. Because then I can leave a nasty message unhampered by actual conversation.*

"Hey?"

Too bad. Oh well. "Yeah. It's Abish."

"Hey." His tone is decidedly unfriendly.

"Stop messing around with Maddie. I told you before, but I mean it, Pen. You're going to drive the girl into a coma."

"Dude, I haven't seen her. Haven't called her. She's the one who keeps leaving me messages."

"Don't tell me you haven't encouraged her."

There's a long silence. "You told me not to mess with her, so I haven't called her back. She's crazy, and she's not even that attractive, to be honest. I mean, she's not a bad kisser, and it's clear she's willing to give up a lot more than most BYU-girls, but—"

"Shut up, Pen," I interrupt him.

"What? You're asking me, and I'm telling."

"You don't know anything about women. Get a clue."

"Why . . ." His next words are kind of muffled, but I can tell they're not ones you'd find in the Bible. Or you would, but not together. "Abish," he says, "I'm sick of playing games with you. Either you want me or you don't. If you don't, then stop calling me. Okay?"

"Okay."

My ear hurts; I realize I'm mashing the phone into it. I press the end button and hand it over.

I take a deep breath to collect my composure. "Thanks, Shell."

Shelley takes the phone. She raises an eyebrow at me.

"I think I should go talk to Maddie," I say. I trudge down the hall, Shelley just a step behind me.

I open the door. She's laying there huddled on her bed, her cell phone on the pillow beside her. "I'm okay," she snaps. "I'm eating."

"Not enough," Shelley says.

"I just want to be a normal size."

"You are a normal size, Mads. You're cute."

"Before I started on the insulin, I was *hot*, not cute."

"Messing with your body's natural balance will only make it worse," I interject. "Don't ruin your body for some guy."

"Guys don't notice 'cute.' Not when there are ten thousand skinny girls walking around campus."

I clear my throat and then remember how I'm incapable of lying. "It's a moot point anyway," I say instead. "Pen said he wants you to stop texting and calling. I'm sorry, Maddie."

Maddie glares at me. "He already told me. But thanks."

"Oh." *One notch up on the scale of responsibility for Pen. And one on the scale of unnecessary jerkiness for me.* "Is there anything I can do?"

Maddie shrugs.

Shelley walks over to sit next to Maddie on the bed. "Do you want to go to a movie together tomorrow, just us girls? And we could order Chinese from New Fong's."

Maddie shakes her head again. She scoots down and pulls the covers over her head.

Guess that's my exit cue.

MILE 21

Actually, wallowing sounds pretty good. I trudge over to my room, grab my journal, and lie down on my bed, but nothing comes to mind that is worth writing. I open my scriptures at random and it's some long list of Jewish genealogy. *Yeah, no answers there.*

I kneel down next to the bed and try to say a prayer, but I feel foolish, like I'm trying to talk to Mark again or something. *Do we really get answers to prayers, or are we just answering ourselves? Is Mark really up there somewhere, or did he just diffuse into the disorganized ether of the universe?*

I mean, I believe. But is there a way I could know *for sure? And while we're at it, is there a way to arrange for us to have a chat so I can find out what he wants me to do?*

Finally I copy Maddie, climbing back into bed, pulling the wedding quilt over my head. I think I smell just the faintest tinge of Old Spice, but that might be my imagination.

Chapter 16

*B*ob brings the kids by early. Anticipating this, I've put on clothes even though it's only seven thirty—an obscene time to be up and dressed on a Saturday morning.

"Hey," Bob says when I open the door.

"Hey," I reply. We just kind of stand there, staring stupidly at each other.

"Can I watch cartoons?" Todd asks, pushing past us.

"Oh. Yeah." I pick him up and plop him onto the couch. "I've got it all queued up and everything. I used to love watching cartoons on Saturday mornings, when my dad didn't make me get up and help him plow fields." I glance over at Bob.

He smiles. "Sounds about right."

"What, me plowing fields?"

"That you're a daddy's girl."

I smile, but there's suddenly a lump in my throat. I take the diaper bag from him, set it on the table, and reach for Gabriel, who's still asleep. As his hot face settles against my collarbone, I turn away from Bob. "You're late. Get going."

MILE 21

He takes my shoulders and turns me back so that he can look at my face. "It makes you sad seeing him. Does he remind you of Amelia?"

"Yeah. I don't know." I try to use my shoulder to get rid of the tear that's made its way down my nose. "Sad, happy. Mostly happy, but sad that I can't . . ." I'm about to say *keep him*, but I manage not to. "Go ahead. See you in a couple of hours. Don't fall off a telephone pole."

"Thanks for taking them. Todd really likes you. You're good at distracting him. It makes things easier for me to know he won't be watching through the window for me to come home. I apologize in advance if Gabe has a hard time again."

My heart is behaving oddly, thumping in my chest like a bass drum. I wonder if he can tell. "Don't worry about it," I reply.

He releases me. "See you in a few hours."

After the door closes behind him, I settle in next to Todd. Gabe stirs a little in my arms but stays asleep.

"Why are you crying?" Todd asks. He's got a finger in his mouth and a slightly worried expression.

I pull up the neckband of my shirt and dry my eyes. "It's not a big deal. I'm just a little crazy like that sometimes."

Todd grins, takes the finger out of his mouth, and uses it to make a loopy sign by his head.

"Yeah. But not so crazy I can't beat your behind at Uno."

"Not until Transformers is done."

"Okay. After Transformers."

Steve's the first of the roommates to wander into the kitchen. She's got a mouthful of lather and a toothbrush. She stops short, gazing at us through the doorway. "'Obshkish?"

"Come again?" I say. "I don't speak toothpaste."

She spits it into the sink and turns on the faucet to rinse it down. I make a mental note to put my dishes through the dishwasher before using them again. "Bob's kids?" she asks.

"This is Todd," I reply, patting Todd on the head. I nod down at my chest, where the baby is nestled, warm and still blissfully unaware that he's being babysat. "And Gabriel."

"It's kind of sick, you know. Worming your way into his affections by targeting his kids."

I turn. "Good morning, Julie. Sleep well?"

Julie, who is leaning in the doorway, shrugs and heads over to the fridge. She opens the freezer door and grabs a cup—I'm guessing one with used ice—and pours herself a glass of orange juice.

"Dude," Steve says. "That was harsh, Jules."

"And I'm betting," Julie continues like nobody has spoken, "that he just likes you because his kids like you. He's vulnerable. Single father, newly divorced. He probably doesn't even know about Pen, does he?"

"Julie!" Steve slams her hand on the table. "Cut it *out*. Okay?"

Julie's back is to both of us, so I can't see her expression, even though I'd really like to at this moment. "I'm just telling the truth," she mutters.

"The truth the way you see it isn't necessarily the truth," I reply, keeping my voice even. "You know, I could tell all kinds of truths about you, but I'm a polite person, not a jerk."

Steve snorts. "You say plenty when you want to, Abe."

"Yes. Well, let's not say any more at this moment." I nod at Todd, who is frowning at me. "Hey," I say to him. "Is Transformers over?"

"Yeah. Blue's Clues is on next."

"Do you want to watch it?"

He shrugs, glancing at Julie, who's sitting at the table with her cereal, and then at Steve, who's leaning against the counter with her arms folded. He's got that bleak, kind of hunted look in his eyes that I remember from Christmas dinner with the Barneses, in that unguarded moment when he role-played with his olive people after the silliness of tap-dancing octopuses. And I'm remembering his words again too: *Don't yell. You're waking up the babies. Please stay.*

I clear my throat. "Let's play that game, okay, Todd?" Carefully, slowly, I lay Gabe on the couch and, miracle of miracles, he stays asleep.

"What are you playing?" Steve asks.

Julie makes a huffy noise and stalks out of the kitchen. I hear a door slam a few seconds later.

"Uno," I reply.

Steve sits with us as I deal the cards, so I deal her a pile too. After a few rounds, I ask the question that's in my mind. "Why are you friends with her?"

"She can be fun. She's good for the one-liners. Kind of like you." Steve grins and slaps a blue three on top of Todd's seven.

Gabe wakes up about halfway through the game, so I have to drop out to comfort him. He howls and stiffens when I pick him up. I sit on the couch and rock him. Steve tries making faces at him. It catches his attention, and he's quiet for a few seconds, but then he takes a shuddering breath and starts wailing again.

Maddie and Shelley wander out.

"Bob's kids?" Shelley asks.

"Yep." Steve and I say it at the same time.

Maddie kneels down next to Todd. "Hey. You're pretty cute."

He gives her a scathing look and lays down another card. "Can you play Uno?"

"I think so." She stands. "But not right now. Shelley and I are going grocery shopping." She glances at me. "I've deleted Pendleton from my address book."

It takes a few seconds for me to absorb the change of subject, and the fact that apparently Maddie's not upset at me. "Good," I say, shifting Gabe to my other side.

"You win, Todd." Steve stands up, laying down her cards. "Sorry. Julie and I have an intramural soccer game to get to." She glances at me. "I'd invite you Abish, if you weren't babysitting."

"Thanks for thinking of me."

One by one they leave. Julie's the last one. I'm expecting a cutting remark as she heads out the door, but she doesn't say anything.

Gabe has finally stopped crying. He's leaning against my arm, keeping his body angled away from me. He's looking up at me with two fingers in his mouth.

"Hi, baby," I say. "Feeling better?"

After a few more seconds of staring, he lays his head on my shoulder. I pat him, feeling in danger of waterworks again.

"When's lunch?" Todd asks.

"Not for a bit," I reply. "You want to try cartoons again?"

Todd doesn't answer. He's murmuring to himself and sliding the cards around, picking them up and letting them scatter over his lap.

I have all of five minutes of peace and quiet before there's a knock on the door. "Come in," I call, startling Gabriel from his half-drowse and setting him wailing again. I stand and begin to rock from foot to foot.

I almost drop him when I see Suzy walk into the living room. "Um, hey."

Suzy looks from me to the baby to Todd, who's sitting and playing with the mess of Uno cards on the floor.

"They're a friend's," I say. "What are you doing here?"

She sighs and flops down on the couch. "I had to get away from Mama. She's totally hounding me about the SAT and prom and finals."

"Yeah, I understand."

"It's worse now that she doesn't have you to talk to. It's like she's taken all her worry about you and poured it out on me so she has something to do about it."

"I'm sorry to hear that. What can I do to help?"

She gives me a nasty look. "You don't have to be rude. I'm just answering your question."

"Okay." I sit, settling Gabe on my chest. He's whimpering, but I think he's falling asleep again. "Let me rephrase that. Why are you here?"

Suzy picks at her nails for a few moments before she answers. "Abish, you have to talk to Dad."

"No, I don't."

"He's eating his heart out over you."

Dad's face pushes its way into my mind in spite of all my attempts to block it. I think of the necklace in the little box at the bottom of my suitcase. "I can't yet." My voice is hoarse.

Suzy flings herself off the couch and glares down at me. "You're not the only person in this world, you know. You're not the only one sad at happened with Mark. People are sad for you too."

"I know."

"And you need to come get your stuff. Mom is starting to look through it to see what she can get rid of. There's a box or two I think you don't want her getting into. It's got all Mark's stuff in it."

It's like a slap to the face. *Mark's stuff.*

Our life, that Mama dismantled when she cleared it all out of the apartment.

What do I do with our life? Am I moving on or what? How can I move on? And yet I've done it, at least a little; somehow I'm not thinking of him as much anymore. I glance down at the dark head on my chest. Baby Gabe is asleep again, his little pink mouth slightly distorted because his face is squished up against me.

I'm thinking of the answering machine, of all things. The message with our voices recorded on it.

The idea of Mama erasing that and giving the machine to D.I. or something makes me feel sick to my stomach. "I didn't know you guys had boxes at home. I thought she put it all in storage."

"Most. Not all."

"Well, that's good to know. Thank you. Tell her not to do anything; I'll come by to get it soon."

Suzy nods curtly and walks out the door, then pauses on the first step. "You know," she says, her voice trembling a little, "I sort of miss you, Abish."

"Thanks for the bracelet," I say quietly.

She nods again without turning to face me and trots down the stairs.

How's that for a load of guilt?

The cynical thought doesn't change how it affects me. *Suzy, who has always been so stoic, so tough.*

Who shared already-chewed-gum with me and used to laugh like crazy when I pushed her high on the swings those summer days that we walked to Keefer Park with Mama. Those bike trips into town and down Bridge Street; sometimes we'd stop in the Book Depot and choose something. Sometimes we'd go by Falls Drug and pick out a candy bar.

I feel a sudden longing for those times when Mama was indisputably the smartest person I knew, and she had the answer to every question. When something as simple as a candy bar was enough to make me feel like the luckiest person in the world.

Gabe dozes for the last hour or so. I'm glad, because I honestly think I can't take more crying without starting in again myself. As it is, Bob immediately asks me if I'm okay when he comes through the door.

"Yeah, I'm fine," I reply, kneeling to help Todd gather up the cards.

"Something's up."

I chuckle. "You're clairvoyant now?" I look up at him and see that he's regarding me calmly. It's that same expression he had when he was cheerfully shoving me down into the mud.

I break eye contact and shove the untidy pile of cards back into their cardboard box.

"Yeah, well, it's okay. Nothing I can't handle."

He folds his arms and leans against the wall. "Shoot. I don't have anything else to do today."

"Except listen to me whine?"

"I can't imagine you whining."

I shrug, quashing the rush of pleasure I feel at the implied compliment. "Well, if you're really that curious, my sister came by. She warned me Mama's going through my stuff. There are a couple boxes I'd rather she didn't touch."

"Let's go get them."

I look up again, startled. "What? You must have better things to do."

"I was going to take the boys to the park, maybe. Where do you live?" He leans over Gabriel. "How did you get him to go to sleep?"

"Saint Anthony. I think he tired himself out crying."

Bob gives me an apologetic look.

"No," I say quickly. "It's okay. Like I said, I don't mind."

"Well"—Bob scoops up the baby and grabs the diaper bag—"at least let me return the favor, okay? I'm betting there are some good parks in Saint Anthony."

I shrug. "Yes. There's a park that's got the river all around it."

"Yeah!" Todd jumps and pumps a fist in the air.

"But you don't have to. I'm sure I'll get up there sometime."

"You're worried about your things," Bob argues. "And you don't have a car. And you'll make me feel better if you let me do you a favor."

"Mark's things," I correct. "Mark's and my things, from when we were married."

He looks a little taken aback. "Okay," he says after a pause. "I can see why you'd rather do that on your own or with your family." He nods at Todd. "Come on, kiddo. We'll head over to Porter Park." He smiles at me. "See you sometime."

"No," I say hastily, imagining myself bent over boxes with Mama breathing down my neck. "I told you everything about Mark already, so maybe I could handle you being there when I sort through stuff too. Yeah, if you could take me, that would be nice."

He hesitates, then nods. "I'd be willing to wait in the car and just help you load stuff."

"I'm not exactly sure what to expect. Suzy just told me there are boxes, and Mama's on a D.I. rampage. Thanks for offering, Bob."

He smiles and holds the door for me, even though one arm is loaded down with baby and diaper bag and I really should be holding it for him. "No problem."

The drive is gorgeous. Bob opens the windows on the way up, and the breeze smells like new alfalfa.

"Don't go above thirty-five in town," I caution as we approach the off-ramp. The memory of my last visit here pops into my mind—how it ended with Pen trying to kiss me and then speeding off in a huff.

We drive through town and wind our way into the fields. There are a few tractors out tilling.

"So, you really know how to drive one of those things?" Bob asks, pointing as we pass one.

"Yeah. I'm not that great at it, though. It's a real skill to drive straight rows. Mine usually end up curved and coming together on either end like a banana. There's where we turn." I point out the white house gleaming in the sunlight. "That's where we're headed."

After he pulls up to the gate, Bob gives me a questioning look.

I glance back at the kids. Gabe is still sleeping, and now Todd is zonked out too, his face pressed to the window.

I smile. "I could use some help carrying the boxes. And you'll be a good buffer."

"Buffer?"

"You'll see."

But it's my dad who answers the door. His eyes gleam when he sees me, and I feel kind of like I've been punched in the stomach. "Hi, Dad."

"Hi," he replies. He looks over my shoulder at Bob.

"This is Robert Hartley from the ward." I explain. "He said he'd help me carry a few boxes. Where did Mama put my stuff?"

"Your things from the apartment?"

I nod.

"Some in the storage unit. Some are in the garage." He leads the way toward the door that leads from the kitchen into the garage. He holds it open for me and Bob to pass. "Do you want any help?"

I hesitate. "No, thank you."

He nods, then turns his ice-blue gaze on Bob. "Hello."

"Hi," Bob replies, and they shake hands.

They're just about the same height, I realize. And build too, except Dad's bulk has traveled from his shoulders and chest to a lower center of gravity.

Dad looks at me again. "If you wanted to go fishing," he says, "I renewed your license. It's in your tackle box." He turns then and heads back into the house.

MILE 21

Several boxes are stacked along the walls in the garage, so it takes a little while to find the right ones. Bob helps me lifts down some that are too tall to reach.

Once I find them, it doesn't take long to go through them. Marks' clothes I leave pretty much as they are. I feel an odd pang when I find his razor—barely used—in a Tupperware tub full of odds-and-ends. I pick it up and look at it for a few seconds, then glance over and see that Bob is watching me. I give him a tight smile and set it down again.

"I understand," Bob says. "Don't worry about me, okay?"

"Yeah. Thanks."

When I'm finished looking, I've got a small shoebox with some stuff: Mark's blue tie—the one he was wearing when I first met him. His journal, which I should probably give to Anne eventually. The answering machine wasn't in any of the boxes, so I have to assume it ended up in the storage unit.

"Do you think your dad might want to take you fishing?" Bob asks as we walk back to the car.

I sigh and fiddle with the door handle. "Yes."

"I'm not telling you to. Just wanted you to know I won't be offended if you don't go back with me."

I look up at him. "Do you have a license?"

"A fishing license? No. Why?"

I give him a grin. "I'll buy you one."

He sputters for a few seconds. "No, you won't."

"This is the best fishing in the world. I bet you haven't been in a while. Do you like to fish?"

"Well, yeah, but—"

"Then come on. It's not that expensive for a day permit. Not much more than the cost of gas to get up and back. Consider it payment."

Bob squints through the window at the backseat, where Todd and Gabe are still asleep. "This trip was to pay you back for helping me."

I shrug. "I guess you still owe me a favor, then. Just so it's out there, I plan to keep you eternally in my debt."

"Well, that's one way to string someone along."

241

I give him a quick glance. There's amusement in his eyes, but he's not smiling. "Todd might like to try too," I add, deciding to let it go. "There's a kid-size rod . . . I'll go get it."

We get the license and some ice cream from Fall's Drug on Bridge Street. Todd wakes up a little grumpy, but a double-scoop of huckleberry cheers him right up. Gabriel grins when he sees his ice cream cone. It's the first time I've seen him smile.

We spend a half hour at the park and then head upriver to a spot that my dad really likes. I feel my skin start to burn, but it's too much fun watching Todd do his excited, wild-flying casts and seeing the way Bob's face relaxes as he watches the flowing river.

I'll rub aloe vera all over me when I get home, I tell myself as I help Todd untangle his line and reel it in for the umpteenth time.

He grins at me and casts again. It goes okay this time. I look over at Gabriel, who is sitting in his carrier in a flat, grassy spot just above where Bob is fishing. The wind gusts, making the baby gasp a little and ruffling Bob's dark curls.

I walk over and stand next to him.

"He likes you a lot," Bob says, nodding in Todd's direction.

"Thanks." I remember Julie's comment this morning about Bob only liking me because his kids like me, and my stomach feels suddenly heavy. "Is that why you . . ." I don't finish the question, and my face turns bright red.

Bob reels in his line, then casts again. "No," he says. "It's not."

"Okay." *Gosh, that was a direct question. Guess I deserved the direct answer.*

"It's nice to see people giving him attention," Bob adds a few minutes later. "My mom spoils him rotten. I let her. I think Todd needs it. That might be the one upside in all of this. Valerie wasn't . . ." He shuts his mouth and does another cast. It's a little crazy, almost catching a bush on the other side.

"Yeah," I say. "That's not fair. I've practically told you my entire life story."

He gives me a look that is half-annoyed, half-resigned. "I guess."

"I mean"—I shrug, feeling suddenly like a complete heel—"I

guess you don't have to talk about it if you don't want to. It's your business. I just can't help but wonder because of some things Todd has said. And just . . ." I shrug again.

There's another long silence. Bob casts one more time, then reels in and carefully sets the rod on the ground. "Let's go sit by Gabe," he says.

We climb up onto the grass and sit there quietly for a few moments. Gabe is cooing and trying to grab at gnats. I pick off a few pieces of grass and start braiding them together to give myself something to look at other than Bob, who is clearly trying to figure out how to begin.

"We met in high school," he finally says. "I was a football star, she was on the drill team." He gives me a sidelong glance. "A cheerleader. You pegged it."

"I didn't mean . . ." I shrug. "Sorry. Go on."

"We dated our junior and senior years. I fell head-over-heels. When I got back from my mission, I proposed. I had a full-ride to the University of Utah. I was going to be pre-med there. She . . . I think she liked the idea of being a doctor's wife and getting out of Rexburg. I mean, I loved her. And I'm pretty sure she loved me too. It just wasn't enough for her. After Todd was born, things got difficult. We'd bought a townhome in Sugarhouse so we wouldn't be renting and planned to sell it when school was done. It was a bad idea. I thought so at the time, but Val insisted it would be a good investment. She came down pretty hard. She can do that, sometimes. So I caved and we signed the papers. And you know how things went from there. The housing bubble, all that. In order to afford payments, we went with a variable interest loan. The payments kept going up each month."

I break a long stick off the bush next to me and stir the water with it. "Yeah."

"We tried for a couple of years to just make do, but finally I had to quit school and get a full-time job to keep up with the mortgage. And then Val decided she would go to school instead. She was a pretty decent dancer and thought she could give lessons from home. So she also took some classes from the U."

"Okay."

"It was really stressful. We knew we were upside down on the house. And then there was the look on Val's face when I'd come home after a day of installing cable and climbing poles. She expected to marry a doctor. Instead she ended up with me—Bob, the cable guy." He gives me a cynical smile. "You know what I mean."

"No."

"Come on. I saw it on your face that first morning we met: *What is this guy doing in my kitchen?*"

"But it wasn't the cable guy thing. It was more . . . a defensive thing."

"Yeah?" He takes the braided grass from my fingers and sets it on the ground. "How?"

My face is heating up again. "Well, I walked in on you in my—uh, pajamas. And then you practically treated me like a harlot."

"Yeah," Bob says. He reaches over and tweaks my ponytail. "Well, I was being defensive too."

It completely startles me. "Of what?" I manage to keep my tone matter-of-fact.

"Well, there I was installing cable, a week after I signed the final papers on my divorce. Some hot girl walks in on me wearing just *pajamas*. You tell me."

My face is burning. "Tell you what?"

"I might be a good guy, but I'm a guy, after all."

I start to stand, but he grabs the cuff of my jeans. I struggle against him. "Cut it out."

He's laughing at me. "Haven't we already tried this? You know how it's going to end."

An image flashes into my mind: Bob, leaning over me, pinning my shoulders to the ground. For a just a moment, I'm tempted.

"Fine," I say, sitting back down.

He scoots closer to me. "Are you still worried about that? You've apologized twice already. Like I said, let's call it even. I was rude enough to you."

"Yeah, it's kind of hard to get over something like that."

"Why?"

"How would *you* feel walking in on a perfect stranger not just in your pajamas, but also looking your absolute worst? And then to top it off, you saw how crazy I was with the pictures and . . . all the stuff."

"But I understand that now." He shrugs. "And if that was your worst . . ." He stops, and it's his turn to go a little red.

"You're just making me feel better. I hadn't shaved my legs in, like, a week."

"That's not an issue. Girls don't realize . . . yeah." He stops again.

I glance up at him. "Don't realize what?"

He shakes his head. "You know, I bet it's hard, dating when you've already been married."

I settle myself more comfortably, crossing my legs in front of me. "Hard being in a singles ward too. Hard to remember what you're allowed to say and not say."

"What you're allowed to *think* and not *think*."

"Yeah." I grimace. "So, did you guys lose the house?"

Bob leans back on his elbows so that he can see me better. "No. We eventually sold it at a loss. It meant I had debt to work off, probably a couple years' worth before I could go to school again. Val wanted to declare bankruptcy. I thought it wasn't right. We fought and fought. Eventually I couldn't take it anymore, so I caved again. It was terrible. People don't realize what a process that is, bankruptcy."

"I don't doubt it."

Gabe stirs a little. I nudge his carrier with my toe, rocking it.

"It woke me up. I started putting my foot down, saying we needed to follow a budget, that we couldn't live beyond our means. I told her I wouldn't be going back to school as a pre-med student because I didn't want to be that much in debt. I told her I wanted to move back home to Rexburg and do a degree in mechanical engineering. My dad is a heating-cooling guy; I figured I could take over the business."

I nod. "That's cool."

"Val couldn't take it. She's used to having things she wants, and like I said, she liked the idea of me being a doctor. She started going off with the friends she met at college, dancing, partying." This bleak expression comes over his face, just like Todd's.

"You don't have to—" I begin.

"No, it's okay. She went on a trip to Vegas once without telling me, or finding a way for Todd to be watched while I was at work. She just left him in his bedroom with the door shut; he was too little to reach the handle. I found him when I came home after work. He was sleeping on the floor in front of the door."

Todd, curled up on the floor all by himself, wondering what he did to deserve it. I do my best to quash my anger because I know it won't help anything.

"We fought a lot toward the end. I'm not proud of it. I know it affected Todd. I said a lot of things I shouldn't have said. I didn't know what to do or say to change things. She left for good three weeks after Gabriel was born. To be a dancer, she said, but I think she was just done."

"Oh." I look over at Gabe. "That must have been hard on him."

"It was. He was nursing and I had to make a fast switch to formula. For a while there, he lost weight. The pediatrician was worried he wasn't thriving. Looks like Todd's headed back."

Sure enough, Todd is approaching with his fishing pole trailing on the ground. I notice that the tackle is missing.

"He cried a lot," Bob continues. "I was up a lot of nights, walking the floor with him."

"Oh," I repeat. I reach out and touch the baby's face. The idea of him . . . a tiny baby, crying on Bob's shoulder, missing his mother, has me choking up a bit.

And then more than a bit. I try to stop, or at least keep it quiet for Todd's sake as well as for the sake of my own dignity, but it's just pouring out. I can't stop, not even as Todd settles next to me on a patch of soft grass.

"Hey." Bob tucks an arm around my shoulder. "Hey, I'm sorry."

"For what?"

"You don't need anything else to cry about. I didn't think how what I was saying might affect you. I guess I tend to do that."

"No, I don't really cry all that much usually. To be honest, it's sort of a relief."

"She's just crazy, Dad," Todd says matter-of-factly. "Don't worry about it."

I reach down and dig my fingers into Todd's thigh just above his knee. He thrashes around on the ground, giggling and getting his leg tangled in the fishing line.

A few minutes later, Bob stands and holds out a hand. After he has lifted me to my feet—a thing I don't need, but don't mind, anyway—he slings Gabe's carrier onto his arm. Todd puts his hand in mine.

"We didn't catch anything," Bob remarks as we walk back through the brush to where we parked the car.

"This isn't the best spot for fishing this time of year. All the good places are closed until June first."

"Okay."

"Fishing's about the experience. Every good fisherman knows that. Being out in nature." I gesture expansively with my free hand. "Enjoying the possibility that you *might* catch a fish."

"You don't have to argue the point. I get it."

Get what? I don't ask.

After we've put my boxes in the trunk and the two kids in the back seat and have settled into the front, there's an odd sense of peace. "Bob," I say as we pass the Sugar City exit.

"Mm-hm." He turns to give me a quick glance and I see the same kind of thing in his face. It makes me happy and also a little frightened.

"You said life is pain. Do you think maybe sometimes Heavenly Father puts people through things so they can experience things, I don't know . . . " I shrug. "Like later, with more joy? Appreciating what they have because they know what it's like to be . . ."

"Lonely?"

My face warms. "Maybe."

"I think that's a possibility."

There's a rough spot in the tread of the tire I'm sitting over. As it turns, it makes a repetitive noise—*Mark, Mark, Mark.*

I find myself saying a little internal prayer as we approach my driveway. *I want to have faith. I do. But I still need to know* what *to do. Please tell me what to do.*

"Heaven," Bob murmurs when he pulls up to the curb.

"What did you say?"

"I just had the thought come to me. I bet the fishing in Saint Anthony is great in the winter too. My dad used to take me out of school to go ice fishing on the Ririe Reservoir. It was like heaven out there with him, watching the snow come down." He pauses. "What's wrong?"

I give him a smile that I hope isn't as conflicted as I feel inside. "Nothing. I'm great. Thanks for the ride, and the . . . yeah."

"You're welcome," Bob says. He's looking at me with those calm, dark eyes. Serious, and a little puzzled. There's something else there too.

I lean closer and put a hand on his shoulder. "Thanks."

He smiles a little. "You already said that."

"Yeah." I shrug. "Well, back to the Freshman Factory, I guess."

"Freshman Factory?"

"It's my name for the incubators that nurture . . ." I gesture to a couple of chattering girls walking toward us on the sidewalk. "Well, that."

Bob shakes his head, studying me with suddenly narrowed eyes. "You're really hard on people, Abish."

"Yeah?" I grin at him. "Rexburg is full of jerks, right? Didn't you say that?"

"Yeah, I guess I did." He leans back, resting his arms on the steering wheel and gazing out the window. "I don't want to stay that way, though. Do you?"

"Stay what way?"

He shrugs. "Jaded." He looks at me again. "I don't think you're really like that, Abish. I've seen how you are with your friends, and with Todd, and Gabe. You really love people. Don't harden yourself. You'll break your own heart in the end."

M ile 21

And suddenly my throat is feeling thick. My heart feels like it might be breaking a little right at that moment.

He reaches over and brushes my cheek with his hand. "See you later, Abish."

I swallow, then nod. "Bye, Bob."

"Ew," someone says—someone from the backseat. I turn and make a face at Todd before I open the door and step out.

I force myself not to stand there and watch him drive away, but I make my walk up the driveway slow on purpose so that I don't get to the door until his car's too far away to hear anymore.

Chapter 17

*D*ead-week always reminds me of one of those fifties-era horror movies about old-school insane asylums. Olivia de Haviland in *The Pit*. We have it all in our apartment the week before finals—weeping, wailing, gnashing of teeth, random outbursts of mania and misplaced frustration, several-days-unwashed bodies, and people obsessively muttering what seem to be nonsensical things under their breath.

Shelley isn't around much. She's had to confine herself to the library so that the random ward members who constantly venture by to speak to the Relief Society president don't interrupt her studying. Steve and Julie are marooned in their room when they're not going off to some wild game or party in the evenings. Julie has taken to ignoring my existence. She walks around me in the hallway and she talks around me too, even if I'm actively participating in a conversation. Maddie is going running a lot in between bouts of studying. She's still not eating enough, but she's not getting noticeably skinnier, either. The upside is, she seems to have set Pen aside. She hasn't mentioned his name for days.

MILE 21

By the time Saturday rolls around again, we're *all* pretty much stewing in our own crazy juices. "If I have to read the conjugations for *instruis* even one more time, I'm fully ripping my head bald," I hear Steve tell Julie.

I'm actually confident for finals. It's been a rather book-centric semester for me with the way I've sidelined myself from all other activities. And now that warm May breezes are blowing through the open windows of our apartment, the old summer hankerings have wakened in me. I walk by Smith Park and think of ice blocking. I run by the Rexburg canal and imagine myself on an inner tube with breezes cooling my skin. But those things aren't as fun when you're by yourself.

I think a few times of calling Bob. Or honestly, more than a few times; I think of it anytime I'm not mentally rehearsing enzymes and their functions for biochemistry. But I don't. Do it, I mean. With going to school, working, and being a full-time dad, Bob definitely doesn't have it in his schedule for frivolous activities like tubing.

Still, it would be nice to see what he looks like in swim trunks.

Bad Abish, I tell myself, turning the pages in my well-battered text. *Focus on nucleotides; there's a good girl.*

A rap sounds on the door, and Steve sticks her head around. She's still got all her hair, so I have to assume she's done studying French. "Hey, your mom's here."

I leap off the bed, sending my textbook crashing to the floor. "*What?*"

"She's in the living room. She's got a box or something for you."

I head down the hall, muttering under my breath. *If it's any of Mark's and my stuff, I will scream. I really will. I'm sure Dad told her I already went through it all.*

". . . use the Scotch-Brite brand," she's saying as I enter the living room. "They aren't much more expensive and they last so much longer, and your landlady will appreciate how much cleaner you get your refrigerator during cleaning checks."

"Uh-huh," Maddie says. She gives me a relieved look. "Hi, Abe."

Mama's expression changes as soon as she sees me. Her eyebrows

251

Sarah Dunster

draw down in the middle and her mouth firms. "*Hija*, I've brought you summer clothes. It's too warm for your sweaters and jeans."

"I can't wear shorts on campus, Mama." I give her a quick kiss on the cheek and grab the box from her. Honestly, I'm so relieved I almost want to kiss her again. *Just summer clothes.*

Mom wrinkles her nose and holds me out at arm's length. "You smell sweaty. You're going to give yourself heatstroke."

"I ran fifteen miles this morning."

She frowns. "Fifteen miles? That's too far. You'll be getting hip replacements by the time you are my age."

"No, Mama. I'm training for a marathon."

Her frown becomes more ferocious, and I'm immediately sorry I confided in her. "And when is this?" she snaps. "Why haven't you told your family you're running a marathon?"

"It's not a big deal. It's not like Boston or St. George or something. Just the Ogden Marathon."

"Well, that's fine. Where's Bob?"

This throws me completely. "What do you know about *Bob*?"

Steve wanders into the kitchen and reaches up into her cupboards for a box of cereal.

"Your father says you brought a boy over. How come you didn't wait until I came home so I could meet him too? Does he live in town?"

"No, Mama. I mean, yes, probably. But it wasn't like that. He was just giving me a ride because I babysat his kids."

Her eyes widen. "He has children already?"

"Yes." I heft the box onto my shoulder. "He's the guy who installed cable into your fourplex. Robert Hartley. Remember?"

"The boy who saw you naked."

Steve and Maddie both freeze. Maddie's mouth drops open.

Great. Now the ward will be hearing all about my secret career as a stripper. "I wasn't naked," I retort. I turn and glare at Maddie. "I walked in on him by accident when he was fixing the cable in my apartment. I was wearing pajamas."

Maddie covers her mouth. I think she's hiding a grin. It just

252

infuriates me more. "I have to get back to studying," I say, trying to keep my tone level. "So, thank you for the clothes, but—"

"Don't hurry me out, Abby. I brought some more empanadas . . . good studying food. Let me go get them."

I roll my eyes.

"Hey, I wouldn't say no to an empanada," Steve says.

After the empanadas are delivered and Mom chats with Steve for a few minutes about the proper cleaning of counter grout, she finally consents to be ushered out the door. I follow her down to the car because I know it's what she expects me to do, and it isn't wise to disappoint Mama's expectations.

"It's not a good idea to get involved with a man with children already," Mama says as she slides into her seat. "Especially one who has seen you naked."

I narrow my eyes at her and shut the door. *Yeah, you'd cooing and fussing over those kids as soon as you met them. And Bob is just your type.* "Don't worry so much, Mama," I say through the open window. "We're not . . ." I can't really finish the sentence, so instead I lean in and give her another peck on the cheek. "Drive safely."

Finals go off without a hitch. Each time I exit the testing center, I feel better about school. When my last final is finished, an enormous weight lifts off my shoulders. *I can do this. I really can. It might not be fun, but it's doable.*

As I head home, feeling lighter and less worried than I have in a long time, there's a new breath of motivation. *Today's the day—I'm going to break through my barrier.* As I put on my socks, I notice that my two little toenails are turning purple again. *Time for new shoes already?*

Well, you have put a lot more mileage on them lately.

I don't make it, though. I'm gasping at fourteen, almost like I can't get enough air, and, once again, barely finish sixteen. It's infinitely more frustrating after the victory of finals. What am I going to do when I'm running my marathon? Stop and walk?

No. Too humiliating.

But how will it be any different then than it is now? I'm simply incapable of running a marathon. I physically cannot do it.

As I enter the apartment, I notice the girls are clustered around the mirrors outside the twin bathroom doors. They're all dressed up as if for a high school prom—even Shelley, who is fussing with Maddie's hair. Her dress has long sleeves, obviously altered from the original design. It looks a little strange.

"Where have you been?" she demands as I walk down the hall.

I shrug.

"You're coming tonight, aren't you, Abish?" Maddie asks.

"To the *Cinderella Ball*?" I reply, employing a fake English accent.

Shelley gives me a look. "You promised."

"I did not."

"Bob will be there."

I stop short. "No, he won't. It sounds like exactly the kind of thing he would hate."

"Bishop strong-armed him into it. Said he needed him to chaperone. I was there at ward council meeting when it happened."

I snort. "Chaperone? What, is he going to go around shoving balloons between people?"

Steve snorts too. Maddie giggles and Julie makes a much more disparaging kind of noise.

Shelley shrugs. "He agreed. Actually, I expected him to argue a little bit. But he seemed okay with going." She glances down at Maddie's hair again. "I wonder why."

Julie sets her mascara wand down and looks up at me. She doesn't say anything. She doesn't need to. A picture's worth a thousand words, after all, and there are a lot of four-letter words in her expression.

Yeah, I have a hard time caring in that moment, though. A shiver is making its way up my spine at the thought of Bob in his Marlon Brando suit, which he will no doubt be wearing.

You'd better go, Abish. You can stand against the wall with him and be company. Give him an excuse to fend off all the annoying freshmen who devour him with their eyes every sacrament meeting.

"I don't have anything to wear," I say finally.

"I've got something that will work. Okay, Mad, I think you're good."

Maddie looks in the mirror and smiles. I notice she's contactless. "Your brown eyes are so great," I tell her. "You look sweet enough to eat."

Her smile disappears. "Sweet," she mutters. "Thanks."

We get there a little early because Shelley is helping set up. Bishop is there, and Dave. And Bob too in his suit and tie. They're all unfolding chairs and arranging them around the room.

I walk over to where Bob is working. "Why do they put the chairs up," I ask, "if the point is to dance? It's like an invitation to be a wallflower."

He turns and smiles at me, and I feel a swooping kind of sensation in my stomach. "Wallflowers deserve a place to sit."

"So what, do they make an estimate beforehand of how many chairs they'll need, based on how many people they think won't be asked?"

"Maybe that's a good way to decide if a dance is worth it or not. Look around the room before you go in, and see how many chairs are out."

I nod. "Good one. I'll remember that if I ever attend another singles' dance."

Bob hands me two folded chairs and grabs two more for himself. "You make it sound like it'd be an unlikely thing," he says as we cross the room.

I unfold one and push it against the wall. "I've never been a fan of dances. I didn't go to homecoming in high school. Didn't go to many in college, either."

"Hmm." Bob sets his down precisely so they're perfectly even with the row. "You missed out."

"Really. How? The spiked punch? The limo ride? The crazy afterparty at my parents' house because they've inexplicably left town the exact night of their kids' prom?"

"Because teen movies are the basis for real life."

"Hey, Bob," Julie cuts in, setting a couple more chairs next to ours. "You look great."

"Thank you," Bob replies, glancing down at his suit. "I wasn't sure this tie was working."

I glance at it and can't hold back a chuckle. It's one of those disturbingly lifelike fish ties I've seen my grandpa wear. "Good strategy," I say. "But I hate to tell you . . . I don't think it'll work."

He shrugs. "Doesn't hurt to try."

I walk back across the gym with him, only vaguely aware that we've left Julie in our metaphorical dust. "Shelley says Bishop roped you in to coming by saying he needed your help. Help with what? Making sure the punch is spiked properly?"

He folds his arms and studies me for a moment. "How about you?"

"Huh?"

"You didn't have to come. How come you're here? You just told me you don't like dances."

I shrug, but my face is growing warm.

He gives me a knowing smile.

"I don't know," I sputter. "Shelley's pretty convincing when she wants to be."

"Right. Well, you look really nice."

"It's Shelley's dress."

"Yellow's a good color on you."

"Yeah, I know."

"Yeah, you *know?*"

"I mean, thank you. Black's a nice . . ." I gesture helplessly. "You look nice too. Of course."

Bob smiles, uncrosses his arms, and takes a step toward me just as the mic lets out a series of excruciating sounds like a herd of dying whales. Bob and I both clap our hands to our ears.

"Okay, folks." Bishop's voice booms into every corner of the room, which is now decently crowded. "The rules are, no looking before you take one. No asking your buddies whose is whose. No trading or otherwise cheating. Men, walk to the left side of the room."

Bob shrugs, smiles at me, and heads up to the front to stand by Bishop.

"Women, you walk to the right side and take off one shoe. Pile them there in the corner."

I glance wildly around. Bob's lucky because he has an excuse for non-participation. *There is no way I'm taking even the slightest chance I'll end up suffering through an entire slow number with Noah-the-zipper-guy.*

Bathroom, I think, sidling through the door. *Woman's universal escape route.*

I wait in a stall for several minutes and take my time walking back to the cultural hall. Cautiously, I walk into the pandemonium of the dance. With the classic standard "At Last," sung by Etta James—one of my grandpa's favorites—as background, the men of the Seventeenth Ward are traveling the room, searching for the mates to all the sweaty pumps they've been forced to handle with their bare hands.

I walk up to Maddie. "Who's got yours?" I ask.

She shrugs. She's chewing her lip and teasing the skirt of her dress with her fingers. Then suddenly her eyes go wide and a giant smile spreads over her face.

Dave Cannon's approaching, holding out her shoe. "This yours?"

"Yes," she says breathlessly.

He gives her a wink. "I'll make sure to take you up on that dance sometime tonight."

And then he walks away.

"But," Maddie stammers, "we're supposed to . . ."

I follow her gaze and see him start chatting with a tall, statuesque brunette. A moment later, he leads the girl onto the floor.

"Yeah, let's go get some punch," I say, taking her by the elbow and leading her to the refreshments. And I do feel like punch, only not the kind we're headed toward. More the verb.

She follows me with a sort of zombie-shocked look on her face. I hand her a cup. She takes it without saying anything and downs it all at once. She ladles another for herself and downs that too. As she's refilling the third time, I put a hand on her wrist. "Hey. Go easy."

She shakes her head and gulps it down. "I don't know what to do different. What can I do, Abe?"

"Don't do anything. Be yourself and forget these guys. Like Bob says, singles wards are full of jerks."

She frowns. "Bob said that?"

The music changes. It's one I remember from stake dances growing up, an oldie by Bryan Adams. It's actually horribly romantic. It takes me back to when I was fourteen and utterly optimistic about stake dances. That feeling of waiting breathlessly for whomever my crush of the week was to come and ask me. Often they didn't, but a few times they did. I shiver, remembering how magical it seemed those times; the music, the dim-ish light, and the kind of dizzy feeling you get turning in repetitive little circles in the middle of a bunch of other whirring couples.

There's a hand on my shoulder. I turn. It's Bob.

Of course.

Bob smiles. "Dance?"

As I take his hand, I feel kind of like I'm having an out-of-body experience. He leads me to the middle of the floor. I have to reach up pretty far to grab his shoulder. His face is mostly the usual serious-calm, but there's just a hint of amusement in his eyes. *This is a little silly*, they seem to say.

I know my face probably looks grim, like I'm not enjoying myself at all. The problem is, I just don't know what to do with myself. The words to the song don't help—they're smarmy and romantic. And they're exactly how I'm feeling, and I'm afraid Bob will see that and know I'm over-interpreting what might just be a friendly gesture. We were, after all, talking about wallflowers. It's like I was begging him to ask me, now that I think about it.

He takes his hand off my waist, whirls me out and around, then pulls me back in. It's kind of a good move. I feel myself relaxing a little. "You're a good dancer."

"So are you. I'm relieved, because it would be a tragedy if you were tone-deaf and also had two left feet."

I can't come up with any witty remarks at that precise moment. I swallow and try to take a deep breath, but my stomach won't relax.

He frowns. "Are you sure you're okay with this?"

"Yeah." My voice is shaky. "Yeah, I'm—I'm fine."

"We can stop."

"No thanks."

He laughs at this and leads us on a path that weaves through the other couples.

We get a whistle from someone. I turn and see Steve grinning at me, and a matching grin spreads across my own face. I'm tempted, so tempted, to lay my head on Bob's shoulder and sway with him as I'd done before with Mark, a position so natural it doesn't take any thought at all. It doesn't even need music. But my own comment about balloons comes back to haunt me.

The song ends.

"Yeah," I say, dropping away from him and tucking a strand of hair behind my ear. "Thank you. That was . . ." I shake my head, afraid I'm going to say something utterly stupid.

"Pretty great," Bob supplies.

"Yep."

We look at each other . . . sort of gaze, actually. Like corny people from a movie. The next song starts up.

I break eye contact. "Well, thanks."

Just as I say it, he puts his hands on my shoulders and draws me in close. He slides his arms around me and just holds me there, pressing his slightly bristly cheek to the top of my head.

When I get my wits about me, I pull away a little so that I can look up into his face. "What?" I ask. "Are you okay?"

He looks down at me, and then he's kissing me, right there in the middle of the dance floor.

Well, not in the middle. More off to the side. In a shadowy corner.

For a moment I'm frozen with astonishment. And then it's like some kind of beast stirs inside of me, rears up, and takes over my body. My arms reach for his neck and I'm kissing him back. His arms slide around my waist and tighten. He pulls me up so I'm resting on his chest, so that my feet leave the floor.

It's nothing like kissing Mark. But it's . . .

Monumental.

Staggering.

He moves his face away from mine, carefully sets me back on the ground, and just looks at me for a few seconds. "Okay," he says finally.

I don't even have that many words. I stare up at him with my mouth hanging slightly open, feeling like my heart is pounding in my eyeballs.

A commotion by the refreshments table breaks the spell. There's a loud thump followed by a collective gasp. A girl shrieks. "She's fainted!"

A group is collecting around something on the floor. It looks in the dim light to be a pile of crumpled pink satin.

"Maddie," I whisper and dash across the room. When I get to the crowd, I elbow my way through the crowd. Two people I don't know are bent over her, grabbing her arms, wiggling them like they're trying to wake her.

"Back up," I say. "She's diabetic. Someone needs to get her purse." I think for a moment. "Find Shelley—the Relief Society president—and tell her to bring Maddie's purse."

It's only a few seconds waiting for Shelley to get to us, but it feels like an eternity. I can tell, even in the dim light, that Maddie is too pale. Her pulse is faint and irregular.

Shelley kneels next to me, pawing through the purse until she finds a blood-sugar test. She nicks Maddie's fingertip and watches for the numbers. "Too high," she says. "Much, much too high." She digs out a syringe and a half-filled glass bottle.

"How much?" I ask.

"All of it. She does half the bottle."

"That's right. Give it to me and go call the ambulance."

I feel Bob's hand on my shoulder again. "What can I do?" he asks.

I shake my head, biting my lip as I draw the clear liquid into the syringe. I flick out the air bubbles and push it up a little, letting a drop or two out of the top.

"Back up," I bark, glaring at the people who have crowded around us. A few move back a little, but most are craning their necks to see.

I look up at Bob. "If you could just sort of shield . . . I'm going to have to get at her abdomen or her hip or something . . ."

Bob glances down at her one-piece dress and nods. He turns to face them. "Give us some privacy, please." He takes off his jacket, kneels, and kind of holds it over us, blocking the rest of the view with his body.

I pull up her dress and inject her just below the belly button, then cover her again. I wait and watch with my palms resting on the floor on either side of her. My heart is going a mile a minute.

"Should we say a prayer?" Bob murmurs. "A blessing, or something?"

I close my eyes tightly. *Please, Heavenly Father. She might be a little foolish, but she doesn't deserve this. Please, if there's anything I can do, tell me.*

I get this overwhelming impulse to touch her hand. My fingers are trembling as I take it in mine. It's ice cold. After a few seconds her mouth stirs a little, and then her eyes open.

I sit back on my heels. "You okay?"

Maddie blinks, then nods.

My relief is accompanied by a weird sort of sadness. I release Maddie's hand and bring mine up to my chest. My heart is still beating like it wants out of my rib cage. I'm suddenly seeing Mark's face, remembering myself bent over him, frantically trying to revive him.

"Hey, Abish," Bob says.

I look over my shoulder just as an EMT guy approaches, followed by a couple others holding a stretcher. "She's awake," he says. "She was passed out before?"

"Oh. Yes." I stand and move aside so he can get past me. "She collapsed. Drank too much punch, I think. She's diabetic."

"You gave her insulin?" The guy nods at the syringe in my other hand.

Shelley comes up behind him. "Her blood sugar was at 741."

"Yes, I gave her insulin. Here." I reach down and grab the bottle that I had dropped on the floor. I hand it to him.

He studies it for a moment. "Do you have her tester?"

Shelley gives him the little contraption and he nicks Maddie's thumb. She just lies there, eyes half-shut. She's breathing, though. I'm watching the rise and fall of her chest through the satin bodice of her dress.

"It's starting to go back down," he says. He turns back to me. "You might have saved her life. She's in shock, but we'll be able to work with it at this point."

I step back to join the crowd.

"Are you okay?" Bob asks.

"Yeah," I reply. "Or I mean actually, not really. Yeah, I'm just going to . . ." I push my way through the crowd.

"Abish." This time it's Bishop Barnes's voice calling me. He's headed toward me across the dance floor. I don't stop. In fact, I go faster. In fact, I'm taking off again. I pass the coatrack on the way out. I dart in and grab mine, sending several others to the floor.

I don't really pay attention where I'm going. The shoes aren't even my Timberlands; they're ballet flats, and so my arches are hating me. I'm stumbling a lot. It's not just the shoes or even the dark, it's the fact that I'm seeing things—images. Mark's face, his eyes staring but not seeing. The EMT's wrestling me off of him, taking him and shutting him up in the ambulance.

Was this what I was supposed to do, then? The big miracle I'm supposed to perform? Then You have a pretty cruel sense of humor. I know, even as I think it, that it's wrong. Maddie's just as important to Heavenly Father as Mark was.

But not to me. Not to me.

At first I'm heading for the hospital automatically. Then I remember. *I said good-bye to everyone. I can't go back.*

262

MILE 21

I'm running without a direction now. The wind is blowing hard, churning the branches of the tall trees lining the street. The yellow light of the streetlamps illuminates their thick trunks. My feet are aching; I can't keep this up in these shoes. I just can't.

I slow to a walk and sit on the first place I can find: a bench made of metal mesh.

Am I crazy? I feel crazy.

I feel like the world is upside down.

I lie down on the bench. The sky seems like it's slowly descending toward me. Like the stars are hanging there, waiting to drop. I can't get the image of Mark's face out of my head. I shut my eyes tight and hug myself. My parka's warm enough, but I'm still shivering.

I don't know how long I've been there, but I must have fallen asleep because a beam of light—directly in my face—startles me awake. "Do you need a ride somewhere?" a voice calls.

A guy, holding a flashlight. I sit up, blocking the light with my hand so that it doesn't blind me. There's a car parked against the curb several yards away. "No."

"The park is closed." The voice is starting to sound familiar; I'm getting a bad feeling about it.

The police officer who found me on campus.

Fear sears through me, and I scramble off the bench. "Sorry," I say, starting to trot away. "Thanks for letting me know. I'll go then."

"Wait."

I stop and turn around slowly.

"Abish, right?"

That's what I get for having a unique name. People remember me when I don't want to be remembered. I bite my lip. "Yeah. Officer—"

"Sanders."

"Right. Officer Sanders. Hello again."

"How have you been?"

It's a totally ludicrous question. "Fine," I say, my voice a little higher-pitched than normal. "I'm not loitering on purpose, I promise. I was just walking, and I found a bench and—"

"Let's talk in the car."

"In the car?"

He walks toward the car and opens the back door closest to the curb.

There's this curdled kind of feeling in my stomach, and my heart is battering itself against my ribs again. Gingerly, I walk over to the car. He holds the door for me, and I step in carefully and sit down.

"I'm going to have to take you in," he says once he's settled himself in the front street. "I'm sorry. You were inside park boundary."

"I didn't think. I was just walking and needed a rest."

"It's past midnight."

"I just came from a stake dance."

He takes in my dress and wildly disheveled hair. "Were you drinking?"

"No!"

He turns around and starts the car.

"By 'take me in,' you mean like, you're *arresting* me?"

"I'm bringing you to the women's detention here in town. You can call people. It's not like in the movies where you only get one phone call." We stop at a red light, and he pulls out his radio thing. "It's Sanders," he says. "I picked up someone. We'll be there in a minute."

After a few seconds there's a crackly reply I can't make out.

"No, just one will be fine."

Just one what? One day? One hypodermic full of tranquilizer? One course of electro-shock therapy? I lean my head against the coolness of the side window. "Heavenly Father," I say, "just let me die."

I don't mean for it to come out that way. I mean it more like, *Take me out of this situation. Help me figure out why I'm here in the first place.* Or something.

"What was that?" Officer Sanders asks.

I sit up, rub the tears off my face, and glare at him through the grate separating us. "Nothing. The ravings of an insane person.

What am I doing in here again?" Anger is starting to well up and replace my shock and confusion.

"You were caught trespassing," he says, giving me a direct look in the rearview mirror, "after you'd already been sentenced on a similar charge. You were given breaks before. Technically we could have brought you in the very first time."

"It's a *park*. It's meant for people to be in. It's not like I was sleeping on someone's porch or something."

"The city curfew is eleven on school nights, midnight on weekends. You were on public property after the official curfew."

"Snowball throwing is also illegal in Rexburg. Have you ever booked someone for that?"

"I've never had a case where I picked someone up for snowball throwing after they'd already been sentenced by a judge. Usually people get scared straight at that point."

My anger flees. My body suddenly feels limp. I lean my head against the metal barrier. "I honestly didn't mean to," I murmur. "It was a mistake. Tonight's been a crazy night."

"That doesn't change the fact you were there and that I found you. I'm sorry. I really can't do it any differently, Abish. But don't worry. You'll probably only be given a few days."

"*Probably*? What else could happen?"

"If the judge is really hard-nosed about it, seeing as you've come before him already and fined, he might decide to give you up to a month. Technically you could be in here a year on a repeat-trespassing charge."

At this point he pulls up to the facility. I can see the gleam of barbed-wire coils along the tops of the walls. My body is itching, longing to leap out of the car and just run, run, run. But that's why the back doors of police cars don't open from the inside.

A giant garage-door thing rises, and we drive in. It closes again behind us before he gets out of the front seat and comes around to me. He opens the door and reaches in as if to put a hand on my head so I don't bump the roof as I come out.

I look him straight in the eyes. "Don't touch me," I say quietly.

He takes a step back and puts his hands on his hips. After a minute or so, another guy comes through a door into the garage area. Slowly, I step out.

"This way," Officer Sanders says, gesturing to a desk and chair. "Do you have any weapons?"

"No."

"I need your cell phone or any other electronic devices. And any jewelry."

I unclasp the chain from around my neck, the necklace that holds my wedding ring. The solitaire diamond glints in the florescent lighting. I coil it up and place it in his palm. He looks down at it for a minute, then at me. "Cell phone?"

"Nope."

"You don't carry a phone."

I give him an evil smile. "It's completely psychotic, I know."

The other officer clears his throat. "What we're going to do now," he says, "is take you in and get your fingerprints, get a picture, and then have you undress in the shower. We'll bring someone over from the women's side to watch you."

"Watch me?"

"She'll have to watch you undress. You'll be given clothes. You can't be wearing anything underneath."

After picture and fingerprints are done, I walk into the shower accompanied by a woman wearing a uniform and a no-nonsense expression. A chill settles over me. *This is real. This is really going to happen.* I undress. She doesn't stare at me, but it's still the most humiliating thing that has ever happened to me.

Finally she hands me over something. I grab it and nearly fall over. "What the crud is *this*?" I ask, holding it to my front and folding my arms across my chest. It's a giant jumper, only padded. Really, really padded. You could almost say it's upholstered. It's sleeveless and it looks like it might come to my shins.

"It's what we give people who are on suicide watch."

"*Suicide* watch? Why am I on suicide watch?"

"Apparently you said something on the way over to make Officer

Sanders feel you were a risk." She gives me a cold look. "Stop arguing and put it on."

I pull it over my head. My shoulders feel naked. I cross my arms tightly over my chest and follow her into the room where the two men are still waiting. I can't look them in the face. Not while I'm wearing this.

"Sit here." Officer Sanders gestures at a stool bolted to the floor, right below a long counter that has more of that metal grilling in front of it. "Are you left handed or right handed?"

"Right."

The mustached guy takes my left wrist, cuffs it, and snaps the other end of the cuff into a metal ring protruding from the surface of the counter. He hands me a pen and a sheaf of papers. "Fill these out," he says. "Mandy, you can head back over. We'll be keeping her in the holding cell on this side for now."

"Okay."

"Scott, I think I've got things covered at this point."

I look up at Officer Sanders. He looks back at me for a few seconds, then nods and follows Mandy out.

The mustached guy turns to me. "I'm Corporal Schmidt, by the way. The paperwork should be pretty straightforward."

"Abish Cavendish Miller," I reply, looking down at the papers.

It only takes me fifteen minutes to finish. When I'm done, I clumsily try to shift them around with my free hand and make them into a neater pile.

"Don't worry about that," Corporal Schmidt says. He uncuffs my wrist. "We'll be putting you in the holding cell. Because you're on suicide watch, you can't have anything in there with you. I will be checking on you every fifteen minutes." He leads me down the hall and opens a door.

It's a tiny room with a concrete floor and a low metal cot with a thin, vinyl-covered mattress. There's a toilet-drinking-fountain-combination-thing cemented to one of the four bare, white walls.

"How long do I have to be in here?"

"Until you're off suicide watch."

"When will that happen?"

"You'd need to get an okay from the doctor."

"When does he come?"

Schmidt pulls the door open wider. I glance at him and take one step, then two, into the room. Knees shaking, I walk over to the cot and sit down.

"Dr. Fairbanks will be in tomorrow," he says. Then he shuts the door.

I lie down on the cot. The mattress is hard, and the bulkiness of the smock makes it a little more awkward. I lie there, feeling the rapid beat of my pulse in my chest and throat. I try to meditate, listening to my own breaths: *in, out. In, out.*

It doesn't work. I'm too tense to go to sleep. Thoughts and images are cramming my mind: Mr. Eems, lying in his bed with wires and tubes like a spider's web, trapping him. Bishop Barnes, holding a sheaf of papers across to me. Mama, with that tired-strained expression on her face. Maddie's eyes opening and finding mine. My dad in his battered plaid robe, sitting next to me in the truck. Mark, with that intense, pleading look on his face just before he fell at my feet. And Bob—laughing at me, throwing me down in the mud, putting his arms around me in the cemetery, lifting me up and kissing me in the middle of the dance floor. *Was that really just a few hours ago?*

Something comes loose in my chest and I'm crying, silently. My whole body is shaking with it. Tears roll off my nose and puddle under my face; it just keeps coming and coming. Finally I shudder to a stop, and the images in my mind blur with the room around me.

Chapter 18

*M*y sleep is a light, fretful one. I keep starting awake. My dreams are more like daydreams. The light in the room never turns off, so I can't tell whether it's still night, or what. After an interminable amount of time the door opens. A guy with a black goatee comes in with a tray of food. "Breakfast," he says.

I sit up. After he gives me the tray, he leans against the door, which is propped just slightly open. I look down at the food: scrambled eggs, a couple pieces of toasted bread, some curls of bacon and orange juice in a plastic container. "I'm not really hungry."

"If you want off suicide watch, you'd better eat all of that," he answers.

I force my way through the eggs and most of the toast. The OJ is the one welcome thing; I take small sips, making it last through the meal. The food feels like a solid brick in my stomach. "When is Dr. Fairbanks coming?" I ask, holding out the empty tray.

He takes it. "Sometime this morning."

I almost say something as he shuts the door behind him—anything to stall him a little—but I think better of it. I sit there looking at the closed door, not sure how long it will be before it opens again. It could be thirty minutes; it could be three hours.

It's not long though, before the handle turns again and the goateed guy enters with another man. "This is Dr. Fairbanks," he says.

The doctor surprises me. I'm expecting a jaded, dour-looking guy, or maybe someone like Bishop Barnes—the drill-sergeant type. But he's round and actually kind of jolly. He's carrying a thick binder under one arm.

"You can go ahead leave us for a few minutes," he says to my jailor, who nods and shuts the door.

I slide my feet over the edge of the bed so they're touching the floor.

He opens the binder. His eyes dart back and forth as he reads something written there. "Hello, Abish. Nice to meet you."

"Nice to meet you. I'm not suicidal."

"You had Officer Sanders worried about you from what he wrote in your chart."

"Chart? They've got a *chart* on me?"

He shuts the binder. "Charting is the law. Just like in a hospital, we are required to keep notes on each of the inmates."

"So people are watching me all the time and writing down what I'm doing?"

He nods. "You seem coherent and stable right now. Are you getting enough sleep lately?"

I raise an eyebrow and glance down at the bed I'm sitting on.

"How about your appetite?"

"Fine," I reply, and then my always-present, always-perverse honesty rises to the surface. "Well, not that great for the last year, but I would think that's normal after what I've gone through."

"And what's that?"

I shrug. "My husband died suddenly of a pulmonary embolism. Then I lost our baby at twenty weeks." I'm a little amazed it comes out so easily, like normal conversation. I'm realizing, though, that in this case openness is the best policy if I want to convince people I'm not a purposeful criminal. "I've been a little weird because of it, but

I've been getting a lot better lately. Falling asleep on the park bench last night was just an accident."

"How long ago did your husband die?"

"December before last. Amelia was born three weeks later, in January. So you see, if I'd been suicidal, it would have happened a long time ago. I'm here talking to you, so clearly I'm not suicidal."

"Clearly," Dr. Fairbanks agrees cheerily, scribbling something in the binder—my *chart*, I guess. "Well, I'll let them know, then." He pauses at the door. "I'll be back tomorrow. I think I feel all right about taking you off suicide watch. Once you're off, you'll be allowed phone calls. Just so you know, your bail is three thousand. That's a little high for your charge, but I hear you've gone before the judge before."

At the word "bail," a chill runs down my spine.

The door shuts behind him, and all I can think is how surreal this whole situation has become. It's like something from a dystopian novel: being forced to strip and wear a hideous and indecent outfit, being put in a cell where I have no way at all of talking to anyone unless they come and find me, and people taking notes about everything I do or say. People not believing a *thing* I say, despite the fact that I'm being, as usual, obnoxiously honest. I feel about as small and undesirable as the fly buzzing around the fluorescent light imbedded in the ceiling.

After a while the door opens again. It's a woman officer this time. "Come on," she says. "I'm taking you to the other side."

I'm tempted to say something about veils and heavenly messengers. "What do you mean?"

"We're on the men's side. You need to head over to the Women's Detention."

"So I'm off suicide watch?"

"Yes, but you'll have to walk across in that." She flicks a glance over my embarrassing attire. "I don't think we have issue small enough for you over here."

Great. I follow her through the building, keeping my eyes on the cement floor. It's cool against my bare feet. We enter the door of the women's detention, and she leads me into another shower and dressing area. She hands me a bundle of cloth and turns her profile to me, keeping me in her peripheral vision as I remove the smock—it's quite a process—and put on the striped cotton pants and shirt. "Why the white and orange?" I ask as I'm pulling on a pair of padded socks.

"So nobody mistakes you for a deer during hunting season."

Okay, it was kind of a dumb question.

She leads me out of the shower and gestures to the telephone on the wall. "You can call people now. The first call will assign you a pin number. You have to speak your name clearly, followed by 'Madison County Jail' when prompted by the message—"

"No thanks."

"You don't want to use the phone."

"No." I fold my arms. "I don't."

"You don't have someone who could post bail? You could be out of here today—until you go before the judge, of course. He'll probably sentence you to a few days. But it will give you a chance to go home for a few hours and get your business in order if you need to. "

A feeling of dread settles in the pit of my stomach. "How long before I go before the judge?"

"This afternoon, probably. They'll arraign you and if you plead guilty, they can sentence you right there."

Arraign. Sentence. It all sounds so serious for illegal park oxygen. "No phone call. Thanks."

She shrugs. "Okay."

She leads me through the doors. We walk past a little room elevated on a platform with a kind of spaceship's prow of glass. Another officer is sitting there surrounded by screens, buttons, dials, and anonymous gadgets that make me wonder if I've accidentally wandered into a *Star Trek* episode. There are long hallways that lead to other glassed-in areas that remind me of fish tanks. I can see through the glass that the rooms all have white-painted cinder block walls. Each area has a little common room and two open doorways leading to bedrooms full of bunk beds. I can see that most of the beds are full. Lots of people are sleeping—I have to wonder how late in the morning it is—and everything smells like bleach and stuffy bedroom.

"Is there any place to exercise?" I ask.

"No." She points at an open space with benches and tables. "This is where you eat meals. We'll be putting you in pod C, but we're full up for the moment, so you'll need to sleep on a cot."

The "cot" is already set up with a blanket. It looks kind of like a giant rectangular Tupperware lid with a mattress. "Thanks," I say, looking down at it.

"We have books you can read. You can do a puzzle if you want. As you can see, most people just sleep."

I look at the women lying in their bunks.

"Your roommates are okay," the officer says. "Aren't you guys?"

One of them mutters something and rolls over, pulling the blanket over her head.

"You'll be fine," the officer reassures me. "Don't cause trouble and trouble won't find you." With this, she walks out.

I glance at the women again. I'm tempted to do something corny like introduce myself and ask all of their names. I have a feeling it won't be well received, so instead I sit in my Tupperware lid, resting my back against the wall. "She said there's stuff to read?" I ask after a few minutes.

"They have them in the control room," one girl replies, sitting up and stretching. "Here, I finished this one." She tosses me a well-used, obviously well-loved copy of *Twilight*.

"I haven't read this yet."

"It's stupid. She should've totally gone with Jacob."

At this, the girl who pulled the blanket over her head emerges and sits up. "You're tripping," she says. "Team Edward."

"If you like making out with a rock."

And it's feeling surreal again. *Here I am in the middle of a prison cell, listening to a conversation that could easily take place in any of the girls' apartments I've lived in.* I clear my throat. "Hey," I venture. "Did any of you come here for school?"

"I was at BYU-Idaho," Team Edward replies. "Got caught smoking pot. What's your name? I'm Alyssa."

"Abish," I say, trying to pretend that this doesn't totally shock me.

"Weird name," Team Jacob comments.

"It's from the Book of Mormon," Alyssa says.

She narrows her eyes. "Even weirder."

"What's *your* name?" I ask.

"Amber. Assault and battery."

I do my best to keep from flinching. "Okay."

Amber points to the girls in the other set of bunks, who are apparently too tired to care what's going on. "And that's Mel on top, and Jerica on the bottom. They're both here for shoplifting."

"How about you?" Alyssa prompts.

"What?"

"What are you here for."

I take a deep breath and blow it out so it ruffles my bangs. "Trespassing," I finally say.

I expect her to laugh scornfully and promptly give me a wedgie, or at least act shocked that something so ridiculous could land someone in jail.

She only shrugs. "Yeah, one of my roommates when I got here was taken in on a trespassing charge too. Don't worry, you'll probably only have to serve a few days. Sometimes the judge will even count time served, so." She smiles and lies back down, gathering the thin blanket around her shoulders. "Guess we won't be getting to know each other very well. Good news for you."

I nod and bury my face in the book. I'm not really seeing words, though. I'm trying to adjust myself to what she has just said—that it's not ludicrous, my being here. Others have been arrested and incarcerated for trespassing.

But it was a mistake. You didn't do it on purpose this time.

A few hours later, we're let out with another pod to eat lunch in the dining area. An officer pulls me aside when we're finished. "Dr. Fairbanks wants to see you again before you leave because he's decided not to come in tomorrow. And you have a visitor scheduled this afternoon."

MILE 21

My heart sinks and my stomach gets tight. "Who?"

"They didn't tell me."

"You can refuse to see them," Alyssa says helpfully as she scrapes out her yogurt carton with a plastic spoon. "But I wouldn't. You've just come off suicide watch. They might put you back on if they think you're isolating."

I'm biting my lip, clenching my hands into tight fists as I follow the guy back to an examination room.

Who knows I'm in jail? I didn't call anyone. One by one, the faces I'm most worried about come to mind.

Mama. Her expression would be grim and disapproving, hiding her real feelings, which would be worry and heartbreak.

Dad. I don't even want to think about that one.

Bishop Barnes.

Bob.

Dear Heavenly Father, please don't let it be Bob.

They give me a hospital gown. Once again I'm watched obliquely by a female officer as I undress. The doctor gives me a cursory examination: weight, height, blood pressure. They do a blood draw. He listens to my heart and lungs and checks my eyes and throat.

"You could use ten more pounds," he says, putting his stethoscope away. "Otherwise you're healthy."

"I'm not usually this skinny. I'm training for a marathon."

He frowns and scribbles something in my chart.

"I haven't eaten enough this last year," I add, watching his pen move across the page, "but it's not because I want to be skinny. It's just been a hard year."

"As you've said," he replies. "But just to make sure, I'll have a test administered to rule out eating disorder."

"The E.D.I? I already know all the questions and how they're scored. I took abnormal psych, and we did a group project on it."

He gives me a smile. "There are several different options." He turns to the female officer. "We're done now. You can have her get dressed."

Have me get dressed. The words kind of underline the dehumanizing humiliation of this entire situation. As I'm putting my striped clothing back on, someone comes to the door. They don't look in, but they talk to the officer watching me. "Her visitor's here. Send her out as soon as she's ready."

My fingers shake as I pull my socks on.

"There will be an officer monitoring," she says as she leads me down a short hallway. "And cameras."

"Thanks," I mutter.

She opens a door, watches me walk in, and then shuts it behind me.

It's a room like any other at the detention: plain, whitewashed cinder block walls. The only difference is there's a large window in one of the walls and a long counter with a plastic chair pushed up against it. There's also a telephone receiver to talk into. On the other side of the window, with the other receiver in hand, is Bishop Barnes.

As I sit down, his stern gaze follows me. I'm utterly relieved it's not any of the others I've been ruminating about. I'm also a little terrified of what he's about to say to me.

Slowly, I pick up the receiver and put it to my ear.

"What on earth happened? I got a notice from the honor code office that you were found trespassing again!"

"I didn't mean to. It was a mistake. I was . . . I mean, I was kind of disoriented. Things were a little crazy."

"Did this happen after you ran out of the dance?"

I nod.

"Robert went after you, but you were too fast for him. You were long gone by the time he'd checked the building and circled around it to see where you went."

I rub my eyes with my free hand. "I was just running, and not really thinking where I was going. When I stopped I found a bench and sat down. I guess I fell asleep. I woke up when Officer Sanders found me. Then he took me here."

There's a long silence. He's staring at me—almost glaring. I lower my gaze to the counter.

"This is ridiculous," he says. "Completely outrageous. You were sitting on a *park bench*—"

"Sleeping. And it was after city curfew." I'm not exactly sure why I'm arguing. I should be glad Bishop Barnes thinks this whole thing is unfair. It's how I feel, isn't it?

"So you basically got arrested for falling asleep. Did you explain what happened at the dance?"

"They weren't interested in explanations. It was the same park I was picked up in before. I've already gone before the judge and paid a hundred-fifty-dollar fine. That's why they didn't ask any questions and just brought me in."

There's no stopping Bishop Barnes once he gets his fire lit. "I'll be speaking to the arresting officer and his supervisor," he growls. "And the honor code office. We're not going to let this stand, Abish. You don't deserve this."

But maybe I do.

The words come to my head; my natural perverse honesty coming out. *If I'd faced things at the dance, if I hadn't run away, I wouldn't have been at the park. I wouldn't have been tired enough to need to fall asleep on a bench.*

And if I hadn't purposefully disobeyed so many times already, then they would have let me off. I used up all my warnings.

"Please don't," I say.

He frowns. "Don't what? You're just going to give in, let this happen to you? You're going to be passive and hide instead of facing things head-on? I'm sorry, Abish, but this is one train wreck I can't allow."

"Bishop, I'm tired." As I say it, I realize how utterly, absolutely true the words are.

I'm exhausted. Mentally, emotionally run-down to the point of breaking. The idea of sleeping for long hours in a quiet, blank space; being fed meals, being cut off from everyone and everything—it actually doesn't sound so bad all of a sudden.

"I know an attorney I think would be willing to try," he argues. "We've got witnesses to what happened at the dance. We could make a case for you being disoriented—upset, and not knowing what you were doing. We'll get you off if you're just willing to fight a little. This doesn't have to go on your record."

I swallow hard and shake my head. "No. Please don't tell anyone if you can help it. I especially don't want my mother to know. She *won't* be able to handle it."

"Your mother would not want you to—"

"I'm supposed to be arraigned today," I interrupt him. "If I plead guilty, they'll just sentence me right there and it'll be over. They'll probably just give me a few days and then I'll be out. If we fight it, it might be a months-long process. Even years. It's not worth it for just a few days in jail."

"You'll be kicked out of school."

"Then I deserve to be. I did trespass, Bishop. Even if I didn't mean to this time, I definitely knew what I was doing all those other times. Anyway, I was kicked out of school as soon as they arrested me."

His mouth gets tight and his eyes narrow. I know that look, and I immediately feel sorry for whoever is going to be on the receiving end of what he's planning. "We'll see about that at least," he says. He stands and holds up a paper bag. "I've brought a couple of your things. They said they would give them to you when you go back to your cell. Apparently they have to check them for concealed weapons."

I don't return his cynical little smile. I just shrug, rise from my chair, and walk through the door when it's opened for me.

I make for my cot immediately. I'm just getting reimmersed in the woes of unrequited vampire love when a jailor guy—they're all blurring into one faceless continuum of blue and gray at this point—walks in.

"Here," he says.

I reach up and take them—my scriptures in their battered leather carrier and the blue journal. Its gilt-edged pages still gleam, shiny and new. They're still mostly blank, kind of like my mind right now.

⁂

MILE 21

Several hours later, as I stand in the elegant courtroom of the Historic Rexburg Courthouse in my striped cotton jammies, I realize that I was wrong to think that undressing in front of a prison guard is the most humiliating thing possible.

I take a deep breath. "Guilty."

The judge considers me through his glasses. It's the same guy I went before last April. I'm sure he recognizes me. Even if he didn't recognize my face, there's my name.

"Seven days," he finally says. "With time served to count for two. And a year of community service."

At this, my jaw drops open.

He raises his eyebrows. *Just give me a reason,* his face seems to say.

"Yes, sir," I murmur, and sit back down.

There are other people at the courthouse. Just a handful, but it's enough, seeing their distasteful expressions as they avoid looking at me when I walk through the room flanked by prison guards. I can almost believe I am one of the bottom-feeders of society and that I'll be forever stuck in this strange state of emotional and societal stasis—prodded from one blank, sterile room to another, whiling away my time with meaningless activities.

I finished *Twilight* already. There was some mild frustration when I found that none of the other books in the series were available at the prison, but honestly I just can't bring myself to care. We get back in time to be served dinner. I force it down because I don't want to be deemed unstable again. We all slog back to our rooms and I curl up in my cot.

For several minutes I stare at the ceiling. Then, sighing, I pull my scriptures out of the space between the cot and the wall where I've jammed them. There's nothing else to read except self-help books and romance novels; two genres I've never been much interested in. And I don't have the presence of mind for Sudoku puzzles right now.

When I open my scriptures, a note falls out. I squint, trying to make sense of the sprawling writing in the dim light.

Abish, you are not alone. Christ descended below all things.

*D&C 122 might be an appropriate thing to read right now, if
you haven't already thought of that.*
  Bishop Barnes

I read it a second time. Slowly, reluctantly, I turn to Doctrine
and Covenants 122. I already know what it is. The passage that was
written by Joseph Smith while he was incarcerated in Liberty Jail.
We studied it extensively in high school seminary. Mark and I also
read and discussed pieces of it for several of our couples' scripture
study sessions. We pretty much squeezed every drop of doctrine
from those words, so I kind of doubt there will be anything new
there for me.

The first few verses make me cringe because they're about virtu-
ous people being betrayed, and honestly, I'm starting to feel more and
more how I deserve to be here. It's not that I've been purposefully bad.
Just criminally careless. Blank to the world and its worldly rules.

I'm starting to remember a lot of other stuff from this last year
too. Crazy stuff I've done, people I've let down and worried. It's painful, realizing how completely self-centered I've been.

*But I wasn't really in my right mind. How can you force yourself to
act functional when you're not functional? Would anyone else have done
any better?*

As I reach verse five—"if thou art called to pass through tribula-
tions"—there's a stir of annoyance. I shut the scriptures abruptly and
zip the cover closed, a vicious movement that catches a few delicate,
tissue-thin page corners. My irritability flares into a real and terrible
anger. *God, you said you wouldn't give us more than we could handle.*

But is that really in scripture?

"I didn't say it would be easy, I only said it would be worth it," I
murmur. *No, that's not in the scriptures, either.*

"Nephi," I whisper. *I will provide a way for you to accomplish the
things I've commanded you.*

*You said that, right? So is that the way you reward the people who
seek out ways to strive for your cause? Dump a load of crap on them and
say, here you go. I'll be watching to see how you handle it. Holler if you*

need anything and I'll decide whether or not to answer you. And by the way, it's for your own good.

I'm grinding my teeth. My jaw wants something to chew to pieces—physically or verbally, I don't really care which. My muscles are twitching unbearably. I stand and begin to pace the room.

Alyssa sits up and regards me sleepily. "You okay?"

I look around and see that the three other girls are also awake, watching me warily from their bunks. I remember the words of the officer when she first brought me here: *Don't make any trouble, and trouble won't find you.*

I relax my jaw and let my hands fall to my sides. "I'm just getting a little cabin fever."

Amber rolls her eyes. "Yeah, it sucks. Just sleep it off. You're lucky; you only got five more days in here." She rolls over, rearranging the blanket.

I lie back down, tucking one of the pillows they issued me between my knees. My legs don't like this level of inactivity. It's like I can't keep from moving them; if I let them lie still for more than a few seconds, they start to feel itchy or like they're burning or something. I wish I could take Amber's advice, but all night I'm moving restlessly, shifting my legs around. My thoughts are turning over and over like a misfiring engine.

If Mark was supposed to die, if I really wasn't supposed to save him, please show me why. If I was really supposed to lose Amelia, please give me a reason, an answer. I deserve it, Heavenly Father. I at least deserve an answer. Father, if this is the way it's supposed to be, you have to show me the way out. If this was supposed to happen to me, show me the way out. God, show me the way out.

My anger starts to dim. Replacing it is the thing I've feared more than anything else: emptiness. An unreachable ache so deep and terrible, so binding, that I can't do much but lie there, restless legs forgotten. Tears are leaking down the side of my face like blood from a wound gone wrong. Like that woman from the Bible with her seven-year-issue, I'm broken. I feel like my life force is slowly bleeding out of me onto the concrete floor.

Chapter
19

*W*hen we get up to shower and go to breakfast the next morning, I've got that hollow, scattered feeling you have when you've had no sleep. I stumble as I walk to the table and fall into the person who is standing in line in front of me.

"Watch it, girl," she says, giving my shoulder a shove that sends me into the table with rib-bruising force. *Girl* isn't the word she really uses.

I look up at her. She is much, much bigger than me, and she's got mean little eyes. "Sorry, didn't mean to be taking up so much space," I mumble.

"What was that?" She puts her hands on her hips and cocks her head. "Are you giving me crap, girl?" Again, not her exact words.

I look over at the two uniformed men who are supposed to be watching us. They're busy dealing with a rail-thin girl who's having some kind of fit, it looks like.

"Selena," a voice booms from the control room. "Back down or you'll end up in solitary again. You don't want to ruin six months' good behavior."

M ɪ ʟ ᴇ 2 1

The big girl narrows her eyes and moves past me, brushing my shoulder none-too-gently as she does so. She finds a seat on the other side of the crowded line of tables. Throughout the meal, I can feel her looking at me.

"Watch out," Alyssa mutters to me as we all head back to our pods. "You don't want to get on Selena's bad side, trust me."

I lay in my cot, shivering. The fear and humiliation of the encounter almost make me want to throw up, but by some miracle, I manage to fall asleep for a while.

Someone jogs my shoulder, waking me. I look up into the face of the woman who checked me in. "Visitor," she says abruptly.

I'm tempted to say no thanks, but I think of that bare, tiny little room and the sleeveless smock.

It's still worse.

I rise to my feet and follow her down the hall to the visiting room. I'm expecting it to be Bishop Barnes, so when I open the door and see who's sitting on the other side of the glass, the shock makes my stomach twist and my scalp tingle. My knees are trembling as I walk over to the chair and lower myself into it. I pick up the phone. "Dad."

He doesn't answer. He just stares at me with his huge hand gripping that phone like it's some kind of lifeline. After a moment he sets it down on the counter and puts his face in his hands.

I have never seen my dad cry.

"I'm sorry," I say into the receiver, even though his is sitting on the counter. "Dad, please don't do this. Please stop." *I can't. I can't cry in front of my dad.*

I don't get direct evidence of the tears until lifts his head again. His eyes are shut, mouth turned down, and his shoulders are shaking. His nose is really red, like mine gets when I cry.

He passes his palm over his face and wipes the moisture away. He reaches over and picks up the phone. "Abish," he chokes. "I'm sorry."

It's like a lance through my heart. "You don't have anything to be sorry for, Dad."

"I'm sorry I wasn't there for you, to help and support you when Mark died."

"Stop it. It was my fault too. I didn't let you. I . . . I didn't know what to do. I thought you were—I didn't know what to feel."

"Look at me, Abish."

I look up and am startled again, not just by the visible signs of weeping on his face, but also by the expression in his eyes. Usually his face is so deadpan, so impassive. Like a brick wall to me. But I can see so many emotions there—worry, sadness, determination. Love, and maybe a little exasperation.

"You thought I was glad when Mark died," he says.

The words sound monstrous. "You didn't like Mark," I finally reply.

"You were my first daughter married. The idea took some getting used to."

"You told me I wasn't being wise." The memory used to bring such mind-numbing anger, but right now I only feel sad.

"I know." He shrugs. "And I was wrong."

"You helped me prepare to serve a mission, but when I decided to get married, you shut me out."

"I was wrong," he repeats, still gazing at me. I want to look away, but I can't. "And I'm asking for your forgiveness. Abish." He sighs, bows his head, and runs his hand through his hair. "I knew on the day you were married, when I saw you coming out of the temple, that you were making the right choice."

The picture of us together—me and Dad, in front of the temple—comes to mind. "Why then?" I ask quietly. "Why didn't you just trust me, Dad? You always trusted me before. I could always talk to you . . ." I shake my head because I can't get any more words out.

"I was worried because you two were so young and I knew what was ahead for you. Life is hard. I've seen your mother's heartbreak over losing our babies. We struggled about money. I was frightened for you. But I knew that day that you were doing the right thing. And I'm more sorry than I can say, now, that I wasn't humble enough to tell it to you then."

MILE 21

I shut my eyes tight and put my hand over my mouth, but there's no hiding the tears spilling down my face. "It's not your fault," I finally manage. "Yeah, of course I forgive you, Dad. I mean, how can I—" and I'm completely gone. It starts him up again too. "It's been so bad," I say after a while. "I love Mama, and she's tried so hard to help me, but I need you. Okay? I've needed you."

"You've got me." Dad puts a hand on the glass, and I put mine there too. It's completely cheesy. Apparently, Dad and I have gone completely off the deep end. I don't want to know what the people looking at the monitors must think of us.

In a way, it's a relief. After being so completely over-the-top emotional with each other, it's easy to sit there and discuss the necessary technicalities of what's going to happen when I'm released. We decide I'll come home to sort things out for a few days and figure out what I'm doing next. It's strange that the idea of going back home doesn't seem awful and destabilizing. Of course, anything is good compared to jail.

"I'll keep it from your mother for as long as I can," Dad says as he rises from his chair.

I stand too. I can feel my pulse thrumming in my temples. "You'll have to tell her," I say. "Please just tell her. I'm kind of done keeping things."

Dad nods. "Me too." He gives me a quick smile—it's like a ray of sunshine, warming me. "Knock 'em dead, Abish."

"Hopefully not. People here are quite capable of returning the favor." I'm immediately sorry for the words as I see the worry on his face. "Just kidding," I amend hastily. "Things here are okay, Dad. I'm safe. I'm fine. I'll be out in four days."

"If you need anything, you can call me. Do you want me to come back tomorrow?"

I swallow hard and shake my head. "I'll see you Friday."

"See you Friday."

I turn my face away from the common area as we pass through on the way to my room so nobody will be able to see the obvious evidence. When I get to my cot, I'm grateful that the two girls in the room are fast asleep. I follow suit, pulling the blanket over my head.

I fall into the prison routine for the next few days: sleep for five hours, and eat. Sleep five more hours, and eat again. Go back to the room and stare at the ceiling for several hours until I finally fall asleep.

I actually spend a lot of time writing in my journal. Not because there's nothing better to do, and not necessarily because of Bishop Barnes. It's more the torture of being full of all these thoughts and worries, with no outlet. In here, I can't run and leave them behind. So I scribble down some of the things that come to mind—about Mark. About life for the past year. About my worries for the future, about my family, about my roommates, about Pen. About Bob, Todd, and Gabe.

I try my scriptures too, but have less success. One time I open directly to the scripture in chapter 19 of the Doctrine and Covenants, "I command you to repent—repent, lest I smite you by the rod of my mouth, and by my wrath, and by my anger, and your sufferings be sore—how sore you know not, how exquisite you know not, yea, how hard to bear you know not."

Repent of what? I write. *What did I do to earn this? Why are you doing this to me, Heavenly Father?*

The anger is constantly there, but sometimes it boils back and leaves me completely bleak and limp and empty. A two-dimensional world isn't hard to imagine while sitting in a jail cell. And it's easy, when you're so bored you've taken to counting your own breaths, to wonder why you're taking them at all.

Selena keeps away from me, even when we're in the common room together, which I generally try to avoid. Sometimes I think I feel her watching me, though. I don't know if it means she's wary of me or she's waiting for a chance to beat the crud out of me. Usually I stay in my cot. At mealtimes I don't look at anyone, don't talk unless someone talks to me.

"Last day," an officer announces one morning as she leads us out for breakfast.

It takes a few seconds of her looking at me, waiting for a response, before I realize what she's saying.

"Really? It doesn't seem like it's been seven days." *It seems like . . . nothing. An eternity or a few hours. Something completely outside temporal bounds.*

"We'll be checking you out tomorrow morning. Do you have someone to come get you?"

"I'll call my dad." My voice is rusty from lack of use. I clear my throat. "I guess I want to use the phones, then."

"You've got a couple of visitors too. They're actually waiting right now. I'll take you to the visiting room as soon as you finish breakfast."

My heart starts racing. "Who?"

"A girl named Shelley Davenport. And a Robert something."

I choke on my milk. "No."

She frowns. "You're not going to see them?"

"I can't. I'll see Shelley if I have to, but . . ." I shake my head.

She shrugs. "That's fine. I'll tell them to let him know."

"Tell him sorry," I add hastily. "Tell him . . ." I shake my head again. *What does it matter, anyway? I don't belong in his life. If he ever dates again, his kids will need someone stable. Someone who doesn't get locked up for seven days. He doesn't deserve to be saddled with someone as clearly broken as I am.*

I finish my breakfast slowly, lingering over my toast crusts. When I'm done, the officer leads me down the hall. I'm relieved when I step into the visiting room and see only Shelley, but I feel a sudden, terrible pang seeing the empty chair next to her.

"Well, that wasn't very nice," are Shelley's first words when I pick up the receiver. "After everything, you just send him away."

"I can't let him see me like this," I reply, looking down at my wrinkled cotton pants and running a hand through my messy bangs.

"I don't think he cares, Abish."

"No, but *I* do. I'm tired of being humiliated in front of him."

"Humiliated?"

"You wouldn't understand," I mutter.

Shelley narrows her eyes. "Oh?"

I glare at her. "Yeah. You wouldn't understand, Shelley. You with your picture-perfect Molly-Mormon little life."

An odd expression crosses her face. She takes a deep breath, then lets it out slowly. "Maddie's doing okay," she says.

I run my hand over my hair again, watching her for a few seconds. She's wearing her usual long-sleeved, collared, sister-missionary blouse. She's got a pink ribbon in her hair. "You didn't have to come," I say, finally.

"No, but I *wanted* to."

"Why?"

She shrugs. "Just wanted you to know people are thinking of you. That I support you."

"How sweet."

"Don't be sarcastic. I also came to tell you that Bishop Barnes is fighting for you. He's got a bunch of people to speak for you at the honor code office."

My annoyance rises. "It's a waste of time. I've been arrested and convicted. Just being arrested alone gets you a permanent boot at BYU-Idaho."

"Don't be so sure. Last I heard they were reconsidering, and Bishop expects an answer within the next week. A lot of people came forward, Abish. One of your professors. Bishop and me and your dad. And Bob came—"

"What did he *say?*"

". . . and I told Bishop how you spend a bunch of time at the hospital, so he went to talk to them too, and a couple of nurses and a receptionist agreed to talk about . . . about what happened to you. And how you've done so much service."

I'm curious in spite of myself. Receptionists actually don't pay much attention to me. The only one who really knows my name is . . . "You don't mean Mara? *Mara* spoke for me."

Shelley nods. "That sounds right. She was pretty forceful, actually. Told them if they didn't keep you in school, they had no heart. That you've gone through a lot and nobody can be expected to function completely when they've had their world torn apart. She talked about how reliable you are, how you follow all the rules even when you don't like to . . ."

"*What?* She's the one who called security on me!"

Shelley shrugs again.

"They *should* kick me out." I shake my head. "I'm not going back, even if they let me in. I mean, how many chances should people have to give me? You guys are all great, but . . ."

"But what?"

"You shouldn't have to do this for me. I don't deserve it, and I'm going to screw up again. I'm messed up, Shelley. Sitting in my cell has given me a lot of time to realize just how messed up."

"We're all messed up."

My anger is stirring, starting to rise to the surface. "Those words sound nice, but you really have no idea what I'm talking about. You don't know what it's like to have your life completely torn apart. Like Mara said. Like mine has been."

Shelley raises an eyebrow. "Okay. Well, you sound to me like you've decided you deserve to be here and to be kicked out of school, so I guess there's not much any of us can do about it. If *you* won't fight—"

"Fight what?" I demand, scooting my chair closer to the desk. "Fight the results of my own mistakes?"

"You didn't *deserve* for your life to be torn apart. You sound like you think you deserved what happened to you. We all get messed up when bad things happen to us, Abish. It's what we do with it, how we come through it, that counts."

"Yeah?" I stand, scraping my chair across the floor, and the screech of the metal on the linoleum is more jarring than if I shouted. "That might be the tritest thing I've heard come out of your mouth, Shelley. And that's saying something. When at some future point you've had a load of dung dumped all over *you*, I'll come and have a talk with you about what *you're* doing with it, okay?" I slam the phone onto the counter and turn to walk out.

"Sit. Down."

Her voice cracks like a whip. I can hear it even though the

phone's not to my ear. I can hear it through the bulletproof glass barrier.

Slowly, I turn back so I'm facing her. I'm astonished at the anger on her face. She's unbuttoning her cuffs and rolling her sleeves up like she's preparing for a fistfight, though how she plans on getting at me through the glass, I'm not sure.

"Is this what I have to do?" she yells. "Do I have to *prove* my suffering to you in order to get you to listen to me?" And she stands, holding up her bare arms.

Shock courses through me when I see the series of dead-white lines—scores of them. They run all the way from her wrist clear to her shoulder. They're precise, perfectly parallel, clustered in areas . . . I can't quite believe it. I can't believe what I'm seeing. *Haven't I seen her arms before?*

No. She always wears long sleeves.

After standing there for a few seconds, she sits again and picks up the receiver.

I slowly walk back to the chair, sit, and pick up mine.

"You think you're the only person on this planet who's ever had pain?" Shelley asks. "You think you're the only one who's not handled things well? You look at me, and you see Molly Mormon. You see what you want to see. What you *don't* want to see is that everybody has pain, Abish. Everybody. You, me, Bob, Maddie, Julie, Steve. And we all deal with it in different ways. Some good, and some terrible." She stops to catch her breath, crossing her arm over her body. "You're embarrassed about a week in jail. Well, *I* ended up in a psychiatric treatment facility for six months."

"What happened?" It comes out before I have a chance to think better of the question. *We both know what made those scars.*

"I was raped when I was sixteen. The guy was my friend; I never would have guessed he'd do something like that. He put something in my drink. I was aware the whole time, but I couldn't do anything about it."

"Oh." It's all I can think to say. Heart pounding, I lower myself back into my chair.

"I felt so ashamed, so dirty. I didn't tell my parents. I didn't talk to anyone. I just . . . retreated. I didn't deal with how I felt. I buried it with this." She touches one particularly thick scar that encircles her wrist. "My mom caught me with the razor one day. The look on her face—horror, revulsion, I could see it so clearly—it was like a reflection of what I felt about myself."

"That . . . stinks." My words sound so inane, so inadequate to me. "She shouldn't . . . she shouldn't have reacted that way."

Shelley shakes her head. "I don't blame her now. I surprised her. I shocked her. To my parents I was the innocent, sweet, put-together person you've assumed me to be." She gives me a smile, but it's *not* a sweet smile—her eyes have this hard, world-weary expression I would never, ever have expected to see from Shelley. She pulls her sleeves down, flips the cuffs over her wrists, and buttons them.

"Are you okay now?" My voice is husky.

"As okay as I'll ever be. What happened will always be something that makes me who I am."

"Okay," I say after a few moments' pause.

"I'll always have the scars, Abish. My mistake was thinking that people didn't love me enough to see that it wasn't my fault. I thought I was dirty, and so I assumed everyone else would feel that way too. I assumed Heavenly Father felt that way. I couldn't see past myself and realize that all around me I had people caring for me. People worried about me—people who would even give their lives to help me. The Savior *did* give his life to help me. He already suffered all of this." She leans forward so her face is almost touching the glass. "Your Savior loves you, Abish."

I can't speak. I can't wrench my eyes away from hers; it's like there's a magnetic current running between us.

Finally she straightens again and stands. "We're holding the spot in the apartment for you." She points an index finger at me. "Fall semester. Plan on it."

I'm feeling rather bemused as I'm escorted back to the common area. "I just got a call from the other side," the officer says when we pass through the doors into the big room where we take our meals. "I trust you'll get back to your pod all right if I let you walk back through on your own. Seeing that you're going home tomorrow and wouldn't want to ruin that for yourself."

"Yeah," I murmur. "Thanks."

I'm not paying much attention to where I'm going as I walk past the tables, and I smack, hard, into someone who suddenly steps across my path.

I look up. It's Selena. "Gosh," I gasp. "I'm so—" I don't quite finish before something yanks my head back so hard that my ears are ringing.

"You need to start watching where you're going, girl." Not her exact words, of course. She's got hold of my hair.

"Dude," I gasp, reaching back and tugging at her relentless grip, "I'm sorry. I wasn't thinking."

"You got that right," she replies, just as a voice through the speaker calls, "Hands off her now, Selena, or you'll go to solitary."

"Yeah, I'm already in solitary with this, though," she retorts. "Might as well finish it."

I hear footsteps approaching—they're not quick enough. Her tiny eyes narrow and she gives me a little smile just before her fist lands in my face.

⌘

"Oh, man," Alyssa says when I come to dinner. "Your nose is probably broken. You've got two black eyes."

"Just what I need," I reply. "An even weirder-looking nose."

It does hurt. The bridge is throbbing with every beat of my pulse, and I have a pretty serious headache. I bled for a while too—they had to bring me an ice pack to get it to stop. I spent lunchtime in the room where the doctor examined me, holding the ice to my face.

"Bad luck it happened just when you were about to leave."

"I don't believe in luck. It's God's will that bad stuff happens to me." As the words come out of my mouth, I feel a nudge of guilt because immediately the image of Shelley—her arms held out, lined with scars—comes back to me.

Amber grins and holds a fist for me to bump. "You said it."

I touch my knuckles to hers, but my heart's not in it.

When dinner's over, I lay with my thin prison-issue blanket tucked under my chin. The words keep coming back: *Your Savior loves you, Abish.*

I see, over and over again, her expression as she leans toward the glass.

After an hour of itchy legs and restless movement, I detangle from the blanket and turn around so that my head falls into the flow of light from the common area. I pull out my scriptures. The page falls open again to chapter 122 in Doctrine and Covenants, probably because of the nicked pages.

That man might not suffer if they repent, but if they would not repent then they must suffer even as I, which suffering caused myself, even God, the greatest of all, to tremble because of pain. Shelley's outstretched arms, a mess of scars.

I close my eyes and rub them with the back of my hand until I see stars. A thought is budding in my mind. *None of us humans are strong enough to be Christ figures because we're not really even strong enough to bear our* own *suffering alone.*

I am making myself suffer more than I can bear. And people around me too.

Suddenly I'm crying again. It's not one of the slow bleeds I've had each night since coming here. It's like it was with Dad—a torrent. My face is swollen, and my nose is aching. The effort to keep quiet is making my ribs ache too.

An image begins to form in my mind, as detailed and clear as if I'm actually seeing it. It feels to me like the dim room must be illuminated by it—*Mark*.

I'm not sure what memory it's from because I can't place it in any of the experiences we've had together. He's smiling with this kind of prodding expression in his eyes like, *Come on, you know the answer. Think a little harder, Abish.*

His features fade away and another picture is materializing, but it's more than an image this time; it's like I'm lying in that hospital bed again. My fingertips feel the soft tissue of her skin, the delicate veins showing through. I see the contrast of her redness against the pale-colored blanket. I smell clean sheets and disinfectant, I feel her slight weight in my arms. I watch her lips and fingers stir. I see her in that moment—passing away from this life.

I bury my head in my blanket to muffle the scream that wants to rise from my throat. *What did I do, Heavenly Father, to deserve this?*

Three words suddenly reverberate off every corner of my skull and catch fire in my chest. *You deserve happiness.*

I spring upright, my heart beating wildly. I look around at all the sleeping girls in their bunks. I take several deep breaths. When my heart has slowed a bit, I shift my legs under me so that I'm sort of kneeling. "What am I supposed to do, then?" I whisper.

Find your happiness. Mine is a plan of happiness.

There's this rush of feeling. It's hard to describe—like I'm seeing the entire world that has been out of joint suddenly snap into place. For a moment I imagine I understand how everything moves perfectly together and the earth is buzzing with life and order.

Faith is what you do when you want something to be true but don't know it is.

Men are that they might have joy.

You can trust me with your happiness.

I zip my scriptures closed and lie down again, tucking them next to my cheek. The cool leather of my scripture holder is like a hand on my face.

$\mathscr{T}$he checkout process is much more complicated than you'd expect. There's the usual sheaf of paperwork, then the doctor has to do a final okay, then they take me in the shower room and give me my clothes back. Nobody watches me this time; I find that rather nice.

When I step out, an officer hands me something. It's my wedding ring on the chain.

I hold it in my palm for a few seconds, then tuck it into my back pocket. I feel relief, but also a pang of grief.

The officer pauses before she opens the door to the lobby. "The police department's fasting for you Sunday," she says abruptly.

It takes me a couple of seconds to ingest this. "Why would they do that?"

"Corporal Schmidt and Officer Sanders organized it. When your bishop asked them to speak at the honor code office for you, he told them your story. I don't know if they'd like me to be telling you, but . . ." She shrugs. "I thought you should know people are rooting for you."

My vision is blurry as I walk out into the parking lot.

Dad's truck is in one of the spaces closest to the entrance. He raises a hand when he sees me and starts the engine.

A police car pulls up next to the truck just as I walk up to it. An officer steps out: the goateed guy who guarded me during my suicide watch. He opens the truck's passenger door and holds it for me while I get in, then gives me a nod before he shuts it.

"I went over to your apartment and packed a couple of boxes for you," Dad says. "I hope I didn't leave out any female essentials."

I nod, not trusting myself to speak.

"Your nose hurting?" Dad asks as we pull onto the road. He's casual, but I can see a grimness about his mouth. I told him yesterday on the phone about the incident, just to prepare him for what my face would look like, and he exploded. It surprised me—not only the height of his emotion, but the revelation that he can get quite creative with vocabulary.

I wipe the moisture off my cheek. "It's not bad. I can breathe okay. If it's a break, it's a clean one."

"You don't look that great."

"It's not the nose. Sorry, I'm pretty much an emotional mess these days."

Dad shrugs. "That's fine," he says, but I can tell it is a little hard for him.

"The officer who let me out told me they're fasting for me," I explain.

"Who is?"

"The police department. I think I might have to bring them cookies or something."

"Cookies for fasting." His dimples make an appearance. "Sounds appropriate."

When we drive up to the house, we sit there for a few minutes. For me, it's because I'm nervous to go inside. I don't know why Dad's hanging out.

He puts a hand on my shoulder. "I didn't tell her, but she knows something is up."

"Of course she does," I snap. "She's Mama." I bite my lip. "Didn't mean to lash out at you."

His eyebrows shoot up.

"Don't look like that. You make me feel like a jerk."

"It's just a little different, hearing you apologize for mouthing off."

"Yeah. Nothing like a broken nose to teach you all kinds of lessons." I open the door and drop to the ground. He gets out too. I shove my hands into my pockets and follow him up the front steps.

"That's a lesson I've been trying to teach you since you were two," he says. "You're saying all I had to do was break your nose once?"

I give him a look, then open the front door.

Suzy's waiting in the little entry area. She saunters over and gives me a one-arm hug. It's about as enthusiastic as she gets about anything without encouragement, so I wrap my arms around her and give her a good squeeze.

"What happened to your eyes?" she asks.

"Nose. It broke. Did you turn my bedroom into your own personal den of iniquity yet?"

"Yeah, I stuck some lewd posters up on the walls and I've been blasting Black Sabbath pretty much constantly."

I pat her head. "Glad to hear it. I'll be needing it back for a few days."

Her face falls. "Only a few days? Dad said you're staying the summer."

I can't help but feel cheerful that she obviously wants me around so much. Cheerful, and also a bit suspicious. "Maybe," I reply, heading down the hall. She follows after me.

I open the door and stop in my tracks.

The room is completely different. It's been painted this light yellow color—so light you can barely tell it's not white—and there's a sun-colored fleece patchwork blanket on the bed. It smells different too. Freesia, or jasmine, or something. *Maybe just new paint.*

"Mama's been busting her behind the last four days." Suzy leans against the doorframe with her arms crossed. "If you don't thank her for it, I'll personally re-break that nose for you."

"Yeah." My voice catches. "I'll do that."

"Well, see you, I guess," she says hastily, stepping out and closing the door.

There are some boxes on the floor by the bed. I open one of them and see my running shoes right at the top.

The marathon, I think. *I completely forgot.* I trot over to the door and open it again. "Suzy," I yell down the hall. "What's the date today?"

"April twenty-second," she calls.

"And it's Friday today?"

"Um, yeah. Where have you been?"

Locked in a jail cell.

I walk over to the bed and fling myself across it. The anxiety has turned to stomach-churning nerves, because unless I'm completely mistaken, I have a marathon to run tomorrow. And I kind of have to run it. For a lot of reasons.

My bib won't be a problem because I stuffed the packet into my purse when I got it in the mail. But it's a three-hour drive, and I have to check in at 5:30 a.m. *How will I get there?*

One thing's certain at least. I've got to break through that twenty-mile barrier.

But I can't run two-thirds of a marathon today and expect to be on form tomorrow.

What do I do?

Faith, Abish. Faith.

Right. Well, I should make sure my muscles haven't completely atro-phied after the seven days I spent lying in my Tupperware lid.

I take the shoes out. When I try to get the left one on, it feels like there's a rock in the toe, so I set the shoe on my lap and feel around inside until my fingers touch something cool and hard. I pull it out: the leather thong necklace Dad gave me for Christmas.

How did it come out of the box at the bottom of my suitcase and end up in there?

MILE 21

Dad had to have put it in there on purpose.

I put it around my neck. The clasp is a knot in the leather and a loop for it to go through. The jade rests perfectly in the hollow of my throat. I dig through the boxes until I find a pair of basketball shorts. I throw them on, tie my shoes, and head down the hall.

"Hey, Lor," Dad says when I enter the living room. "Look what I brought home."

Mama doesn't say a word. She just sits there, looking at me.

"Hi," I say. "Thanks for the room, Mama."

She nods, just a tiny movement.

I have to tell her.

I clear my throat and cross my arms over my stomach. "Want to go for a walk?"

She nods again. "I would like that, thank you. Let me get my exercising clothes on."

I fall into the space she has vacated, my heart going a mile a minute.

Dad looks at me over his newspaper. He gives me an encouraging, grim sort of smile. He glances at the necklace, and it softens.

My chest feels tight.

"Hey, I'm going over to Acklers'," Suzy calls, trotting into the living room. "We're studying for the final. Abish, do you need the truck tomorrow?"

I narrow my eyes at her. "Why would I?"

"I don't know. Just being polite and asking before I plan a whole day."

I look at Dad, or really, his newspaper, which is covering his face again. "Don't you need it?"

"I don't have anything except to make sure the fields get watered."

A plan is forming in my mind. "I might use it in the morning. When do you need it, Suzy?"

"Saturday night."

"I'll definitely be done with it by then."

"What are you doing?" Dad asks, still not lowering his newspaper.

"I've got some stuff I'd like to take care of. I'll repay gas—I've still got something in my bank account."

Just then Mama walks into the living room. She's got on a pair of spanking-new Nikes and white running shorts, and her hair is pulled back in a ponytail. She looks fabulous, of course.

"Where were you thinking of going?" she asks as we step outside.

I shrug. "The greenway by the river?"

We get into her little Mazda. The silence on the drive is painful. I keep thinking through the words, but there is no gentle way to tell your mother that you've spent the last week in jail.

At the trailhead, I let her lead out. She sets a good pace, pumping her arms and her stride extremely businesslike. It's a little fast for me, to be honest. I'm used to running, not walking. There are different muscle groups involved. "So," I say.

"The water is pretty."

"It is." I quicken my steps again to try to match hers.

A guy runs by. He whistles, and my mom gives him a look that could tarnish steel. "The birds sound nice," she says.

"They do." I break into a jog. "Mama, what are you doing?"

"Power walking. I've started going with a group from the ward every Wednesday."

"Well, could you stop . . . power walking . . . for just a minute?"

"Yes." She stops so suddenly I have to double back a few steps.

I take a moment to catch my breath. "So, Mama."

"Yes?"

"There's something you need to know. I wish I didn't have to tell you this, but . . ." Again, I'm searching for the words.

She glares at me. "You were in the women's jail. I know."

I blink. "Okay."

"And a fat girl punched you in the eye. Your father talks loud when he's upset. I heard from the kitchen."

I sigh and bend, stretching my hamstrings. "It was my nose, not my eye."

"You should get it looked at."

"It's fine."

We both stand there, arms folded, glaring at each other.

"Okay," I say, breaking the silence again. "Well, you should know

300

it wasn't anything . . . like, I'm not on drugs or something. I was caught trespassing."

She's still glaring. "Anything else?"

"What?"

"Anything else you haven't told me that you might want to, now that you're telling me things?"

There's something about the way she says it.

"Like what?" I ask warily.

"Like something a daughter should tell a mother. Something women should share together."

I shake my head. "What, Mama? I . . ."

A tear trickles down the side of her nose. "The baby." The words come out in a whisper.

Slowly, I walk over to a bench that is a little off the trail, closer to the river. She follows and sits down next to me. We both watch the water rushing over the rocks. There's a giant white bird crouched in the middle, a trumpeter swan, I think. Hunting for trout. It lifts is head in a startling, graceful movement, eyes us beadily, then goes back to business.

"How long have you known?" I ask.

"I knew when you were expecting."

"How did you know? I never really showed much at all."

"You don't with your first. Your eyes had"—she traces around her eye with a fingertip—"dark rings. The same thing happens to me when I am carrying a baby. And also a mother just knows."

My chest seizes and my face crumples. It's completely mortifying, and my nose is hurting.

Immediately her arms are around me. "You don't have to, *hija*, but I've gone through the pain too. I lost four. Did you know that?"

"I didn't," I manage. It comes out muffled because my face is pressed to her shoulder.

"Yes. It was David and Cynthia, then you. Then Stephen. Then Andrew. And then Susannah."

I pull away and wipe at my eyes. "I knew about Stephen. And I remember Andrew. It was terrible. We were all so sad."

She digs through her shorts pocket and offers me a Kleenex.

"It's not that I didn't want you to know."

She nods but doesn't meet my gaze.

"It's not that I didn't trust you. It was just so much for me at the time. And I didn't want you or Dad to have to . . ."

"Suffer with you? But we suffer whether you let us do it with you or not."

We take a few moments there by the river. The swan takes off, scattering droplets almost to the shoreline.

"Okay," I say, finally. "Well, let's get back to the car. I've got stuff to do."

We start back in the direction we came from, stepping off the path to let a bicyclist spin by. "Amelia," I say. "That was her name."

Mama nods. "Do you want to tell me?"

I relate the story of Amelia's birth, haltingly at first. When I finish, she sighs. "Women carry a lot. Our children take a piece of us with them, whether they are living on this side or the other."

I nod.

"You know you should tell your father. He deserves to know he is a grandparent."

"Yeah."

"Heavenly Father will give you more chances. I was told I couldn't carry a baby to terms, but you and Susannah are here with me. And now they have more things they can do to help."

I glance over at her. "To term," I correct.

"Does that Bob know you went to jail?"

"Yes. He does."

She doesn't push the issue farther even though I can tell she really wants to.

"I made empanadas," she says when we get back to the car. "I hid them from your father in the pantry. They're your favorite kind— caramel apple."

I'm laughing as we pull onto the road. I try to do it quietly, but it's impossible to hide anything from Mama. She frowns at me.

Mile 21

"They're good empanadas. As good as my grandmother's. You are lucky."

"Yeah, I know."

❧

The familiar tones of my alarm clock wake me at a not-so-familiar time: 2:00 a.m. For just a moment, I'm debating internally. *This is insane. Go back to sleep, Abish.*

And then my gut takes over. *No. You have to do this.*

I shower quickly and dig through my boxes to find my sports bra and the thin, tight-fitting cotton shirt I selected a while ago. I pull on a pair of black running shorts, then add a pair of track pants on top. I pull my hair into a tight ponytail and glance at myself in the mirror. The eyes are still pretty colorful, but there's not much I can do about that. *I'm ready*, I tell myself as I walk into the kitchen to fill my water bottle.

I stop short at the doorway. "Hi."

Dad's sitting on a stool at the kitchen bar, sipping something from a mug. Probably Postum; it's his favorite. "You're up pretty early," he says.

"Uh, yeah." I shuffle over to the sink. "I've got a lot of stuff to do this morning. Thanks for letting me borrow your truck."

"No problem."

I reach over for his mug. "You finished with that? Why are *you* up? It's, like, the middle of the night."

"Thanks." He hands it to me and stretches his arms. "Couldn't sleep."

"Okay."

"You'll be out for a while then?"

"Yeah, I think I might be back mid-afternoon, maybe."

He tilts his head and considers me for a moment. "You must be driving quite a ways, then."

I bite my lip. "Yeah."

"But I'll see you tonight?"

"Yup."

303

He shrugs and gives me a sudden, disarming smile. "Okay."

I trot out of the room, swatting his back as I pass him. "Bye, Dad."

The drive is long and boring. Plenty of time and opportunity to stress, in other words. *What if I just can't handle it? What if I end up walking?*

Well, what if?

I'll hate myself. That's what.

I pull into downtown Ogden at a little past 5:00 a.m. The directions I printed off the Internet said to go to the parking lot of Comfort Inn & Suites, so I scan the lit-up signs on the main city streets until I find it. It's kind of hard to miss. There's a mob in the parking lot—hundreds waiting, and several busses coming and going. It's a little surreal seeing so much activity and so many people awake at such an ungodly hour.

I grab the fleece jacket my dad keeps behind the seat of the truck and pull it on. It smells like him. I'm very grateful for it as I step out onto the concrete. I wait several minutes and finally board a bus, taking a seat over one of the heaters.

We drive out of the bright city lights and up into the canyon.

There's a lady sitting next to me—older. She's lean, and her face has the weathered look of someone who spends a lot of time outside. *Running, maybe.*

She turns suddenly and gives me a smile. I catch a glint of silver—one of her eyeteeth is false. "Is this your first marathon?"

I wrap my arms around my waist. "How could you tell?"

"You look like you're about to lose your breakfast. You aren't, are you?"

I swallow. "I'll be fine."

"It's chaotic. So many people. Just block it all out and remember what you're here for." She pats my shoulder.

The ride seems to take an eternity. With each bend of the road going up the canyon, my stomach tightens more. The sky is dark periwinkle-blue by the time the bus pulls into a parking lot milling with people. I step out of the bus and look around, feeling suddenly at a loss.

The lady who sat next to me is standing not far away. She unzips her jacket and pins her bib to the front of her shirt. "Do you need some?" she asks, handing me two safety pins.

I nod and take them. *What am I supposed to be doing? Where am I supposed to be going?*

It is really cold.

There are several trash cans with fires lit in them, and people are huddled around them, shivering and chatting. It seems like everyone is with people they know. It brings Mark to mind in a powerful way. I'm thinking of the days we trained together. There's a moment when I almost imagine I see him running across the parking lot toward me. I realize when he gets closer that it's some other blond-haired guy, and he's headed toward a woman warming her hands over the fire next to mine.

The sky slowly gets brighter. Birds are chirping. The air is rich with pine, and a sharp tinge that makes me wonder if it might snow on us. I do things to distract myself: wander away from the fire and grab a bottle of water; use the deluxe Honeybucket restroom/sink combo just to make sure. The hand soap smells excessively fruity.

People start gathering in the road. With a lurch of my stomach I wander over, stepping further and further toward the back as more people pour out of the parking lot to the place where the race will start. It's shoulder-to-shoulder, mosh pit–like crowding, except everyone is tense, focused. Some bend to stretch a little. We're all waiting for the gun to go off. And then it does, the crack echoing through the canyon and sending a shock through me. I stumble a little as I start.

About a quarter mile in, just as I get my comfortable pace back and the crowd is thinning and stretching out a bit, I feel a spatter on the top of my head, then another.

About three miles in, and it's a done deal. The scenery is beautiful—forest, rushing river—but I'm not paying much attention because pouring rain has soaked my clothing entirely, making it stick to my skin. Water is streaming off the ends of my hair. My socks and shoes are a sodden, chafing mess. By mile seven, my breath is already catching in my chest and my thighs ache. I think I might be going a faster pace than usual; it's a lot harder to keep my gait steady when people are passing me on either side. I brush my wet bangs out of my eyes for the umpteenth time and slow a bit. Six more people pass me in the next few minutes. Running downhill is harder than the level runs I've been doing too, taxing my quadriceps more than they're used to. *I never would have predicted that the downhill would be my problem.*

I start to veer a little bit as I come up on mile thirteen. We're passing through a little town—Eden, the signs say. The streets are crowded, cheering on the runners.

"You doing all right?" a guy in one of the race uniforms calls out to me. I nod and slow almost to a walk. "Something to eat?" he adds, passing me a foil tube.

I grimace after I empty it into my mouth. I hate Gu. It's pretty much like eating vanilla-flavored phlegm. I nod my thanks and quicken my pace again, though my muscles are asking me in no uncertain terms to stop. As I leave the cheering crowds and enter into deepest, solitary forest once more, I feel a wave of despair. Half a dozen other runners are keeping pace with me. We couldn't get any wetter. *If it would just stop raining. If I could dry out a bit.*

As if in answer, the rain is suddenly hail. It pings down on my skull and lands in the collar of my shirt, chilling my neck.

I force myself to keep running on the balls of my feet and not sink into the heel-slapping gait I had as a beginner.

A little while later I lift my face toward the sky to shake my bangs off my forehead, and a thumbnail-sized piece of hail clocks me on the bridge of my nose, right on my sore spot. It brings tears to my eyes and several words to my mind that I'd never say aloud. It also blesses me with a surge of angry adrenaline that somehow takes me through to mile seventeen before it peters out, right about the time the path starts slanting upward at an alarmingly steep angle.

My mind is telling me it's time to quit, I'll never be able to make it up that hill with legs of rubber, but I force myself to keep putting one foot in front of the other. My quads burn, my knees wobble. "This . . . completely . . . stinks," I mumble with each step.

When I get to the top, there's another brief rush of triumphant energy, but I can already tell I'm approaching my barrier. I'm coughing. It tastes metallic and salty, almost bringing up the non-contents of my stomach. I'm straining my neck and gritting my teeth, forcing myself to keep going. *Water,* I think as I round the corner. And there it is—a checkpoint with water. I actually quicken my pace a little, seeing it. I swoop in and grab a cup, guzzle it, and toss it in the trash without slowing to a walk because I'm afraid if I do, I won't be able to get going again.

I'm good for another couple miles, though every step is agony. Another spate of coughing takes me, and I'm thinking I'm going to have to stop and walk. There's no way around it. *My body was just not made to run more. It's my limit. Everybody has one; mine just happens to be twenty miles. If I had to run twenty-one miles to escape from a rabid tiger hungry for my blood, I'd be dinner.*

You can do it. You've lived for twenty-one years, and you can run twenty-one miles. You just don't want to finish.

That's ridiculous, I argue. *Why did I come here if I don't want to finish? The next bend, you can stop and walk. Go ahead and walk after you've rounded the next bend in the road.*

The next mile feels like what I imagine hell must be like—burning. My legs are on fire. *And I'm doing this to myself! How stupid am I.*

A couple minutes later, the canyon starts opening up, and I see the valley below. *It looks so far away. Impossible. Impossible.* I start to slow a bit.

And then I hear a bunch of screaming. My heart sinks. It's another crowd of people, there to watch the runners come out of the mouth of the canyon. *I'll walk after the* next *bend in the road,* I amend. *Stopping here will just induce a bunch of well-intentioned, humiliating, screamed encouragements.*

"Abish!" a bunch of voices call through the melee. I blink and glance at the crowd as I jog past. It's kind of impossible that anyone who knows me is here, but there aren't many Abishes on the planet.

I nearly stop, out of sheer shock, as I see them: Mom. Dad. Suzy, who's punching the air with her fist and snarling at me. And more startling, Shelley's here too, and Bishop Barnes. It takes me a moment to believe I'm not hallucinating them.

"How you doing, Abish?" Dad calls.

I shake my head. "I—I'm . . ."

He must see something of how I'm feeling in my expression because he pushes through the crowd and catches up with me. "You okay?" he asks, jogging next to me.

"I'm fine . . . I think I have to stop," I manage. "I've never done more than eighteen. I'm never going to get past twenty—"

"I'll get you past twenty," Dad says, a grim determination coming to his face.

"No. Dad, you're not wearing running shoes."

"These steel-toe boots are twenty years broken in." He's already gasping a little. "Traction's okay too."

"But you haven't *run* in twenty years."

He doesn't answer because he's too out of breath.

It sort of works, because I don't have the heart to stop with him loping beside me. I'm hurting, and I feel like my lungs might voluntarily exorcize themselves from my chest at any moment, but I keep going.

"You doing okay, Dad?" I ask when we've made it another mile and a half. He's breathing heavily, in through the nose and out through the mouth, like any good athlete, but I can hear the strain with each intake.

"Fine," he grunts. "You?"

I force my knees a little higher. I'm starting to feel disconnected from my legs. "I don't know, I might be able to make it now I've got past twenty. We've probably got four miles left. I'll be okay—you can stop."

"I noticed most people are running with partners," Dad grunts, laboring over each word. "Does it help for me to run with you?"

MILE 21

I open my mouth to speak, then shut it, because it would be a lie to say it didn't help, and I have never, ever lied to my Dad. "It's not necessary," I gasp.

"I'll see if I can get you to the next checkpoint."

We pass the next checkpoint, and he doesn't stop.

"Dad," I say.

"Three miles left. I ran three miles every week when I was on the track team," he wheezes.

I don't have the breath to argue. The horizon is wavering in front of me. I can't feel my feet anymore, and there's this curious floating sensation in my head.

I'm hurting. It's hurting. Not just my legs, not just my feet. It's a terrible ache, somewhere deep inside me. I'm seeing Mark again. Memories, things I haven't really thought about in a long time. Conversations we had—snatches of them—are floating into my mind. We had a fight once about where to put the glasses and plates. It was just after we first moved into the apartment. I remember getting really frustrated and leaving in a huff.

I remember a time when Mark made dinner and it turned out to be a disaster, but I ate it anyway and never said anything. It made me love him more, I think.

There was the time Mark cleaned my side of the closet for me, and I felt horribly guilty about it.

My shins feel like they might actually splinter if I keep doing this.

Mark and me running together. Him urging me on, goading me through the next mile. He got me up to thirteen.

Keep your heels high, Abish.

I've never done this before.

Yes, you have. You do it all the time.

Do what?

Finish. Get through it, even when it hurts. Even if you might die.

Am I going to die?

No, you're not going to die. You're going to live.

Am I? Can I?

Yes, you can.

The ground seems like it's not under my feet anymore. I feel like I'm running on air.

Can I really?

"Yes," Dad growls, "you can. I can't talk and run at the same time. Can we save . . . this conversation . . . until after we're done? Look, we're headed for the finish-line chute."

We're headed for the finish-line chute.

Almost over, Abish.

You're almost there.

The crowd is insane—huge, like at the open house for the LDS Conference Center I attended when I was nine, only very much less reverent. There are cowbells, air-horns, and screaming worthy of an NFL football event.

As I leap over the finish line, I feel like my heart is ready to come loose in my chest. Tears are leaking out over my face. The world feels unreal. Everything smells so intense with the rain, and yet everything is hazy in my vision. I feel like I'm dreaming.

Next to me, Dad stumbles. He's on his knees and people are teeming all around us. I drop down next to him. He's shaking. "You're okay, Dad," I murmur, putting an arm under his shoulder. Slowly he gets back to his feet, and we walk through the crowd together.

The first familiar face I see is Shelley's. She's jogging toward me carrying an enormous bouquet of daisies, which she presses into my arms. It's exactly like Shelley: flowers for a marathon. "Thanks, Shel," I croak, bending my head to sniff at them.

"They're not just from me," she says.

The pulse in my neck thrums oddly as Bob's face comes to mind. "Oh," I reply after a few seconds.

"Bishop chipped in half."

"Oh," I say, managing a smile.

"Abish!" someone screams.

In my bleary state, it takes me a few seconds to register that it was Suzy's voice. Then something hurtles into me with a bruising force, nearly sending me to the ground. "Hey," I manage, patting Suzy's back.

"Good job," she says, pulling away and giving me a fierce look.

I grin at her.

"Abby," I hear Mama call.

I turn and nod at her. "Thank you for coming."

"Of course I would come," she snaps.

"Hey," Dad says, holding an arm out.

I let him gather me to his side. "Dad," I say, and my throat catches. "I love you."

"Me too," Suzy adds. "Both."

I narrow my eyes and give her my evil smile. "Both what?"

She rolls her eyes. "You know what I mean."

Mama suddenly leans into Dad's other side. She reaches out for Suzy and slides an arm around my shoulders too. She's got an amazing span of embrace for such a small woman. It's a small miracle. We're not a family that enjoys such displays even in private, and here we are in the middle of a crowded parking lot full of people.

"Abish," Dad says. His chest rumbles with his voice, tickling my face.

I pull away and look up at him. "Yeah?"

"I don't know how you were going to drive back alone. I've only run six miles and I don't think I'm capable of operating the gas pedal in that old truck for a two-hour drive." He pulls away and looks me up and down. "You're shaking. Go get some of that slimy stuff."

"I think I'm okay," I say, taking a couple steps. "Yes, a little shaky, but . . ." I shrug. "I'm not really a fan of Gu. I'd kind of like some real food."

"We'll see how you feel in about thirty minutes," someone calls. It's Bishop Barnes's voice. I turn and see him wending his way toward us through the crowd, holding fistfuls of foil packets, several water bottles tucked in his arms. He hands me a several Gus and gives a couple to Dad. I make a face, but I break one open and squeeze the contents into my mouth. "Yum. Orange snotsickle."

$\mathcal{T}$here's not enough room for all of us in Bishop Barnes's car," Suzy says. A devilish gleam comes to her dark eyes. "I could drive the truck home. Mom doesn't know stick."

"Sounds like a good plan to me," Dad replies. "I think I've burned enough calories to offset a stop for ice cream on the way home."

"I'll go with Suzy," Shelley says quickly.

"Also me," Mama puts in. "I don't have time for ice cream. We must leave now, Susannah, because I promised to help decorate for the Keanes' wedding reception."

As we walk back to the hotel parking lot, I have my first inkling of what Bishop Barnes was talking about. My muscles don't feel like they can support my weight. I make it to the car okay, but I've never been more relieved to arrive at a destination. *Well, okay; maybe finishing the marathon.*

"Don't just sit," Bishop cautions as I reach for the door handle. "Stretch out, or tomorrow you'll be more sorry than you can imagine."

I roll my eyes slightly, but I've learned my lesson about taking Bishop Barnes's advice. I sit down on the asphalt and do some quad and hamstring stretches. Dad does a couple lunges and then climbs into the front seat. "I only ran six," he says by way of explanation, but I'm thinking it's more that he feels silly sitting in the parking lot in his jeans and work boots because that's exactly how I would have felt. My often-foolish pride didn't come from nowhere.

We stop at a Dairy Queen, which is my dad's favorite. The ice cream is nice, but I'm still really thirsty even after guzzling two full water bottles. Again, Bishop came prepared. And I'm feeling pretty grateful he did.

But I'm also feeling a little out of sorts. I gaze out at the green folds of hilly Pocatello, and I'm missing someone pretty badly. In fact, I'm feeling quite emotional about it. *Likely aftereffects of the race,* I tell myself.

But I'm not fooling anyone. Dad looks at me in the rearview mirror. I shake my head and hide my face in my hand, propping my forehead against the window. My nose is stinging.

"So . . . thanks for coming, Dad." I say when I've got hold of myself. "And Bishop. Thanks for bringing all the stuff we'd need. I guess it was sort of foolish of me to try to run my first marathon by myself without really knowing what to expect."

"It was your father's doing," Bishop Barnes replies.

"How did you guys know about it?"

Dad leans back against his seat. "You told us, remember? When your mother and I came to visit. You your mother that you were signed up for the Ogden marathon. I looked it up. Marked it on the calendar. I wasn't sure if you were still planning on it after . . ."

"Being in jail," I supply. "Well, thanks for coming. It was a real surprise. And for inviting Bishop Barnes. And Shelley."

"Robert was going to come too," Bishop Barnes says. "But he bowed out at the last minute. He had an emergency at work. Or so he said."

I look up, startled. His eyes have that steely glint. "Yeah."

"He was hurt when you turned him away. He'd never say so, but I could see it."

"I couldn't let him see me in jail," I murmur.

"I can see how you'd feel that way," Bishop replies. "But Robert has a hard time putting himself out there like he did for you. He's had enough difficult things happen to him. I think that you're going to have to do something to show him you want his friendship at this point. If that's the case."

I can't think of anything to say in response. Certainly the words that come to my head—*friendship's really not what I had in mind*—aren't the kind to speak aloud.

"I'm a little lost here," Dad says.

I shrug and shake my head. We lapse into silence. I fall asleep for a while, then wake up with a huge headache. We're almost to Rexburg. I see Bishop flip the blinker on at exit 333.

"Where are we going?" I ask.

"You need to get back to the apartment," Dad replies. "Much as I like having you around, Abish. Spring term starts in a couple of days."

"I'm kicked out!"

"No."

I look at the rearview mirror again. Bishop Barnes nods at me.

"There's no way they let me back in school," I say slowly, "after I spent a week in jail. No way."

"If it hasn't, it has now. After reevaluating your case, they're letting you continue, but you are going to have to be on your best behavior from here on out." Bishop Barnes narrows his eyes, then turns his attention back to the road. "I expect you to function, Abish."

"Okay. Well, one problem. I'm not on Spring track; I'm Fall-Winter."

"Good," Dad remarks. "I was disappointed we weren't getting our summer with you."

"Then I'll hold your place in the apartment," Bishop Barnes says. "Until fall."

I squirm. "You don't have to do that."

"No, but I would like to."

As we come up on Fifth West, a sudden impulse overtakes me. "Turn here."

Dad looks over his shoulder and squints at me.

"Please," I amend. "There's something I've got to take care of."

We drive a block down Fifth, and I direct the bishop to pull into a certain driveway. I hop down, wince, and nearly collapse right there. I try not to pant as I make my way around the car. They're watching me through the window with amused expressions. I give them a good glare.

Somehow I make it down the stairs to the basement door.

I knock, and Pen answers. His hair is a little disheveled—not studiously, just plain disheveled—and his face has that bleary just-woken-up look. When he sees me, he blinks and takes a step back. "Hey," he says, only it comes out more like a question.

It's a littler harder now that I'm coming down to it. "Hey," I reply. "I . . . yeah."

He leans against the doorframe.

I take a deep breath. "I came by to tell you I'm sorry for treating you how I did," I say, keeping my gaze in the vicinity of his feet.

"Yeah?"

"I—letting you kiss me. Leading you on and making you think that . . ." I shrug. "I took you for granted and kind of . . . yeah."

There's a long silence. "I'm not going to do this," Pen says.

I look up. "Do what?"

"It was just a little fun. Making out. I'm not going to sit here and have some big DTR or whatever you BYU chicks call it."

I frown at him. "You're a BYU student too. Why do you always act like it's some bad thing?"

He shrugs. "I'm not anymore."

"You got kicked out?"

He doesn't answer, so I try another one. "So the dinner you made . . . the apologies . . . all that was for show? You weren't really changing? You didn't really like me as more than a make-out partner?"

He doesn't answer this question either; he just takes a step back and shuts the door, harder than necessary.

I stand there for a few more seconds, my heart pounding.

The walk back is, if possible, even more excruciating. "You okay?" Dad asks as I slowly work my way back into my seat.

"Yeah. Fine." My voice sounds dull even to me.

Bishop Barnes glances at me as he turns his head to back out of the driveway. "Do you mind if we take another detour?"

"Of course not," Dad replies for me.

When we get to the school crosswalk, Bishop pulls his cell phone from his pocket, punches in a number, and puts it to his ear. "Where are they right now?" he mutters into the phone. "The intersection . . . you mean over by the old high school? Okay. No, I just had a question for them. See you in a minute."

We zigzag through several blocks and park on the shoulder behind a giant truck.

"Interesting," Dad remarks. "Someone's up on the pole."

I frown at Bishop Barnes. He gives me a pointed look and nods at the figure on the telephone pole.

My heart quickens. "Just a sec." I stumble out of the car, bracing myself on the door for a moment. It's starting to drizzle a little bit, but my socks and shoes are still drenched from before, so it's not a big deal, really.

There's a guy standing at the base of the pole, looking up and watching the other guy climb. I make my way over to him. "Hey."

He turns.

I point. "Is that Robert Hartley up there?"

"He'll be down in a little while," he says. "Do you need him for something? He's just splicing a cable together."

"Um," I reply, "I guess I can wait." We stand there for a few seconds, gazing up at the figure on the pole. I glance back at the car. Dad is giving me another puzzled look. He rolls down the window. "We've got to get back home," he calls. "Your mother needs my help with the lattices for the reception."

I turn to the guy again. "Can you ask him—" I shake my head. "When do you think he'll be done?"

He shrugs. "It must be a trickier repair than we thought it would be. He doesn't have his cell on him, or I'd call and tell him he has a visitor." There's a tinge of sarcasm in his tone.

My face is heating up. "I just have to talk to him. I guess it's not that important." My gaze lights on the bucket lifter folded in the back of the giant truck. "Well, actually it kind of is. Do you think I could . . . ?" I gesture to it.

He frowns. "You want to go *up?*"

I shrug. "Just for a minute. I wouldn't want to interrupt him. I could just talk to him while he works."

"Is it really that much of an emergency?"

I lift my gaze to the small dark figure clinging to the telephone pole. Every fiber of my being wants to be up there with Bob, and that's saying something, because I'm actually terrified of heights. The one time I went rappelling at a Young Women camp, I got so freaked out that I froze halfway down the cliff face. They had to set up another rope so someone could take me down.

I look back at the car. Bishop makes an impatient gesture and points up at the pole, and my dad looks at him like he's nuts.

"Yeah," I say. "I've got a very important message from his bishop."

"Oh." He glances at the car too with an uncertain expression. "Well, I guess that's all right."

He leads me over to the truck. It takes me a while. He stops a couple of times and waits for me to catch up. He boosts me into the bucket—quite an endeavor, because my legs are useless appendages at this point.

"No," I say when he climbs in next to me. "I mean, could you just show me how to work the controls? This is kind of a confidential message."

He gives me an exasperated look. "I can't let you operate this machine. You haven't had training, and I'm breaking a hundred rules just taking you up in it, so it's this or nothing, okay?"

"Okay," I reply meekly.

He fiddles with some switches and pulls on a lever. I gasp and grab the side as we rise up into the air.

"Abish," I hear Dad yell. "What on earth?"

"An errand!" I call, watching Bob's small dark blob of a figure grow slowly larger and clearer as we rise into the air. I don't look down; I keep my gaze squarely focused on him.

Finally we're resting against the telephone pole about five feet below Bob. He's noticed us by now of course. He turns his body and glances down at us; just a quick glance, but when I see his face, I think my heart does a full 360 in my chest. "Can you get us higher?" I ask.

"It's as high as it goes," the guy says. "Look, he's coming down."

I bite my lip, watching him descend. He's got some kind of special tool on his boots to help him climb, but I'm afraid every second I'm going to see him stumble and fall to his death.

"You didn't have to come up to get me, Ernie," Bob says as he takes his last few steps down to where our bucket is waiting. "I just finished, and with the rain, I don't think . . ." He stops short as he sees me.

"Interesting job you've got," I say.

I don't know what my problem is. Those are just the first words that come to mind, which is still entirely fuzzy from endorphins or lack of ketones or whatever it is.

Bob looks down at the ground. "How did you get up here?"

"There's this machine, it lifts people up in the—" He gives me a look that warns me it's no time for sarcasm. "I just had to," I amend. "I don't know. I'm still kind of messed up from the run. Maybe I'm being a little crazy."

The other guy—Ernie—sighs. "Sorry, Bob. I brought her up because she says there's an urgent message from your bishop, and you left your cell in the truck."

Bob narrows his eyes. "Ernie, do you think that you could give us a moment? Maybe switch me places?"

Ernie gives me an extremely sour look.

"I'll take the next job. This repair's done, so all you have to do is climb down right now."

"Lucky I've got my equipment on," Ernie mutters.

Bob edges up a few feet, allowing Ernie to shift from bucket to pole, and then Ernie climbs down several feet so Bob has a clear path to the bucket. It's a very complicated process. I'd feel bad about putting them through so much trouble if I weren't completely overwhelmed already with other emotions.

MILE 21

When Bob climbs in beside me, one emotion in particular warms my chest. All I can do is stare at him for a few seconds. "Hi," I say.

His expression changes from perturbed, maybe frustrated, to slightly amused. "Hi. Fancy meeting you up here."

"Sorry for interrupting your work."

Bob looks down at my hands, which are gripping the edge of the bucket.

"I'm kind of scared of heights," I admit. "And I just ran a marathon. And also . . . yeah."

"No yeah," he retorts. "And also . . . what?"

"I don't know. Like I said, I'm not thinking very clearly." I sigh and lean my body up against the side of the bucket. "I'm sorry for not seeing you the other day."

He shrugs, and the smile lines around his eyes disappear. "So you just came up here to apologize?"

"Sort of."

"You could have waited until Sunday."

My heart sinks. "I'm glad you wanted to come," I say hastily. "But, I mean, I couldn't handle the thought of you seeing me."

He raises his eyebrows. "Seeing you in jail is worse than seeing you in your pajamas?"

"I was in orange striped scrub things, and my hair was a mess." I take one of my hands from the rim and run it through my utterly sodden bangs. "I mean, I was in *jail*. It was completely humiliating. And like you just said, you've already seen me in some pretty humiliating situations."

Bob narrows his eyes again, and a small smile forms. "How'd you get the eye?"

"Eyes . . . nose. It was a parting gift."

"Making friends wherever you go."

I frown. "I don't mean to sound snarky; it just comes out that way sometimes."

"I know," Bob says. His eyes soften, and he gives me a real smile. It's too much. I feel like I should look away. "So how was your race?" he asks.

I bat a strand of hair out of my face. "What, the marathon?" *This is turning out to be a pretty casual conversation to be having thirty feet in the air.*

He reaches over tucks the piece of hair behind my ear. He leaves his hand there on my cheek and I reach up and touch it. We stand there for a couple seconds—his hand on my face, my hand on his. It's a little awkward.

"Bishop was trying to convince me to go," Bob says, taking a step closer. He moves his hand from my face, turning it and closing his fingers around my palm. "But I wasn't sure you'd want me there."

"I did want you there." I manage to say the words, though I think they might choke me coming out.

The rain is coming down pretty hard now, streaming his hair down his cheeks and plastering mine to my head. In one sudden movement he slides his arms around my back, pulling me tight to him.

He's warm. He smells good—wet wool, clean sweat. I can feel his heart beating. "Bob, I feel like I'm being really selfish."

"Selfish how? You're shivering."

"You *know* my situation. We could never be sealed. And we can never know for sure how things would work out. And any kids we'd have would—"

Bob's laughing silently; I can feel the vibrations in his chest.

I try to pull away from him. His hold tightens. "What's so funny?" I snap.

"Just that we're getting a little ahead of ourselves."

I gaze up at him. It's hard, because I'm so close to him that it means craning my neck almost as far back as it will go. "But don't we kind of have to?"

"I don't know," he replies. His dark eyes look serious, but I've learned at this point that his serious expression could mean any combination of things, most of them far from serious. "Why don't we try this first?" he adds. And then he leans down and kisses me.

"We've already tried that," I say when I get a chance.

"Not enough."

M I L E 2 1

Bob, like my dad, doesn't show a whole lot of emotion in his words, but he expresses himself very well in some ways. Well enough that, in spite of the fact that I'm still worried about how high up were are and I'm all-out frightened about the future, I can't help but reach up and put my arms around his neck and kiss him back. In fact, after several minutes I am teetering on the conclusion that staying up there with him—maybe even permanently—might be all right.

But then there's a clap of thunder and some indistinct shouting from the ground. Bob lifts his head and starts struggling out of his coat.

"You don't have to do that," I say as he puts it around my shoulders.

"But you want me to," he says.

I roll my eyes. He grins. "We'd better get down. Lightning and tall metal structures don't mix very well."

"So I've heard."

Back on the ground, I feel suddenly self-conscious. Or to be more accurate, completely embarrassed. I mean, we were up there for the whole world to see: Dad, Bishop Barnes, Ernie the cable guy. Any random passing freshmen.

Without really meaning to, I take a step away from Bob, but he steps with me, keeping an arm around my shoulders. "Time to call it quits," he says to Ernie, who's not quite looking at us. "See you Monday."

My legs are noticeably wobbly as we walk to the car. Bob opens the door, scoops me up, and lifts me into the backseat. "Sorry we're getting your upholstery all wet," he says, sliding in beside me.

Bishop Barnes doesn't say anything, but he's got a small, annoyingly self-satisfied smile as he turns the key in the ignition. Dad is really quiet for several minutes. As we approach the South Saint Anthony exit he looks over his shoulder, glances at me, and offers Bob his right hand. "Nice to see you again," he says. Then he turns back around.

I'm laughing silently; I can't help it. Bob smiles and crooks his arm around my waist, pulling me tight to his side.

Epilogue

Bob was right. It's not easy to date once you've been married. There are times we have to decide to hang out a little less while we get our heads around things. It's too tempting to just fall into something comfortable without asking the important questions when you're lonely and when you've had some real difficulty.

There are those moments of despair, struggling with the whole faith thing. It's hard, when you're completely falling in love with someone, not to worry about the eternal nature of things. Luckily Bishop Barnes is there to talk sense into both of us when we need it.

There's also randomly awkward stuff that would only happen to a previously married person trying to date again. Like the time I'm sitting in Bob's car and I'm describing this bruise I got on my thigh. Without thinking, I fling up my skirt to show him like I would have with Mark when we were married. And then I immediately flip it back down, cover my face, and want to die for a few minutes. Bob nearly drives into the other lane, he is laughing so hard. "What was that again?" he says once he's gotten himself under control. "I think I missed it the first time." And he tells everyone about it too: Mama,

Dad, *his* mom, *his* dad, and Bishop Barnes. Luckily they all laugh instead of being scandalized like they should.

But it's completely worth it. I can say that even now, after standing in a line for two hours with bobby pins digging into my scalp. "How much longer?" I ask Mama, massaging my smile muscles.

"As long as we need to, Abby," she snaps, looking down at Gabriel and bouncing him on her hip. "It's what a wedding reception is *for*."

Gabe laughs, a completely delicious low chuckle that I discovered a month ago playing peek-a-boo with him. Bob was worried he wasn't laughing, but Gabe laughs and smiles enough now for three babies. He must be making up for lost time.

"I thought it was for the cake," I mutter.

Bob catches this and gives me a sly grin.

"You're totally going to shove it in my face, aren't you?"

"I'm expecting chocolate will taste good on you."

"I . . . hope so," is all I can manage to reply because he's looking handsome and Marlon Brando–like at that moment.

"Abish." A pair of arms closes tightly around me and I think I feel my sternum crack a little.

"Aunt Cindy," I say, only it comes out more like "Am Synf," because my face is smashed into her shoulder.

"I guess missions really aren't your thing," she adds, pulling away and holding me at arm's length.

Her smile doesn't fool me. "Oh, we'll go on one someday," I reply sweetly, taking Bob's elbow and jerking him an inch closer to me.

"She's chosen her mission, Cyn." Dad's voice, behind us, startles me. I glance up and am surprised to see sternness in his expression.

"Of course," she chirps after a pause. She leans in to hug Bob. "You seem like a worthy young man. Good for you two."

After she moves on, I look up at Dad again. He's smiling. It's that same smile from the picture: Pride. Joy. I don't know how I missed it before. I'm worried that, in a minute, there might be some kind of embarrassing display on either or both of our parts.

Mama elbows me in the ribs. "Abby," she says in her reception-smile voice.

I turn, and a tingle of shock runs through me. "Andy. Anne. Thank you so much for coming.

"We're glad you invited us," Andy says, leaning in for a hug. "It's been a while."

I nudge Bob. "These are Mark's parents."

Bob shakes each of their hands.

Andy moves on to shake the next set of hands, but Anne turns back again and puts her arms around me. "It's nice to see you happy," she murmurs. I realize in that moment that I need to tell her too about Amelia. Not now, because a reception line's not the time or place, but soon. She also has a right to know she's a grandmother.

I hear my sister laughing somewhere. I scan the room and spot her sitting at a table with Bishop Barnes's freshman son; I forget his name. Steve's at the same table, and Shelley. Shelley sees me looking at her. She gives me a smile and a little wave.

They're the only Manor roomies that came. Maddie couldn't because her family is in town, and Julie . . . well. I'm not sure she *would* have come even if she weren't swamped with Relief Society president duties. That first Sunday of Fall semester when the Bishop read her name from the stand, I admit I let off a rather sadistic chuckle. It hasn't been an easy job for her, but she's gotten noticeably more civil. Being forced to love people can do that to you.

And Pen. He's my only real unsolvable regret. I never see him, and I don't know if he'll ever forgive me. Because I know I hurt him. *I know I did.*

Adrian walks up to me. "Hello," she says, and glances down at my dress. "Your mom picked that out, didn't she?"

I smooth the beaded silk overskirt of my actually quite-gorgeous A-line dress. "Where did you get yours? From the JC Penney fifty-percent-off-nothing-but-boring-black-sheaths rack?"

Bob frowns.

"She likes it," I whisper.

And indeed, I can see her barely-restrained smirk as she leans past me to give Bob a hug. "Hm. Nice." She makes a sudden grab for one of his biceps and gives it a squeeze. "Good job, Abe."

Bob flinches and then watches her walk away, a bewildered expression on his face. His gaze travels to our fathers, who are standing close together in what looks to be rather intense conversation. "Uh-oh. I think they're talking politics."

"It'll be okay. When my Dad disagrees with people, he nods and smiles and thinks his own thoughts. Kind of like you." I punch him lightly on the arm. "It can be annoying sometimes."

"Yeah? Nobody could ever accuse *you* of not speaking your mind."

"Congratulations, Abish Hartley," a voice cuts in.

It's Bishop Barnes. And, relief of reliefs, he's the last person in line.

"Abish Cavendish *Miller*-Hartley," I correct him, reaching up to pull out a hairpin. "Thank you. For marrying us too."

He nods and leans in to give me a sideways hug. "It was a pleasure."

My vision blurs a bit. "Yes, it was."

When he moves over to congratulate Bob, Marylin, Bob's mother, taps me on the shoulder. "I'm going to take Todd to get some food. He's hungry." She gives me a smile every bit as devastating as Bob's. "He's going to miss you two while you're gone. Gabe too, though it looks like he's pretty happy where he is."

I glance at Mama, who is murmuring incomprehensible Spanish phrases into Gabe's dark curls. "It's only two weeks," I reply. "But I'll miss them."

Bob puts his arm around my shoulders. "Yes, but we won't miss them too much."

I look up at Bob. The smile just happens, I can't keep it in.

Bob's arm tightens, pulling me close to him, and he smiles back. I see so many things in that smile: the usual amusement mixed with tenderness, but also something that brings that tightness to my chest. It's a look of wonder, of complete and utter joy. *How did we get here?* His eyes seem to say.

Sometimes it's best not to ask questions, I want to tell him. *Sometimes you just have to trust in your own happiness. That the plan is a plan of happiness.*

Yes, thank you, Mark. Thank you, Heavenly Father. But please, keep teaching me.

I take his face in my two hands. "I love you," I whisper.

"Ew."

I look over and see Todd, standing there observing us with a finger tucked in his mouth. *He must have escaped Grandma Hartley.*

I start to move my hands away, but Bob takes them and puts them up around his neck. He leans in and kisses me, bending me backward over his arm, just like in movies. I think there are cheers, a few catcalls, even. Honestly, I don't know. The building could be falling down on us, and I'd still be hard-pressed to notice much at all other than Bob, showing me all he's worth.

Oh, man. I'll say it—

He's worth a lot.

Discussion
Questions

1. Abish is obviously struggling. Why do you think she has such a hard time realizing her situation and need to change?

2. What about her husband's death has made it harder for Abish to grieve?

3. LDS doctrine about eternal marriage is sometimes difficult to understand and apply in unconventional situations like divorce and death. What can help people like Abish and Bob to feel good about moving on with their lives?

4. Sometimes when people struggle, they aren't easy to be around. Which of Abish's friends or relatives have handled her situation well and helped her the most? What did they do?

5. What do you think about how Aunt Cindy was trying to help Abish? Would you have reacted the way Abish did?

6. Abish's family has a difficult time being vulnerable with each other. Is this something you can identify with?

DISCUSSION QUESTIONS

7. Do you think Abish's time in jail was productive or unproductive? Have you ever wondered why something has happened and then found later that it was a blessing?

8. Do you think Bob, Abish, Todd, and Gabriel have a good chance at being happy together? What are the challenges they will have to face as they become a family?

About the Author

Sarah Dunster is wife to one, mother to seven, and an award-winning poet and novelist. Her poems have appeared in several LDS literary journals. Her first novel, *Lightning Tree,* was released by Cedar Fort Publishing in April 2012. When she is not writing, Sarah can often be found cleaning, cooking vegetarian meals, holding small people in her lap, or taking long, risky walks during thunderstorms.